W9-ACZ-261

Praise for *Assassin's Game*

"A tightly woven story line that builds to a series of bombshell concluding twists."

—*Publishers Weekly*

"An Iranian scientist only weeks away from a viable nuclear warhead, a superb Mossad assassin on the hunt, the fate of Israel hanging in the balance—popular fiction doesn't get any better."

—Stephen Coonts,
New York Times bestselling author of
Saucer: Savage Planet

"Sharp as a dagger and swift as a sudden blow, *Assassin's Game* is a first-rate thriller with a plot that grabs you hard and won't let go. Ward Larsen is bound to attract devotees." —Ralph Peters,
New York Times bestselling author of
Valley of the Shadow

"Mideast tensions, nuclear threats, and double crosses laced with surprises makes this Larsen's very best in a series of page-turners. Well done, Ward!"

—David Hagberg,
New York Times bestselling author of
The Fourth Horseman

ASSASSIN'S GAME

WARD LARSEN

FORGE®

A TOM DOHERTY ASSOCIATES BOOK
NEW YORK

This is a work of fiction. All of the characters, organizations, and events portrayed in this novel are either products of the author's imagination or are used fictitiously.

ASSASSIN'S GAME

Copyright © 2014 by Ward Larsen

A Forge Book
Published by Tom Doherty Associates, LLC
175 Fifth Avenue
New York, NY 10010

www.tor-forge.com

Forge® is a registered trademark of Tom Doherty Associates, LLC.

ISBN 978-0-7653-8809-4

Our books may be purchased in bulk for promotional, educational, or business use. Please contact your local bookseller or the Macmillan Corporate and Premium Sales Department at 1-800-221-7945, extension 5442, or by e-mail at MacmillanSpecialMarkets@macmillan.com.

First Edition: August 2014
First Mass Market Edition: April 2016

Printed in the United States of America

0 9 8 7 6 5 4 3 2 1

For Bob and Pat Gussin

ACKNOWLEDGMENTS

My most sincere thanks to those who helped bring this story to life. To my editor, Bob Gleason, for his support and encouragement. To Kelly Quinn and the entire staff at Tor/Forge—there are none better. To those who helped me early on, Deb Stowell and Kevin Kremer, your contributions were essential. I would be hard-pressed to find a more hardworking and knowledgeable agent than Susan Gleason.

Finally, thanks to my family for their patience and support over the years.

ASSASSIN'S GAME

PROLOGUE

One could only expect so much from a stolen donkey.

Nearing the crest of an extended rise, Yaniv Stein watched the creature slowly buckle. Struggling beneath three hundred pounds of guns, ammunition, and explosives, its legs began to wobble. Then, fifty yards to go, it did what donkeys did when they reached their limit—the beast dropped to its haunches and froze, statue-like and immovable. Stein heaved on the harness, trying to coax forward momentum, but he might as well have been pulling against an oak tree. His years of training in the Israeli Special Forces had covered a great many contingencies. No one had ever thought to include this in the curriculum.

He left the donkey where it was and padded ahead, his boots scuffing over sand and loose stones. He gave a hand signal and the others appeared out of the darkness, three vibrant silhouettes clear under a half-moon that split the night sky. The obstinate donkey was only the latest in a series of misfortunes to befall the mission. To begin, their military flight from Israel to Turkmenistan had suffered a ten-hour delay, cursed by not one but two airplanes with mechanical issues. Arriving in Ashgabat behind schedule, their promised transportation to the Iranian border, a pair of jeeps obtained by an advance party, had never materialized, and they'd been forced to negotiate the purchase of a decrepit van from an Armenian used car salesman—yet another shortcoming in the training syllabus.

Then had come the most serious setback: three nights ago their most lethal marksman had broken an ankle while scouting a washed-out road. The only option was to have the field medic drive him a hundred miles back to the Turkmen border using their only vehicle. That had put the squad down two men, a one-third reduction in firepower. The rest of them could shoot well enough—and they would—but their meticulously rehearsed plan would require significant adjustments. The loss had also placed an unacceptable equipment load on the remaining four. Thus the stolen donkey. Now, five days and four hundred miles since injecting themselves into Iran, the men were tired. They had moved on foot the last three nights, fourteen-hour treks separated by daytime rest periods in the concealment of sandstone formations. Still, all hardship aside, they were on the verge of success.

The air was still and sweet, the desert almost agreeable with the sun no longer pounding overhead. Stein rendezvoused with his team. The two men from the flanks were waiting, the point man the last to arrive. All wore dark robes and sandals. Their beards, cultivated for months, were long and unkempt in the most pious Muslim tradition. As a group, the four infiltrators blended in as well as four men could in this part of the world. They arranged themselves in a circle, and Stein tried to meet their eyes one by one. He had no success as the others' gazes shifted constantly. Watching and alert.

"What now?" Dani, the second in command asked, not taking his eyes off the horizon.

Stein referenced the luminous green screen on his GPS receiver. "We still have five kilometers to go. There's no way we can haul all the equipment ourselves and be in place before dawn."

Standing under a faultless night sky, Stein gauged the terrain ahead. Fifty yards remained to the top of the rise, and after that the choppy topography would give way to a dry lake bed as hard and flat as a billiards table. From that point there would be little cover.

"Come on," Stein said, slapping Dani in the middle of his armored vest. "Maybe we can see it."

Stein led Dani ahead. Without being told, the other soldiers stayed with the gear. The hill of sand that had defeated their donkey was the highest ground in any direction, and nearing the crest the two commandos crouched low to keep their profiles masked. They took turns with the night vision glasses, studying a dim island of light that seemed to float on the far horizon.

"There it is," said Stein. "Lit up like a damned amusement park."

He handed over the optics, and after a look Dani said, "It looks like they're having a party. We planned on eight bodyguards, Yaniv. If there is a special event tonight, with dignitaries, we could be facing four times that number."

"You worry too much, Dani. The fact that there's a party only tells me our intelligence is correct. He's there now. Even better, they're probably all drunk."

Dani shot Stein a hard look. "And you worry too little. We need to do it before sunrise."

"You have something in mind?"

"There's a party tonight," Dani said. "Maybe we can catch him outside having a smoke. I say we split up. Mayer and I go ahead fast, just take the SR-25." He was referring to the big sniper rifle. "You and Goldman bring the assault gear in case we don't get a shot. We can all crash the place later if it comes to that."

"Room to room in broad daylight?" Stein shook his head doubtfully. They had planned a predawn raid—always the favored hour for residential takedowns—but the new twist in logistics put that schedule out of reach. "And I don't like the idea of splitting up."

An extended silence ensued, what passed for a debate between two battle-hardened men. The sounds of the night seemed to amplify, chirping insects and the distant howl of a jackal. Stein was about to speak when Dani suddenly put up a hand. Both men froze.

After a long ten seconds, Dani asked, "Did you hear something?"

Stein shook his head to say he had not.

Dani sighed, shrugging it off. "I say we split now. But it's your call, Yaniv."

There were few people in the world Yaniv Stein listened to. Dani was one of them. "All right. We'll do it your way. Let's just hope to hell he's there."

The two men scrambled down from their perch, and Stein relayed his decision to Goldman and Mayer. Neither showed a glimmer of opinion on the matter. They pulled everything off the donkey, yet even after being relieved of its burden the beast kept stubbornly on its haunches. As the four men began sorting through the gear, Dani addressed Stein in a low voice, "Once it is done, how will we egress, Yaniv?"

The lack of transportation had been an ongoing problem, but this time Stein had an answer. "There must be vehicles at the compound. We'll take our pick. Maybe something luxurious like a—" He stopped abruptly when Dani's hand came up a second time.

They both heard it this time, an almost imperceptible click. Metal on metal.

And then hell came to earth.

Dr. Ibrahim Hamedi gazed out into the still night, his ears reaching for any further sound. He heard nothing, as had been the case for a full twenty minutes.

Standing on the patio, Hamedi was centered in a quarter acre of smooth stone, this fronting a swimming pool the size of a tennis court. The whole arrangement was framed by verdant landscaping, plantings incorporated in flagrant contradiction to the desert flora outside the perimeter wall. It was all quite symbolic, he supposed, representing well the detachment that those who frequented this place held with their country. The palace—a boy from the squalor of south Tehran could think of it as nothing less—was twenty miles from the Qom facility. Rarely were those who worked the technical side of the operation permitted here. The compound was reserved, Hamedi knew, for visiting dignitaries, the religious and political elite who came to either marvel at Iran's great technical achievement, or complain about the billions of petrodollars being funneled so deep into a pit in the earth. Hamedi had been here twice in the last months, once for an audience with the president himself, and tonight invited by the Guardian Council to speak to a group of concerned Majlis legislators. That job done, he'd left the legislators inside to posture and gossip and drink—as such men did when clear of the mullahs.

Hamedi tilted his head to one side and kept listening. The distant crackling noises that had frayed the night air were completely gone. The racket had carried on for a full ten minutes, ebbing in the last seconds at a decisive rate to be finally absorbed by the desert's indifference. The ensuing silence seemed resounding, even if the outcome had never been in question. All the same, Hamedi closed his eyes and listened. He heard cicadas buzzing and the soft flush of the breeze though palms that had likely been imported from Africa or Indochina. Then his eyes flicked open as he registered a new sound over his shoulder, something even more out of place than the tropical landscaping. The tinkle of ice cubes in an empty glass.

"I think our excitement has ended," said Farzad Behrouz.

Hamedi did not turn, preferring to imagine the rutted image of the man who headed Iran's state security apparatus. It had long been Hamedi's opinion that men of prominence were carved from one of two blocks. They were either imposing and handsome, or caricature oddities, men who had likely suffered cruel childhoods and were thus numb to life's trials. Behrouz was firmly in the latter group. He was small and pale, short legs carrying an androgynous torso. His eyes were too close together, split by a pinched nose and framed by shallow, pockmarked cheeks. Presently, Hamedi pictured that face in a mask of cruel satisfaction. If a troll could be made to smile, that would be Farzad Behrouz.

"You must brim with confidence to be so close to the action," Hamedi said. A brief silence ran and he sensed a mistake, that these words might imply a degree of cowardice. "Your intelligence source has again proved reliable," he added quickly.

"Mossad is not what it once was," Behrouz replied.

"No, certainly not. But they have never been what the world believes. If you ask me, Mossad is more legend than reality. The Jews, for all their faults, are wondrous storytellers."

Hamedi sensed Behrouz fall still behind him, just out of sight, a geometry that served them both. Again ice tinkled in a glass.

"Our guests from Tehran are asking where you've gone. After your enlightening speech they have many questions about the project."

"They always do," Hamedi said derisively.

"Yes, yes. I too find them insufferable. Still, they have their place. Neither of us can do our work without funding."

Hamedi said nothing.

"We are not so different, Professor. We have both risen to great achievements, the pinnacle of our respective disciplines."

Hamedi could in no way equate his work to that of the thug standing behind him. Behrouz had risen through the military, climbing ranks with an appetite for brutality and sadism, qualities that translated well to a battlefield. After twenty years of thuggery, and with any remnants of civility certainly ruined, he had joined the secret police. Hamedi, on the other hand, had excelled academically, in particular math and science. He had attended universities and performed research, both at home and abroad. *My intellect is respected while your fist is feared*, he thought. *Otherwise, we could not be more alike*. What he said was, "This is the second attempt on my life this year."

"And the second failure."

"Do you think they will give up?"

Behrouz sighed. "That is the trouble with Jews. They never give up."

"Quite so," Hamedi agreed. "Which is why we must fight them on level ground."

"Precisely. I've been told that your work is reaching fruition. This is fortunate for you. Once you've given us the ultimate weapon, I can't imagine you will be at risk any longer. A year, Dr. Hamedi, perhaps two, and you will no longer require such heavy security. Who knows—you may never see me again."

Finally, Hamedi turned to face the ugly little man. He smiled thinly.

Behrouz's phone trilled a happy little ringtone, and Hamedi watched him pick up the call. After stating his name, the security chief only listened, his impervious, sunken expression giving nothing away.

Behrouz ended the connection, and said, "It is done. There were four commandos. All are dead."

"Four," Hamedi remarked.

"You expected more? A regiment, perhaps?"

"I am Israel's greatest nightmare. I think I might warrant it. Did we suffer casualties?"

"Yes." For the first time Behrouz seemed tentative. "Twenty-four dead, eighteen wounded."

Hamedi stiffened, then turned back to face the desert. Neither man spoke for a time. But then, what could be said to such a thing? Behrouz had at his disposal the most experienced, well-trained soldiers in Iran. They had known exactly where and when to wait. And still a casualty ratio of ten to one.

"How will it be presented?" Hamedi asked.

"Must you ask? The news tomorrow will shout of a great victory over Israeli assassins. The mechanics of how it came to be? No one will care about that."

A wave of laughter rolled from the house, disrupting the still desert night.

"Come," Behrouz said. "We should return. Your expertise is in great demand."

"Yes," Hamedi agreed. "Isn't it, though?"

With that the two men went inside, each riding his own thoughts.

What neither could know at that moment was that the attack just beaten down was not the end. Quite to the contrary, Israel's latest failure would soon prompt decisions at the highest levels in Tel Aviv to approach things from an altogether different angle. The strike of September 25, having come within five miles of its target, would not be the last.

Nor would it be the most successful.

ONE

⊕ Three days later

Anton Bloch walked briskly along King George Street, leaning into a stiff wind that had swept in over the course of the morning. In most of the world, autumn winds brought change. Cold fronts to separate leaves from branches, gunmetal gray skies, and the breaking out of mothballed winter gear. In Tel Aviv, the last Friday of September did little more than stir the dust of yet another heat-stricken summer.

Had Bloch gone for a walk a year ago, it would have been a very different project. He would have been shadowed by two armored limousines and a dozen bodyguards, every street on his route mapped in advance and monitored. Even now, long removed from office, he generally warranted two men. But not today. The unusual request had come this morning, a handwritten note delivered by his successor's aide de camp: *9:15, Meir Garden. Come alone.* So, for the first time in recent memory, Anton Bloch was walking by himself on a public street. He found it oddly liberating. Were he more of a pessimist, he might imagine Arab assassins around every corner. But then, no man who has served as director of Mossad can exist as a pessimist.

Bloch rounded a corner and turned left into the

main entrance of Meir Garden. He spotted a familiar face—or rather, a familiar silhouette. A massive man with a flattop haircut materialized to greet him. He was wearing a suit and tie, cheap material but nicely pressed, the jacket either two sizes too small or fitted in a way to accentuate his muscular arms and shoulders. Bloch suspected the latter.

"Good morning, sir."

On hearing his voice, Bloch remembered a first name. "Hello, Amos."

Bloch had clearly gotten it right—Amos produced a smile that was at odds with his intimidating appearance. He spoke again through a tightly clenched jaw, "The director is expecting you, sir. Straight ahead, then the first path on your right."

Bloch did as instructed.

He found the incumbent director of Mossad feeding peanuts to an obese squirrel. If the human form could have a generic equivalent, it would be Raymond Nurin. He was average in height and build, hair thinning but not bald, a trace of gray at the edges commensurate with his fifty-something years. His facial features were completely unremarkable, no hooked nose or brilliant eyes or distinguishing marks. The clothing was in line with the man, neither expensive nor cheap, neither bright nor drab. Raymond Nurin was the man you would meet at a cocktail party whose name escaped you ten minutes later. For an insurance salesman or an actor, a certain detriment. For a spy chief? He was the model of somatic perfection.

Nurin had taken over Mossad when Bloch was forced out. They'd had a few meetings in the weeks after the transfer of command, sessions intended to cover ongoing operations and facilitate a smooth transition. Bloch had barely known the man going in, and he'd expected little. Nurin had surprised him with an intellect that belied his unexceptional appearance. Since those initial meetings they'd had no contact whatsoever. Consequently, Bloch had no idea what sort of empire his successor might have built. Even less an idea of what he wanted today.

"Good morning, Anton."

"Raymond."

The two exchanged a polite handshake.

"Thank you for coming," Nurin said. "I know it was short notice, but I can assure you my reasons are sound."

Bloch said nothing. He looked idly around the park and saw no one else. No widows with grocery sacks or spandex-clad mothers pushing strollers on a trot. Bloch hadn't spent much of his career in the field, but enough to recognize a sterile perimeter that reached at least two hundred yards. Even the bodyguards—there had to be an army—were keeping out of sight. Not for the first time, his opinion of Nurin shifted slightly, and in the same direction it always seemed to.

Nurin tossed his bag of peanuts into a trash can and began strolling the pressed gravel path. Bloch kept pace.

"How do you like the job?" Bloch asked.

"I would expect that question from anyone else."

Bloch allowed a rare grin.

Nurin said, "Tell me, did you ever call on your predecessor for advice?"

"Is that why I'm here? Advice?"

"Of course not. That would imply certain inadequacies on my part." It was Nurin's chance to grin, but he passed and said, "Tell me what you've heard about our recent failure in Iran."

"Qom? Only what was in the newspapers."

"Come, Anton."

Bloch paused on the path. Nurin turned to face him.

"All right," Bloch said, "I still have a few friends, and we talk over a Guinness now and again. It was a disaster. We lost four good men, two of whom I knew well. Hamedi was untouched."

"Four of our best, I won't deny it. A terrible loss. It would have been six, but two were forced to abort the mission and return due to an injury."

"What really happened?" Bloch asked.

"Essentially what you've read in the papers, a botched attempt at Hamedi. There was little hard evidence in the aftermath, of course. The men had no identification and we've denied all involvement. Still—"

"The world does not believe it."

"Would you?"

Bloch didn't bother to answer.

"Iran, as you would expect, has been gloating over the entire affair. Much like the attack in Tehran six months ago."

"And that catastrophe was also as reported? Two assassins on motorcycles, both shot dead by security forces before they were within a mile of Hamedi?"

"Yes," Nurin said.

"And so his legend grows." Bloch mused, "One such failure and I think it is bad luck. Twice, however—" the old director's voice faded off.

They began walking again, silence prevailing. A whirl of dust stirred over a nearby playground, sweeping past like a miniature tornado.

"You have a leak," Bloch finally said.

"Clearly."

"It happens—with some regularity, I fear, although usually at lower levels."

"The missions against Hamedi were kept very high, exclusive need to know."

Bloch nodded.

"It is the first such problem under my watch," Nurin said. "I've begun a quiet investigation, but these things take time."

"Yes, and always more than you think. Worse yet, there is no guarantee you will ever find your traitor."

Nurin led them to a bench.

Bloch settled beside him, put an index finger to his temple, and said, "It is too bad you missed him. Yet I find myself wondering—if you did succeed would it really change Iran's timetable? Is one man so important?"

"Hamedi is their Oppenheimer. Since taking control of the Atomic Energy Organization of Iran, two years ago, he has become our worst nightmare. Prior to his watch, the program had fallen into complete disarray. In order to mask the program from international inspectors, the Iranians divided the program, burying twenty facilities deeper than ever. Missile components and stockpiles of nuclear material were shuffled like a deck of cards. The result was that each working group knew little about what the other was doing, and progress suffered. There was a time when our Stuxnet and Flame viruses brought things to a virtual standstill. Centrifuges were destroyed by the thousands, and their entire network of software controls ruined. It was wonderful. But Hamedi has brought great change. On one hand, he is a raving anti-Semite whose speeches parrot their former president, the lunatic who denies that the Holocaust ever occurred.

But Hamedi is also a brilliant engineer and an organizational genius."

"As with Hitler and his oratory prowess," Bloch reflected. "Why does God grant madmen such gifts?"

"Hamedi has publicly stated that Iran's ballistic nuclear capability, should the country be so blessed, will be aimed squarely at Israel."

"When I resigned, the estimate for Iran mating their first weapon to a Shahab-4 ballistic missile was three years. Has this changed?"

"We have only a matter of months. The critical components are being gathered at a new facility outside Qom. The Iranians long ago cleared the hurdle of distilling uranium to weapons-grade purity. That is the only reason they came to the negotiating table, agreeing to slow the program if sanctions were removed."

"How much material do you estimate they have?" Block asked.

"Enough for a half dozen warheads, possibly more. Yet putting this material to use, achieving a scaled-down device that can be mounted atop a ballistic missile—that is a more elusive challenge. Hamedi, unfortunately, has nearly brought success."

"Will there be a demonstration? An underground test?" Bloch asked.

"Of course, just as the North Koreans performed for the benefit of America. To test an efficient, small-scale weapon in the ground is like issuing a birth certificate, an announcement of your new child."

"Our defenses?"

"Upgrades to our Arrow ballistic missile defense system will not be ready soon enough. The engineers can't guarantee it will ever be capable of defending against such a long-range weapon. They talk about percentages and probabilities, not the kind of measurements one wants to hear with regard to the annihilation of Tel Aviv."

Nurin fell quiet, and Bloch eyed him more closely. "Am I to take it that you wish to make another attempt against Hamedi?"

Nurin nodded.

"Surely you realize your problem. These two failed missions have not only caused great embarrassment, but they spoil the chance for further attempts. With a target pinned on his back, Hamedi will be more cautious than ever."

Bloch waited, but Nurin did not speak. The new Mossad director was allowing his predecessor to work things through, perhaps as a test to his own ideas. To see if the same conclusion was reached.

Bloch looked skyward and whispered aloud, fashioning a path as he would have a year earlier, "You need to eliminate a man who is very well guarded. You have a security leak in your organization at a high level, one you cannot cut out in time to make a difference. Given this, I'd say your only option is to use an outsider. A solo operator, I think. Someone reliable and certainly discreet. There are such men for hire in the world . . ." Bloch hesitated, "or so I've heard."

Nurin remained silent.

"Yet the chance of failure is high. Escape would be difficult, and even if achieved the assassin would have to disappear completely. You would need a man who is—" Bloch stumbled for a moment, and when the answer fell he understood why he was here. He looked at Nurin with a piercing glare.

"There—you see it, Anton. What more perfect assassin than a man who is already dead."

Nurin again went quiet, allowing Bloch to consider

every aspect. In the interim, he produced a pack of cigarettes and selected one. He made no offer to Bloch, so Nurin knew he'd recently quit. The director lit up, took a deep pull, and exhaled a steady stream of smoke that was instantly carried away on the breeze.

"No," Bloch said. "It would never work."

"I disagree. He is perfect, Anton. His new life was facilitated by the Americans, but even they do not know his true background. Only three people in the world know what David Slaton once was. Two are seated on this bench. The third, of course, is immaterial. Slaton died one year ago—I can even show you a headstone in a quiet cemetery outside London. He does not exist. Not on paper, not in computers. Many years ago, Mossad made sure that his past was wiped clean. He became our most lethal *kidon*, an assassin who existed for years as no more than a shadow. Now that shadow itself has disappeared. He is an apparition, I tell you, as pure and absolute as can be."

Bloch did not respond.

"More to the point, he is the most effective, lethal *kidon* we have ever created."

Those words returned Bloch to an uncomfortable place, a long-buried sense of conflict. The appraisal of Slaton was more accurate than even Nurin could know. Still, Bloch had never decided whether Israel should find pride or shame in having created such a killer. What did it say about his country? What did it do to the man? "He is an assassin second to none, I grant you that. Or at least he was. But there is one overriding flaw in your plan, Director—he would never do it. He has a new life. No patriotic plea, no amount of money will pique his interest, I assure you."

"He is still a Jew. We are his people."

Bloch did not reply.

Nurin hunched forward on the bench and seemed to inspect the brown gravel. He took another long draw, then dropped his cigarette to the earth and crushed it under the heel of his nondescript Oxford.

"Anyway," Bloch said, "what makes you think he would be more successful than the others?"

"Our internal security has been compromised, that much is clear. Slaton would operate outside the organization. He would report only to me, thus isolating the leak. The larger problem, the one that has vexed us all along, is that Hamedi remains in Iran. However, a singular opportunity has arisen."

"He is going abroad?"

Nurin nodded.

"Where?"

"That is something only Slaton and I should know, Anton. I'm sure you understand. It will be public knowledge soon enough. But I can tell you that our chance will come in just over three weeks."

"Three weeks? Not much time to plan a mission."

Nurin gave him a plaintive look.

Bloch met his gaze, then turned away to look across the park. "That is the very same look I used to get from the prime minister. I am a fountain of the negative, am I not?"

"You are—at least that's what everyone on the third floor tells me."

"And what else do they say?"

"They say you will always do what is best for Israel."

Bloch said nothing.

"There is a way to bring Slaton back, Anton."

For twenty minutes Bloch listened. At the end, he wished he had not.

"So it begins in Stockholm?" Bloch asked.

Nurin nodded.

"And Slaton? Where will he be?"

Like a good spy chief, Nurin had that answer as well.

TWO

Earl Long steered his Ford F-150 up the service path to the estate, wet gravel crunching under the truck's tires. On the trailer behind him was the morning's third pallet of rock, which was considerable headway for having a work crew of one. The big new home came into view, a colonial monstrosity. It sat high on a manicured hill, framed by rows of freshly plugged chestnut and elm saplings. Long wasn't a landscaper, but he imagined the trees must have set the owners back two or three times the fifteen thousand they were blowing on his hundred-foot retaining wall. It would all look stately in about fifty years, he thought. Some people just pissed it away.

The job site was on the far side of the house, and Long kept to the service road as long as he could, not wanting to damage the new lawn that had to be soft after last night's rain. He spotted his lone employee at the base of the hill hauling an eighty-pound block of cut granite. Just as he'd been doing all summer.

Edmund Deadmarsh had answered the Craigslist ad back in June. Long had lost an entire crew overnight—deported to Honduras—and he'd hired Deadmarsh for the usual twelve bucks an hour, reckoning he'd still need two more replacements. On the first day the man had moved four tons of rock. Not only that, he'd put it down with a set and finish that was nearly a work of art. After a week, Long had bumped his new man up to fifteen an hour and pulled the ad. Deadmarsh had been showing up for three straight months now, working through the height of summer when crews rarely lasted more than three jobs. The man just kept going, day after sweltering day, never slowing or asking for help. It was almost as if he was punishing himself.

Long backed the truck into place and stepped down from the cab. He nodded at Deadmarsh and got one in return. Cranking the Bobcat, he pulled the pallet off the trailer and placed it as close as possible to the wall. *Gotta give the man some kind of help*, he thought. He parked the machine, then went back in his truck and began fiddling with invoices as he sipped his Starbucks. Soon, however, Long found himself watching Deadmarsh. It was the damnedest thing, the way the guy moved around a worksite. He was quick, but never rushed. Never slipped in the mud or lost his balance setting a stone into place. And the strangest thing of all—he did it in near silence. No huffing or grunting or shuffling over the ground. Only yesterday, a surprised Long had turned around to find Deadmarsh right behind him with a boulder in his arms. Never made a sound. *The damnedest thing.*

Long got out of the truck when his cup ran dry. "Looks good," he said, sidestepping down the embankment.

Deadmarsh slid a block into place, and asked, "Is the height what you wanted?"

"Looks about right. Did you measure it?"

"You took the measuring tape when you drove off for that last load."

Long fished into his pocket and felt the metal square. "Oh yeah, so I did." He took it out, pulled four feet from the reel, and set one end at the base of the wall. "Yep, right on."

Deadmarsh nodded, but there was no apparent satisfaction. He just turned for another stone.

"You're pretty darned good at this," Long said. "You been in the line of work long?"

Deadmarsh pulled a stone from the pallet and turned smoothly. "About three months."

Long grinned. "What'd you do before that?"

The stone slid perfectly into place. "Government work."

"Civil service?"

"Yeah. You could say that."

Long nodded. "My wife wanted me to get into that a few years back. I had a buddy who said he could hook me into a nice desk job with the county—building code administrator." He shook his head. "Couldn't do it though. You know, sitting in one of those damned cubicles all day."

Deadmarsh grabbed another block of granite and turned on the mud without the slightest waver. "Benefits might have been good," he said. "You've got two kids to look after."

"Yeah, that's what my wife said. But guys like us are born to work outside, right? Blue sky and green grass."

Deadmarsh said nothing. His T-shirt was soaked in sweat, clinging like a second skin. Long remembered thinking the man had been in good shape when he'd started—wouldn't have hired him otherwise—but after a summer spent humping granite slabs up and down hills he looked like a cruiserweight boxer. Thick, lean muscle, not an ounce of fat anywhere.

"So just what part of the government did you work for?" Long pressed.

Deadmarsh dropped another block into place, and turned to look at him. He seemed to think about it, then said, "The part that worked."

Long stared for a moment, then began to chuckle. "Ain't no such thing."

Deadmarsh's phone chirped, and they both looked toward his motorcycle. The phone rarely went off, but when it did Deadmarsh always dropped what he was doing and checked the call. He vaulted up over the wall and went to the bike, a big BMW that somehow didn't seem right to Long. He'd once asked Deadmarsh how he could afford a bike like that, and gotten the answer that his wife was a doctor. Long had nearly laughed out loud, thinking, *Yeah, and that's why you're out here busting rock in ninety-degree heat.*

Deadmarsh picked up the phone and checked the screen. He went very still, then typed a reply and waited. After less than a minute, he pocketed his phone and said, "I've got to go."

That was all. No explanation or timeframe. Without another word, he swung a leg over the BMW and reached for the key.

"Go? What do you mean, go?"

Deadmarsh said nothing.

"I need you back in an hour to finish this pallet. I told the irrigation guy we'd be done this afternoon."

"You'll have to do it." Deadmarsh cranked the engine and the big bike purred to life.

Incredulous, Long strode over and got in his face. He pointed to the pallet of rock. "You think I'm gonna haul that? To hell with you, mister! If you want your paycheck next week, you'd better be back by—"

"Look! I'm sorry to put you in a bind, but I quit. Keep the paycheck." Deadmarsh leaned the bike straight and kicked up the stand. He reached for a helmet that was hooked onto the back.

"Quit? Now hang on a minute!" Long reached out and grabbed the handlebar.

That was when it happened. A sharp pain in the back of his legs, as if a club had swept in just below his knees. Before he knew what was happening, Long was on his ass in the gravel and staring up at Deadmarsh.

Earl Long was a big man, and not unaccustomed to physical challenges. On and off the job he'd seen his share of confrontation, and usually with favorable results. At six-five, two-sixty, he had three inches and at least forty pounds on the man hovering over him. Even so, Long didn't move. There was something in the stare that kept him planted right where he was. He'd seen men full of hate and whiskey. Even craziness. This was none of those things. He was looking at eyes that were hard and impenetrable, like a steel-gray sky on the coldest winter day.

Long sat still.

The big bike jumped and a fountain of stone spewed behind, peppering his face. Long heard the engine wind up to the redline, then shift. It happened again, and again, until the motorcycle and its rider became a collective blur. Earl Long just sat on the ground and watched, and from that vantage point he predicted—quite correctly, as it turned out—that he would never see Edmund Deadmarsh again.

THREE

Stockholm, Sweden

Christine Palmer sat looking at her watch. The auditorium was less than half full, so she suspected the other physicians attending the conference had known what was coming. Dr. Adolphus Breen, professor emeritus of internal medicine at the University of Oslo, had been prattling for an hour on the issue of bacterial prostatitis. To make it even more excruciating, the afternoon outside was glorious.

She had been at the conference for three days, attending seminars in a dutiful way that would have made her sponsoring organization, The Physician's Group of Eastern Virginia, smile with pride. Even so, when the esteemed Dr. Breen shifted to his well-trod treatise, "The Role of Bacterial Overgrowth in Chronic Diarrhea," Christine could take no more. She made her move, breaking discreetly from her chair at the end of a row.

Outside, the sun struck like a wave of warm liquid, fresh and exhilarating on her face. Having recently completed her residency, this was her first medical conference, and she now saw why her colleagues had recommended this particular seminar. In a display of right-mindedness, it had been based at the Strand Hotel, a magnificent venue overlooking Stockholm's harbor and the Strandvägen. The timing was equally superlative. In a few months, the sidewalk she was strolling would be carpeted with snow and ice.

Christine crossed the street, and began wandering the granite footpath that skirted the waterfront. Not for the first time, she wished David were here. She instinctively reached into her back pocket, but her phone wasn't there. She'd been unable to find it in her room this morning, and running late, she'd shrugged and gone downstairs without it. David would be furious if he knew.

He hadn't wanted her to come in the first place, and Christine knew his reservations went beyond the simple fact that they were newlyweds. When she invited him to join her, David only made excuses. He mentioned the cost—the physicians group, in recent belt tightening, no longer funded the inclusion of spouses on such boondoggles. Then he'd brought up the issue of his own work, and on that Christine had bitten her tongue. In the end, she knew it was something deeper. Given his fluency in Swedish, she suspected he had served here at some point as an agent for Mossad. If so, his reluctance to come might be a way of forgetting his past, akin to the way her grandfather, a D-Day veteran, had waited decades before returning to the beaches of Normandy. So it was, Christine had come alone.

The sidewalks along the waterfront were busy. Couples walking aimlessly, families with strollers, blond children running teetering circles around grandparents. Christine appraised the buildings along the Strandvägen, and saw noble facades given to grand towers and domes and exposed brickwork. Lining the wide esplanade were rows of massive trees that had likely once shaded horse-drawn carriages, but now were relegated to bursting foliage every spring over electric trams and bumper-to-bumper Volvos. Altogether, she saw a vibrant and contemporary city, but with the bones of Old World dignity.

Christine had skipped breakfast after rising with an unsettled stomach, and lunch at the conference had been less than inspiring, a smorgasbord where she'd nibbled lightly while weighing the bleak afternoon lecture lineup. Now, washed in full sun and a brisk October breeze, she found her appetite rekindled. Christine drifted into a café and was given a table overlooking the waterway. She ordered coffee and a pastry, the traditional Swedish fika, and amused herself by watching the crowds. She noted an unusual number of men pushing strollers, and she remembered being told that this was a product of Sweden's liberal parenting laws. On the birth of a child, fathers were granted generous paternity leave, and many took advantage to spend time with their newborns. She tried to picture David behind an umbrella stroller. He had come a long way in the last year, but she couldn't fix that vision in her mind. Not yet, anyway. Christine sweetened and creamed her coffee, and watched the tan swirl blend as she stirred.

When she looked up, a man had appeared out of nowhere.

Her hand jerked, and in some distant recess she felt warm liquid splatter onto her wrist, heard a spoon clatter to the table. He was just on the other side of the gilt railing, standing as still and fixed as a statue in a square. He was staring at her.

It was the last person in the world she wanted to see.

Christine felt like she was falling into an abyss. She tried to breath, yet somehow couldn't, as if the surrounding atmosphere had drawn to a vacuum. Anton Bloch said nothing. He simply stood there, blunt and immovable. Knowing the effect he was having.

A decorative railing was all that separated them. Christine wanted more. She wanted iron bars or bulletproof glass. A thousand miles. His face, stony and dour, was just as she remembered. That he made no effort to feign surprise was the only positive, no what-a-small-world lie pressed into his expression. Bloch waited for her shock to run its course. When it did, he said, "Hello, Christine."

She took a deep breath to gather herself. "Anton."

"Do you mind if I join you?" he asked, his accent a crush of consonants.

"If I said no?"

He ignored this and circled around to the entrance. Bloch had a quick word with the hostess, and thirty seconds later he was there, easing his bulk onto the delicate white chair across the table. He started to speak, but the waitress swooped in and took his order. Coffee, black.

The moment the waitress was away, Christine seized the initiative. "What do you want?"

Bloch hesitated, and Christine took that moment to study him. He'd changed little in a year, perhaps a few pounds heavier in retirement, but retaining the sober gaze and furrowed brow she'd come to know in their brief association. A brooding Buddha.

"How is the conference at the Strand?" he asked.

A question that was no question at all, Christine thought. More a statement to announce that there would be no pretenses. *I know why you are here. Where you are staying. What you are doing.* Spies, she'd learned, by some strange paradox, had a way of being succinct.

"The conference? I'd been enjoying it until now."

"Why didn't David come with you?"

"Edmund, you mean?"

"Do you really call him that?"

"When I have to. Cocktail parties, dinner with friends. Lying has become a way of life for me."

Bloch said nothing.

That silence weighed on Christine. At essence, she knew Bloch to be a decent man. He had once been David's boss, ordering him to do Israel's dirtiest work. But he had also helped David leave that impossible life and disappear. What really bothered her, she supposed, was what Bloch represented—her husband's past.

"I'm sorry, Anton."

"I know this must be a shock, but I'll take it as a good sign. You've had no other . . . surprises in the last year?"

"Surprises? You mean like assassins breaking into our home in the middle of the night to settle old scores? No, nothing like that. David Slaton, the *kidon*, has disappeared. He's fallen off the face of the earth." She then added, "Just like you promised."

Bloch grinned, an awkward undertaking where his face came creased, little-used muscles finding recall. He moved his thick hands to the table in front of him, a space occupied by flatware and a napkin that had been folded in the shape of a boat. Bloch pushed it all aside and the tiny boat capsized.

She said, "I tried to bring David with me, actually. He made excuses."

"The passport would have held up."

"I don't think it was that. Tell me—did he ever spend time here?"

"He spent much of his childhood in Stockholm. David speaks fluent Swedish, you know."

"That's not what I mean. Did he work here for you? For Mossad?"

After a pause, Bloch said, "Yes."

And there it was, the simplest of answers. Part of her wanted to know more. She understood what David had been to Mossad, but the details of her husband's past were largely left unsaid between them. Here was a chance to learn more, yet she hesitated mightily. Did she really want to know?

As if sensing her uncertainty, Bloch said, "I had to find you, Christine. Something important has come up."

Her eyes fell to her coffee. *Something important.* For most people, a newly diagnosed heart murmur, a bent fender on the Toyota. She straightened in her chair and clasped her hands deliberately in her lap. More than ever, she wished David were here.

Bloch's tone was strictly business. "The current director of Mossad, a man named Raymond Nurin, recently asked to meet with me. A few weeks ago a team of our operatives was lost in Iran. Did you hear about it?"

"I remember David showing me an article in the *Post*. He wondered if anyone he knew had been involved."

"I'm sure he knew at least one of the men—they worked together some years ago, when I was in charge of things. His name was Yaniv Stein." Bloch explained a few details of the attack, things that hadn't been in the *Post*. Then he mentioned another mission that had failed some months prior. He explained that Mossad was desperate to stop Iran's headlong charge toward nuclear-tipped madness.

"The key to stopping them," he continued, "involves the head of the program, Dr. Ibrahim Hamedi. He was the target of both failed missions."

"Anton, I really don't need to know any of this because—"

"Next week," he cut in, "Hamedi will leave Iran. The director believes he will be vulnerable and is determined to try again. The problem is—"

"I don't give a damn about your director's problems! I am here for a medical conference. David and I have a life, and we don't need anything from you or Israel."

Bloch's coffee came, forcing a pause. When the waitress left he didn't pretend to address his cup. "Christine, *please* listen to me. Mossad is in crisis. The missions I told you about failed because there is a traitor, a leak somewhere in the agency—it has frozen them. They can't act directly on this opportunity, and Nurin believes there is only one other way to go after Hamedi. They must use someone outside the organization."

Christine went rigid. Her voice struck an arctic whisper that surprised even her, "Don't you even say it!" She pushed back from the table and stood. "You stay away from him!" Her voice kept rising. "Stay away from us!"

Bloch rose and grabbed her arm, his hand a vice. "That's what I told Nurin!" Bloch whispered harshly. "I am on your side in this!"

People were staring.

He repeated it slowly. "I am on your side."

Hesitantly, Christine eased back into her seat.

Bloch said, "I told him David would never do it, that nothing could make him go back. I suspected Nurin had called me in as a recruiter—to try and talk David into doing the job. He didn't even try."

Her gaze narrowed. "So what did he want?"

"He believes there is a way to force David into taking this assignment. He told me that . . . that you would be here in Stockholm today. Alone."

Christine didn't understand at first. As a physician she was accustomed to directness, not trained to search for snares. But finally she saw what Bloch was suggesting, and the cold realization swept her away. He kept talking, but the words barely registered.

"Can't you see it?" he said. "I am the only person in Israel you would trust. The director asked me to help—he thought I might be able to bring you in quietly. I told him I would."

Her world was spinning, but Bloch's eyes held her in a grip harsher than the one that had just bruised her arm. "That's what I *told* him. But the truth is that I came here to help you. I am going to get you out of this."

She shook her head. "Whatever you are trying to tell me—"

"Listen very carefully, Christine. I want you to look discreetly across the street. You will see a silver Audi, two men. One is standing on the curb, the other sitting in the driver's seat."

Trying to be casual in a world gone mad, Christine tilted her head and saw them, two men and a car framed by the shimmering waterfront. The one standing was tall and heavy, dark hair. The man at the wheel, bald and thick-necked.

Bloch continued, "A third man is positioned near the café entrance, on the sidewalk. He's talking on his phone."

She looked and there he was, smiling and chatting in a most carefree manner. He might have been asking his girlfriend on a date, or perhaps scheduling a tennis match.

Bloch's words fell to a slow, measured clip. "You

must do as I say, Christine. For your sake. For *David's* sake."

Christine was holding the table by its edges. She had to hold something. Bloch leveled a still, somber gaze, and she imagined it was a look he had used before with David—right before sending him into the world as Israel's killing machine.

"They intend to put you in that car. A private jet is waiting at the airport. Right now they're assuming that I will act out a ruse to deliver you calmly to the car."

Her eyes flicked across the street.

"What I am going to do is pay our bill, then stand up. When I do, take my arm as we head to the exit. When I give you the order, turn and run. Go inside the main restaurant, straight back through the central hallway. Past the kitchen you'll find a door at the back. It leads to an alley."

The table began trembling under her grip. She focused on a glass of water on the table, mesmerized by the concentric rings inside.

"In the alley, turn left." Bloch pried one of her hands from the table, the one out of sight from the street, and Christine felt him press something into it. She looked down and saw a car key.

"Dark blue Saab, near the mouth of the alley. Drive straight ahead, turn right. There's no need to go fast, you'll have a head start and they won't know what to look for. I'll hold them here as long as I can."

She looked at him pleadingly, willing him to stop.

He implored in a low voice, "There is no other way, Christine!"

"But—then what?"

She saw his hand come around the side of the table again. This time it held her missing cell phone.

He answered her question before she could ask it. "We took it from your room last night to isolate you. I've powered it down for now—leave it that way. You can be tracked when the phone is on. Just put it in your pocket."

She did so, not even bothering to ask how they'd invaded her hotel room.

"I've already sent a message to David. He's on the way."

"David is coming here? What did you tell him?"

"Wait until tomorrow," Bloch said, ignoring her question, "then use your phone to contact him. Do it from a cab or a bus, something mobile. If he doesn't answer, turn it back off and keep moving. Try again one day later, at the same time. Whatever you do in the meantime, don't go back to your hotel. If I can't stop them, it's the first place they'll look."

"If you can't—" Her thoughts froze, stilled like a metronome hitting a stop. "Why are you doing this, Anton?"

He seemed to take care in choosing his words. "I've asked a great deal of David over the years. This is a decision I made just over a week ago, during Yom Kippur. It is our Day of Atonement."

The waitress came with the check. Bloch took it, settled in cash, and stood. "Now," he ordered.

Christine pushed away from the table, but her legs seemed weak. He put a hand under her elbow and she rose, falling in beside him. The man on the sidewalk was still chatting on his phone. He was thirty feet away.

"Are you ready?" Bloch whispered, adding a staged smile. He might have been escorting his daughter to a high school dance.

Christine responded by looking squarely at the man

outside. It was a mistake. When he recognized her eye contact, his manufactured smile disappeared. He slipped the phone under the lapel of his jacket. His hand came back out with a gun.

"Go!" Bloch yelled, pushing her aside.

Christine stumbled, but caught her balance. Frozen with indecision, she saw Bloch draw his own gun, then heard a crash of shots. The man on the sidewalk went down and gunfire burst in from the street. The legs that had wobbled only moments ago found new strength. Christine broke into a run, shouldering past scrambling patrons into the shadowed dining room. People were screaming, trying to get away. She slowed down and turned, caught a glimpse of Bloch aiming his gun at something—no, someone—and then his body rocked once, twice, and he dropped like a stone. Stunned, Christine's first urge was to go to his side. But then she was stepping backward, all the while watching, willing him to rise. He didn't move.

The gunfire paused.

Christine whipped around and slammed straight into a waiter, his tray clattering to the ground in an explosion of food and china and cutlery. If the men on the street had lost track of her in the confusion of the firefight, that advantage was gone. Sure enough, she spotted the heavy man who'd been standing by the car. He was running across the street and pointing a finger at her.

She shoved past a frantic chef into the hallway. Then, just as Bloch had said, she saw the door at the end. Christine picked up speed and burst through without slowing. She pitched into an alley and immediately tripped over a box of kitchen garbage, sprawling to the ground and taking a mouthful of asphalt. But when she looked up it was right in front of her—a blue car. She scrambled to her feet and reached it in seconds. The door was unlocked and she clambered in. Amazingly, the key was still in her fist, clutched like a token of salvation. Christine shoved it in the ignition.

The key didn't fit.

FOUR

Christine slammed the key with the palm of her hand. It sank awkwardly and jammed in the lock.

"God, no! No, no, no!"

She looked over her shoulder. No one yet. Christine kept trying, but the key wouldn't turn. Frantically, she checked the gearshift. Already in park. Her foot was on the brake. *What else?* The steering lock. So many damned safety mechanisms. She twisted the wheel and turned the key simultaneously. Still jammed.

A clatter from behind.

She turned and saw the big man, his eyes sweeping the alley, gun drawn. She slid down in the seat, and that was when she recognized the problem—the emblem on the steering wheel. Ford. Christine smacked the seat, remembering what Bloch had said. *In the alley, turn left.* She had fallen, looked up, and seen a blue car. But she'd gone the wrong way. Peering between the headrests, she saw the man walking guardedly in the other direction. Eyes moving, gun level. A hundred feet beyond was a second blue car, a Saab whose key was wedged in the ignition in front of her. Christine reached up and tried to pull the key, but it was hopelessly stuck. There was no time to deal with it. The man would soon reverse and come her way, or possibly his partner would take this side of the alley. She had to move.

Christine slid to the passenger side of the Ford, which was better shielded from where the man stood. She checked again and saw her pursuer at the far end of the alley peering into the Saab. In front of her, the side street was only twenty feet away. It seemed like a mile, but if she could turn that corner without being seen, she'd be in the clear.

She pulled the door handle like it was made of glass. The mechanism gave, barely audible, and she eased the door open. Crawling out, she stayed low, leaving the door ajar as a visual screen. She was two steps from the corner when she heard a shout.

"Stop!"

Christine sprinted toward the waterfront, dodging bicycles and skirting bystanders who were gawking at the wrecked café behind her. The café where Anton Bloch was lying in a pool of blood. She looked back and saw the big man giving chase, negotiating cars as he crossed the street. One nearly hit him, horn blaring, and Dr. Christine Palmer, avowed healer, wished it had done so. She was moving fast now, not the sloppy gait of a frightened woman, but the driving stride of the hurdler she'd been in high school. Even so, the man was gaining. She didn't see his partner, the driver. Had Bloch shot him? Christine decided it made no difference. One man with a gun was enough.

Her feet pounded the path along the water's edge. On her left was a busy street, the far side lined with hotels and shops. On her right was the harbor, tour boats tied along a short pier, a passenger ferry unloading. Her lungs were heaving. Christine was in good shape—she jogged fifteen miles a week. But running for your life was different.

She heard the alternating wail of a siren in the distance. The police had to be speeding toward the café—but that was the one direction she couldn't go. Nearing a congested crosswalk, Christine spun to avoid a collision with a woman on a bicycle. She'd just gotten back in stride when she saw something that brought her skidding to a stop. A hundred feet ahead—a car with its hood raised. A silver Audi. The second Mossad man was leaning into the engine compartment, but he was looking directly at her.

For the first time Christine felt a moment of panic. These were professionals like David. The car was perfectly positioned, and since it was illegally parked on the shoulder, the driver had raised the hood to feign a mechanical issue. It would work for a minute, maybe two, and that was all they needed. Probably right out of the Mossad field agent handbook. The big man was fifty feet away, skirting the street. He'd slowed to a quick walk and was panting with the grace of a bull.

Her head kept wheeling, left and right. No way out. They had the angles covered perfectly. All too late, Christine realized her mistake—by going to the waterfront she had boxed herself in, made their geometric problem that much easier. She could scream, call for help, but the police were busy elsewhere—shots fired, bodies in the street. And anyway, these two Mossad operatives would handle a hysterical woman as smoothly as they'd positioned their car on the curb with a raised hood.

They closed in, but didn't show their weapons. There was no need. The three of them knew, and that was all that mattered. Christine turned toward the harbor. The water looked cold and uninviting. Then, amid the street noise and bustle of the city, she distinguished a singular sound. A low rumble. She looked down the short pier where tour boats were moored and saw a different kind of boat pushing clear of the dock. Thirty feet long, it was blunt and businesslike, perhaps a harbor master's utility vessel. The deck was crowded with cables and winches and fifty-five-gallon drums. She saw a crewman on deck stowing a line. There had to be another in the wheelhouse. Black smoke coughed from the stern.

Christine broke into a sprint. She hit the wooden dock in stride and watched the boat accelerate, a cloud of diesel exhaust billowing in its wake. The deckhand disappeared into the cabin. Christine was twenty feet from the end of the dock. She kept running and didn't look back—she knew the men were coming. The aft gunnel of the harbor boat was five feet from the dock and moving away. The engines rumbled higher as the skipper added power. Eight feet now? Ten? What did it matter?

At full sprint, Christine focused completely on two things: the last plank on the dock, and the thick, greasy rail of the boat. She never hesitated, hitting the last board like a long jumper taking flight. She soared over the void with arms outstretched and slammed into the side of the boat. On impact she bounced away, and Christine clawed out for a handhold. Her right hand found something and she clamped down for all she was worth, fingers and nails biting into a coarse mesh. She was hanging over the side, hips and legs dragging through the icy harbor, upper body wrapped to the steel hull. Her hand began to slip, and she groped with the other until she felt a second handful of thick hemp. A docking line. Christine reasserted her grip, then pulled and kicked and twisted until she got a leg up. Finally, she pulled herself up over the rail and collapsed to a wet steel deck.

Her ribs stung with pain. Doubled over, she stumbled amidships along the port side. There was no sign of the crew. The boat kept gaining speed, muscling through the water and building a stiff breeze over the deck. Christine collapsed, her back against the wheelhouse, and tried to catch her breath. Only then did she venture a look back. The two men were on the dock, talking and gesturing. One pulled out a phone. She closed her eyes and pushed back against the cabin, drawing her knees into her aching chest. Christine reached into her back pocket and pulled out her phone. It was soaking wet and the screen was cracked.

"No!"

Ignoring what Bloch had told her, she turned it on. Nothing happened—the shattered screen didn't even flicker.

Her spirits crumbled. "Oh, David," she murmured breathlessly. "Now what do I do?"

The two men on the pier were still watching, but getting smaller as the boat pulled away. Looking ahead, over the bowsprit of the boat and across the waterway, Christine saw a maze of city streets and seawalls. Beyond that, in the distance, the urban canals gave way to a more natural flow. Evergreen islands and winding channels. And just like that, the answer came.

Exactly as David had said it would.

FIVE

Nineteen hours later, a Scandinavian Airlines A-340 touched down smoothly at Stockholm's Arlanda Airport, the last act of a four-thousand-mile journey. The big jet taxied in, took its place at the terminal, and three hundred and twelve passengers began the customary odyssey, steering through jet bridges, corridors, and crowd-control stanchions toward the human repository marked ARRIVALS.

Among them, fixed in the middle of the pack, was a tall and slightly disheveled man. He was tan and fit, but clearly fatigued. Wearing an untucked polo shirt and wrinkled cotton slacks, he had the look of a man returning from a well-spent vacation. His tousled, sun-bleached hair merged into the unshaven roughage of a few days' beard. His casual shoes were untied, thin laces dragging across the polished stone floor. Everything in between these ends corresponded, weary and beaten, all easily attributable to a nine-hour red-eye flight. At a glance, he was a nondescript traveler among a sea of the same. Yet were anyone to look more closely—and no one did—certain marks might have distinguished him from the crowd. He moved quietly, with no wasted motion. He carried a bag in one hand, his left, yet there was no hint of awkwardness or imbalance. His stride was easy and controlled, even precise, and he neatly avoided contact with those around him, never bumping shoulders or locking glances. Most telling of all, his eyes were discreetly active.

The queue came to a stop at the roadblock that was immigration, and David Slaton stood patiently behind fifty other souls in the NON-EU line. For the second time since landing he checked his phone. There was still nothing from Christine. He called up the message he'd received yesterday and stared at it: Help! Only one word, yet that very simplicity made it ring even louder. Since then, she had not answered his calls, nor had she sent any texts or emails. For what seemed the hundredth time, Slaton tried to imagine what had happened. Any number of dire scenarios came to mind, but they all distilled to one source—his former life with Mossad had come back with a vengeance.

This was the day he'd hoped would never come. The contingency he had wanted to prepare for and Christine had wanted to deny. As he'd been doing all the way across an ocean, Slaton tried to shape his response. He was a product of training and methods that strove for predictability, because the predictable could be controlled. Yet for the first time ever, his attempts at thoughtful design seemed to drift. Unmoored by last words and gestures, things left unsaid. He had seen others wrestle such complications. A spotter on his sniper team with a sick child. A surveillance partner going through an ugly divorce. Personal issues always got in the way—that was a determination Slaton had long ago made. This time, however, it was different. This time it was happening to him.

To have gotten this far was simple enough—it had been the only course. *Get to Stockholm as quickly as possible.* But now what? Unlike the old days, he could expect no help. Funding, intelligence briefings, embassy staff, diplomatic immunity. Those were the things Slaton had once taken for granted. The things that someone in an office, deep in Mossad's engine room, had always made happen. Now, whatever he and Christine were facing, they were facing it alone.

The line inched forward, branching into five smaller lines. As Slaton approached the podium he studied the immigration officer. She was middle-aged, attractive in a peroxide-over-tortoiseshell-glasses kind of way. There was no wedding ring on her well-manicured left hand. Her uniform was crisp and neat, her physique trim. Perhaps a runner. He saw a faint tan line around her eyes, as if she'd recently spent time outside wearing sunglasses. If he were to venture a guess, a 10K race over the weekend. It struck Slaton then how long it had been since he'd appraised a person in such a way.

He moved to the podium.

"Passport," she said, her words clipped and precise.

He handed over the document and she swiped it into her machine. Her eyes lingered on a display that would be full of information on an American named Edmund Deadmarsh. Full legal name, place of birth, age, vital statistics. Might there also be a flag? Slaton wondered. To this point, he'd had no reception. No police, no Ministry of Justice, no Swedish Security Service. The longer it stayed that way, he decided, the better.

She asked, "How long will you be staying, sir?"

"Only a few days."

She handed his passport back and smiled, this time holding his gaze a bit longer than necessary. "Enjoy your stay in Sweden, Mr. Deadmarsh."

And that was the moment it struck Slaton.

Yesterday he had gotten a desperate message from his wife, and in the intervening hours he had vacillated. Sensed tremors of conflict, even indecision. Yet right then, standing at an immigration counter, everything crystallized. There was now but one objective in his life—to find Christine and take her to safety. And if that required a complete reversion to what he had once been?

So be it.

The transition came with alarming ease. David Slaton had no interest in a casual flirtation with a nice-looking woman. Edmund Deadmarsh, on the other hand, seen at that moment as a rumpled but rather attractive traveler, could have only one response. He gave the woman his most engaging smile.

"Thank you. I'm sure I will."

And with that, the *kidon* turned toward the exit and disappeared.

Slaton slipped into a taxi five minutes later.

"Strand Hotel, please."

"Strand Hotel," the driver repeated.

The cabbie was a burly sort, a man in need of both a smile and a sharper razor. He made a stab at conversation in troubled English, the usual weather observations and have-you-been-here-before banter. By his accent, Slaton pegged him as Eastern European, Bulgarian perhaps. Slaton was minimally receptive, and the chatter soon ended.

For most, a backseat ride in a cab is an idle affair. For an assassin it is something else. Of primary importance is position. Slaton sat where he could see the driver's hands, wanting to know if they were on the wheel or elsewhere. The rearview mirror held greater nuance—he had to be able to see the driver's eyes when it suited him, but fall out of the reciprocal view with a shift of his shoulders. He checked his line of sight to each sideview mirror, not to watch the following traffic—a discreet turn of the head was always better—but rather to monitor the blind spots along either rear quarter-panel, particularly when stopped. The cab's physical security measures were standard issue. The doors were not the type to lock automatically—some did—and Slaton noted the positions of the mechanical latches. All the windows were presently raised, except for the driver's. The man apparently did his best work with an elbow hanging over the rail. There was a Plexiglas bulkhead between the front and back seats with an opening too small for a man to pass through. Yet it did allow access. A strong arm. A hand to the wheel. That was all the control Slaton could assume in an emergency. On most days, details that amounted to nothing. But one day details that might matter very much.

The ride took thirty minutes, and approaching downtown Slaton began to study his surroundings. How long since he'd been to Stockholm? Eight years? Ten? Things would have changed. Things like how you bought a bus ticket and which local football clubs were playing well. He supposed surveillance cameras were everywhere now, watching businesses and municipal parking lots and traffic corridors. His Swedish would hold up, he was sure of that, but for the moment it was of little use. Edmund Deadmarsh, a man who lugged stone blocks across well-manicured Virginia lawns, ought not be fluent in six languages.

The cab turned onto a busy thoroughfare. Slaton soon saw the harbor, and with another turn he spotted his objective in the distance. It stood wide and tall, like a granite throne at the water's edge—the Strand Hotel. He settled back and sequenced his thoughts. Christine was here, somewhere, yet he had no more than a starting point. It struck him that he didn't even know her room number. Again Slaton admonished himself. For a year he had relaxed, allowed his skills to tarnish. He had practiced recycling instead of marksmanship. Planned grocery lists instead of countersurveillance. Now Christine was suffering, and it was a direct result of his half-measures. A direct result of his carelessness.

He would not be careless again.

Slaton was dropped at the hotel awning at 1:14 in the afternoon. He settled with the driver, then gave the bellman his bag and a ten-dollar bill, saying he'd be back shortly. The size of the gratuity was well considered. Enough to be remembered when he claimed his bag in an hour or two. Not enough to be remembered tomorrow.

Slaton turned sharply away from the entrance and started up the street. He was already quite sure he was not being followed. In truth, he wished it were the case, because any tail would likely be a lead to Christine. He walked straight to Berzelii Park, at the head of the waterway, and turned right. He navigated a misaligned web of streets, making two brief stops, and paused to marvel at the nouveau architecture of the Royal Dramatic Theater. Changing course, he weaved westward until he came to the Kungsträdgården, and there he passed a statue of Charles XIII, the much maligned king of the early nineteenth century, before meandering the park's well-manicured gardens with an approving eye. With one more left turn, at the Strömbron bridge, Slaton picked up his pace. He ended back at the Strand Hotel at 1:41, twenty-seven minutes after he'd started.

Slaton considered the time well spent. He had located two separate curbs where cabs congregated, their drivers leaning on fenders and drawing down cigarettes. He'd purchased an unrestricted day pass for both the water taxi and subway, and was aware of seven access points for trolley and bus service. At a nearby parking garage he'd noted a valet stand where the keys to no fewer than fifty late-model vehicles resided on a pegboard. Irregular flows of traffic—points of congestion and one-way streets—were fixed in his mind, as were the two security guards with Steyr TMP machine pistols stationed obviously outside a bank on Stallgatan. Slaton knew that a mobile police station had been situated near the Kungsträdgården, and was staffed by two officers, both carrying SIG Sauer semi-automatics and spare magazines, who could reach the hotel in no less than four minutes on a dead run. He also knew that the hotel had one service entrance, six fire escapes, and an entire north-facing wing with unbarred windows at street level.

Then, and only then, did Slaton walk into the Strand Hotel.

He stepped though the entrance, paused, and began a carefully governed survey.

Belying the hotel's stately, ivy-covered exterior, the lobby was a contrast in Scandinavian contemporary: maple hardwood floors under Finnish Rya rugs; mid-century modern chairs and fixtures, all glass and angles and polished chrome. Aside from their physical arrangement, however, Slaton had no interest in the furnishings. He instead plotted the room's landscape: counters, staircases, elevators, lounge areas. He took in the sounds and registered the general mood. His practiced eyes brushed over each guest and employee, hoping to capture any gaze that seemed equally practiced. Nothing drew his attention.

Slaton saw two clerks at the reception desk, both women, and an older man staffing the adjacent concierge station. The concierge was deeply engaged with a guest, so his choices were narrow. He walked to the desk, veering toward the younger of the two women. Early twenties, blond, dazzling smile. Eager to please.

She looked up as he approached, and said, *"Kan jag hjälpa dig?"*

Slaton was not unprepared. His blue-gray eyes and sandy hair—lighter than usual after a summer outdoors—certainly made him appear more Swedish than American. Or, for that matter, Israeli. Yet another reason Mossad had found him so useful.

"Sorry," he said, "I'm American."

She shifted effortlessly to English, "Of course. How can I help you?"

"I'm trying to locate one of your guests, but I don't know the room number. Could you look it up for me?"

"I am not permitted to give out such information," she said, telling Slaton what he already knew. "But if you like I can dial the room and let you speak with the guest."

"That would be fine."

"What is the name?"

"Christine Palmer. Dr. Christine Palmer."

Watching closely, Slaton sensed a hesitation. Her thin fingers typed the name into her computer.

"Here it is," she said.

The clerk turned an adjacent house phone to face Slaton and performed the connection, again using her computer. For the second time he watched her type, and happily she used the number pad on the keyboard as opposed to the upper numeric bar. By some quirk of memory, inputs to ten-digit keypads were easily recalled by pattern alone. Seven, three, two, four. The seven was almost certainly a prefix to denote an internal line, which meant that Christine was in room 324.

Or had been.

Slaton picked up the house phone and listened as it rang. A dim hope rose that Christine would answer, that he would wake her from a midafternoon nap and they'd be laughing about the grand misunderstanding over dinner. On the eighth ring he hung up, both the phone and the idea.

"I'm afraid she's not in," he said. "I'll try again later. Thank you for your help."

"My pleasure," she beamed.

Slaton was about to turn when she added, "One moment, sir . . ." Another hesitation.

He went to full alert, and saw her eyes flick to the right—toward the other receptionist. The second woman stood stiffly, her gaze locked to a spot behind him in the lobby.

The pretty young clerk began to say something, but Slaton didn't hear it. His attention was padlocked to a reflective strip of stainless-steel trim on the wall behind the counter. In the mirror-like surface he saw three men approaching.

Slaton did not turn, but he moved. Ever so slightly, his stance widened and his left foot edged back in preparation. His hands were already free, so there was no need to set down a briefcase or pocket a mobile phone. As he braced his body, his eyes searched for improvised weapons, but he was standing at the front desk of a noble hotel. There was nothing.

When the men were ten steps away they spread left and right. This told Slaton they were trained. He saw two possibilities. Unfortunately, two possibilities that demanded very different reactions. Slaton planned for the worst case and rehearsed a flow in his mind. With a half step back, he could pivot to his left and strike the man on the right, the biggest, with a heel to the head. Next, he would rotate a right elbow to the center target. He ended his blueprint there, knowing that was as far as it would realistically hold.

Seconds from launching into a melee, he took one more look at the older clerk. Slaton weighed her expression very carefully. She was concerned, but in a controlled way. Guarded, yet not preparing to dive behind the counter. That made his decision.

With the men positioned three steps behind him, Slaton slowly turned.

The one in the middle, the smallest and a man who had ten years on the other two, put a hand under the lapel of his jacket. It came back out, as Slaton had hoped, with a well-worn set of credentials.

"*Polisen. Vi vill prata med dig.*"

Slaton gave the man a questioning look. "English?"

"Police. We'd like to have a word with you."

SIX

"Might I see some identification, sir?"

Slaton gave his passport to the man in the middle and watched him type E-D-M-U-N-D D-E-A-D-M-A-R-S-H into his phone. The two bookends stood motionless and appeared unconcerned. In truth, Slaton was happy to see the police—they were next on his list to contact. He was not, however, happy to find them here. Slaton was sure he'd been highlighted by the receptionist after inquiring about Christine, and it struck him as ominous that this had earned him special recognition. It meant the police were at the Strand for reasons relating to her, and committing three officers to such a quest would not be done lightly.

"I'm trying to find my wife," Slaton said, his voice perfectly askew.

"Her name?"

"Dr. Christine Palmer. She's here for a medical conference."

The man in the middle seemed to study him for a moment, then handed back his passport. He said, "Mr. Deadmarsh, I think we should talk."

They moved to a quiet corner of the lobby where two couches were separated by a glass table. The lead man introduced himself as Detective Inspector Sanderson. He was late fifties, a small man with a crooked nose and more than his share of scars. A bantam scrapper if Slaton had ever seen one. He sensed a toughness about the man, along with a manner that implied there was little he hadn't seen, nothing he hadn't heard. His most striking feature was a set of ice-blue eyes that ran clear and sharp. After a businesslike handshake, Sanderson settled onto one of the couches. The two supporting men—twin monuments of bulk, sinew, and seriousness—drifted to the perimeter.

"What can you tell me about Christine?" Slaton asked, not having to manufacture the edge in his voice.

"I can tell you we're looking for her."

"Why?"

"Actually, I was going to ask you that same question. Why are you here?"

"I got a text from Christine yesterday. I was back in the States." Slaton pulled out his phone and showed Sanderson the message.

The inspector studied the display with apparent interest, although Slaton suspected the message was something he'd already seen. If the man was indeed searching for Christine, the first thing he would have done was acquire a record of her mobile traffic.

"And based on this one-word text," Sanderson surmised, "you booked the first available flight to Stockholm?"

"Yes," Slaton said matter-of-factly. "My wife said she needed help. I tried to contact her, but she didn't answer. So I took the first flight." All true, and once again points that Sanderson, if he was thorough, had already verified.

"Has anything like this happened before?" the inspector asked.

"My wife calling for help? No, never. This scares the hell out of me, Inspector. Why are the police involved?"

The cool blue eyes probed. "First I should tell you that we have no reason to believe your wife is in immediate danger."

"*Immediate* danger? What the hell does that mean?"

"Yesterday there was a shooting at a café nearby. Two men were gunned down. Your wife was at that café."

"Was she injured?"

"No," Sanderson said, "at least not that we know of. But she was seen talking with one of the victims right before the shooting began."

"Who?"

"I'm afraid that has been vexing us. We're not sure, which is why we'd very much like to talk to her. Unfortunately . . ." Another heavy pause.

Another dead stare from Edmund Deadmarsh.

"Soon after this shooting took place, a woman—we believe your wife—was seen by a number of witnesses running across the waterfront."

"Running?"

"She was being pursued by a man, we think one of the assailants."

Slaton put his head in his hands, a reaction that was part theater. But only part. He tried to incorporate what he was learning with what he already knew, yet the possibilities remained overwhelming. He needed more information. "A man was chasing Christine? Why? Was this a robbery or something?"

"At the moment, I'd say not. But we really aren't sure."

Slaton sensed a degree of honesty in that answer,

laced perhaps with frustration. "All right, so this man was seen chasing my wife—what happened then?"

"Again, we have a number of witnesses, and their statements all correlate. They saw your wife jump onto a departing boat to escape her pursuer."

For the first time Slaton saw an answer he liked, but he gave no tell. Remaining in character, he pulled an incredulous tone. "She jumped onto a boat? Where did she go from there?"

The policeman turned his palms up to say he didn't know.

"Have you identified any of these people?"

"Not yet, I'm afraid."

"But you said two men were shot. Don't people in Sweden carry driver's licenses or identity cards?"

To his credit, Sanderson remained steady. "We strongly suspect that these men are not Swedish. And this is where I was hoping you might be able to add something."

"What could I tell you? My wife is a doctor and she came here for a conference." Slaton held up his phone like a lawyer holding an exhibit to a jury. "She called me for help, and now you're telling me a man with a gun was chasing her."

"Did I say the man had a gun?" Sanderson countered quickly.

"You said there were shootings."

Both fell silent for a moment, and the policeman leveled his cool stare, probing for any glimmer of deceit or indecision. Slaton showed him desperation, rising anger.

Sanderson sighed. "Well, Mr. Deadmarsh, it appears you don't understand what's happening any more than we do."

"I wish I did."

"All the same, there might be something you can do to help us find your wife."

"Anything."

Minutes later they were weaving through traffic in an unmarked police car. Slaton was in the backseat, shouldered next to the larger of the two bookends, a massive and unsmiling man with a blond crew cut. He supposed they were trying to intimidate him, trying to force the right mind-set. At that moment, Slaton imagined he was going to waste the rest of his day answering questions. He expected photographs and stale coffee in a room that stank of sweat and fear. He expected takeout food on a scratched wooden table. He expected police headquarters.

He was wrong.

SEVEN

Inspector Arne Sanderson tried to be discreet as he eyed the man in the backseat of his unmarked car. He was intrigued by the American in the mirror.

For the last twenty-four hours Sanderson had run an ambitious investigation. The first hours of any inquiry were critical, the time when cases were broken, yet this particular quest had hit a wall. His overall assessment was one of disconnects. He had a double shooting, but no apparent motive. A doctor with a spotless background who'd been chased through the streets, and who was concerned enough about her safety to have leapt onto a moving boat. And the most troubling thing of all—of the five people involved, the only one he'd identified was the doctor, and she seemed more a victim than a suspect. They had found driver's licenses and passports on the two men who'd been collected by ambulances at the scene. All were Turkish items and all patently forged. Yet it was quality work, or so Sanderson had been told—biometric chips, color-changing ink, fluorescent fibers—all certainly fashioned by the same artist. Drug smuggling was his first inclination, and that could still be the case. But there was a niggling doubt. A doubt further driven by the man seated behind him.

Driving fast and distracted by thoughts of his passenger, Sanderson missed the turn at the Kungsbron bridge. He made a hasty correction, and nearly ran down a pedestrian outside the Belgian embassy. Cursing silently, he eased off the accelerator. For thirty-five years Sanderson had watched policemen near the end of their careers, and he knew there were two distinct leanings. Most pulled back and coasted onto the off-ramp of retirement. They put checkmarks in boxes and answered phones when it suited them, showed up at the station a few minutes later each morning. When the halfhearted party finally came, with its backslapping and cake and embarrassing gifts, it was no more than a ripple, quickly lost in the ongoing storm of day-to-day operations. But there was a second path. Men and women who went out on less subdued terms, the results either noble or ruinous, but always spectacular.

Is that where I'm headed? he wondered.

Sanderson looked in the mirror again, but the man had somehow slipped from view. In what was becoming a recurring mental exercise, he challenged himself to recall details about Edmund Deadmarsh: a bricklayer from Virginia, calluses on his hands to prove it. What color were his eyes? Blue-gray, unusual. *Too easy.* What color were his shoes? Sanderson thought, but drew a blank. *What color?*

Brown, tan laces, well-worn. Boat shoes, but not a name brand, U.S. size eleven or twelve.

Yes, he thought, *that's it.*

He pressed a bit harder on the gas, and took a policeman's liberties against a newly red traffic light. He made it through the intersection unscathed, but with horns blaring behind him. Arne Sanderson grinned ever so slightly.

———

Minutes later Sanderson turned sharply into the parking lot of Saint Göran Hospital. On appearances a contemporary affair of burnt brick and glass, the facility was in fact one of the oldest in Sweden, with a pedigree dating back to the thirteenth century. As an institution, it had survived war, famine, and no fewer than eight hundred Nordic winters, which was more than could be said for the monarchies and governments that had overseen its administration.

Sanderson led inside, flashed his identification to a security guard, and entered the elevator with Deadmarsh and Sergeant Blix in trail. When the door closed, he sank the only button that would take them down.

Deadmarsh watched closely. "Why are we at a hospital?" he asked.

"The two victims of this shooting are here, but we haven't been able to identify either. Both men were carrying false papers—very high-quality documents, in fact." Sanderson saw no reaction to this as the elevator bottomed out. The door opened, and he noticed Deadmarsh eyeing a sign on the wall that said in Swedish, MORGUE. If he didn't know better, he might have thought the American was reading it.

He said, "We'd like you to take a look at these men, see if you recognize either of them."

"What makes you think I'd know who they are?" Deadmarsh asked.

"We know your wife had an acquaintance with one of them, so there must be some chance. How long have the two of you been married?"

"About six months."

"Did you know each other long before that?"

"No, actually. Only a few months."

"So you wouldn't have a lot of mutual friends," Sanderson suggested.

"Fewer than most couples."

They arrived at a heavy metal door, and Sanderson sent Blix ahead. He turned and said, "All the same, I'd like you to have a look. But I must warn you, this is the morgue. Are you up to it?"

"If it will help find my wife—absolutely."

Sanderson engaged his most somber smile. "Good. It always helps to have that kind of cooperation."

EIGHT

Slaton followed the inspector through a steel door that looked like something from a prison. Here, on the lowest level, the contemporary architecture of the building's outer facade gave way to more original underpinnings. As was common practice in Europe, the ancient foundation had been shored up, and the old skeleton dressed with new fixtures and fittings. The room in which he was standing was dated by a hard stone floor that seemed to go straight to the earth's core. He saw naked ventilation ducts strapped to a plaster ceiling, Internet wiring tacked across wall slabs that had been laid down centuries before. Noting the thickness of the jointed stone, Slaton was happy to have taken up masonry in the twenty-first century.

Weak lighting sprayed the unpainted walls in an eerie yellow hue. The room was cold and damp, fitting to its function, and the smell of an acrid cleaning agent didn't quite overpower the stench of death. Slaton had been in morgues before, bigger versions overflowing with the aftermath of bombings and war. Here there were no more than a dozen tables reserved for the newly departed, a waiting room for earthly remains until they could be disposed of with that proper balance of decency and sanitation. Slaton did not see an attendant, but he heard music from a nearby office, something with a Euro-pop techno beat that added to the room's bizarre texture.

A drawer had already been pulled, presenting a body covered by an off-white sheet. The inspector led Slaton to one side of the long gray tray, and his sergeant pulled back the cover. Slaton studied the body. As he did, he felt Sanderson studying him.

"He was alive when the paramedics arrived," the inspector said. "Survived for nine hours in the critical care unit before giving up."

Slaton said nothing.

"Well? Do you know him?" Sanderson asked.

"No, I've never seen him."

Sanderson stared for a long moment but didn't ask again.

Slaton turned away and swept his eyes over the dank room. "Where's the second body?"

"Upstairs," Sanderson replied. "Fortunately for everyone, that one is a bit warmer."

On the way to the elevator Sanderson's phone rang. He excused himself and asked Sergeant Blix to escort Slaton to the sixth floor. When they arrived, the hulking Norseman told Slaton it would be a few minutes, and then he struck up a conversation with a pretty young attendant at the nurse's station.

Slaton found a row of chairs and took a seat. The body downstairs had told him little. He'd seen only the face, and truly had not recognized it. Dark hair and complexion, perhaps thirty years old, and judging by the lay of the covering sheet a man in reasonably good shape. He might have been Israeli. Then again, he might have been Turkish, Greek, or Egyptian.

Slaton had been unable to think of a justifiable reason to view the rest of the body, which might have been more useful: Had the fatal wounds struck in the chest, the center of mass? How many rounds and how were they grouped? Such details, in the correct presentation, might signify a professional strike, giving Slaton some direction as to who he was dealing with. Yet as much as he wanted to ask questions of his own, Slaton knew that was a delicate game. If he seemed too curious, Sanderson would become suspicious. Consequently, he resigned himself to the role of passive intelligence gathering for the time being.

Sanderson reappeared and beckoned Slaton to follow.

They walked down a bright corridor, everything white and antiseptic. Turning into a room, Slaton saw a nurse tending an IV, and in the adjacent bed he saw the second victim. This one told him a great deal more. He was looking at his former boss, Anton Bloch.

Bloch lay motionless, trussed in tubes and wires. His swarthy face was pale, distorted by a ventilator pipe that had been taped into his mouth. But there was no doubt—it *was* him. Slaton did his best to not react, knowing Sanderson was watching. He certainly failed. There were shocks in life that could not be tempered by any amount of training or self-discipline, and seeing an old friend on the edge of an untimely death was one of them.

"What's his condition?" Slaton asked.

"He's been placed in a drug-induced coma. He was shot three times. The surgeons were able to remove two of the bullets, but the last is lodged close to his spine. They've stabilized him until they decide how to proceed. The doctors want very much to talk to his family." Sanderson paused before prompting, "So? Any idea who he is?"

"No," Slaton said. He felt the policeman's eyes drill in from the periphery. "You said my wife was seen talking to one of these men. Was this the one?"

"Yes, a very good guess."

Slaton took one last look at Bloch, a mental snapshot, then turned to the hallway.

Sanderson followed him out, and said, "Too bad you weren't able to help us."

"I wish I could, Inspector."

"Yes, well—not to worry. We'll just figure it out some other way, won't we? Oh, there is one other thing that's come up, Mr. Deadmarsh."

"Something about Christine?"

"Unfortunately, no. More of an administrative matter involving your passport."

"What about it?"

"Would you mind if I took another look?"

Slaton reached into his back pocket and handed the document over. Sanderson made a show of inspecting it, holding it up to the corridor's bright fluorescent lights like a radiologist with an X-ray.

"Is there a problem?" Slaton asked.

Sanderson frowned and handed it back. "With the document, no. It looks perfectly in order." He shoved his hands into his pockets. "But I just took a rather curious phone call. One of our people back at headquarters performed a check on your immigration status—it's only standard practice. You arrived at Arlanda earlier today, is that right?"

"Yes."

"It seems that the electronic record of your arrival has somehow disappeared. The name on your passport brings up nothing now. The only Edmund Deadmarsh we could find in our backlog is an eighty-nine-year-old Englishman who hasn't visited Sweden in thirty years."

Slaton shrugged. "What can I tell you? It must be a computer glitch. I walked right through immigration and gave them my passport. I can even describe the officer I gave it to," he added, guessing that Sanderson's people had already verified that video.

"Yes, as you say, I'm sure it's only some kind of computer foul-up. I have to get back to headquarters now. Why don't you give me your mobile number. I'll call you if we learn anything as to your wife's whereabouts."

Slaton gave his number. Sanderson handed over a business card in return, and said, "If you should hear from her, please let me know right away."

"I will." Slaton glanced toward the room they'd just left, and said, "I do have one question, Inspector."

Sanderson cocked his head, inviting him to go on.

"The two men you showed me—did one of them shoot the other?"

The answer came quickly, "We don't have that ballistics information yet."

"But you said this happened in a public place, a café. Surely there were witnesses."

Sanderson eyed him. "When I have everything sorted, I promise to let you know. Sergeant Blix will give you a lift wherever you like."

"I'd like to go back to the Strand Hotel."

Sanderson gave Blix the order.

Slaton asked, "Is it all right if I use Christine's room at the hotel? I am paying for it, after all."

Sanderson seemed to think about this, then said, "I

don't see why not. I'll make sure the front desk knows about it."

Slaton was dropped at the Strand Hotel for the second time at six that evening. The massive building hovered at the water's edge, seeming almost medieval as framed by the enduring Scandinavian twilight. He retrieved his bag from the bellman, went to the front desk, and just as Sanderson had promised was given a key to Christine's room.

As soon as he stepped into room 324, Slaton knew it was hers. Obvious enough were her familiar things—a blue sweater in the closet, her father's old suitcase on a chair. But her perfume was also there. He saw Christine's effects laid out with intimate signatures—the way her comb and hairbrush were nested together, and the way her shoes were set in a perfect line. He was equally sure the police had been here, and he imagined Sanderson and his brutes plodding through the place with big boots and gloved hands. In a drawer he saw carefully folded shirts overturned, toiletries in the bathroom scattered and disorganized. He looked for her passport but didn't find it. Slaton guessed she would not have taken it to a café—not unless she'd known what was coming. Was that a possibility? Might Bloch have arranged a meeting and forewarned her to bring it? Had he been trying to help her escape from something? From someone?

He found a conference welcome bag on a table stuffed with brochures, along with pens and lanyards emblazoned with the names of pharmaceutical conglomerates. A lecture schedule was on the adjacent desk, and he recognized her brisk check marks next to certain presentations, these ending yesterday afternoon. After that, nothing. Slaton scanned the margins of the schedule for scribbled notes, and checked the scratchpad near the phone for names or numbers. He picked up the hotel phone and dialed the code to retrieve messages. There were none, of course.

The bed was made, but Slaton noted a lengthwise impression where Christine must have laid down, an indentation in the pillow where her head had been. He sat on it and pulled in the air, searching for any remnants of her presence.

"Where are you?" he whispered.

Slaton eased back on the bed, into the day-old crease, and closed his eyes. He had little solid information, but more than when he'd arrived. Anton Bloch had come here to meet Christine. Then he'd been shot and Christine was forced to run. Had Bloch shot the other man? Had he been protecting Christine? If it came to that, Slaton was sure he would have. But more importantly, who had Bloch been facing? The usual suspects? Arabs? Iranians? Israel had her share of enemies. Slaton saw but one unbreakable strand: Bloch, and whoever else was involved, had come to Sweden because Christine was here. And Christine had been targeted because of him. Of this he was sure.

Slaton felt a numbness begin to fall. He needed sleep, needed it every bit as much as he would soon need more conventional weapons. He considered his options for the next morning. His first idea was simplistic—find Inspector Sanderson and press him for every scrap of information. That was what Edmund Deadmarsh would do. But Sanderson had shared little so far, indeed no more than necessary to prod his witness down the desired paths. Slaton doubted the inspector was going to be more forthcoming, no matter how outraged the American stonemason became. His prognosis for that course of action: poor.

He searched for Plan B. Past experience had taught him that for all Israel's enemies, there was often none more treacherous than Israel herself. Slaton had one confirmed character in the disaster that was playing out—Anton Bloch, former director of Mossad. Centering on this, and disregarding who else might be involved, his answer fell into place. He knew precisely what his next step had to be.

That settled, Slaton allowed his body to relax. He heard the sounds of the city outside his window— passing cars, shouted greetings, a far-off siren. Then, amid the asynchronous din, he extracted another sound, this more constant. It was deep and resonating, a distinctive signature to anyone who was familiar— the diesel rumble of a boat on the waterway. He knew nothing of the boat's function, nothing about its destination, but that steady sound gave Slaton a fleeting peace of mind.

Minutes later, he was fast asleep.

NINE

Slaton woke at six-thirty. He'd slept well but was hardly refreshed, his body still in arrears to the tune of six time zones. At the bathroom mirror he weighed the question of whether to shave his thickening beard. He'd not bothered since Christine had left for the conference, almost a week now. Slaton decided to leave it as it was, reasoning that a disheveled look was ideal for a man in his circumstances.

He showered and donned fresh clothes, a pair of tan cotton pants and a long-sleeve button-down shirt. The shirt was a shade of red so bright it might have doubled as a bullfighter's cape. He pocketed his passport and a wallet full of identification attesting him to be Edmund Deadmarsh, along with the grand sum of thirty-seven hundred dollars—he had cleaned out his and Christine's joint checking account before leaving Virginia. Everything else went into his suitcase, and that went into the closet.

He passed under the Strand's front awning at 6:55, turned left, and took up a leisurely pace. Rounding the waterway, Slaton passed the café where Christine had last been seen two days ago. The establishment, which he imagined had been cordoned off by police tape yesterday, was again open for business, the maître d' ignoring a pressure cleaning crew that was busy removing a dark stain from the nearby sidewalk. Slaton might have stopped to take a seat, and from there sketch what had happened. He could ask questions of employees and regular customers, and study the hasty repairs.

He didn't because his strategy precluded it.

Farther up the street, he stopped at a news kiosk and purchased the only English language newspaper on the stand, a day-old copy of the *New York Times*. He put the paper under his arm and walked toward the waterfront, stopping now and again as if taking in the sights. The air was still and crisp, and the sidewalks quiet on a languid Sunday morning. Along the waterfront he saw tour boats, water taxis, and a lone police runabout. Sanderson had not mentioned the type of vessel Christine used to escape her pursuers, and Slaton made a mental note to ask that question when the chance came. *If* the chance came.

He began moving again, a red-shirted sightseer keeping a predictable pace. He never once looked behind him or reversed direction, and made not a single abrupt turn. He nodded cordially to two policemen riding past on bicycles, and ignored a white panel van that was parked crookedly at the mouth of an alley. Two blocks from the first café he paused at the entrance of a second, the Renaissance Tea Room, and pretended to study a breakfast menu that was posted on a stand. As if finding the fare agreeable, he turned inside and asked for a specific table, a request the host was happy to accommodate on what was clearly a slow morning.

Slaton sat overlooking the waterway and Strandvägen, much as Christine had done two days earlier only a few hundred yards away. Morning smells filled the air, coffee brewing and bacon on the grill. He lingered over the menu, and on the waiter's third pass ordered a comprehensive breakfast—fresh fruit, eggs, sausage, and toast. As his meal was being prepared, Slaton addressed a pot of English Breakfast tea. He found it a nicely robust and flavorful blend, as one would expect from a tearoom.

He unfolded the *Times* and began to read.

When Sanderson arrived at work the air was stamped with the usual aromas of a waking police department— sweat, shoe polish, burnt coffee, all accented by more objectionable risings from the drunk tank on the backside of a Saturday night. He had dodged television reporters at the entrance, two attractive young women with enamel hair and blond smiles who were tethered to news vans sprouting tall, telescoping antennas. It was all to be expected. Two men had been shot nearly forty-eight hours ago, and so far neither the victims nor the assailants had been identified. Sweden's nerves were increasingly thin when it came to terrorism, and this crime was looking more and more the part.

At his desk Sanderson searched for his cell phone, which he hadn't been able to find at home this morning. He didn't see it, but a check of his computer revealed a dozen messages. He scanned through, saw nothing of interest, and decided to press ahead with his most disagreeable task of the morning.

Assistant Commissioner Paul Sjoberg headed up the Criminal Investigation Unit of the Stockholm County Police. Younger than Sanderson by three years, and five years junior on the force, he was a man who lacked the edges of a street cop. Fair-skinned and carrying twenty more pounds than he should have, his well-tended wave of silvering blond hair framed an indoor face. This was all at odds with the image he tried to project. Sjoberg had started a career in Sweden's navy before trading uniforms, dark blue for light, and signing on with the Stockholm police. It was a circumstance he played to great effect in his office—the room was brimming with bottled ships and rope-framed oil paintings depicting great sea battles. He was a decent man and a competent policeman—Sanderson would never say otherwise—but a better politician.

Sanderson paused at the door and saw Sjoberg pecking at his computer—an emphatic dagger to his swashbuckling image. Noting the helmsman's wheel stuck to the far wall, Sanderson had a mischievous urge to ask permission to come aboard. What little careerism remained in him quashed the idea. "A word, sir?"

Sjoberg noticed him and clicked off his computer. "Arne—just the man I wanted to see. Have the bastards over at SÄPO given us anything yet?" He was referring to the Swedish Security Service, who handled matters of counterterrorism—the sea to which their investigation seemed to be drifting.

"Actually, they have. I told you yesterday that I'd had a few words with Edmund Deadmarsh, the husband of our damsel in distress."

"Yes, I remember you said something about it."

"When I ran a check on Deadmarsh's passport there were some odd results. To put it simply, his information has disappeared from our immigration system. I asked SÄPO to take a look, since it seemed more up their street, and they contacted the American FBI."

"And?"

With Sjoberg already sitting down, Sanderson said, "The FBI responded almost immediately. They claim that the U.S. has never issued a passport to anyone named Edmund Deadmarsh."

"How could that be?" Sjoberg said in a rising inflection.

"I don't know. They did find a driving record and two speeding tickets in the name, but a crosscheck of the corresponding driver's license number came up blank."

"So he's using forged documents."

Sanderson hesitated. "I'm not so sure. I saw the passport myself, and while I'm no expert, it looked quite authentic. There's something here I don't like."

"Such as?"

"Deadmarsh entered Sweden yesterday at Arlanda. His passport cleared perfectly—we have him on video passing through immigration. Yet a few hours later, a search for his name in the records showed nothing. It's as if the damned file vaporized. I talked to a man at Immigration who said it could only be a glitch at the source, on the American end. It's almost as if . . ." Sanderson paused and rubbed his chin, "as if once he'd entered Sweden, his documents were somehow wiped clean. They were legitimate at one point, but now have gone lost in cyberspace."

"Is that possible?" Sjoberg asked witheringly.

"I don't know—we're looking into it. In the meantime, I've asked Sergeant Elmander to keep an eye on Deadmarsh."

"On a Sunday? You realize our extra pay accounts are already overextended this quarter."

Sanderson bit down hard on the reply that was welling up.

Sjoberg raised his chin theatrically, in a way that made Sanderson think he might order canvas put to the mizzenmast. "Arne, I'm counting on you—we can't drop the ball on this one."

"Is that something I've made a habit of?"

"No, of course not. I put you in charge with every confidence. It's just that . . ." Sjoberg hesitated, "well, this is a high-profile inquiry. I want you to know what's at stake."

Sanderson knew precisely what was at stake—Assistant Commissioner Paul Sjoberg's step up to National. He said, "I think I have a good idea."

"Good. Give me an update this afternoon. Three o'clock?"

"Three o'clock," Sanderson repeated, retreating to the door.

Paul Sjoberg stared at the threshold long after Sanderson was gone, his fingers tapping the blotter on his desk. After a full minute, he went back to his computer. He called up his email and reopened a file near the top.

From: Dr. Ernst Samuels, M.D./NPMS
Subject: D/I Sanderson
Please be advised that Detective Inspector
Sanderson has no-showed a second appointment.
Given the nature of his evaluation, I recommend that
he reschedule immediately, and if necessary be pulled
from duty to accommodate. A third event will result in
a formal letter of complaint through department
channels.
Regards,
E. Samuels, M.D.
NPB Health Services

Sjoberg composed the most conciliatory reply he could muster and hit the Send button. He then wondered what the hell to do.

It took nearly two hours for Slaton to be proved correct. He was scanning a review for a thriller he would never read when a man sat down at his table. Slaton didn't look up right away, but instead tipped the last of the tea into his cup, the dregs of the pot thick and flavorful. It was a good ten seconds before he lowered the *Times*.

"It took you long enough," he said in Hebrew.

He was looking at a man roughly his equal in height, but considerably heavier. He had dark eyes, curly black hair shot with threads of gray, and was casually dressed in jeans and a polo shirt. One hand gripped the arm of his chair while the other, in an awkward set, was positioned near the open zipper of his dark windbreaker. Outside, there was not a breath of wind. The man responded to Slaton's taunt by simply sliding a black iPhone across the table, angling between a spent glass of orange juice and a bowl of sweetener packets.

Slaton put the *Times* on the table. He ignored the phone and gave the man a level, dispassionate stare. The same look a headmaster might give a recidivist truant.

"How long have you been in country?" Slaton asked.

The man obviously didn't want to chat, but Slaton waited, making it clear who was in charge.

"A week," the man replied, keeping with Hebrew.

Slaton's eyes drifted obviously to the street. "Where is your partner?"

To his credit, the man didn't flinch. "Just take the damned phone."

The waiter was bearing down. Slaton waved him away, and while his right hand swiped the air dismissively, his left foot inched forward under the table.

"Who will I be talking to?" Slaton asked.

"It's a secure line." The courier offered nothing more.

Slaton picked up the phone and saw that it was ready to connect to a number labeled HOME. He tapped the screen, and the call was answered before even a single ring had rattled the handset. "This is the director." The voice was flat and featureless, like an ocean in the doldrums.

"How do I know that?" Slaton said. "We've never met."

"No, but you were well acquainted with my predecessor."

"Your predecessor is in a hospital fighting for his life. Why?"

"Anton put himself in a bad position."

"I think *you* put him in a bad position," said Slaton.

"That was never my intent. We are doing what we can for him."

Slaton did not doubt that he was talking to Raymond Nurin. If he didn't know the man, he recognized the thought process. A pragmatic viper.

"Who approached Christine?" he asked.

"We did."

"Why? If Mossad saw a threat to her safety, I should have been told. Is she in danger?"

Nurin did not reply right away.

"Dammit! What's going on here? Where is my wife?"

"Your wife is safe," Nurin said.

There was a lengthy pause as Slaton interpreted.

Your wife is safe. Four simple words, but the implication was stunning. His world, so long predictable, seemed to invert. All that was known became unknown. All that was controlled became uncontrolled.

"Are you telling me Mossad has *taken* Christine?"

"She is safe."

"Safe? You put her in the middle of a goddamn firefight. Christine ran through traffic and threw herself into a boat."

"None of that was planned."

"And what *was* planned? Mossad is branching out into kidnapping and extortion? If that's your new organization, Director, I'm glad I left."

"Actually, David, that is my point. You can never leave. Not with your background. You will always be what we trained you to be."

Slaton felt anger welling. "Is that the point of all this? You want me back? For what?"

Nurin answered with silence.

Still focused on the man across the table, Slaton said, "All right, Director, I'll go that far with you. Who do you want me to kill?"

TEN

Sitting in an unmarked police car a hundred yards away, Sergeant Lars Elmander was becoming increasingly agitated. To begin with, he was unhappy he'd been forced to work on a Sunday morning—his twelve-year-old son had an important soccer match. Then there was the assignment itself. It had started out easily enough when he'd spotted Deadmarsh leaving the Strand Hotel. For two hours Elmander had watched him stroll the waterfront like any tourist, taking in the sights at a casual pace, chatting with a vendor at a news kiosk. This was followed by an extended breakfast on the patio of the Renaissance Tea Room.

Yet the very ease of the job had begun to bother Elmander. He was watching Deadmarsh flick casually through a newspaper, teacup in hand, when the disconnect mushroomed to sufficient mass in his policeman's brain. Elmander had been given a briefing on his target, and he decided that for a man who'd just flown across an ocean to find his missing wife, Edmund Deadmarsh was acting in an improbably casual manner. His concerns were magnified when a second man arrived and, with no apparent invitation, took a seat at Deadmarsh's table.

He watched closely, yet saw little interaction

between the two. Soon Deadmarsh began talking on a mobile phone, and it was then that the final revelation thumped into Elmander's head. It occurred to him that the stranger who'd just arrived matched the description of a man they were looking for—the shooter of two days prior.

Elmander straightened in his seat and pulled out his phone. He dialed Sanderson's number, but the inspector didn't pick up. "Come on, come on . . ."

In a move that would save his life in a matter of minutes, he ended the call, rang the dispatcher, and requested backup.

"Your target is Dr. Ibrahim Hamedi," Nurin said, "the head of the Atomic Energy Organization of Iran."

"I should have known," Slaton said.

"Hamedi will soon be traveling outside Iran. He will be vulnerable. The phone you are holding contains a file of information. It will tell you where and when to strike, including details on a tactical opening that is ideal for a man with your gift. Use it."

These words rang in Slaton's head like a klaxon, and he stamped them to memory without trying to understand. Nothing made sense. An assassination planned, but then subcontracted? Christine abducted to make it happen?

"Why?" Slaton asked. "If you have such a great opening, do it yourself. You have others like me."

"No, David. Not like you. Think about what has happened recently and everything will make sense."

Slaton considered what he knew, and he did find a way to make it work. "You've failed twice. A leak?"

"Yes," Nurin said.

"All the more reason for me to not get involved."

"I will be your only contact, David. No one in Mossad knows your intent, not even the man sitting across the table from you. Do this one job and it will be your last."

"No. I've already done my last job."

"Christine will—"

"Christine will be safe very soon," Slaton cut in, "because you don't have her. If you did, you'd already have given me proof."

After a pause, Nurin said, "You're right, of course. But we're looking for her."

"So am I."

"Don't overestimate your abilities, *kidon*. You are alone with no support. We have dozens of operatives in country, and every airport terminal and rail station in Stockholm is covered. We will find her first."

"And then what—hold her in an undisclosed location? Interrogation?"

"Please, David, believe me when I say that I am a practical man. This is no more than a demonstration. You and Christine are in a tenuous position. Anonymity is what keeps your past at bay, and Mossad controls that anonymity. We have gone to great trouble and expense to ensure it. But there is a price for our continued support. You need us, and we need you."

"And if I don't agree, then what? Mossad will give me up? Expose me for what I once was? That sounds like a threat."

"A threat against you would be—how should I say it? Counterproductive? I dare say I might be putting my own personal safety at risk."

Slaton said nothing. He put his free forearm on the lip of the table, curled his fingers underneath, and leaned forward.

"This isn't about your safety or mine," Nurin

continued, "and certainly not your wife's. This is about Israel." He explained that Iran was close to achieving its ultimate nuclear ambition, the development of a fission device that could be coupled to a long-range ballistic missile. Israel's air force and cyberwarriors, for all their offensive capability, could not end that threat. Hamedi was the key. "The architect of Qom is vulnerable. We must act because this is our last chance. Israel is desperate, David, so I am desperate."

"You don't represent the Israel I knew. Not with a scheme like this."

"And if I had come to Virginia and asked for your help? Would you have acted?"

No reply.

"You know we'll find Christine. Do as I ask, and in a week Israel will be rescued. You and your wife can then be safe for the long term. You have my word."

"Your word?" Slaton spat, his anger rising. "You and your organization can go to hell!"

His thumb ended the call. He took a deep breath and tried to right his thoughts. There was something he wasn't seeing. Something in Nurin's reasoning that didn't make sense. Slaton had no chance to decipher what it was because the man across the table moved.

It wasn't his hand, but his gaze, flicking toward the street for an instant. Slaton was sure he was a Mossad field operative, a *katsa*, presumably armed with a company-issued .22 Beretta in a company-issued shoulder holster. The man had been here roughly five minutes, and until a moment ago his eyes had been locked squarely across the table. There was caution in every facet of the man, his stiff posture and overcasual stare, and so the *katsa* knew who Slaton was. Knew *what* Slaton was. According to Nurin, the man hadn't been told why he was here, and this was likely true. *Give him the phone. He is dangerous, but not a threat to you.* Those would have been his instructions. But the phone call to the director had obviously not gone well, and so the *katsa* was double-checking that his backup was nearby. A partner, or even a team.

Where? Slaton wondered. Close in, on the sidewalk? Across the street in a car? How many? He imagined it was the same setup they'd used two days ago with Christine. Unfortunately, that thought took Slaton to an unexpected place, to a vision of Christine running for her life across the waterfront. The control he'd been fighting for was suddenly lost.

Pocketing the phone, Slaton looked across the table and said in a clear voice, "Tell me one thing. Were you the one who went after my wife?"

He got a dark stare in return, an attempt at bravado. But no answer.

"Did you shoot Anton Bloch?"

Ten full seconds of silence.

Slaton kept perfectly still. Perfectly.

Fifteen seconds.

Nothing.

At twenty seconds the *katsa* lost his nerve. He moved for his gun in a rush.

ELEVEN

Krav Maga, literally "contact combat," is a style of fighting developed in Israel. Emphasizing the art of counterattack, it is the embodiment of street-fighting. There are no rules, and any and all resources are used to neutralize opponents. In training, emphasis is placed on reacting to unexpected and immediate threats, the worst-case scenario. In the real world, however, the preference is to recognize potential adversaries in advance and formulate preemptive strikes.

Operating under this mind-set, Slaton had been positioning for his assault ever since the *katsa* had sat down. In truth, even before the *katsa* had sat down. He knew a great deal about the table in front of him. He knew that it weighed very near fifteen pounds and was not secured to the floor. He knew it rested on three legs, two of which were now perfectly bracketing the *katsa*'s chair. He understood the table's distribution of weight, and that its center of gravity lay just below a blunt edge that was situated between the *katsa*'s solar plexus and his holstered gun. The *katsa*'s chair was identical to his own, a typical four-legged affair, but atypically light and unstable. Slaton knew all of this because he had studied and weighed and measured for the better part of two hours. He also knew that the area behind the chair was clear, nothing but five feet of cold, hard concrete.

So before the *katsa*'s hand had even reached his windbreaker, Slaton was countering. Perfectly balanced by his right foot and left arm, his left foot hooked a front leg of the *katsa*'s chair and pulled, while at the same time his right hand pushed the tabletop in the opposite direction. The only possible result was for the man to rotate uncontrollably in his chair. The *katsa*'s free hand went up and back, a foreseeable reaction to falling blindly backward. His right hand cleared his jacket as he fell, and the predicted Beretta was there. But he was completely off balance, more flying than sitting, and his head slammed into the concrete.

Everything on the table flew to the floor, a clatter of breaking china and spinning utensils. Slaton moved instantly over the stunned *katsa*, but the man recovered quickly. He still had the Beretta, and started swinging it forward. Slaton lunged for the gun but got only a wrist. He grappled with his other hand and reached the weapon, covering the *katsa*'s desperate grip. The gun was frozen between them, two big men, but gravity was on Slaton's side. He levered all his weight, and applied the hand and arm strength of a man who in the last months had moved three hundred tons of stone. The *katsa* buckled, and Slaton forced the barrel away from his own chest and toward his opponent.

Both men were grasping and pulling when the gun went off.

Slaton held firm, unrelenting.

The man below him went slack.

He wrestled the gun free, and saw a wound at the *katsa*'s throat pulsing blood. This, he knew, was no more than a mechanical aftereffect, fluid dynamics taking its course. The upward angle of the shot had sent the round into his head, and the man's eyes were already lifeless and wide, staring at the sky. With bright red blood pooling on the floor, Slaton stood with the gun in his hand. He quickly gauged the movement around him, and registered nothing as a threat. Briefly, he considered searching the body for documents or identification, but knew it was pointless. And there was no time. He had completed his objective, made the sought connection. Now the situation had digressed, and only one thing mattered.

Get clear.

Slaton had backed one step away when he was struck by an opportunity. He pulled the phone from his pocket and took a quick photograph. Then he ran.

He dodged tables amid cries of shock and outrage. The chaos around him, on appearances random and uncontrolled, was in fact quite predictable. Those nearest the fray were leaning away and trying for distance, while others, farther back and with the illusion of security, dialed 112 on their mobile phones to reach the police. Slaton ignored them all. In the last hour he had studied every man and woman in the place, and seen no one with the air of a would-be hero. No off-duty policeman or soldier on leave. If a threat remained, it would be outside.

Reaching the sidewalk with the gun still in hand, he palmed it discreetly to his thigh. A voice from the past played in his head. *A man moving fast generates attention. A man moving fast with a gun generates panic.* Slaton broke into a purposeful jog, the pace of a man trying to reach a stopped bus before the door closed. He'd gone no more than five steps when he skidded to a stop.

Two men had him perfectly bracketed.

If there is a recipe for disaster it is to put three men who are armed and trained in one place, and then fix that each is unaware of the others' motives.

Of the three, it was Sergeant Elmander who was taken completely by surprise. He'd been completing the call to dispatch, his mobile stuck to his ear, when he saw flashes of movement under the café's cheerful yellow awning. He'd seen the table go flying, and watched Deadmarsh jump to his feet. The man who'd been sitting across from him disappeared in a burst of commotion.

Then Elmander heard the gunshot.

He knew he had to do something, so he clambered out of his car. He heard the reassuring sound of a siren in the distance. Backup was on the way. His hand went under his jacket and he performed an awkward exchange—his phone for his SIG Sauer. At a cautious trot, Lars Elmander began moving toward the Renaissance Tea Room.

One hundred yards away, on an opposite diagonal to the café, a stocky and nearly bald man burst from a black Mercedes sedan. He too began moving, though at a decidedly more purposeful clip. His eyes alternated between the café and a blond man with a crew cut who had just come into play—judging by his dress, the bald man decided, almost certainly a policeman. As if to prove the point, the crew-cut man drew a weapon as he ran, and his other hand fumbled in a back pocket for what had to be his credentials.

The bald man altered his vector slightly, but he didn't slow—not until he reached the street. The traffic was heavy, a nearby light having cycled to green at precisely the wrong time. That, he knew, could be fixed. He held up an open palm to stop oncoming traffic, and reinforced the directive with what was brandished in his other hand—a heavy handgun with a long barrel.

An approaching delivery truck skidded to a stop.

Slaton saw them both.

The policeman was closer, thirty yards and closing. He was holding his ID toward Slaton, but his gun was low, pointed at the pavement—a configuration that might prove fatal in a matter of seconds. The bald man's weapon was ready, held steady and high. Slaton couldn't identify the type of gun from forty yards, but it was a heavy piece.

Only the policeman seemed unaware of the triangular nature of the battlefield. Any of the three might shoot, and all had two targets from which to choose. It was a tactical riddle the likes of which Slaton had never experienced, indeed never imagined. The kind of situation his old instructors at the schoolhouse loved to conjure. In an instant, he narrowed his focus to one thing—*his* desired outcome. He had to separate from this place and get safe. Countless variables came into play—crowds, traffic, a low sun—all things that might or might not push an engagement in his favor. There was simply no time to compute it all. Slaton's principal advantage was that he had faced such dilemmas before, and so he took immediate control.

With the Beretta still palmed tightly to his hip, he looked squarely at the cop. Slaton raised his empty left hand and pointed toward the third man in the street.

Elmander didn't stop. But he looked where Deadmarsh was pointing. He saw a stocky man with a gun in the middle of the road.

On locking gazes both froze.

Elmander watched the bald man square his shoulders and raise his weapon. His policeman's response was instantaneous, a sequence beaten into his head through years of training. He shouted, "Police, drop your weapon!" and set himself in a good platform as he brought his own weapon to bear. It was a motion he had practiced a thousand times on the firing range.

But this was not a firing range.

Elmander felt like he was moving in slow motion, like his limbs were stuck in quicksand. He saw the massive barrel being leveled at him, and knew that his own gun was coming up too late. His sited his target, but the picture was uncontrolled and wavering. Elmander tried to settle for a shot, knowing speed was nothing without accuracy. He watched the bald man doing the same. His finger began to squeeze, but the gun's hammer never fell.

He was hit.

Excruciating pain seared into his right thigh, and before he knew it he was toppling sideways like a two-hundred-pound bowling pin. Strangely, in that instant, with the pavement rushing toward his left ear in an uncontrolled descent, Elmander swore he heard a second bullet whistle past his head. As he hit hard and rolled, every conscious effort went to one thing. *Hold on to your gun, you idiot!*

Elmander did. The hard steel stock was there in his hand, but when he tried to stand again his right leg buckled. Half sitting, half kneeling, he scanned for the bald man and saw him, just a flash disappearing behind the frame of a parked car. Elmander trained his gun in that direction—a terrible position from which to fire, but at least a deterrent. Something for the man to think about. He looked for Deadmarsh but didn't see him anywhere.

Christ.

His leg felt as if it was on fire, but through either honed discipline or visceral fear Elmander ignored his wound. The siren was getting closer, echoing off the surrounding buildings in the most beautiful symphony he'd ever heard. He kept alert, his weapon poised, knowing that if he could just keep the assailant at bay for another minute, maybe two, help would arrive. Scanning the streets and sidewalks, he saw no sign of either Deadmarsh or the bald man. As it turned out, Elmander would never see either again.

He did, however, hear their shots.

With the policeman out of the fight, Slaton ran an arc around the bald man, pulling him away from the wounded officer. He was moving at full speed, skirting the busy street. The .22 Beretta is a light weapon, and even in his practiced hand a handicap in terms of range, accuracy, and stopping power. Slaton fired from fifty feet on a hard run, and the fact that he scored any hits at all was testament that his marksmanship had not faded. Of the three rounds he sent, two found their mark.

His target rocked once, twice, and almost fell.

Almost.

He's wearing a vest, Slaton thought.

The stocky man returned fire, and a round smacked into the wall just in front of Slaton, concrete chips stinging his face.

Move, move!

Slaton fired across his body, but missed. At this range, on the run, the odds of a successful headshot were virtually nil. With two rounds remaining, and no spare magazine, he was on the defensive. There was nothing to be gained from an engagement—only risk. He changed his angle and sprinted toward a corner that would put him clear. A bus wheeled around from the side street, giving momentary cover, and Slaton lowered his weapon and went for flat-out speed. He was two steps from safety when another shot came. Another miss.

He never saw the scooter.

He would later surmise that it was a kid trying to get away. Whatever the case, the scooter appeared in a flash and hit him like an express train. Slaton clattered to the ground and slammed into a lamppost stanchion. Something slashed his arm. He was facedown on the sidewalk, arms and legs sprawled wide. The killer had to be right behind him, closing fast with a capable weapon—and now at a range where he wouldn't miss.

With all the self-discipline he had, Slaton lay perfectly still.

He imagined the bald man nearing, imagined him focusing on his downed target and closing for a coup de grâce. Amid the raucous street noise, Slaton discerned the sound of slowing footsteps.

One . . .

Absolute stillness, his body relaxed. He sensed the footsteps shuffle to a pause.

Two . . .

A vision of the bald man raising his weapon, settling his sight.

Three.

Slaton snap-rolled left, and in the next instant a

bullet smacked the concrete where his head had just been. The Beretta moved in a flash, his right hand sweeping a high arc to intersect the man's head. At precisely the right instant—

Fire.

Flat on his back, Slaton again went still. The recoiling Beretta was calm in his hand, ready with one round remaining. He didn't need it.

The killer, with a new and neat hole in his forehead, crumpled to the concrete and didn't move.

Slaton did.

With the gunfire at an end, order would soon be restored. And order was his enemy. He scrambled to his feet and turned onto the side street. Were there any others? he wondered. Slaton hoped he'd been facing a team of two, but there was no way to be sure. He ran a block east, then a block south, glancing over his shoulder at every turn. He kept up the zigzag pattern, east then south, for five minutes. His arm stung, but he was moving fluently, adrenaline doing its job. He kept an eye on the cars and people around him, watching for movement that was abrupt or counter to the natural flow. Nothing drew his attention.

Spotting an in-service taxi at a stoplight, he hailed it with his good arm. The driver waved him in and Slaton careened into the backseat, whipping the door shut behind him.

"Gustav Vasa church," he said breathlessly. "I'm late. How long will it take?"

"Fifteen minutes," the driver said, not questioning the idea of being late for church on a Sunday morning.

Slaton threw a hundred-dollar bill through the Plexiglas window—there was no time for subtly. He caught the man's eyes in the mirror. "Make it ten."

Not another word was spoken. The cab jumped ahead.

Slaton examined his arm. Pain, moderate bleeding, but his shirt helped mask the damage—red on red. He settled back into the seat and felt his heart thumping, something you never noticed until the downside of a firefight.

The driver was worthy. He ran two red lights and hurtled over a curb to reach the church in nine minutes. Slaton got out and started toward the main chapel where a large crowd was spilling into the street. Tourists perhaps, or well-blessed parishioners leaving the midmorning service. He didn't bother to differentiate. As soon as the cab was out of sight, Slaton reversed course and walked fifty yards to the Odenplan subway entrance. He quick-stepped down and disappeared.

TWELVE

Sanderson was concentrating on a computer screen in the criminal forensics division, a video that had been captured two days earlier by the security camera of a Strandvägen bank. A silver Audi was parked along the street, blurry and distant, and the technician seated beside him tinkered with the image until the license plate became clear.

"And you ran it?" Sanderson asked.

"The number doesn't exist—it's probably been altered."

Sanderson frowned, but was not surprised. "What about the car? Any luck identifying it?"

"No reports of that make and model being stolen, and we haven't found anything similar abandoned."

"What about our suspects? We could really use a good photograph or two."

The tech sorted computer files like a magician running a card trick. He pulled up a half dozen photos. "These are the best we've been able to find."

The images, again extracted from video footage, were grainy and of marginal use. Nothing Sanderson would bother to distribute, and probably nothing a prosecutor could ever use in a court of law. The only consolation was that two of the men were already

ASSASSIN'S GAME | 95

accounted for, one in hospital and one in the morgue. The best image captured was one they did not need— they already had an excellent passport photo of Dr. Christine Palmer, along with a high-resolution image from the website run by her physician's group. She was an attractive woman with soft features under medium-length auburn hair, and on the website she was presented as doctors invariably were—compassionate smile over the requisite white lab coat. The fact that she was apparently married to a manual laborer registered as a curiosity to Sanderson, but nothing more. He was pondering it all when a young woman from the command center rushed into the room.

"Inspector Sanderson! We've just had more trouble on the waterfront, sir!"

"What now?"

"The Renaissance Tea Room. Shots fired, two dead. And one of ours is injured, on his way to the hospital now."

Sanderson's stomach knotted. "Do we know who?"

"I believe it's Elmander."

Slaton was seated behind a partition on a nearly empty Metro train, the Blue Line bound for Tensta. White shafts from passing floodlights flicked through the windows as the car swayed smooth and quick over the tracks. There were two other passengers in his car, a teenage couple who'd gotten on at the last stop in a rush of laughter and fumbling limbs. A pair so absorbed in each other, Slaton doubted they had even noticed him.

His first order of business was a self-appraisal, and the only damage he saw was a three-inch gash to his upper arm, his shirtsleeve torn to correlate. A bullet?

he wondered. A ricochet? Most likely not. As was usually the case, something less dramatic, even mundane— a broken beer bottle or a sharp edge from the scooter he'd tackled. Behind the partition he bandaged the wound with what he'd been able to scavenge from the departure platform, a pile of discarded napkins and a strip of packing tape ripped from a cardboard box. That stopped the bleeding, but it was no use against infection. He rolled up the long sleeve of his shirt to cover the bloodstained section, then did the same with the other side for the sake of symmetry. This turned out to be the most painful part, flexing his injured bicep, but he got the job done.

Slaton took the iPhone from his pocket and turned it in his hand. On appearances it seemed a generic device, but he was sure it had been loaded with any number of applications that Apple had never imagined. Mossad was certainly tracking it, his position likely pinging on a display somewhere in Tel Aviv at this very moment, like a beacon out of a dark night. He also allowed that the phone had been modified in such a way that turning it off, or even removing the battery, was not a solution. For the moment, however, Slaton knew he was safe—a train was a moving target, and this offered a certain latitude. To get rid of the thing was the only answer, but first he had to see what was in Nurin's files. He woke the phone and saw the usual icons for web browsers, music, and games. Only one was unfamiliar, a bright red square with a capital N. A spymaster's sense of humor? he wondered.

Slaton tapped the icon and a list of files came into view. He opened the first and saw a map of Geneva marked with reference numbers for associated notes. He navigated through and saw that the assassination was to take place the following Sunday, seven days from today. Another file contained an op plan, complete with diagrams and schedules. Slaton read quickly and took mental pictures. He considered forwarding the files to another computer, but quickly discarded the idea—trying to outmaneuver Mossad's clever computer technicians was a fool's game. The files were certainly tagged, tied like so many fishing lures to mainframes in Tel Aviv. Waiting to be reeled in. So Slaton reverted to basics, cataloging in his mind the vital details: times, dates, and locations, all stamped into gray matter behind closed eyes.

The train slowed nearing Rissne Station. Slaton decided he'd kept the phone long enough, but he was not quite finished. He called up the picture he'd taken at the café. It was a wobbly composition, suffering from poor lighting and the urgency of the moment, but the subject was clear enough: Nurin's agent strewn on the floor, his eyes rolled back and a jagged wound on his throat, all against a backdrop of blood-covered concrete. Going in, it had not been Slaton's intent to kill anyone. Now both members of Nurin's contact team were dead. As was so often the case, a well-orchestrated sketch had gone down in flames. The reasons were equally classic—complications resulting from the human element. Mistrust, fear, anger. All had played a part, and now the tragic outcome was summed in one high-resolution image.

Slaton had no way to know if anyone else—another Mossad operative or perhaps an embassy employee—had already reported in to Tel Aviv with a damage assessment. If not, this picture would provide all the debriefing necessary. Slaton considered a text message to accompany the image, but on this he hesitated. He'd already made one mistake. Angered that Nurin had pulled Christine into his scheme, Slaton had lost his temper with the director. He had rejected the assassination plot out of hand. Now, however, he saw a better course, one that might relieve some of the pressure. Using carefully measured words, he typed a brief and succinct message.

The train pulled to a stop and Slaton disembarked. He climbed the stairs to street level and immediately turned right. Confirming he had good reception, he hit the phone's Send button. Two minutes later Slaton stood on a curb next to a bicyclist, an older man who was waiting for a green crossing light. Up and down the street there wasn't a car in sight. An orderly people, the Swedes. The old man was hauling groceries in twin baskets that outriggered his rear tire.

"Lovely weather," Slaton said, speaking Swedish for the first time since his arrival.

The old man looked at him, then up to a sullen, darkening sky. He shrugged before noticing that the light had changed. As the old man cast off, Slaton slipped the phone deftly into his starboard basket. He turned the other way and began to walk.

Thirty minutes later and seven miles west, Slaton stepped off a bus in the working-class suburb of Jakobsberg. He estimated he was twelve miles from downtown, well clear of the morning's chaos. He walked until he found a convenience shop, and there paid cash for three prepaid, disposable cell phones, a long-sleeve sweatshirt emblazoned with the logo of the Swedish National Rugby team, and a large bottle of water. His next stop was a pharmacy where he purchased disinfectant, proper bandages, and alcohol wipes.

From there he scouted for a public restroom, the

quietest he could find being in the basement of a dark and nearly vacant pub. The place stunk of piss and stale beer, but it met his most important constraint—he was alone. At the sink he wet a handful of paper towels before locking himself into one of the two toilet stalls. He sat down, pulled off his shirt and carefully removed the improvised bandage. The wound was more painful now, and he cleaned it using the disinfectant. Slaton did his best with a field dressing, keeping a portion of the supplies in reserve for a better job when he had more time and better conditions. Gingerly, he pulled the new sweatshirt over his head, happy he'd gone with an extra-large. Finished, he took a long drink from the water bottle.

With two plastic bags in hand, Slaton divided his worldly possessions. In one he put the cell phones and clinical supplies, and in the other went a torn and bloody shirt. He flushed the old bandage down the toilet, and buried the plastic bag with the shirt deep into a repulsive trash bin. Seconds later he was climbing the stairs back to the street, taking two at a time, the beaten restroom door swinging loosely behind him.

THIRTEEN

Raymond Nurin sat in his bunker an unhappy man. He lived, or so it seemed, deep in the bowels of Mossad headquarters. He kept a proper office, of course, one with heavy furniture and a decent view, but that was a place for formal occasions—meetings with Knesset members and the issuance of citations to the rank and file. The bunker was where Nurin's real work was done.

The room had been designed under his exacting eye. There was a single workstation to display information, data that had already been sorted and scrubbed by the army of technicians one floor above. There was also a modest conference table with six chairs, this being the number of opinions at which Nurin drew a line—any more, in his view, generated a level of noise that was no more than static.

He was sitting alone at the conference table when the knock came, forceful and impatient. The kind of knock that would come if the building was on fire.

"Come."

Two men appeared. Rolling in the lead, predictably, was the tanklike form of Oded Veron. Though a man of average height, Veron exceeded the human mean in every other dimension. His hulking shoulders and massive head were fitted over a thick base, all of it advancing with an air of unstoppable momentum. Sharply pressed desert fatigues, sans insignia, covered chain-mail skin that paraded forty years of sun, sand, and scar tissue. Bringing up the rear was Nurin's second in command, Mossad's director of operations, Ezra Zacharias. Zacharias had been promoted only recently, after the previous operations chief, a known tyrant who openly aspired to Nurin's post, was forced to retire in the face of a life-threatening illness. Nurin had chosen Zacharias for his softer, more malleable countenance, not to mention his loyalty. Physically he was Veron's counterpoint—small, round, and nearsighted—yet what he lacked in physical presence was more than compensated for by an unbending work ethic.

"Well?" Nurin prodded, his voice raised in a rare display of temper. "What the hell happened in Stockholm?"

Veron remained stoic. He silently set a stack of papers on the conference table and spread them out like a poker dealer fanning a deck of cards.

Zacharias filled the void, his voice measured as always, "There hasn't been much information through our usual channels, at least not yet. It appears the target became violent. He attacked our team."

"I told you specifically there was to be no engagement. This man is someone we need!"

"With all respect, sir, your instructions were narrow. The man was to be contacted, given a phone, and we were to track him afterward if we could do so discreetly."

"And this is what you call discreet?"

Veron stepped in, "We don't know what happened. One of the men was from my section, and he would not have engaged without cause."

Nurin stared at Veron. The old soldier headed up his recent creation, a cell uncompromisingly called Direct Action. DA took on special projects for, and reported solely to, the director. It kept in its ranks not a single analyst or interpreter, but was comprised of individuals handpicked from IDF Special Forces units, Shin Bet, and Mossad's own operations arm. Direct Action, as the name implied, was a group of individuals who got things done. Except, it seemed, today.

Nurin said, "Whatever his reasons, your man made a fatal mistake."

The turret that was Veron's head swiveled. "The target was fortunate."

"No, *we* are fortunate to have sent only two."

"Who is he?" Veron asked flatly.

"I've already told you, I can't say."

Veron stiffened, but demurred to Nurin's authority with a stony silence.

"What about the girl?" Nurin asked. "Have we made any progress in finding her?"

This was Zacharias's ground. "We have four operatives in country and eight on the way. The embassy provided six. So far they've found nothing."

"She is an amateur! How could she disappear so completely?"

"Sometimes to be an amateur is the best thing," Veron suggested. "They are unpredictable."

Zacharias added, "The Swedes have no record of her exit, so she's still there somewhere. We'll find her, but I can't say how long it will take."

Nurin drummed his fingers on the table. He'd completely misread Anton Bloch's loyalties, and now the man had thrown a wrench into the most important operation in years. "Do we have anything new on Bloch's condition?"

"No change," said Zacharias. "The embassy is keeping a discreet eye on him. At the moment, I would say it's in our favor that he's in a coma. It will give us time to arrange his extraction." Clearly trying to set a more hopeful tone, he added, "We did recover the phone."

"Where was it?"

"We tracked it to an old pensioner's flat. One of our people slipped in and found it on the kitchen counter. The target had clearly ditched it."

"Did he access the file?"

"He looked at it once."

Nurin felt a ray of hope in an otherwise dismal situation.

"And he used it to send one message," Veron added. His meaty hands fumbled through the papers he'd set on the table, a clearly foreign task. He pulled one clear and dropped it at an angle so it slid across the table and came to rest in front of Nurin. "You've seen this?"

Nurin glanced at the photograph, then averted his eyes. "Yes, yes. I've seen it."

The room fell silent—two men waiting for an explanation, the third not giving it.

Veron broke the impasse by saying, "We will do whatever you ask, sir. But it would be a great help if we knew who we were dealing with. I must ask again— who is this man?"

Nurin glanced at his subordinates in turn, settling on Veron. "I will put it like this, Oded. In different circumstances, he might well be in your shoes."

Veron stood very still, almost as if at attention,

until Nurin said, "Go, both of you. Find this woman. She is our priority."

"And the man?" Zacharias asked.

"I don't think you'll find him."

"But if we do?"

Nurin considered it. "If you do . . . let him run."

Veron and Zacharias walked out, both clearly unhappy but with jobs to do.

Alone, Nurin's eyes fell to the photograph in front of him. The question he'd been riding all afternoon came back. Could Slaton still be convinced to carry through? In spite of their fumbling, a chance remained. If things fell perfectly. He reasoned that even if Slaton was the first to reach his wife, the threat was now implicit. Nurin might find a way to push, to manipulate one last mission from the *kidon*. One last sacrifice for Israel. There were alternatives, of course—Veron and his DA squad. That was a last resort, and one Nurin didn't like, but he would issue the order if necessary. The pursuit of Dr. Ibrahim Hamedi was the most important operation of his tenure, indeed the most important in decades. There was time for one more mission, and it had to be in Geneva. The engineer of Qom would be vulnerable. The Iranians, of course, knew it as well. Farzad Behrouz, Nurin's counterpart in Tehran, would be on high alert for a last try. Even expecting it.

But then other concerns came to mind. Concerns of a more personal nature.

Nurin looked at the photo on the table with more than a shred of anxiety. It showed the *katsa*, bloody and glassy-eyed in death. He understood that the photograph was no more than posturing. He was less sure, however, about the attached text message.

HEADING TO GENEVA. DO NOT PURSUE CHRISTINE.
IF SHE IS HARMED IN ANY WAY, DEAR DIRECTOR,
YOU WILL BE NEXT.

Slaton knew what he needed next, but walked a
brisk mile before asking a passerby for directions. He
selected a young man who looked Middle Eastern,
perhaps even Iranian, and was given friendly instructions. Slaton reached the Internet café three minutes
later.

Knowing he could no longer use Edmund Deadmarsh's credit card, he paid cash for an access code.
He surveyed the place and saw a vacant workstation
at the end of a row, and as he made his way there Slaton noticed a nearby computer that had been turned
off, an OUT OF SERVICE placard topping its keyboard.
He stopped at this machine, set his bag on the table
and began rummaging through its contents. No one
seemed to notice when moments later he left with
the placard in his bag.

He took a seat at the last console and established a
connection. Slaton called up the local Stockholm news
feeds and read everything he could find about the
shooting of two days prior. He read six stories, three
of which quoted Detective Inspector Arne Sanderson.
Every article put suspicion on foreign-hatched terrorism, disregarding Sanderson's quote that "We can't
yet rule anything out." Nothing Slaton saw gave a
lead to Christine's whereabouts.

He next went to the Stockholm police website and
performed a search of recently stolen property, but
didn't find what he was looking for. Slaton switched
to a commercial mapping program and zoomed in on

the Strandvägen. From there he dragged the cursor north, and then east along the waterways, following the Stockholm-Riga passage and weaving through a maze of islands until the widening channel was finally swallowed by the Baltic Sea. From that point Slaton reversed. He studied the largest islands and primary tributaries. He tried to imprint a mental picture, but the geography was overwhelming amid an endless network of coves and estuaries. Without knowing where to begin it was a vexing problem, but also satisfying—because that had been the idea all along.

Finished with the maps, he called up a search engine and typed in: Sweden, seaplane, charter. He was rewarded with six hits, and after cross-checking locations he narrowed his options to three. He studied the respective websites, made his choice, and entered the contact number for Magnussen Air Charters into one of the phones he'd just purchased.

The timer in his head rang, as it systematically did, and Slaton took a moment to scan the room. He saw perhaps twenty people engaged at computer stations, ranging from deeply engrossed loners, these hunched and wearing earbuds, to casual surfers with friends at their shoulders. The coffee bar ran a short line, and behind the counter a steaming espresso machine hissed and spewed. Nothing felt wrong.

Slaton returned to the computer, his last task being the most delicate. He called up the website for the Physician's Group of Eastern Virginia, and logged in with Christine's username and password. As the machine whirred and the connect icon circled, he felt a surge of anticipation. Or was it dread? After an interminable wait, the log of Christine's messages from work finally lit the screen. He saw three contacts from patients and four from associates, subject lines ranging from "My Gallbladder" to "Softball Canceled." There was also one message from an unknown address, nothing in the subject line. It seemed the only possibility. His finger hovered over the mouse button, and then one click later Slaton was staring at the simplest of messages: BRICKLAYER111029.

The release of tension was massive and immediate. Those sixteen characters brought Slaton's eyes closed, and the air that had been locked in his chest purged. Only then did he realize how heavily Christine's disappearance had been weighing on him. He had fallen so readily into his old rhythms—op plans, objectives, contacts—that he'd lost sight of what was truly at stake. The simple message in front of him brought undeniable relief, yet there was also a sense of unease. It served as a reminder that he was walking a very narrow wire. No room for error.

Slaton again referenced mapping software before typing a final group of characters into the browser window, an impossibly obscure sequence of numbers and special characters. He doubted the site had been disabled because its function was as relevant now as it had been a year ago. The page that came to the screen was like a million others—an advertisement for cheap Viagra, complete with a picture of a little blue pill. Below that, highlighted in red, was a lone file available for download. It was the kind of web link that anyone in their right mind, on the miniscule chance they should navigate here to begin with, would immediately write off as spam. They would close the page and never go back. More to the point, the download link would be treated by any casual user as the web equivalent of a bomb. Which, as it turned out, was exactly what it was.

Slaton clicked on the download and the computer

began to hum, extracting a Mossad-designed malware that worked with ruthless efficiency. First, all information on the hard drive would be destroyed. Subsequently, the program would corrupt the operating system in a manner that left it useless and completely unrecoverable. After three minutes—or so Slaton had been briefed—the machine he was using might as well have spent a month at the bottom of the sea. He pushed back from the workstation and placed the OUT OF SERVICE placard on the keyboard.

Sixty seconds later Slaton was back on the street. It was time to leave Stockholm. With each passing hour Inspector Sanderson, or someone like him, would start making connections. When that happened his ability to move within the city would be severely constrained. Fortunately, there was no longer a need for him to be here. Slaton had a new destination, albeit ground that would be difficult to cover. His immediate need—to separate cleanly with no hint of where he was heading. Walking down a cobblestone sidewalk under an azure sky, his pace seemed to quicken with every step.

FOURTEEN

That a second shooting had occurred in the space of forty-eight hours, in the same block of picturesque waterfront, generated a storm of critique around Stockholm. The press was swarming both the scene and police headquarters. The mayor was asking questions. The prime minister of Sweden had even called the National Police commissioner to his luxurious carpet for an explanation. All of this rolled downhill, of course, to land at the well-worn Birkenstocks of Arne Sanderson.

He spent an hour at the scene watching his men string yellow tape around the shambles of yet another Strandvägen café. One look at the victims confirmed what Sanderson already suspected—these were the two men being sought in relation to Friday's shootings, the same pair who had chased Christine Palmer across the waterfront. Initial eyewitness interviews, including Elmander from his hospital bed, made it clear who they should now be looking for—the American stonemason. *Two steps forward, one step back*, Sanderson mused. *Progress in a sense*. He gave careful directions to the on-scene forensic team, and was back at the station by one that afternoon. He had not yet reached his desk when Sergeant Blix intercepted him.

"Assistant commissioner wants to see you, boss."

Sanderson rolled his eyes, but did not feign surprise. "God, not again. How am I supposed to get anything done? While I've got you, Gunnar, check with Metro for any new surveillance footage on today's disaster—I know it's a Sunday but get them out of bed. This one looks a lot like the last, and I'm tired of spinning our wheels."

"Ah . . . right," Blix said. "I'll get on it." The sergeant turned away, and Sanderson watched him go with a sense that something wasn't right.

He approached Sjoberg's open door with caution, and saw the assistant commissioner frowning at his laptop. His mild exterior had acquired new edges, reddened eyes and a furrowed brow—the sea captain was enduring some heavy weather. Sanderson supposed he was getting heat from above. Sjoberg did not like high-profile cases, and this one was nearing critical mass.

With his mouth already set in an upside down *U*, Sjoberg's glare deepened when Sanderson breached the door. "Arne, please come in."

"I was just down at the waterfront," Sanderson began. "It's a damned war zone out there. Has National given us—"

"Arne," Sjoberg interrupted, "please sit down. And close the door, would you?"

A cautious Sanderson did both. "Is something wrong?" he asked. "Is it Elmander? Has he taken a turn for the worse?"

"No, no," Sjoberg said, "nothing like that. He's stable."

"I'm told it might have been serious the way he was bleeding. It was a damned good decision that dispatcher made to scramble EMTs along with the uniformed backup. She should be put up for a citation, if you ask me."

Sjoberg said nothing.

Sanderson asked again, "What's wrong? Have I botched something up?"

Sjoberg reached into his desk and pulled out a mobile phone. Sanderson's mobile phone.

"Thank God! I've been looking for that all morning. Where on earth was it?"

"In the unmarked department car you were using yesterday."

Sanderson reached out and took his phone.

"An officer found it this morning," said Sjoberg. "It was in the ashtray."

Sanderson pocketed his phone and said, "Silly of me—that's where I keep it in my car."

"But it wasn't your car."

Sanderson didn't like the trajectory of the conversation. "What are you trying to say?"

"I think you know."

"You can take that idea and—" he squelched the words rising in his throat, words sure to earn a reprimand.

"Friday I took a call from Dr. Samuels, Arne. Your preliminary evaluation was inconclusive, and he feels he must follow up. Unfortunately, you haven't done your part."

A silent Sanderson watched Sjoberg steel himself with a deep breath.

"I'm afraid my hands are tied. You're off the case, effective immediately."

"*What?*"

"I've booked you in with Samuels tomorrow morning—nine o'clock sharp."

Sanderson was incredulous. It had all started this summer with a regular physical examination. Sanderson had mentioned that he'd seemed forgetful lately, and the department physician began asking questions. His interest came acute on learning that Sanderson's mother had suffered from early-onset Alzheimer's. Now it had come to this. A few misplaced bills had snowballed into a false crisis.

"First of all," Sanderson insisted, "I would expect a little privacy when it comes to consultations with my doctor. Second, what gives you the right to—"

"To what? To reschedule your Alzheimer's evaluation because you forgot about another appointment?"

Sanderson shot from his chair. "I did not forget! I was called unexpectedly into court to give evidence!"

Sjoberg stood and met him face to face. "Do you know *why* your mobile was found earlier? It was ringing. Ringing because Sergeant Elmander, who is now in the hospital, called you to ask for instructions. The man he was tailing on your orders engaged in a conversation with a suspicious character, and Elmander wanted advice on how to proceed. He needed to talk to his superior, and his superior was nowhere to be found!"

Sanderson turned away, stung by the idea that he'd let a fellow officer down. He said nothing for a moment, then, "This is ridiculous. Tell me you've never misplaced your mobile."

"Arne . . . I'm sorry. There's probably nothing to this, but I can't take the chance. This inquiry has become very high profile."

Sanderson's urge was to battle, but he knew it

would only work against him. He asked quietly, "Who will take over?"

"Anna Forsten from National."

"A rising star, that one. Ambitious, telegenic. Not suffering from dementia."

"Please . . . let's not make this more difficult than it is. SÄPO has gotten involved. The terrorism angle is getting a lot of play."

"It's not terrorism," Sanderson said quietly. "At least not in the way SÄPO thinks about it."

"Which brings me to my next point—you've got a meeting after lunch with all of them. I want you to get them up to speed on everything we have so far."

Sanderson sank back into his chair. Sjoberg did the same.

"Please understand my position, Arne. I know this can't be easy for you."

Sanderson stared blankly at a display of knotted ropes under glass hanging on the far wall. "And after I brief them? Then what?"

"You'll be on medical leave until I have an evaluation from the department physician clearing you for full duty."

Sanderson forced a quiet calm. "All right. I will go see the doctor, do whatever testing is necessary to clear up this nonsense. But I want to stay involved in this inquiry."

"I don't see how—"

"Put me on desk duty, whatever you want to call it." Sanderson looked across the divide and swallowed his pride. "Paul, please—don't pull me off this one."

"I'm sorry, Arne, my hands are tied. The sooner you clear this up, the sooner you'll be reinstated." Sjoberg looked at him sympathetically.

It was all Sanderson could do to not leap for the

man's throat. With an exaggerated vitality, he rose and strode to the door.

He was reaching for the handle when Sjoberg said, "Arne—"

Sanderson paused.

"Expand on what you said."

"About what?"

"About SÄPO being convinced this is terrorism. You think otherwise. Why?"

His answer was some time in coming. "By definition terrorism is violence in the pursuit of political aims. Intimidation of the masses. If you look at these shootings no one has been terrorized. This is something else, more like a gang war in our front yard. Everyone involved seems to be a foreign national, but I don't see anything directed at Sweden."

Sjoberg nodded. "Yes, I see your point."

"We should be working with Interpol and the foreign intelligence services. The Americans, to begin—we have to find out who the hell Edmund Deadmarsh is. The man is clearly at the center of it all, but he's a damned enigma. All the information we have on him has either been disproved or vaporized in the last twenty-four hours."

Sanderson kept talking for five minutes, rattling off what was essentially a dress rehearsal for his afternoon meeting. He saw Sjoberg actually taking notes. When he was done, he said, "Anything else?"

"No, Arne, that's all for now. Carry on."

FIFTEEN

The man they were looking for was, at that moment, thirty miles southwest on an express train paralleling the E4. The window at Slaton's shoulder framed an interlaced mesh of freshly turned fields and conifer forest, brown leaves tumbling across land that was done with the business of summer and preparing for another season of survival. The *kidon* noticed none of it, his eyes a blank as they floated over the ever-changing portrait. His lost gaze was in part due to distraction, his thoughts managing the next few hours, but it also served to disengage the passengers around him. Happily, they all seemed similarly inclined, silently grappling ill-timed investments, marital disharmony, or whatever crisis had turned up on the threshold of their lives.

Everyone had problems. It was simply a matter of degree.

The train arrived after an hour in Nyköping, and there Slaton bore a ninety-minute layover at a station-side restaurant, taking espresso and a robust Smörgåstårta of ham, cucumber, and caviar on rye, before stepping onto his connection. The second train arrived at the village of Oxelösund, by the station clock, at 4:21.

Outside the terminal, Slaton stopped to get his bearings. To his right he saw an expansive iron mill fronting the Baltic Sea, acre upon acre of piping and machinery, mountains of ore rising from the scarred ground, all of it burnt rust-red by a windswept sea. Adjacent to the mill were working neighborhoods that had sprung up to house the attendant workforce. The homes reflected the mill—dated and worn, but soldiering on tenaciously in a changing world.

Slaton reckoned what he needed would be in the center of town, and a five-minute walk put him in Oxelösund's market district, a modest arrangement of shops and restaurants. Turning left onto the main boulevard, Slaton saw a shoe repair shop, its faded sign overlaid by a banner for mobile phone service. Farther on, a sandwich board in the middle of the sidewalk advertised a restaurant's new menu, traditional fare having given way to pizza and cappuccino. Slaton recognized the commerce of survival, and it was an inclination that suited him well. Unlike Stockholm, strangers here would not be regarded with suspicion. Quite the opposite, they would be welcomed openly for the kronor that might be in their pockets. And the chances of anyone on Oxelösund's Esplanaden linking Slaton with a rash of terrorism on Stockholm's Strandvägen? That was a chasm he was more than comfortable with. Better yet, there was probably not a Mossad operative within fifty miles.

On a waning Sunday afternoon the less robust establishments had already closed for the day, but Slaton was lucky to catch the owner of the local outfitter as he was reaching for the sign in his window. Even better, the man steered him to a rack where summer gear had been marked down for quick clearance. Assassins appreciate a bargain like anyone else, although

Slaton's direct reasoning—that he would not soon be forced to steal more money—was less than conventional.

Explaining to the proprietor that he was gearing up for some late-season hiking, Slaton selected a good set of trail boots, two pairs of heavy socks, a small backpack, and a GPS navigation device. From a half-price rack he selected a pair of trousers with multiple pockets down the side of each leg, and paired it with a thick cotton shirt and a rain-resistant jacket of medium thickness. That done, he turned to the main counter and committed to full price for a compact set of Zeiss field glasses and a handful of energy bars. His bill was driven higher by taxes—always the case in Scandinavia—but the owner allowed a reasonable exchange rate. Slaton walked out of the shop four hundred dollars lighter than when he'd gone in.

His final chore in Oxelösund was fixed in his mind as more of a question. *How to hide a lie?* The answer came in the voice of another long-forgotten Mossad instructor—*With a smaller, more obvious one.* Walking along the esplanade, this fluid pretense came solid in the form of a brassy lingerie boutique. Slaton dealt with a woman in her thirties who could well have modeled her wares, and he left the shop with a tiny pink bag in hand that contained one miniscule red negligee, matching panties, and two absurdly expensive chocolate bars. Back on the street, he initiated the GPS device and saw that Magnussen Air Charters was roughly a ten-minute walk from his present position.

Slaton set a quick pace, realizing that business hours for the day were nearing an end. The directions took him away from town, and he was soon drifting under long shadows in the low western hills. Evergreen walls swallowed a road that went from asphalt to crushed gravel, and finally, rutted dirt. Rounding a switchback turn, he broke into a clearing and saw the place he was looking for, a lone clapboard building, weathered and gray, and labeled with a hand-painted sign—MAGNUSSEN AIR CHARTERS. Above the sign he saw a second floor that likely doubled as a residence.

There were two small seaplanes. One was secured to a floating dock and bobbed aimlessly back and forth on tight mooring lines. The second craft was of the same type, a Cessna he thought, but this one stabled landside beneath an unwalled shed. The second craft was missing its engine, wheels, and the port float. Its innards had clearly been stripped, and open access panels swayed in the breeze. The approach seemed simple enough. One airplane was a flyer, and the other derelict and grounded, scavenged for spare parts like a wrecked car in a salvage yard.

Slaton walked to the building and knocked on the only door in sight, a wooden item in a bent frame that rattled under his knuckles. There was no answer, but he heard a small dog bark from the upstairs unit. Then from behind, "Can I help you?"

He turned to see a woman no more than five foot two. She was probably late fifties, blond hair giving to gray and a firm gaze that didn't give a damn. She had a wrench in one hand, and grease stains on the sleeve of her navy coveralls. She looked like a diminutive Rosie the Riveter.

Keeping to the Swedish she'd begun, he said, "Yes, I'd like to inquire about a charter."

"You've come to the right place." She came closer, wiped her hand on a rag, and they shook hands. "Janna Magnussen."

"Nils Lindstrom," he said. "Are you the owner?"

"Owner, pilot." She lifted the wrench and added, "Occasional mechanic."

Her blue eyes were spirited and lively, and Slaton grinned as he corrected himself. A diminutive Amelia Earhart.

"Are you and your airplane available tomorrow?"

"We are. This time of year is slow. I don't have anything until a supply drop to an island near Arholma on Wednesday."

"Excellent. I represent CLT Associates. We're a small company that contracts for private geological surveys. I need to reach an area near Bulleron Island tomorrow morning. I'd like to be dropped there for a day, then picked up and flown out the next morning."

Janna Magnussen nodded as she considered it. Slaton was sure his request was not unusual. Bush pilots made their living flying people and supplies into places that couldn't be reached any other way. Parts of Sweden were remote, islands and mountain lakes that might take a week to reach by more conventional means, some cut off completely in the winter. She walked toward the carcass of the dilapidated parts aircraft, bent down, and started working her wrench on the remaining float.

A woman with no time to waste, Slaton thought. That was good.

She said over her shoulder, "I charge fourteen hundred kronor per flight hour whether you're on the aircraft or not. Bulleron is one hour north, so for two round trips . . ." she paused to calculate, "let's say five thousand."

Slaton converted to dollars and came up with approximately seven hundred. "Actually," he said, "I may need more time. I want to do a visual survey when we get to the area, perhaps take a few pictures. Let's plan for another hour tomorrow, two on Tuesday. The airplane seats four, is that right?"

"Yes."

"I may need to bring a team member out on the return trip. Shall we call it seven hours?"

Now banging distractedly with a hammer, she said, "Eight thousand, then. Half up front."

"Is cash all right?"

Janna Magnussen stopped what she was doing. She stood and stared at Slaton, her once-lively eyes stilled by suspicion. "Cash you say?"

Slaton stiffened noticeably. He'd carefully arranged his recent purchases in the outfitter's shopping bag, now resting obviously on the ground by his knee. Magnussen came closer and her eyes slipped to the bag, or more succinctly, to what was in plain view on top—the red negligee held in a delicate shell of crimson tissue.

He sighed. "I'm sorry. I'm not really a geologist. I'm a—"

"A married man?" she suggested.

"Barely. I've arranged to meet someone I haven't seen in a long time. Someone I care about very much."

She eyed the bag. "Yes, I can see exactly how much you care. Tell me—how long have you been married?"

"Nine years. The first two were happy."

She studied him for a long moment, and Slaton tried to look the part—no longer a man with a business proposition, but a caught-out philanderer. Janna Magnussen had the upper hand. Just as he'd planned.

"Join the club," she finally said. "My bastard husband left me five years ago for a twenty-nine-year-old harpsichordist. But I got the last laugh."

"How is that?"

She pointed to the rusted hulk behind her, an untidy skeleton of scrap metal that had once been a sleek seaplane. "I got her in the divorce settlement," she said, a wisp of victory creasing her lips. "That was *his* airplane."

They agreed to an eight o'clock departure the next morning. Slaton was doubly happy when Magnussen mentioned that her sister ran a small bed and breakfast only a short walk up the road, and given the season could likely be persuaded to accept a modest sum for a room and two meals. After a five-minute walk and the briefest of introductions, Slaton was shown to a room with a view of the harbor and Stjärnholms-slott Bay. He dined alone on authentic sjomansbiff, a hearty stew of potatoes in beef stock and dark beer. After dinner he took Aquavit, complimented Greta Magnussen on her cooking and hospitality, and arranged for an early-morning wakeup followed by breakfast. Back in his room by ten, Slaton organized his gear, and by ten-thirty, with the low sun creasing the western horizon over the bay, he shut his eyes for the last time that day.

As Slaton drifted to sleep, a deflated Arne Sanderson was walking into his apartment. He hung his overcoat on a hook by the door, making sure to pull out his cell phone and place it on the charger. It had been a wretched day, first getting bumped from the investigation and then suffering the humiliation of briefing his replacements.

The house seemed more quiet than usual and he turned on the television for company, only to find a press conference pertaining to the recent terrorist at-tacks. Sanderson turned the television off. Having just spent two hours explaining things to Anna Forsten, he was in no mood to watch her—lovely as she might be—preen in front of the camera.

He could not remember being more tired after a day of work, and to top it off he had a smashing head-ache. Overwhelmed by the idea of cooking a proper supper, he shoved a frozen beef entrée into the micro-wave and pulled a bottle of wine from his cabinet. Sanderson searched for the corkscrew but was unable to find it. Annoyed, he considered using a knife or a screwdriver, but in the end simply repulled the cork on the stale remains of a Merlot he'd begun a week earlier. He issued a tall serving, and by the time he'd sorted out the wine his main course was severely over-cooked.

Sanderson ate in silence, stabbing and sawing at a slab of vulcanized beef. Divorced five years ago, he was accustomed to dining alone. The marriage had lasted nineteen years, and produced one daughter, two affairs, and considerable suffering all around. To this day the cause of the split escaped him. The infidelities—bilateral and concurrent—were an obvious enough excuse, but in fact only a symptom of some greater ill. He knew he shouldered much of the blame, his career having taken its predictable toll, but in the end the decision to separate had been a mutual one.

Ingrid, then fifty-two, had remarried quickly and well, latching on to a seventy-year-old bathroom fix-ture magnate whose relative age still permitted her trophy status. Sanderson saw her now and again, when she and the toilet king wintered in the city, and they remained friendly, always able to talk about their daughter who, in spite of her parents' sufferings, had blossomed into a remarkably well-adjusted kindergarten teacher. Yet for all of Ingrid's shortcomings, Sanderson did miss her cooking—and, if he were honest, her intermittent good humor. He'd seen a few women in the intervening years, but none who could make him laugh like Ingrid on a good day. And this was the time—quiet dinners over stale wine—when Ingrid had always been at her best. Not for the first time, he hoped the toilet king was an utter bore behind her braised veal and Chardonnay.

He finished dinner quickly and, relishing the one recompense of frozen entrées, tossed the plastic tray into an overflowing trash bin. Realizing that misery was getting the better of him, Sanderson did what he always did when he was feeling low—he poured a second glass of wine and turned his thoughts to work. He might have been put off the case, but it was not so easy to jettison the routines of a thirty-five-year career.

His instincts about Edmund Deadmarsh had been accurate. Unfortunately, he had not acted on them. He should have ordered comprehensive surveillance, not just a single man to watch over a target who was an unknown entity; indeed, one whose very identity had become an open question. As he'd been doing for hours, Sanderson thought about Sergeant Elmander. Had he put the man at risk? It was a discomforting idea, and one that made his head hurt even more.

He went to the medicine cabinet for ibuprofen, and in the mirror saw a tired man. He'd not been sleeping well in recent weeks, and today's events weren't going to help matters. Returning to the kitchen, he considered his schedule for the next day. He was to see Dr. Samuels at nine in the morning, with any mercy no more than an hour. After that, for the first time in thirty-five years, Sanderson had nothing on his agenda.

He supposed he would go to the station. On principle he did not dispute Sjoberg's authority to pull him from the case, yet as a practical matter he could never sit still while Edmund Deadmarsh, or whoever the man was, remained at large. Even more, Sanderson knew his vindication wasn't going to come from any crackpot medical evaluation. Far better it should come from finishing the job he'd today put on a platter for Anna Forsten.

Tired, but increasingly restless, Sanderson checked the clock. Quarter past eight. It took no more than a minute of silence, a minute of staring at the dregs of the Merlot, to make up his mind. *I might as well go back in. Sjoberg won't be anywhere near the place. An hour, maybe two. Long enough for the ibuprofen to kick in. After that I might get some sleep.*

There were still three fingers in the bottle when Sanderson recorked it. He put his coat back on and tapped the pockets to make sure everything was where it ought to be. Credentials, phone, wallet. He then cursed himself for succumbing to Sjoberg's accusations. *Alzheimer's my ass.*

Sanderson stepped outside and set a brisk pace in the cool evening air.

SIXTEEN

Hamedi watched the video feed with intense interest. The half-cut spherical encasement turned slowly as it was sprayed with an etching solution, the composite cubic boron nitride cutting tools performing their work with computer precision. When the casings were complete, they would be shaved to a precision measured in thousandths of an inch. Hamedi knew the value of such demanding specifications. The issue was not a matter of function—to initiate a reaction was simple enough—but rather efficiency. Once the fission began, every minute flaw brought a resultant decrease in yield. And Hamedi, with all his heart, was determined to maximize the weapon's yield.

"Gently," he ordered. "Bring down the speed."

The technician seated next to him entered a command, and the machine tools three floors below decreased their revolutions. The machining vault was on the lowest level of the complex outside Qom. Sealed and secure, the entire room was built on dampers to resist the slightest seismic tremor, and the climate was stabilized to provide constant temperature and humidity. But most importantly, the vault lay beneath eighty yards of earth and reinforced concrete, making it safe from Israeli and even American warplanes.

"There, yes. Now let's measure."

More commands were sent. The cutting tools pulled away, and seconds later the surfaces were measured using laser interferometers. The numbers that lit to the control display fell just outside the desired tolerances.

"Almost," Hamedi said. "Keep going."

The operator took the control stick in hand and was about to reengage the grinding surfaces when Hamedi saw him hesitate. The man seemed frozen, his face twisted in an odd expression.

"What is wrong, Ahmed?" Hamedi demanded.

The man almost answered, but then his head rocked back and he sneezed. The sudden muscle contractions caused his hand to jolt the control grip. The alarm sounded instantly, red lights and an audible warning blaring from the console, as the emergency system began its automated shutdown sequence. Hamedi sucked in a deep breath and watched the video feed in horror. He saw the mechanical arms pull away cleanly from the hemispheric casing, and watched the grinding heads spin to a stop. Only then did he begin to breathe again.

"You fool!" he shouted.

"I am sorry, Doctor. I . . . I went home to see my family last weekend, the first time in a month. My son had a cold. I promise it will not happen again."

Hamedi rubbed his temples with thumb and forefinger before fixing an icy stare. "No, Ahmed, it most certainly will not happen again! Get out of here, and send in Faisal! You are the filthy Jews' best friend!"

The technician stood slowly.

"And if you make a mistake like that again, you will not answer to me. I will feed you to Behrouz. I can assure you he is not of my forgiving nature."

Ahmed's eyes glazed over.

"Go!" Hamedi shouted.

The technician scurried away, and Hamedi waited until the door behind him latched shut.

He closed his eyes. Time was getting short, as was his patience. He knew he would have to smooth things over later with Ahmed—the man was actually one of his more competent operators. Still, these were the kinds of mistakes they could not afford, not when success was so near. The pressure was getting to him, robbing him of sleep, but at least he was spared Ahmed's complications. For Hamedi, family was not a concern. He had no wife, no children, not even any brothers or sisters. His only blood relation was his old mother, and he was no longer welcome at her door. Aside from his work, Hamedi was alone, and for the moment that was a good thing. A distraction avoided.

Hamedi went to work resetting the system, yet his thoughts were elsewhere. After the project was complete? he wondered. Would things change for him then?

That was a question only God could answer.

Hamedi was back in his office ten minutes later, sorting through the most recent internal messages. By his orders, all critical communications, both between the facilities and within the Qom compound, were restricted to paper copy and military courier. Email and electronic file transfers were no longer an option—Israel's hackers had penetrated their supposedly secure server on three occasions. Three that they knew of, anyway. The result of Hamedi's directive, of course, was that the movement of information had slowed to a crawl. But at least it was a secure crawl.

A knock came at the door.

"Come."

Hamedi looked up to see Farzad Behrouz, and it struck him that something about the man seemed more distorted than usual. If he didn't know better he might think Behrouz was pleased. Hamedi wrote it off to the harsh subterranean lighting.

"Is it true?" Behrouz asked.

"Is what true?"

"I've been told you are getting very close."

Hamedi's eyes went back to his desk. "We are on schedule. In truth, we would be ahead of schedule if I had more competent technicians."

"What do you mean?"

"A few minutes ago one of my machinists nearly dented three weeks' work."

"Did you make an example of him?"

Hamedi broke from his reading. "I didn't shoot him in the back of the head, if that's what you mean."

Behrouz smiled, or at least gave his troll's equivalent.

"I cannot fault a man for inexperience," Hamedi continued. "Six months ago he was working in a factory grinding lenses for reading glasses. Now he is manufacturing nuclear bombs. Such a leap cannot rely on faith alone—even if the black robes in Tehran tell you otherwise."

"Are more experienced workers not available?"

"A few, yes, and I requested them."

"But?"

Hamedi let his frustration vent. "But most of them work in universities, and this makes them unreliable. Or so I am repeatedly told."

Behrouz did not falter at the accusation, which was directed, if not at him personally, at the ideology of the imams he served. He said, "And you, Professor?

Not so long ago you were lecturing at one of our finest institutions. Surely you are reliable."

Hamedi glared, his contempt obvious. "What do you want?"

"Your trip to Geneva is near. We should discuss security arrangements."

"Please don't tell me the Israelis will be senseless enough to try again."

"No, nothing I've heard about, but I am always listening." Behrouz let that hang before launching into the details of his precautions. He would have fifty men at his disposal in Geneva, and Hamedi was sure this was not a complete accounting—a man like Behrouz always kept something in reserve. The plans seemed solid enough, and at the end Behrouz said, "I am concerned about the event you've added after your speech."

"What of it?"

"It seems unnecessary. Must you attend?"

Hamedi leaned back in his chair. He had been working terrifically hard, but there were still a great many details to be resolved. "I am deluged with work, and had no desire to go to Geneva in the first place. But what can I do? The international inspectors have insisted on this special meeting. Apparently they do not trust our latest inventory numbers. The good news for us is that this trip will be our last. Once the test has taken place, I shall never again have to conjure up ridiculous lies to deny our development of this weapon. As for the event I've added—yes, I am going. I don't expect you to understand, but as a member of the world academic community these things are expected. Besides, I find little time to socialize here in Qom, something I'm sure you are well aware of."

Behrouz shrugged. "The world academic community—yes, very impressive. It will be a night to remember for a boy from south Tehran, no?"

Hamedi said nothing.

"Tell me again," the security man said, "what neighborhood was it that you grew up in? Udlajan?"

"No," Hamedi said, "Molavi."

"Of course, that was it." Behrouz moved toward the door. "All right, I will make the preparations, including your evening out. Oh yes . . . the president has asked for an advance draft of your presentation to the inspectors."

Hamedi managed a smile as he said, "Is he worried that I will give away our state secrets?"

Behrouz raised an admonishing finger.

"All right," Hamedi relented. "I will have it for you tomorrow . . . since I have nothing better to do."

"Thank you for understanding."

Behrouz closed the door, and air seemed to refill the room.

Hamedi turned back to his desk and again reviewed the sequence of events that would lead to the underground test. Only ten days remained. Three for work here, three in Geneva, and then four final days in Qom to complete his preparations. And finally—the culmination of all his work.

There was only one task lagging behind in his demanding schedule, the placement of a seismic array to measure the blast's yield. Sensors were being sunk into the earth all around the test site, but progress was glacial. Hamedi could not imagine how a country whose life's blood involved drilling holes in the ground could fail such a challenge. Fortunately, the work was not critical. By his own estimate the yield would be five kilotons—seismic arrays or not, there would be no missing it. The test had been carefully timed so that an Israeli satellite would be overhead. The Americans, of course, were always watching. Soon all the world would see his project succeed in a blaze of glory.

He wondered for a moment what his old professors might think, and his colleagues from graduate school. Most were now making a respectable living in private industry, others doing research at the best universities. Hamedi could not deny that virtually all had found some measure of wealth and prestige. Yet none would make a mark on the world as he soon would. Hamedi had taken the harder path, something he never shied from, and the result of his work would be a blaze to rock the Middle East, indeed a shift of power to last a generation. Hamedi supposed he would get his name in the history books—either honored or reviled, depending on the language.

And is that why I am doing it? he wondered. In all honesty, he had to say yes, that was part of it. His scientist's ego.

But then there was the other part.

Slaton woke at seven, enjoyed two of Greta Magnussen's best waffles and a deep pot of coffee, and by eight o'clock he was climbing into the right seat of the Cessna next to her sister.

"Do you have coordinates for our destination?" his pilot asked. "Or are you going to give me progressive vectors?"

"Do you have a map?"

Janna Magnussen toggled up a map display on the central screen of the instrument panel.

"Can you expand it?" he asked.

She pressed a button twice and the map graduated

to cover more of Sweden. Slaton got his bearings as the captain went through her preflight checks, and he applied the message he'd found on Christine's work message board: BRICKLAYER111029.

"Here," he said, pointing to the islands east of Stockholm. "Get me that far and I can be more precise. Will the weather be good?"

"The whole country is in the clear today. But tomorrow may be different—there is a cold front approaching. If you still want to depart then, we should make it no later than midday. Otherwise you may be stranded for some time." She seasoned this with a distinctly Bohemian grin.

"My friend and I will be staying in a remote location, so we should have a contingency plan. If you can't reach us tomorrow then wait for me to call."

"Do you have a satellite phone?"

"No, but I'll find a way to get in touch." Slaton reached into his pocket and pulled out a wad of cash. "The first installment."

She took it, not bothering to count. "Do you want a receipt?" she asked, adding mischievously, "For tax purposes?"

He gave her a good-natured smile. "Remember—bring extra fuel tomorrow. We may want to do some sightseeing."

Magnussen put the money into a sidewall storage pocket, wedging it against an aircraft operating manual that looked as if it had never been opened. "I'll bring full fuel tanks," she said. "But if we go beyond the agreed flight time the price will go up."

"Done. Let's get going."

Minutes later the engine was straining and rattling as the Cessna skimmed over the faultless morning calm of Stjärnholmsslott Bay. The wings took a grip on the air, tenuous at first, and soon the twin creases of wake behind them came to an end. An easy sea was replaced by an easy sky, and Magnussen's hands were soft on the controls, sure and familiar. Slaton watched the glowing map display rotate in perfect synchronization to the heading of the airplane. Once established on a heading of north by northeast, everything settled. Magnussen made an effort to chat, pointing out a few sights, but Slaton was minimally receptive and she soon gave up. The only sound then was the steady drone of the engine.

Slaton began to feel restless.

He had gotten this far using the contingency procedures he'd forced on Christine months earlier. At the time she'd not seen a need for it, convinced that his past with Mossad was permanently buried. Slaton had feared otherwise, a fear now proven correct. But clearly she'd listened, because the agreed upon message was there. Christine had done her part, and now the rest was up to him. Tactically, his execution had been good, though not without mistakes. How easy would it be for someone else to check her message board at work? The meeting with Nurin's men had gone horribly wrong, and now the Swedish police were looking for him. And then there was Mossad. Would they give up? Perhaps coerce another retired assassin to do their bidding? Or was Nurin sitting patiently, waiting for Slaton to show up in Geneva? There was no way to tell. The more he thought about it, the more faults he saw in his and Christine's escape plan.

All the same, he was close. *She* was close.

He looked at the seascape ahead and saw a vast archipelago, hundreds of square miles of rock and forest and dark water. It seemed overwhelming. He didn't know what he was looking for—not exactly, anyway. He had no more than a rough starting point and two sets of sharp eyes, his and Janna Magnussen's. Slaton didn't want to carry his plan any farther—every time he tried to imagine where he and Christine could go next, doubt rolled in like a heavy fog. He simply had to find her. Would she be where he hoped? What was she doing right now? For Slaton there was only one certainty.

The next hour would be the longest of his life.

SEVENTEEN

Christine Palmer was, at that moment, waist deep in the very cold Baltic Sea.

The sailboat she'd appropriated, a vessel that normally drew five feet of water to the base of the keel, was heeling markedly in three briny feet on a rising low tide. Standing on the rocky bottom of a nameless bay, Christine had a paintbrush in hand and was mopping a wide blue line around the waist of the boat using bottom paint she'd found in a storage bin. The heavy stripe was the final touch. She had already removed a set of faded red sail covers and made slight alterations to the boat's registration number. Taken together, the changes gave a markedly different appearance from the craft she'd spirited away from a private dock outside Stockholm. That was the word she'd settled on: spirited. Far preferable to stolen, pilfered, or the overrationalized borrowed.

With one last stroke, she reached the stern of the boat and backed away to appraise her work. The detailing was awful, edges smeared and uneven, and a dozen drip marks ran down to the waterline. It hardly mattered. She was following David's instructions to the letter. *Do what you can to make it look different. Think large scale, so that no one looking from a mile away will recognize it.* Christine dropped the brush into the paint bucket and used her wrist to wipe a strand of hair from her face. She regarded the stern, where she'd worked for thirty minutes with a barnacle scraper to take off the old name, a Swedish word that meant nothing to her. After scratching right down to bare fiberglass, she had christened the boat with its new name, struck in bold blue lettering: *Bricklayer*.

Noticing an uneven C, Christine reached out to perform a touchup. At that moment, three feet underwater, the rock she was standing on wobbled. She nearly tumbled into the sea, but caught herself at the expense of a wayward paintbrush. When she regained her balance Christine was staring at a fresh streak of blue that snaked nearly to the waterline. Between the block letters *K* and *L* was what looked like a drunken *S*.

Brickslayer.

At that moment, Dr. Christine Palmer was struck by the absurdity of her situation. This was what her life had come to—standing in the Baltic Sea to paint a new name on the boat she'd stolen so it wouldn't be recognized by Israeli spies.

"What the hell am I doing?"

She smacked the transom with the wet brush, paint splattering across the deck like the droppings of some massive blue bird. She climbed up the boarding steps, and dropped the bucket and brush as cool air bit into her exposed legs and hips—she had stripped down to her panties to go into the sea, the only option for a sailor with one set of dry clothes. Mercifully, the owner kept a tall stack of towels on board.

Christine went below. There was no shower on the boat, so she soaked a hand towel with warm water from the sink and dragged it over the lower half of her body to cut the saltwater. It felt warm and wonderful. Using a fresh towel to dry, she dressed before turning to the table where a nautical chart was rolled open, anchored on opposing corners by two empty coffee mugs. The boat was fitted with receptacles for an electronic navigation suite, but the owner had clearly removed the system for the season—only the most hardened sailors bothered to cruise Scandinavia in the winter. The chart bore a single heavy line that was drawn from the center of Stockholm to her present position. Magnetic bearing, 111 degrees. Distance, 29 miles. The numbers had not worked out perfectly—as usual, variables had come into play, the most significant being the anchorage she'd settled on which was nearly a mile from the precise distance and bearing. David would also have to work out the beginning reference point of her last known position—the Strandvägen. And of course, all this assumed that he'd gotten to Sweden and found her message to begin with. From there it was simple. Find a way to reach her in the middle of nowhere.

What could go wrong?

Christine went above and stood on deck. A chilly breeze swept across the cockpit of the little boat, a basic and reliable Pearson 26. She scanned the horizon as she'd been doing all morning, but saw nothing new. Indeed she saw not a single man-made thing. Her last encounter with civilization had been yesterday morning, the seaside village of Runmarö eight miles north. There she had spent every penny in her pocket, mostly on food, and sent one message to her work email account. Then she had sailed here, to the back side of a remote island, and dropped anchor. With her part of the bargain done, there was nothing to do but wait. This was where David's plan ended, a windswept natural harbor at the end of the earth, winter bearing down like a frigid anvil.

She looked ashore, to the tiny island called Bulleron. It was no different from a thousand others in the Stockholm Archipelago, barren rock outcroppings, a few hardy trees and shrubs clinging for life. It looked a jagged and inhospitable place. The other three cardinal points of the compass were equally discouraging—open water, a few remote islands floating in the marine haze. That was all Christine saw. No boats, no barges, no ferries.

And no David.

"I'd like you to draw a clock showing the time as nine twenty-one," Dr. Samuels said.

"Digital or analog?" Sanderson asked.

The doctor stared at him with the solemnness of an undertaker.

Sanderson weighed asking if he wanted a.m. or p.m., but decided there was no point in antagonizing the man. Samuels was a nuisance, but in the end only a man doing his job. They'd been at it for the better part of an hour. *What is the date? Can you tell me the year? Where are we?* Ridiculous hoops, but hoops he had to jump through all the same. It hadn't helped that when he'd been asked to count backward by sevens, starting with one hundred, Sanderson had stumbled at seventy-nine. But then, he wasn't taking any of it very seriously. To make his misery complete, he'd woken with another headache. He'd be damned if he was going to mention that to the doctor.

Sanderson drew a clock with Mickey Mouse hands and handed it over.

Dr. Samuels frowned. He was a tall man, balding

and with a beard that looked positively Freudian. It seemed as if every shrink Sanderson had ever known tried for the same look, a manifestation of transference or repression or some damned thing that made them all, in his view, no better than the poor sods they were passing judgment on.

"How old was your mother when she was diagnosed with early-onset Alzheimer's?"

"I can't remember."

The doctor looked at him uncertainly.

"Sixty, maybe sixty-one."

A sigh. "Do you have any trouble balancing your checkbook?"

"Yes, but only because I need a raise."

"Please, Inspector. We're nearly done. I'm going to give you three words. Please say them back to me in reverse order. Cashier, lumber, gable."

"*Pignon, bois, caissier.*"

The doctor stared at him blankly.

"Gable, lumber, cashier—in French, because you didn't specify a language. Doctor, perhaps we could continue these parlor games later over a pint, but I really should be going. The streets are not as safe as they ought to be lately, and my oath obliges me to do something about it, notwithstanding the off-chance that there may be beta-amyloid proteins clogging my brain."

"All right," Samuels said. "I think I have enough to work with. But I will insist on an MRI."

Sanderson nearly protested, but decided it would do no good. He heaved a sigh and said, "Let's get on with it then."

EIGHTEEN

Janna Magnussen banked the Cessna into another tight turn.

"There are fifty thousand cabins in the Stockholm Archipelago," she said. "I don't see a single one here."

"This is the place," Slaton said. "I'm sure of it."

They'd been circling the area for thirty minutes, a peninsula at the top of a rabbit-shaped island named Bulleron. Starting with the bearing and range from Stockholm that Christine had given, Slaton instructed Magnussen to fly outward in an ever-expanding pattern. The weather was not cooperating, a broken marine layer having risen to obscure things below. With a bit of bad luck, Slaton knew they could fly right over Christine and never realize it. He'd asked Magnussen to search for a cabin along Bulleron's eastern shoreline, while he looked for the true objective—a small boat, probably anchored in the natural harbor along the western shore. It might be a sailboat or a power cruiser, even an open runabout. Slaton would be thrilled with a rowboat if Christine was in it.

The peninsula was a mile wide and perhaps three miles long, an evergreen carpet broken by patches of dirt and rock. Slaton saw no roads or power lines, indeed no sign of civilization at all. They were five hundred feet above the eastern shore, skimming the cloud layer, when he caught a flash of white. Slaton watched the spot intently and saw it again—no more than a hundred yards offshore, a sleek profile flickering through the clouds. As casually as he could, he trained the field glasses on the sea, willing the clouds to break one more time. They did, long enough for him to make out a small sailboat. He quickly focused the glasses and read the name on the stern: *Bricklayer*.

In his years with Mossad, Slaton had endured countless stressful situations, and so he was an expert at compartmentalizing emotion. It didn't matter. When he saw the name of the boat he felt a surge from the depths of his soul. He shifted the glasses to the far end of the peninsula and began searching for landmarks by which he could crosscheck the position.

"I see it!" he said, pointing to the area. "Just inside that stand of trees."

Magnussen followed his finger to the forest five hundred feet below. "I don't see anything," she said.

"This is the place. Can you put it down near the eastern shore?"

Magnussen gauged the waters. Then she gauged him. "The western side is in the lee—the water is calmer there."

He gave her an unwavering look.

"Yes, I can manage either way," she affirmed. "But you're *sure* this is the place?"

"I'm sure."

"All right—it's your kronor." Magnussen maneuvered the aircraft, and minutes later made a smooth touchdown, the twin floats settling like a pair of high-speed canoes. From that point, the aircraft became a boat.

"I can't maneuver very well once she's in the water,"

she said. "If you want to get close to the shoreline I see only one stretch of beach that looks approachable. Even there I'm going to need your help."

On her instructions, Slaton got out and stood at the midpoint of the starboard float, clear of the idling propeller. Ten yards from shore Magnussen killed the engine. Slaton moved forward, jumped into knee-deep water with his backpack in hand, and then pushed and pulled until the Cessna was pointed back out to sea.

Magnussen called through the open door, "Remember, tomorrow we have to fly in the morning if we're going to beat the weather. Eleven o'clock, here?"

Slaton gave a thumbs-up, and after a final shove the engine chugged to life and Magnussen added power. Already running into the wind, the little airplane skipped nimbly over the waves and rose into the sky.

Slaton turned ashore, and as soon as his feet hit sand he broke into a jog. The terrain was rough—rock and brambles and fallen timber. A mile that would have taken six minutes over level ground took fifteen. When the western shore came into view he didn't see the boat, and for a terrible moment he feared she might have gotten under way to a new anchorage. Finally, closer to shore, he spotted the white hull.

And then he saw Christine.

He could barely see her face, but there was no mistaking his wife's willowy build and upright posture. She'd come ashore, probably having seen or heard the seaplane. The boat was moored close to shore, an anchor off the stern and a bow line secured to a fallen tree. Christine was standing on a patch of rocks and searching the sky.

Slaton ran faster, battering through brush and vaulting boulders. The noise drew her attention, and finally they locked eyes.

Only she didn't move.

Christine stood her ground and let him come to her. Slaton didn't care—after five thousand miles what were a few more yards? When he came near she didn't raise her arms, and he stopped a few steps away. Slaton stood completely out of breath and tried to read her face. He saw hope and pain and worry. Finally, Christine cocked her head ever so slightly and leaned toward him. Arms at her side, she virtually fell into his chest.

Slaton caught her and held on, her body conforming to his like clay in search of a form. They were still for a long, long moment until the inevitable came. Her uncontrollable sobs began welling into his chest. He began to kiss her, first the top of her head, and then her upturned face. She pulled him down and soon they were on their knees in the sand, just holding one another.

Hanging on tenaciously against the spiraling world.

Sanderson's MRI was scheduled for eleven o'clock that morning, to be conducted in a radiology annex near Saint Göran Hospital. The technicians were running behind, but after an aggravating thirty-minute wait a young man stripped Sanderson of his possessions and shoved him into a clattering tube. When the test was done, he was given his clothing along with solemn assurances that the results would soon find his doctor, who in turn would find him.

His morning wasted, Sanderson got dressed and, after a pitched fight with his necktie at the bathroom mirror, decided to walk two blocks to Saint Göran to check on Sergeant Elmander. Of all Sjoberg's accusations at their last meeting, the thing to strike Sanderson hardest was the idea that he'd not been there to back up a fellow officer in a moment of need. Nearing the hospital he considered buying a takeout meal, recalling that Elmander was mad about some kind of ethnic food. The variety, however, escaped him. Had it been Thai? Chinese perhaps? Sanderson couldn't remember, and another stitch of worry sank in. Was this how it would be from now on? Every time something didn't snap into his mind, more anxiety? No, he decided. He would not let that happen.

As luck would have it, he found Elmander sitting up in bed, his wife and son at his side, and his face buried deep in a takeout container of spaghetti. *Italian*, Sanderson thought.

"Afternoon, Inspector," said a chipper Elmander.

"Hello, Lars. How are you?"

Elmander gestured to a heavily bandaged leg. "Up and running in a few days, they tell me."

Elmander and his son began bantering about which of them would now be faster on the soccer pitch, a sparring contest that Sanderson found even more encouraging than the official medical prognosis.

"I'm sorry I didn't answer when you called," Sanderson said.

"Not to worry, Inspector," Elmander replied in a mercifully carefree tone. "Blix tells me they've bumped you off the case."

Sanderson nodded.

"Big mistake on the assistant commissioner's part, if you ask me. Of course, it wouldn't be his first, eh?"

They exchanged the kind of smile shared between subordinates, but Sanderson was left wondering how much else had made its way to the rumor mill. He supposed that news of his advanced dementia had swept the station by now. They talked for ten more minutes about work and sports, and agreed to meet for a pint at Black and Brown next week.

Sanderson left the room feeling much better than when he'd gone in. He was nearing the elevator when it occurred to him that he should check on their mystery patient, the man who was presumably still in a coma. At the nurse's station Sanderson pulled his credentials—Sjoberg, by either good grace or gross oversight, had not confiscated them—and a young man directed him to the correct room.

He arrived to find a nurse tending an IV. The patient looked no different, still and lifeless, but an array of monitors beeped rhythmically to prove otherwise.

"Any change?" Sanderson asked, again showing his identification.

"No," the nurse replied. "I expect it will be a few days before any decisions are made." She was a matronly sort, roughly his age, and Sanderson suspected she knew what she was talking about.

He stood with his hands on his hips, and thought aloud, "Too bad we never got a word with him."

"There were a few moments when you might have."

"A few moments?"

"He was conscious when he arrived. Even muttering a bit."

"Muttering?" Sanderson repeated.

"He kept saying something over and over, but it made no sense to me."

"Can you remember the words?"

She shrugged. "They were very distinct, but it wasn't Swedish. And not English either. My only two languages." She made a stab at sounding it out.

Sanderson took out his notepad. "Say it again as precisely as you can."

The nurse did, and Sanderson wrote down the words phonetically. "Who else was on duty when he came in?"

"Dr. Gould down in ER. I think he's working now if you want to talk to him."

Five minutes later Sanderson was doing just that. Gould was nearing the end of his shift, but happy to help a policeman on a quest.

"Yes," the doctor said, "I did hear what he said. It didn't make much sense, but that's not unusual around here—the man had incurred severe trauma."

Sanderson again took out his notepad, ready to scribble. "Tell me anyway."

The words the doctor gave were very near those he'd gotten from the nurse, perhaps a harsher edge to a few of the consonants.

"One more time," Sanderson said.

"Would you like it in English?"

Sanderson looked up, nonplussed.

"It's Hebrew," Gould said. "I recognized it immediately. He was saying, 'Let the bayonet go.' As for what that means—I wish you luck, Inspector."

NINETEEN

Slaton watched Christine start a pot of coffee aboard the newly christened *Bricklayer*, and as she went about the job neither tried to discuss their predicament. Her smooth face was strained, the usual easy smile gone. Her weariness was accentuated by the rumpled clothes she'd certainly been wearing for days. Being well versed in stressful situations, he knew to let her lead the conversation.

Christine rummaged through a storage bin and made small talk about the weather, eventually progressing to a rundown of her short voyage here, this no more than a sailor's account of an uneventful passage. Dividing her narrations, however, were long moments of silence. When the coffee was brewed she found two mismatched cups, poured, and sat down at the small table to face him.

"What are we going to do?" she asked.

"We're going to get you safe. Then we're going to keep it that way."

"How?" Her voice was uncharacteristically flat and direct—as if she was in doctor mode.

"I don't know exactly, but I'll make it happen."

"Anton was trying to help me."

"I know, I figured that much out. He wanted to ruin this whole Mossad scheme."

She nodded. "He's dead, isn't he?"

"No."

Christine's face came alight, and for the first time she looked at him with something near hope.

"He's alive, but there's a bullet lodged near his spine. He's in the hospital and in serious condition, but there's a good chance he'll pull through."

She was silent for a time. "You want to hear my story, don't you?"

"Only when you're ready."

"A debriefing—isn't that what they call it in your line of work?"

"Christine, please don't—"

"No, no," she interrupted. "I should tell you everything. I know that."

And she did, beginning with a mundane physician's conference, and ending with the Stockholm to Riga Passage and a stolen sailboat anchored in a remote cove. She included Bloch's account of Mossad's failed mission in Iran and the loss of four men, including Yaniv Stein whom Slaton had known well. She gave the abduction attempt particular emphasis, and when she recounted the details of Bloch being shot her voice wavered. But she carried on. Christine explained that three men had been involved, and by her descriptions Slaton was sure he'd seen them all—one on a slab in the morgue, and the other two at the Renaissance Tea Room. Without a doubt, all Mossad. Without a doubt, all dead.

Slaton responded with his own story, beginning with the call for help Bloch had made from her phone, and ending with Magnussen Air Charters. When he was done, he paused long enough to refill their cups.

"You killed two men?" she asked.

"That wasn't my plan—but yes."

"And you shot a policeman?"

"One round in his leg. I had to put him on the ground because he was about to be killed."

She laughed nervously. "I would not believe that from anyone else on God's earth. Why do I trust you so unfailingly?"

He didn't answer.

"This assassination Mossad is pursuing—where is it to take place?"

"Do you really want to know?"

She nodded.

"Geneva. Six days from today."

Christine went silent, and Slaton had an urge to change tack. Looking around the cabin, he said, "Tell me again where you got this boat."

"I stole it."

"From who?"

"How should I know?"

He waited patiently.

Christine pitched a heavy sigh, and said, "It was at a private dock near the marina. I saw a moving truck at the house above—a crew was hauling out some clothing and books, boxes of pots and pans. It seemed like a nice house, well-kept. I figured the owners were moving south for the winter, maybe to a place in France or Spain. If that was the case, the boat wasn't going anywhere. I figured it would probably just sit there until somebody from the marina came and hauled it out for dry storage in a month or so. After the movers drove off, I waited until dark. There were no locks, so it was easy. I pulled two mooring lines and she was mine."

"You're right—the boat probably won't be missed anytime soon. That was a good move."

"No, David. I did it, but it was *not* a good move. It was grand theft, or whatever they call it here. I stole someone's boat. I'm using their food and fuel and supplies, and it's not right. I know how I'd feel if it was my boat."

"Even if the person who stole it was facing what you were?"

"That doesn't justify it."

Slaton recognized an argument he wasn't going to win. He also sensed an irregular edge to her tone. Christine was a doctor, typically steady under pressure. He'd even seen her handle situations like this before. Something had his wife uncharacteristically rattled.

She gripped her mug with both hands, and after a full minute picked up with, "What are we going to do, David? We can't just keep running from Mossad and the Swedish police and . . . and whoever else wants to ruin our lives."

"We think of a way out."

"Well, you'll have to do it because I don't understand what's going on. This whole thing is like a damned game, nothing but smoke and mirrors. Mossad actually thinks that by kidnapping me they'll force you into one last assassination? Does that make sense?"

"If you understand how people like Nurin think—maybe. But you have a point. There's something more going on here."

He remembered Nurin's words. *Think about it and everything will make sense . . . Do this one job and it will be your last.* The more Slaton thought about it, the more confusing everything seemed. He had sent Nurin a message saying he would go to Geneva, all along knowing there was only one obvious course—to find Christine. Yet now that he had, it seemed a tenuous victory. Even if he could protect her and evade Mossad in the days ahead, what would happen next week or next year?

Try as he might, Slaton could not find an answer.

Not everyone at SÄPO was an idiot.

This point had settled in Sanderson's mind five years ago when he'd met Elin Almgren. In the course of a particularly maddening investigation, Almgren had helped him track down a killer, passing critical information that others in her service might have held as proprietary. Sanderson had since reciprocated, most recently helping Almgren and SÄPO make a solid case against an international money-laundering network. It was the kind of intergovernmental cooperation that was vital to effective law enforcement, yet rarely seen as a result of turf wars. Fortunately, a handful of midlevel people like Sanderson and Almgren knew how to bend the system in favor of results.

He had arranged to meet Almgren for lunch at The Flying Horse Pub, and in keeping with their private tradition, since Sanderson had made the request he was obliged to pick up the bill.

"The Flying Horse Chipotle Burger?" he asked.

"Best burger in town," she said, adding, "and the most expensive." She was a decent-looking woman with fair hair, blue eyes, and the prominent worry lines that came from twenty years of surveillance, late meetings, and otherwise keeping crown and country secure.

"If you don't mind my saying so, Arne, you don't look well."

"I've been having trouble sleeping."

"You need more sex."

Sanderson grinned. This was Almgren's answer to all things amiss in his life. She'd said it when he and Ingrid were near a split, and again afterward when he'd fallen into a miserable funk. Less credibly, it was also her advice when his arthritic knee acted up. Given that Almgren was a lesbian in a long-term relationship, there was no hint of suggestiveness or hidden meaning. And along these same lines, her recommendation carried the weight of what one might find in the middle of a fortune cookie.

"I'm working on it," Sanderson said.

"No you're not. You're repressed. Always have been."

The waitress swooped in with two pints of ale. She was a slim, tattooed girl of no more than twenty, and as she walked away Sanderson made a point of leering at her bottom.

"Oh, please," Almgren said, addressing her beer. "I hear you've been taken off these two shootings."

"That's right. Sjoberg is convinced I'm going daft."

"Going? You've been that way for years, darling. He's just now realizing it? My opinion of the man slips another notch."

Sanderson responded by taking a long pull of his own beer.

"All right, what do you need?" she asked.

"I think this man we're looking for is Israeli."

"Israeli? What makes you say that?"

"The victim who ended up in a coma in the hospital—he was conscious when they first brought him to the emergency room. The staff heard him speaking Hebrew."

"Hebrew? You're sure?"

"Yes."

Almgren gave this some thought. "There *are* Jews in Sweden, Arne."

He gave her a suffering look.

"Lillehammer?" she said tentatively.

"It puts everything in a different light, doesn't it?"

That event, occurring long before either of them had entered their respective academies, was the stuff of legend in Scandinavian law enforcement. In the summer of 1973, Israel was hunting Ali Hassan Salameh, leader of the group responsible for the previous year's Munich Massacre. Thinking they'd found their man, a Mossad team was dispatched to the village of Lillehammer, Norway, to assassinate Salameh, but mistakenly murdered an innocent Moroccan waiter as he walked home from a theater with his pregnant wife. The next day, two members of the assassination squad were arrested, and soon the entire team was in custody, later to be put on trial. It was the blackest of days for Mossad, and a debacle that exposed Israel's brazen will to operate in Europe as never before imagined.

"It's been a long time," Almgren said. "Perhaps the new administration in Tel Aviv is too young to remember."

"Or perhaps Israel is desperate."

"In what way?"

Sanderson shook his head. "I don't know. I'm trying to work that out."

"They always have a list of extremists they're after—Hamas or Hezbollah. Maybe one of them turned up here."

"No. That's not it."

"How do you know?"

"The first shooting. All the witnesses said it was a

case of one versus three. The man who is now in the hospital was by himself. He shot the man who died, and was exchanging fire with the other two on the street."

"And he's the one who was spouting Hebrew? So then we have the reverse—one of Israel's enemies tracked this man here. Perhaps he's a Mossad operative or an Israeli general. Even a politician."

Again Sanderson shook his head. "That's not it either. The two who escaped that first incident were gunned down yesterday. We now have identity documents from all four. They're good quality forgeries . . ." he hesitated, "but nearly identical. The same manufacture."

Almgren thought about it. "Yes, I see what you mean."

The young waitress dropped a plate on the table that held a massive burger with jalapeños and pepperoni spilling from under the bun.

"Good God," Sanderson said. "Just looking at it gives me acid reflux."

"You don't have acid reflux. You just need more sex." Almgren, relishing her cast-iron constitution, dug into the burger with gusto. With a partially full mouth, she said, "This man in a coma—maybe he was a rogue of some kind. The others could have been sent here to eliminate him."

Sanderson took a handful of chips from her plate. "Possibly. But I still don't understand where the girl comes in. There's nothing sordid in her background, yet this Israeli was talking to her in the café for at least ten minutes. Witnesses said the two of them seemed tense but familiar."

"What else then?"

Sanderson thought about it. "The man now in a coma. He was attended to by a doctor who spoke Hebrew—that's why I'm certain about the language."

"Does the doctor remember what he said?"

"Yes. He said, 'Let the bayonet go.'"

Almgren set her burger on the plate and stared at him. "Bayonet?"

"Yes. The doctor was quite sure."

"As in 'kidon'?"

Sanderson eyed her. "You speak Hebrew?"

"No. I speak Mossad—we all do where I live. Israeli intelligence is a big organization, but most of their employees are a straightforward bunch. Field operatives, linguists, communications specialists. There is, however, a very elite unit. A handful known as *kidons*."

"And what do they do?"

"They're a very special division. The *kidonim* are Mossad's assassins."

Sanderson stared blankly across the table. He considered the first shooting, the man in the hospital and the three he'd been up against. Had there been an assassin among them? It was not until he considered the second attack that the thunderbolt struck.

It settled in his mind in a familiar way, a recurring instinct he never doubted. It was none of the first four, but the other, the lone survivor. A man he'd met at the Strand Hotel and interviewed at length. One who had yesterday stolen a gun at a café and used it to kill twice. Sanderson remembered watching him read signs in a language he supposedly didn't know. Remembered the blue-gray eyes that reflected like polished steel, taking everything in yet letting nothing out. In the car, the way he'd moved to see and not be seen. It had been right there in front of him all along, like staring at the sun but not seeing it for the brilliance.

The stonemason.

Edmund Deadmarsh was an assassin.

TWENTY

The early-afternoon sky over Bulleron had turned to a full overcast, a steel gray curtain that promised rain. The wind kept still and the seas were quiet, soft waves lapping the boat's hull with barely audible authority. For Slaton these were no idle observations. Weather conditions at high latitudes were subject to volatile change, and right now meteorology was critical to his near-term planning. Janna Magnussen had said a cold front would arrive tomorrow, but he wondered if things were turning sooner. Could tomorrow morning's extraction be delayed? Part of him hoped for the worst, a maelstrom that would last a week and cover him and Christine like an impenetrable blanket. A storm formidable enough to curtail the other path that was forming in his mind.

They were going over nautical charts when Slaton broached a subject he knew would be delicate.

"I need your help," he said. "In a professional capacity."

Her stare began as curious, but shifted to grim when he removed his shirt to display the wound on his bicep.

"It's not a gunshot," he said.

"Very reassuring—but I can see that. I did a turn in the emergency room at a big hospital in Boston." She left it at that, not asking what *had* caused it. "I'm afraid the boat isn't very well stocked with first-aid supplies."

Slaton reached into his backpack and handed over the remainder of what he'd purchased in Stockholm.

"You always have an answer, don't you?"

He presented his arm. "Obviously not."

She set to work, removing the old dressing and cleaning the wound as best she could. Christine was normally chatty and chipper, but she carried on now in a discomforting silence. Slaton found it unbearable—one more good thing trampled by his intractable problems.

The quiet lasted until she tied off the outer bandage.

"Anything else?" she asked, pulling away.

"Is there a toothbrush on board?"

She shook her head, and said dismally, "It's a hell of a way to live, Deadmarsh."

"And I am a little hungry."

"I docked for provisions in a village yesterday. Spent all the cash I had on cheap calories—pasta, rice, eggs, some canned vegetables."

"I've seen you work with a box of rice. You're good."

Christine didn't smile, and again his marital radar sensed something amiss. Slaton wondered if there was some complication he'd not yet seen. She pulled a pot from a cabinet and started fiddling with the tiny gas stove. He watched her work, knowing that simple chores could bring a sense of normalcy. It was a thing Slaton had learned during nerve-racking stays in safe houses and treacherous surveillance stakeouts: washing a load of laundry or doing the dishes was a simple way to cut the tension. Christine probably hadn't recognized it yet. But she would. She was learning.

"How long will the provisions last?" he asked.

"For both of us? A few days, a week if we want to lose some weight. Is that the plan? To wait Nurin out until this assassination scheme is past its shelf life?"

"That was my original idea."

She went still. "But not anymore?"

"Things have changed. Staying here, or sailing someplace else . . . it wouldn't work. Mossad is looking for us. And of course the police—I've killed two men and shot an officer, and I'd rather not have to explain my reasons in a court of law. As for Mossad, it's true that Nurin's plan will be dead in a week, but who's to say the director won't come up with something better next week or next month. Hamedi might go abroad again, or perhaps Mossad will find an opening in Iran that has a better chance of succeeding than the last two. No," he said with certainty, "laying low for a few days doesn't fix anything. It only postpones the inevitable."

"The inevitable? And what is that?"

Slaton didn't answer.

The rain promised by the darkening skies began to fall, tapping against the boat's fiberglass shell. Christine went to the companionway and slid the top shell closed as drizzle swirled into the cabin. She sank next to him at the built-in dining table, and again he sensed something amiss in her pained expression.

He met her eyes. "What's wrong, Christine?"

After a long pause, she said, "There's something you should know."

"You mean it gets better?"

He'd hoped for a good-natured smile, but didn't get it.

"When I was in the village yesterday, I bought one thing besides the food." Christine reached into her pocket and pulled out a small plastic strip. It looked like a Popsicle stick, blue and with two colored bands on one end. She set the stick on the table and Slaton stared at it blankly. Only when he correlated the depth of her gaze did he realize what he was looking at.

"Is that a . . . you mean we . . . ?"

Christine nodded. "Yes, David. We're going to have a child."

At 4:05 that Monday afternoon Sanderson was waiting in Sjoberg's office while the assistant commissioner was tied up in something called the Interdepartmental Coordination Group. Sanderson briefly considered bursting in on the meeting with his revelations about Deadmarsh, but in the end he decided against it—given his present standing, he supposed drama would not work in his favor.

A ship's clock somewhere in the room rang eight bells. He thought it sounded silly in a police department, and certainly not fitting for an AC's office. Sanderson looked around the place and admitted, not for the first time, that he had once aspired to this room. The nameplate on the door might well have been his had he kept a more careerist outlook. He noted two pictures behind the desk. A younger Sjoberg standing on a golfer's tee box with a commissioner long since retired, both brandishing long-shafted clubs. Another of Sjoberg accepting a plaque of commendation from the mayor, probably for some groundbreaking administrative achievement. Sanderson asked himself the familiar questions. Should he have made more appearances at the moving-up parties? Spent his weekends on the charity fund-raiser circuit? Those were the unwritten rules of the game of advancement, and Sanderson had not played by them. He supposed it was natural to find a few regrets at the end of a career, and he couldn't deny this was one of his. Still, if he hadn't achieved rank, he knew he'd earned the respect of the men and women he worked with on a day-to-day basis. If the inspectors and sergeants and constables at Kungsholmsgatan 43 were faced with a challenging case, he was the man they'd want to run it. Of this he was sure.

The door behind him rattled, breaking his musings, and Sjoberg walked in. He was followed by a woman whose self-important air and yellow identification badge indicted her as being from National.

"Arne—" Sjoberg looked at him with unmasked surprise. "What are you doing here?"

"I'd just like a minute of your time. I've come across something important." Sanderson saw the woman hesitate at the door.

A befuddled Sjoberg addressed her, "Would you give us a minute?"

She backed outside with a gracious smile, leaving the door open.

"Arne, we're very busy. I'd think you of all people would realize it."

"I talked to a doctor today at Saint Göran."

"Good, it's about damn time."

"No, no. Not Samuels. It was a physician from the emergency room. He told me that the victim brought into the ER Saturday—"

"*What?*" Sjoberg said, cutting him off in a coarse whisper. "You went to Saint Göran on a matter relating to this investigation?"

"Yes."

"Have you forgotten my orders? Or are you simply ignoring them? You are not involved in this anymore!"

"But the man was Israeli, I'm sure of it. Don't you see how this fits? This man we're looking for is—"

"Enough! Arne, you are on medical leave. What must I do to make this clear? We are perfectly capable of handling things."

"Are you? Then how could you miss something like this?"

Sjoberg's voice rose, "I will not listen to the accusations of a dysfunctional detective who can't even keep track of his—" His words faltered there, and the two glared at one another.

The office door was still open, and Sanderson sensed a hush outside. Phone calls paused, keyboards gone still.

In steady, drawn-out words, Sjoberg said, "Out of my office this minute or I'll have your credentials."

Without thinking, Sanderson reached into his pocket, pulled them out, and threw them at Sjoberg, striking him in the chest. He turned on a heel and walked out.

There were a dozen police officers in the outer room, men and women standing like statues between desks, planted motionless in chairs. They were detectives and sergeants and constables. One and all, they looked at Sanderson with something he had never seen before. They looked at him with pity.

Slaton was swept away. Joy, dread, hope, fear. All of it washed through his head in a single, tumultuous wave. He didn't know what to do, what to say, and so he reached out and took Christine in his arms. He wanted her to clutch him back, but that didn't happen. She pushed him away with tears welling in her eyes.

"So what the hell do we do now?" she said harshly. "You're going to be a father, David. Is there a procedure for that?"

His mouth dropped open but nothing came. It was just as she'd said. His thoughts were a blank. No contingency plan, no tactical recourse. Slaton sat there shaking his head, stunned to inaction for the first time in his life.

"I just want this to end," she said. "I know you've tried to escape your past, but it hasn't worked. And now you're doing just what they want, falling into this trap. The *kidon* is back—and I'm losing David Slaton."

"No, Christine. I'm not going anywhere."

"Yes, you are. I *know* you are."

He said nothing.

"When can we just live like everyone else, David? When?"

After a long pause, he said, "Right now."

Finally her face softened, and for the first time since arriving she looked at him as she last had—on the porch in Virginia with her suitcase in her hand. Having to go but not wanting to leave.

"I'm sorry," she said.

"No, there's nothing for you to be sorry about."

"If I didn't love you like I do . . ."

He leaned in and kissed her.

She responded, tentatively at first, then becoming more insistent. Slaton pressed back and was met with more. Desperation gave way to relief. Relief brought comfort. And finally—the familiar anticipation. Soon they were holding and fumbling, kissing necks and raking careless hands through one another's hair.

They'd only been apart for days, but it felt like years. The strain that had been building, cresting like a wave, suddenly expelled in a frantic rush. They half shuffled, half fell onto the bunk. An empty coffee mug got kicked to the floor. Hands went under clothing and shoes thumped to the deck.

And for the briefest of times, the hostile world outside was forgotten.

TWENTY-ONE

They made love in a frenzy, to the point of exhaustion. Afterward, they went to the galley and indulged their other cravings, putting a far bigger dent in the provisions than they should have.

Then they did it all over again.

Slaton devoured every second, every sensation with an air of desperation, in the way a condemned man takes his last earthly meal. By midnight both were sated, having wasted time and food and energy in the most wondrous of ways. It was what they both needed, and afterward Christine collapsed into a profoundly deep sleep.

The *kidon* did not.

The night was black and the seas calm, and the little boat swung lightly on her deep-water anchor. Slaton should have relaxed. He was right where he wanted to be—free of the outside world and with his wife in his arms. He should have slept, but didn't want to sacrifice an instant of what he had right now. They were naked and intertwined, her breathing rhythmic, his hand flat on her belly. He knew better than to expect a heartbeat or a kick, but their child was there—of this Slaton was sure. He imagined he was holding it, protecting them both. He wondered if he would ever get this close again.

He lay very still, not wanting to wake Christine. Not wanting to change anything. Yet if his body was motionless, his mind was reeling. He was losing count of the variables, and tomorrow would only bring more, threats and complications like no mission he'd ever seen. Tonight's revelation raised the stakes immeasurably, and this brought a sobering realization. He was at a precipice, a point of no return. He was on the verge of losing control. Slaton had confidence in his abilities—he would never have survived this long otherwise—but he was not infallible. He had seen it happen before to good men. Hard men. The odds had a way of catching up.

Laying in near silence, with the boat enveloped in a sheath of mist, it struck Slaton that he had been out of the life for nearly a year. In his absence, he wondered what had changed. Had Israel become a more or less secure place? Not likely. Probably no more change than he'd seen during his years on the job. So what had it all been for? Others had taken his place—the men on the Strandvägen?—and soon others would take their place. The futility seemed overwhelming. His mood darkened, and at that moment, with Christine pressed against him and their child in her womb, he felt a protective instinct he'd never before experienced. One overriding question came to the forefront: How could he keep them safe?

He suspected there was a way, but it would be more difficult than anything he'd ever done. And the more he thought about it, the more he knew it was the only way.

How could he keep them safe?

He would have to let them go.

Four in the morning is a distinctive time of day. A singular time zone of tranquility, it circles the earth as continuous witness to the low point of human activity. Nightclubs are closed and parties have fizzled. The previous night's contestants have largely found their ends, some snoring contentedly next to husbands or wives, others laying spent in hotel rooms, having finalized proceedings with mistresses or prostitutes. Friends can be found crashed on friend's couches, and those without means simply sprawl in alleyways. Those unfortunate enough to work the night shift are at their circadian bottoms, bleary-eyed and searching the drawer under the coffee machine for one more creamer packet. Conversely, four in the morning is an hour to challenge even the most industrious early riser. Those already awake are still at home, busy breakfasting, dressing, and performing necessary tasks of personal hygiene.

For all these reasons, four in the morning holds one inescapable certainty. It is the hour in which a city's streets will be at their most quiet. And for all these reasons, across the world, it is the hour when secret police units are at their energetic best.

Farzad Behrouz sat in a black car parked quietly along Palestine Street in south Tehran. The synagogue he was watching appeared quiet, but it was a markedly false impression—at the moment, his ten-man team was laying siege inside. The head of state security sat lamenting what is a little known paradox: Iran, the most virulently anti-Semitic country on earth, in fact hosts the largest Jewish population of any Muslim state. The Jews of Iran are granted solid constitutional protections, and are on paper equal to

Muslims. Here, of course, Behrouz took his own interpretation—paper was of little use against steel and leather.

He looked at his watch and saw that the squad had been inside for twenty minutes. It was time to make an appearance. He got out and buttoned his overcoat, nothing to do with the cool desert night, and walked purposefully toward the entrance. He was met at the ornate portico by a man who was shorter than he was, albeit built like a cinder block.

"Well?" Behrouz asked.

"Two. We have them out back," the man replied.

The stout sergeant led Behrouz through the central building, past the Torah ark and a tile mosaic depicting a menorah, and finally outside to a gated courtyard. Two Jews, one presumably a rabbi, and the other younger and wearing a yarmulke, were seated on the ground. If the men were wide-eyed to begin with, the arrival of the thick-coated head of state security did nothing to quell their anxiety. Behrouz hovered over the pair like a farmer with a shouldered ax.

"You know who I am?" he asked.

"Yes," they said in near unison.

"Do you know why I am here?"

The Jews looked at one another haltingly. Behrouz knew they did not, at least not specifically. In truth, neither did his own men. He had been ordering searches of synagogues at a breakneck pace for the last month. His crews would burst in and gather papers, files, and computers. On appearances it was madness without methods, a roughshod turnover that seemed absent any cohesive objective. Favored were property deeds, construction blueprints, bar mitzvah records, and flash drives. Less in vogue were service calendars, garbage collection bills, and prayer book invoices. In the end, the keepers of the holy proceedings were simply left to sweep up, reorganize, and carry on in brooding silence. Complaints were regularly filed, of course, but ignored with an equal consistency that took no one by surprise.

Just to keep things straight, Behrouz gave his stock explanation.

"I am here because Jew assassins have been infiltrating our country. Even though their hopeless plots fail, I am left to wonder if they will try again. I am left to wonder if they are getting assistance from traitors inside our blessed country. Would either of you be aware of such treachery?"

Neither man responded, which actually pleased Behrouz—it was better for everyone to keep things simple. A rabbi had gotten demanding last week, and the only person to benefit in the end was a reconstructive dentist. Behrouz decided there was no more to be said. Just as he was about to leave, a scrawny dog padded into the courtyard. The mutt made a beeline for the two interviewees, but before it could identify a master the squat sergeant lashed out and kicked it with a heavy boot.

The dog yelped, and it was the rabbi who reached out to the cowering creature.

"Sit still!" the sergeant barked at the rabbi.

The dog skittered away with a limp that may or may not have already been there. Behrouz stepped closer, his face etched in a new severity. He put out an empty hand, and the sergeant filled it with the thick baton from his belt. Behrouz slapped the nightstick once in his palm, then whipped around and struck the sergeant a savage backhand blow to the head.

The man fell like the brick he resembled. He was still for a time, then groggily began to roll back and forth. Two of Behrouz's other minions watched from a distance. Neither moved, clearly unsure how to react.

"We are not animals," Behrouz muttered under his breath.

Ten minutes later they were all back in the sedan, the woozy sergeant in the backseat next to Behrouz. He rubbed the side of his head, his expression asking, *What was that for?*

Behrouz only said, "Did you get everything?"

The answer came from the front seat, a man with a stack of papers and files in his lap. "Yes, enough to keep us busy for days."

Behrouz nodded, silently wondering if they had that much time. The baton was still in his hand, and he dropped it into the squat sergeant's lap before addressing the driver. "All right then, headquarters—quickly!"

They woke with the sun, at this latitude not a few minutes of glory but a process of hours, light feeding the eastern sky in a slow burn. Slaton didn't want to move, but a look at the clock brought reality down like a hammer. It was nine-fifteen, and Janna Magnussen's seaplane would be splashing down in the nearby cove in less than two hours.

He got up and looked out the port window. The weather was cooperating, high clouds and good visibility. Slaton didn't know whether to be happy or disheartened. He began cooking breakfast, wondering what was appropriate for a prenatal menu. He knew Christine needed to eat: for her health, for that of their child, and perhaps most importantly, to instill a sense of normalcy.

Once breakfast was on the stove, and with Christine stirring slowly, Slaton ran his eyes over the tiny cabin. He began checking cupboards and compartments, and found what he was looking for in a portside utensil drawer. At the back, wrapped in a piece of oilskin, a .38 revolver. He had seen a single bullet yesterday in another drawer, and so he knew it was here. He wanted something better than the .22, yet when Slaton inspected the piece it was a disappointment. With difficulty, he pried the cylinder open and saw that the gun wasn't loaded. He tried to work the firing mechanism but it had long ago seized. The gun was crusted in rust, and probably hadn't been used in ten years, maybe twenty. Even with a good cleaning it would be unreliable, and a weapon in such condition was worse than none at all. It was a distraction, a thing you might be tempted to trust in a critical moment.

He climbed to the top of the companionway steps and was about to toss it into the sea when he heard, "What are you doing?"

Slaton turned.

Christine was staring at him, as beautiful as ever with bent morning hair and bleary eyes. He stepped back down into the cabin and showed her the weapon. "I'm polluting—heavy metal into the marine environment. They can add that to my rap sheet."

She frowned at the gun. "Please get rid of it."

He did so, a neat fling out the hatch that ended in a decisive splash. She came closer, but just as Slaton moved in for an embrace, Christine turned and rushed to the marine head, flinging the door closed behind her. He heard her retching.

He waited at the door, and when she came out he succeeded in getting his arms around her the second time. She was tense and rigid.

"What can I do to help?"

"It will pass," she said. "I should try to eat something."

Ten minutes later he slid a plate on the table, scrambled eggs and toast, and next to it a pot of coffee. He gave her the lion's share, only to watch her spin her fork aimlessly in the center of the plate.

He said, "Yesterday we were talking about options. Aside from staying here, you asked what else we could do."

"And?"

"I've had some time to think. There may be a way out. To begin with, we can't sit here. Sooner or later we'll be found."

Her eyes cast down. "I know."

"There might be a way to make everything work—but I can only do it from Geneva."

Her gaze snapped up. "Geneva?"

He hesitated. "If I go there, if I *start* that process . . . maybe I can find an opening, some other way. But it has to begin there. And I'll need your help to pull it off."

"My help?" She cocked her head uneasily. "What do you want me to do?"

He gave her what was essentially a mission briefing, details he'd nailed down in the silent hours as he'd laid awake and held her. "It probably won't work exactly as I've said, but do what you can, improvise. None of it should be dangerous, but if you see something you don't like, anything at all, just go to the authorities."

"Is a wife protected from testifying against her husband in Sweden?"

"Probably. But it doesn't matter. Go ahead and tell them the truth. There's only one thing I need you to hold back—tell them you don't know where I've gone. The rest is in your favor. They'll threaten to prosecute if you don't cooperate, but that's only a bluff. The worst thing you've done is take this boat, and your reasons were justifiable."

"How encouraging." She locked her eyes to his. "But you haven't told me what you're going to do."

"It's probably better you don't know."

"I don't think you even know."

"Not exactly."

There was a pause as she weighed it all. "All right. Once again I will trust you, David. But you have to promise me one thing in return. Tell me you will not go through with this assassination. Tell me you're only going through the motions in order to find a better way."

"It's not that simple to—"

"Yes, it is! It's *just* that simple—don't kill anyone!"

He let out a deep breath. "I can only promise one thing. I will do whatever it takes for you to be safe. I will get you and our child out of the mess I've created."

After a long stare, Christine turned away in silence.

Their last minutes together were awkward as Slaton gave a crash course on tradecraft. That he was schooling his newly pregnant wife, in the little time they had together, on methods to evade authorities was a sorry reflection on the capsized state of their marriage. Christine listened tensely, rarely asking questions.

"You'll need a place to stay," he said. "Is there someone in Stockholm you can trust?"

"Ulrika Torsten. She's a doctor, a friend from residency. She lives in town and we had dinner together the first night I was in Stockholm."

"Was it just the two of you?"

"Yes."

"Who knew about that meeting?"

"Her husband, I suppose."

"Anyone else?"

She glared impatiently. "The waiter."

"Please—where does she live?"

"The east side I think, near . . ." she hesitated, "I don't know. But David, she must know the police are looking for me. Aren't I a 'person of interest' or something?"

"You were a witness to what took place that first day on the Strandvägen. But that investigation has probably become secondary. Bloch is in the hospital, and the other suspects are . . ." he paused.

"Dead?" she offered.

"The police will want to interview you, Christine, but there's no manhunt under way. Not for you—I'm the one they're after."

"I don't like bringing Ulrika into this, David. She's married. She has a child."

"So do you."

He took a hard glare.

"Christine, you won't be putting anyone at risk. All you need is a place to stay for a night or two. Would she do it?"

She crossed her arms sullenly, but relented. "If I can think of a good lie about why the police want to question me . . . yes, probably."

Slaton checked the time. "All right, I have to go. Do you have any questions?"

She laughed nervously.

He gave her a serious look.

"No, no questions."

He brought her close and held her, and she responded. He felt her contours, and felt her hands grip his shoulders. Slaton drew in Christine's familiar scent with her head buried in his chest. He sensed a mutual desperation, a veil of uncertainty—neither knew when such a moment would come again. Or even *if* such a moment would come. She pushed away abruptly.

With edged words, Christine said, "I will do what you ask. I will lie and steal because I love you and there is no other choice. But know one thing, David Slaton. Everything you did for your country—I can leave that in the past and not pass judgment. But I will not allow you to do harm in my name, or worse in our child's."

He nodded.

"If you kill this man in Geneva . . . don't ever come back to me."

TWENTY-TWO

Evita Levine stood in front of her dressing mirror with her nightdress hanging open. She was not unhappy with what she saw. On the lee side of forty, she remained an exceptionally attractive woman. There was not yet a line on her exquisite face, and her wide-set olive eyes shone as vibrant as ever. Her body, once lithe and thin, had come full in recent years, but she'd adapted well, learning to present her new curves to considerable advantage. Perhaps to prove the point, she had recently begun a running count of sidewalk stares and unsolicited smiles. Had she been of a more empirical nature, Evita would have foreseen that she kept no baseline survey against which to compare her tally. All the same, her analysis did uncover one unexpected new truth—the men who noticed her nowadays were of greater maturity themselves, and this she took as a positive. Like fine wine to a connoisseur's palate, she had bettered with age.

A shuffling in the hallway outside the room, most likely her husband, caused her to close the folds of her nightdress. She registered the familiar squeak of the back door swinging open, and amid the midday Tel Aviv traffic Evita heard a hard clatter as he emptied the kitchen garbage into a can outside. It was the most initiative he'd shown in a month.

She went to her closet and dragged a long index finger across her options. There was the new set of black undergarments, but that would require stockings and heels. Or she could take a more virginal approach, a white slip under her beige satin dress, perhaps with the new pearls, the ones she kept hidden in the toe of an old tennis shoe. She sighed, knowing what he would want, and reached for the black stockings.

The phone call that put her into action had come yesterday. There was a time long ago—three years to be exact—when she would have gone through these same motions with breathless anticipation. Evita had married when she was eighteen, a consignment arranged by an ancient matchmaker, approved by her rabbi, and encouraged by virtually everyone. Her husband, sixteen years her senior, had in the beginning been wealthy, fit, and relatively kind. All this faded soon after he lost his job at the export bank. The drinking came first, followed by surliness and, when it came to her, disinterest. She tried to meet him halfway for a time, to mend their relationship. He'd responded with more drinking and ill moods that bordered on psychosis. She could today think of only two positives in their relationship—that they had not manufactured children, and that he had not sought a mistress. The later was a given, actually, as he'd not been able to perform in years, even with the colorful pills. Evita had fallen increasingly despondent, sensing she was doomed to a life of misery from which there was no escape. Then, one magnificent day, she had found salvation. His name was Saud.

The first time she saw him was at a showing for

promising young artists at the Ashdod Museum of Art. He was the most beautiful thing she had ever seen. He worked in stone, yet Evita thought this a problematic medium for a man whose chiseled features paled anything he might create. His work was good, as far as she knew, and critics raved about his potential. But for a young Palestinian boy from Jibaliya, potential meant little. To his credit, Saud never wavered. He worked day after day, his strong hands chipping and smoothing, his keen brown eyes appraising his creations with an intensity that could not have been bettered by Da Vinci or Michelangelo. And those sharp eyes held Evita in the same way, running brazenly over her body as if contemplating a work of art. That was how Saud made her feel—like a masterpiece.

They chatted at the reception that first day, and went for coffee afterward. A lunch two days later ran three hours, both of them lingering shamelessly. The next week she offered to pose naked for him, a project that took twice as long as it should have for predictable reasons, and the product of which was destroyed when knocked from its stand during a particularly enthusiastic sitting. For six months and two days, Evita Levine was happier than she had ever been. She and Saud made plans as best a married Israeli woman and a poor Palestinian sculptor could. In hopeful moments they imagined divorce and artistic discovery, and in the rest they plotted desperate trysts in attic flats.

Then had come the airstrike.

If Saud knew that his studio was adjacent to a Hamas safe house, he'd never let on. The bomb struck neatly, but failed to fuse correctly—or so Evita had later been told—penetrating one additional wall to explode in Saud's kitchen as he was preparing a celebratory dinner to mark their sixth month of love.

Evita had been crushed. She had never been a political creature, yet when Israel claimed Saud to be a terrorist, and thus a legitimate target, any residual affinity for her homeland was lost. She cursed Israel. She cried for a month. Even her husband, dolt that he was, noticed something amiss. He did what he could, more than once pulling down a second tumbler from the wet bar and offering a shot of whiskey to "dull whatever ache that's found you." Evita supposed he knew, in a general way, the source of her unhappiness, but if there was anger or pity she could never discern it amid his despairing nature.

Then a new man came into her life. He called himself Rafi, and said he was from Netanya, but she thought he might be Syrian. Perhaps even Hezbollah. Evita didn't care. She listened to his stories of other Arab boys, like Saud gentle young artists and scholars who had nothing to do with Israel's war yet were imprisoned and shot and vaporized all the same. From there, the rest was a small step for a woman of advancing age who had married misery and lost love. What began as an off-the-cuff suggestion by Rafi spurred her mind to action. Without asking who she might be aiding, Evita told him she wanted to hurt Israel. She told him there was nothing she wouldn't do.

This Rafi had put to the test.

Evita was still at the open closet when her husband came into the room. She pulled her most dreary house frock from the rack and held it in front of the mirror.

"I thought you were going out to lunch," she said.

"Yes, soon. The boys will wait," he said, using his preferred term for the revolting band of sixty-something alcoholics with whom he spent most of his day. "What about you? Are you going out?"

"I may go to the market later," she said.

"Get me some cigarettes, would you?"

He stripped off a filthy T-shirt and threw it onto a pile of the same.

Evita watched him disappear into the bathroom. She hoped he'd brush his teeth. Around the corner she heard him pissing, then a pause, and the toothbrush starting working. When he seemed done, rinsing and spitting noisily, Evita did something that surprised her. Pretending not to notice his reappearance, and with the dreary house frock in hand, she let her nightdress drop to the floor. She put her shoulders back and arched gently with a pile of worn cotton around her ankles. Sensing his pause, she turned to look.

He was there, his eyes on her naked ass—he was still a man, wasn't he? Yet there was something in his expression she didn't like. Frustration? No, anger.

"Teasing bitch," he muttered. He pulled a fresh undershirt from his drawer and walked out.

Evita stood still for a very long time. She remained in front of the mirror, yet her eyes were fixed to the floor. Her stupor was broken by the sound of the front door slamming shut.

On hearing that, Evita Levine began to prepare.

If Sanderson had not been sleeping well to begin with, the idea that he'd just quit his job of thirty-five years did nothing to help. He stayed in bed past nine that first morning of his retirement, rose unrefreshed, and went straight to the medicine cabinet. He saw nothing stronger than ibuprofen, and minutes later was washing down a small handful with his first cup of coffee. He sat heavily at the kitchen table and wondered, perhaps with a dash of self-pity, what to do with himself.

For the first time in his adult life he had nowhere to go. His resignation was not yet official, of course. He had filed no paperwork, and certainly could go to Sjoberg's office with his tail between his legs and smooth things over. He would be sent home for a week or two, as long as it took to straighten out the reckless quacks, and then be assigned to a desk. His email inbox would overflow with interdepartmental memos, and he'd be granted authority enough to write a new policy manual on social tolerance, or perhaps if he was lucky, draft an update to the station's Emergency Action Plan. He would bandy long-forgotten names and stories with the other hangers-on at the other desks, and in the months to come Sanderson would show up a little later each day. Answer the phone when it suited him. And then the party.

Not wishing to dwell on these dismal prospects, he skimmed the morning paper. He made every attempt to ignore articles relating to the investigation, yet failed as his eye was unavoidably caught by a police sketch of the suspect Deadmarsh. It had been drawn, of course, with the input of Blix and Officer Petersen, the two men who had stood at his side at the Strand Hotel. The image was just a bit off—it always was—and for Sanderson served as no more than another twist of the knife. He'd spent more time with Deadmarsh than anyone, yet his addled brain had clearly not been worth consulting. He tossed the paper into the rubbish.

Sanderson did a load of laundry, and for an hour he clattered around the house looking for chores, finding a few, and ignoring them without exception.

He ended where he'd begun, seated at the kitchen table and rubbing fingers on his temples, soothing circles that worked wonders. With a newfound clarity he succumbed to the inescapable.

There was really no question. He had to go in to headquarters. All he needed was a sound excuse, and he settled on the most obvious. It was time to clean out his desk.

He arrived at the station at ten forty-five. Sanderson's gait was well known around the place—quick and direct, or as he'd once overheard, "like a short train on a narrow-gauge track"—and he passed through the entrance unchallenged, nodding to the familiar face at the security podium.

On the third floor he circumnavigated Sjoberg's office, and in the hallways a few of his coworkers said "Good morning," although some with more sympathy than they should have. The rumors had to be rampant by now, he supposed. *Have you heard why the old man was pulled? He's gone daft. Can't keep track of his car keys, poor bugger.* Worse still were those who seemed not to notice him, men and women half-sitting on desks as they volleyed theories back and forth, much as he'd done back in the day—a fond and familiar diversion he would never take part in again. Sanderson was ruminating on that cheerless thought when the man he was looking for came up from behind him in the main hallway.

"Hello, Inspector," Blix said.

Sanderson turned. If anyone on the force was going to help, it was his well-versed deputy Gunnar Blix.

"Good morning, Gunnar. Do you have a minute?"

"Of course."

Sanderson shunted Blix toward an empty conference room and closed the door. "I suppose you heard about my blow-up with Sjoberg yesterday?"

Blix grinned. "I only wish I'd been there to see it."

"I'm clearly persona non grata around here for the time being. They've told me to go home and not be seen. Honestly, I'm rather warming to the idea."

"You? Sit around the house? Please."

"A doctor has told me, however, that mental exercise is just the thing for my deteriorating condition."

"You're going to work the case on your own."

"I might make an inquiry or two . . . in the name of my recovering mental health, you understand."

"And it would help if you had someone inside the department with a sharp ear?"

Sanderson regarded his protégé. "I knew I saw something in you."

"Consider it done, Inspector. Least I can do. Call me anytime on my mobile—but we will have to be discreet."

"Done. Anything new today?"

"No headway at all with Deadmarsh. SÄPO has asked the FBI for more information. They've been on a hunt for friends and family, and found few of the former—neighbors and his most recent employer—but none of the latter. The official records are all a blank. His driver's license and passport seem to have never existed. He and Dr. Palmer keep a joint bank account that was recently drawn down, but there's nothing in their credit report that speaks of money problems. He and the missus took out a mortgage for a small home a few months back. We've researched him the usual ways, search engines and social networking sites. Everything's a blank. The man entered

Sweden a few days ago like a million other tourists, and since then he's faded to nothing."

"I'm not surprised."

"Why is that?"

"Because—"

A young constable with a stack of files under her arm burst through the door. "Oh—sorry," she said. "Didn't know the room was in use."

"No, we were just leaving," Sanderson said. He walked out with Blix, and once in the hallway whispered, "Sjoberg won't listen to anything I say, but if an astute investigator were to go to Saint Göran Hospital and ask for Dr. Gould he might find something useful. Apparently the man who's now in a coma was babbling in tongues when he first arrived."

"An astute investigator, you say? Not sure where I'd find one of those round here, but I'll keep an eye out."

Sanderson smiled, and added, "Yes, do that."

He broke away and made straight for his desk. Along the way he picked up an empty cardboard box that had been discarded near the printer. When he reached his desk, Sanderson set the box on top and began filling it. The first thing in was a framed picture, at least twenty years old, of him and Ingrid and their daughter—they were all smiling stupidly and standing on snow skis at Sunne. He lifted files from the bottom drawer without even looking at their labels, and from the middle drawer he removed a mildewed address book, a dog-eared calendar from 1997, and an alarm clock he didn't even recognize. He then went to the top drawer, felt toward the back, and found what he was looking for. Sanderson pulled the item clear palmed beneath an old calculator with long-dead batteries.

Fixing a look of winsome nostalgia on his face, he then closed the box, took it under his arm, and gave a chain of somber nods all the way to the elevator.

The seaplane touched down sharply at eleven o'clock. Minutes later Slaton was shin deep in cold water, his hands pushing on the wing struts to steer the craft's nose back out to sea. He pulled open the passenger door and was greeted by a smiling Janna Magnussen.

"Good morning!"

Slaton slid inside. "Good morning. Thanks for being on time."

"We were correct to have not waited any longer. There is a heavy marine layer slipping down from the north—in another hour it will cover everything." She seemed to gauge him for a moment, then remarked, "I see you are alone."

"Yes. Things didn't go as I'd planned."

Magnussen paused, perhaps waiting for more. Slaton suspected she was enjoying this contract more than most, her usual crowd likely being hunters who would stuff rifles and tents and slabs of bloody venison into her airplane. Tangled romance was undoubtedly more entertaining.

She finally said, "Does this mean you won't be doing any sightseeing?"

His eyes flicked to the fuel gauges. As promised, he saw nearly full tanks. "Actually, I was still planning on it. Let's start with an aerial tour of Stockholm."

"You won't see anything. North and west, the cloud cover is nearly a solid undercast."

"I'd like to try anyway. That was our agreement, and I've already paid half, haven't I?"

She gave me a shrug that said *It's your money,* and

pushed the throttle forward. The Cessna began to accelerate, and was soon stepping onto the light waves and rising into the air. Slaton saw the altimeter register a thousand feet, then two. His eyes scanned to the north, and he did see a heavy cloud layer sweeping in low over the blackening Baltic. Christine had already weighed anchor and was under way, moving north to a different island. He'd given her most of his cash and specific instructions on how to get more. Slaton knew he was asking a lot from his wife, but he hoped it would be the last time.

"It's a quick trip, twenty miles," Magnussen said. She pointed ahead. "As you can see, the clouds are nearly covering the city."

In fact Slaton did not see, because at that moment his eyes were riveted elsewhere. Just over his right shoulder, through a slim break in the undercast, he saw a tiny boat bobbing northward. He could even make out the name on the stern, prominent block letters in fresh blue paint. Slaton watched as long as he could, but soon the image fragmented, broken by thickening wisps of gray vapor.

Then all at once, she was lost to the mist.

TWENTY-THREE

Magnussen was busy talking to air traffic controllers as the little seaplane ventured into what had to be unfamiliar territory—the busy air corridor over Stockholm. The view was exactly as she'd promised, the leaden topside of a cloudbank with only a few breaks, the highest buildings and a few radio antennae stabbing through like so many urban periscopes. Slaton didn't mind the featureless cityscape. He had not come to sightsee.

He pulled the three prepaid cell phones from his backpack, pocketing two and waking the third.

"Do you mind?" he asked.

Magnussen laughed. "This airplane doesn't have many instruments to interfere with. Go ahead and call. You should get good reception as low as we are."

The phone was already activated, and indeed he saw good signal strength. Slaton pulled a business card from his pocket and dialed Detective Inspector Arne Sanderson.

Sanderson was closing the trunk of his car when it dawned on him that he should check his email one last time—Sjoberg had likely forgotten to pull up that anchor. He had just entered the headquarters building when his phone vibrated. He looked at the number but didn't recognize it. Thinking it might involve one of his mandatory medical probings, he answered reluctantly.

"Sanderson."

He heard a great deal of background noise, and then, "Hello, Inspector."

The voice registered instantly—one he had first heard three days prior in the lobby of the Strand Hotel. "Where are you?"

"I'm very near, actually."

Sanderson began trotting up the hallway that led to the operations center.

The man whose name was certainly not Edmund Deadmarsh said, "I thought we should talk."

"You realize you're in a great deal of trouble."

"How is the policeman?"

"His leg was damaged, but he's expected to make a full recovery. Unlike the other two." Sanderson shoved his way into the room and skidded to a stop in front of the duty officer's desk. He switched the phone to his left hand and began scribbling on a notepad.

"I'm glad to hear he's recovering," said the familiar voice. "Please give him my apologies. At the time I didn't see any other way. He was about to get far worse."

Sanderson finished his note and shoved it toward the duty officer. *Talking to suspect Deadmarsh on my duty number! Triangulate this call immediately!* He then readdressed the phone with, "Are you trying to tell me you shot our man in the leg to rescue him from another assailant? Do you expect me to believe that?"

"Believe whatever you like, Inspector. I was having a leisurely breakfast when I was forced to defend myself. Have you identified the other two, the ones who initiated things?"

"I think you know we haven't."

"How is Anton?"

"Who?"

"The man you showed me in Saint Göran, the one in a coma. Has his condition improved?"

"There's been no change." Sanderson looked expectantly at the desk man who was multitasking between a phone and a computer. He scribbled a reply to Sanderson. *Pinging now. Need thirty more seconds.*

Sanderson said, "Who is he?"

"You really have no idea? Tell me you're better than that, Inspector."

"Please. Let's not play games."

"All right. His name is Anton Bloch. One year ago he was the director of Mossad."

Sanderson wanted to respond, but his thoughts fell into a tailspin. As incredible as this sounded, it made perfect sense. An Israeli, and certainly a man with enemies.

"I'll assume by your silence that you really didn't know," Deadmarsh prompted.

"Are you saying this was some kind of attempted assassination?"

"You figure it out. I want to talk about my wife."

Sanderson half-listened as Deadmarsh made her case, the fugitive stonemason explaining that his wife was only a victim in some ill-defined scheme. The tech gave a wild thumbs-up and wrote another note. *We have him locked! Near Frihamnen Ferry Terminal!*

Sanderson issued an order he was in no position to give—he made a circular carry-on motion with his free hand to indicate that the duty officer should launch the fleet. The man complied, and within seconds every available unit on the east side of Stockholm was descending on the computed position.

Deadmarsh chose that moment to say, "Sorry, Inspector, but let me call you right back."

The line went dead.

"You can't do that!" Janna Magnussen shouted.

Slaton had opened the side window of the Cessna. It was an easy thing to do, a single latch, and had raised the level of wind noise considerably. What had his pilot's attention, however, was that he was holding the mobile phone outside with one hand as he studied the breaks in the clouds below. When they were over a clear section of the Lilla Värtan Strait, he let fly.

"No! You cannot do that!"

Slaton watched the handset flutter down behind them, but quickly lost sight.

"It is against the law to drop things from an aircraft!" she protested.

Slaton eyed her. The cockpit was loud, but it was a small space, so he was sure Magnussen had heard at least some of his conversation with Inspector Sanderson. Now he'd begun dropping objects on the city below. It was a pivotal moment, and one that Slaton had anticipated, indeed planned. Before calling Sanderson again, there was a need to amend his relationship with his pilot. He pulled the Beretta from his right thigh pocket and pointed it across his body. Magnussen's scowl shifted, annoyance giving way to concern. But the pilot kept her cool, as pilots were prone to do. She had certainly faced moments of more immediate peril—terrible thunderstorms, ice-covered wings, oncoming aircraft. All the same, Slaton had her undivided attention.

"I need your help," he said.

"This is how you ask for help?"

"I don't have the luxury of asking. Please understand that I have no interest in harming you, Janna. But I won't hesitate if you make it necessary. And before you declare this illogical, that a passenger would disable an airplane's only pilot, I should explain. I'm not an experienced aviator, but I have had some training. If I needed to land this airplane I could. I wouldn't attempt it in the water because I've never done that. I'd just hold a speed of eighty knots, fly south until the weather clears, and then find a nice open field or a dirt road. A place with no power lines or trees. It wouldn't be pretty, and I'd probably wreck your airplane. But I would walk away. I'm very confident of that."

Magnussen alternated, watching him one moment, and her instruments and path the next.

He continued, "I won't let you change the transponder code to indicate a hijacking, and I will be listening to every radio call you make. All I ask is that you fly over two more points here in Stockholm, and then take me south."

"Where?" she asked.

"I'll let you know when the time comes. When we arrive, I'll get off your airplane and you'll never see me again. You can go wherever you like, and I will still pay you the balance of our agreed upon fee. Once I'm gone you can alert the authorities or not—that's up to you. But if you delay that contact for a few hours, say the time it will take you to return to Oxelösund from our destination, then two weeks from now I'll send you a check in the amount of twenty thousand U.S. dollars."

She looked at him suspiciously, but not without interest. Mossad agents were trained to operate in a sequence—manipulate, persuade, coerce, and as a last resort, threaten and deliver bodily harm. As an assassin, Slaton had long resided on the backside of this continuum, but he was not incapable of lesser means.

"This is where you calculate probabilities, Janna."

They locked eyes and he could see her doing exactly that. The gun was now pointed at the floorboard, having served its purpose.

"Do as I ask for a few hours," he said. "The rest is up to you."

The more Magnussen thought about it, the less worried she appeared. Skeptical certainly, but not immediately fearful for her life. She said, "I saw something on television yesterday. There have been shootings in Stockholm. A manhunt is under way. You are the one they're looking for."

"Yes. And so you know I'm serious. But I also think you believe me—you know I won't harm you. I only need to leave Sweden, Janna. Doesn't that make sense?"

He watched her consider it all, likely adding in the circumstance of having dropped him off on a remote island yesterday.

"All right," she said. "Tell me where you want to go."

"For the moment, let's turn west."

Sanderson listened intently as the units reported in. He was still in the operations center, his phone in hand and a thumb poised over the Answer button.

He was sure the primary revelation was now rising up the chain of command—that the man lying in a coma at Saint Göran was a former director of Mossad. As explosive as this was, Sanderson viewed it as a distraction for the moment, a piece of a larger, more theoretical puzzle that was secondary to finding Deadmarsh. Get the American in custody, he decided, and the intriguing details could be sorted at will.

The duty officer in charge of the operations center, Assistant Commander Eilsen, was giving a status report on a secure phone. "We've got eight cars establishing blockades around the Frihamnen terminal. All the access roads are covered, and six teams on foot have begun flushing the passenger boarding area. We've also recalled a ferry that just left for Riga. No one's spotted Deadmarsh yet, but he's got to be there somewhere."

Sanderson's phone rang, again an unknown number. He answered by saying, "Give it up!"

"I could say the same to you, Inspector."

Sanderson heard the same background noise he'd registered earlier, and thought, *He's moving. The boat to Riga?*

Eilsen tapped his computer display and whispered, "He's using a different number!"

"Let's end the hide and seek, shall we?" Sanderson said. "You claim that you didn't shoot that policeman with malicious intent. I'm inclined to believe you. And you imply the others were shot in self-defense. If this can all be proven, you'll be shown leniency. Come in quietly, *kidon*."

The line went quiet, nothing but the low mechanical buzz.

Their second triangulation went more quickly, everyone having been forewarned. Sanderson saw a red circle blossom to the map display. It was ten miles from the first plot. His eyes narrowed.

"What the hell?" Eilsen mumbled. He immediately began redirecting units toward the new fix.

Deadmarsh was talking again, something about his wife's innocence. Sanderson covered the mouthpiece and said, "I can hear an engine in the background. He's traveling. A truck or a motorcycle. It's the only way he could have moved like that. Tell everyone to watch for a vehicle running north!"

The call suddenly ended.

Sanderson cursed.

Three miles east of police headquarters at Kungsholmsgatan 43, a white mobile phone traveling at its terminal velocity struck the pavement of a nearly empty municipal parking lot near the Vasa Museum. The handset exploded into shards of plastic and circuitry, and scattered across the tarmac, no piece larger than a one-kronor coin surviving. Ten minutes later and eight miles west, after another brief conversation, the third phone fared marginally better. It bounced off the vaulted roof of the rectory at Brännkyrka Church, streaked past a priceless stained-glass window, and finally came to rest under eighteen inches of well-consecrated earth in the adjacent cemetery.

By the time Deadmarsh's third call ended, cars in blue and yellow Battenburg markings were racing a patternless weave across greater Stockholm. Sanderson was immediately summoned to Sjoberg's office, and found the new investigator-in-charge already there.

"Why did he call you of all people?" Anna Forsten asked before he'd even crossed the threshold.

"I'd given him my number. I'm probably the only policeman in Sweden he knows."

Sjoberg said, "SÄPO is going to be all over this. Can it be true? The former director of Mossad is sitting in a coma at Saint Göran?"

"It sounds incredible," Sanderson said, "but I expect it's true."

Forsten flicked a well-manicured finger through a printed transcript of the calls Sanderson had just taken. "What does this mean—'Come in quietly, *kidon*.' What the devil is a *kidon*?"

"A *kidon* is a Mossad assassin."

Sjoberg stared incredulously. "And where did this revelation come from?"

"That's what I was trying to tell you when you—" Sanderson hesitated. He looked at each of them in turn. "Am I to understand that I'm back on this investigation?"

An agitated Sjoberg said, "No, Arne, you most certainly are not. I just need to know how—"

"Then figure it out for yourselves!" Sanderson turned on a heel and started for the door.

"Wait! I want your phone."

Sanderson stopped.

Forsten said, "We'll give it back once we've routed your number through the operations center switchboard."

"Brilliant. And when he calls again expecting to speak to me, how will you answer?"

"He doesn't give a damn about you. This man is obviously trying to throw us off. I wouldn't be surprised if this whole Mossad angle is no more than misdirection."

"I agree," Sjoberg said. "All he's done is prove what we already suspected—that he's right here in Stockholm."

"Is he?" Sanderson countered.

"Arne," Sjoberg said, "let's not make this more difficult than it has to be. Give me the phone."

Sanderson pulled out his mobile and dropped it on

Sjoberg's desk. "Do what you like. But I'll tell you this. If you . . . if you . . ." Sanderson stood still, trying to remember what he was about to say. He felt suddenly dizzy.

And then everything went blank.

TWENTY-FOUR

When Sanderson regained consciousness he was lying on the couch in Sjoberg's office. Looking down at him were Sjoberg and a uniformed EMT.

He blinked, and said, "What happened?"

Sjoberg said, "You passed out, Arne."

"Passed out?" He wrestled up to a sitting position, only then realizing that a blood pressure cuff was wrapped around his arm.

"Are you on any medication?" the EMT asked.

"No."

"Has anything like this happened before?"

"No, of course not."

The EMT removed the blood pressure cuff.

"How long was I out?" Sanderson asked.

"Only a few minutes," Sjoberg said. "You went pale as a ghost and over you went. Forsten caught you before you hit."

With that picture in his mind, Sanderson's humiliation was complete. He rubbed his forehead and tried to stand.

"Easy," said Sjoberg. "There's no hurry."

"I'm fine," Sanderson said. He felt the EMT at his elbow, and on reaching his feet made every attempt not to waver.

"Did you eat anything this morning?" the EMT asked.

"No—I'm sure that's all it was. And I have been working hard."

"Yes," Sjoberg agreed, "he's been under considerable stress."

"Have you ever had a seizure of any sort?"

"Seizure? No, never."

The EMT addressed Sjoberg. "Well, he seems all right. I'll leave you now, but I'm just downstairs if you need me." He turned to Sanderson. "Get something in your belly, and then rest. If anything like this happens again you should see your doctor."

The man left, and Sjoberg said, "Well, Arne, if this doesn't convince you I don't know what will. Go home and get some sleep. I'll have Blix drive you."

Sanderson did not argue.

Evita was given a ride to her assignation by a friend from work, an undependable woman who for once showed up on time. Traffic was light, and when they arrived Evita asked to be dropped two blocks away from the hotel. She thanked her friend and checked the time. As feared, she was early. Seeing no upside in punctuality, Evita spotted a pub nearby and decided to shore up her nerve.

She took a seat at the nearly vacant bar, and in no more time than it took for a double vodka to be pushed in front of her, Evita found herself sandwiched between a pair of afternoon regulars, a thrice-divorced lawyer and an old man named Yehud whose breath smelled like a camel's crotch. The lawyer tried to chat about his ex-wives, while old Yehud, unshaven and unwashed and with beer foam on his lips, simply propositioned her in the most vulgar of terms. She was equally unreceptive, though found the old beggar's honesty refreshing in a way. Yet as she sat in silence, Evita felt a tremor of unease—even if she was miles from home, there was a chance one of them might know her husband, a man on terms with a good share of the city's connoisseurs. As it turned out, the far-off look in her eyes was enough to deflect their advances.

The vodka worked wonders. As always, Evita was repulsed by what she was about to do, yet there was never a question of following through. This morning, like every morning, she had spent her ritual moment with the picture of Saud and the tender poem he'd written for her. These were her only remembrances, and she kept both hidden deep in a dresser drawer. For a few minutes each day he was hers again—a man whose beauty would never fade, an artist whose talent would never diminish, and a lover whose soul would always be faithful. That daily tribute gave her the steel to go forward, gave her the will to take vengeance for a crime that would never be pursued in any court.

Evita would undertake her justice. But to do it with the requisite smile? That required a little something extra. She lifted her glass, snapped her head back one last time, and bid her courters good-bye.

The Baltic, five thousand feet below, was in a pitched battle, wind versus water. Slaton watched the white-caps come and go, creases of white bursting to life, then fading quickly into the matte-black sea. The skies above were equally ominous, hard gray clouds that blotted the sun into submission and fragmented the horizon. He could see rain to the west and north, sweeping gray curtains reaching down to the sea. Dramatic as the scene was, it held little relevance. The visibility ahead and below—that was the critical thing, and right now it was suitable for what Slaton had in mind.

They'd struck a course of south by southwest, and the little Cessna plowed obediently at a steady one hundred knots. Janna Magnussen was equally steady. Two hours removed from Stockholm, the tension had dissipated. Their conversation had turned almost casual, as if the dynamics of their relationship had never been skewed by a hijacking. The gun was back in Slaton's right pocket, but both knew it was readily presentable. They began by discussing Magnussen: her upbringing near Oxelösund, her sister, even her failed marriage. Then, in a clear breach of professional standards, Slaton found himself contributing to the conversation. He gave a candid account of his own childhood in Sweden. Keeping light on detail, he reflected on schoolyard memories—pranks conspired with long-forgotten friends, sporting matches gloriously won or comically lost.

To be drawn into such an exchange, even intrigued by it, was a long-lost response for Slaton, yet a proficiency that had been restored during his months in Virginia. There he had begun to strike up conversations with waitresses, pizza delivery kids, and concrete truck drivers, regaining the everyday skill of talking to a stranger without sizing them up for fighting ability, without filtering every word for deceit or logging character flaws fit for blackmail. To simply sit and talk was a long-forgotten pleasure, and something Christine had given him back.

Magnussen said, "I took up flying ten years ago when I retired from my civil service job. After twenty-one years in the same building I had an irresistible urge to be outside. There's nothing as liberating as flying."

"I can understand that."

"It's not much of a business, mind you. Most years I break even, maybe clear enough for a few weeks in Spain during the holidays."

"And that's all you need?"

She thought about it. "Yes, I suppose it is. Last year I had a chance to buy out a competitor in Malmö at an excellent price. I would have gotten four airplanes, six pilots, and a backlog of contracts."

"And all the headaches that go with it?"

"Exactly. It was the second easiest decision I ever made."

Slaton took the bait. "And the first?"

"Leaving my bastard husband, of course."

He smiled.

"And you?" she asked.

"What about me?"

"Do you really have a wife?"

Slaton looked ahead. The brooding contour of Germany was rising out of the sea, low hills strung along the coastline, unseen rivers knuckling through valleys. This was their destination, and the sight had a sobering effect on his disposition.

When he didn't answer, she said, "You wear a ring. If you're having troubles perhaps we could talk about it. It can be very helpful to—"

"Janna," he interrupted. "You said you were civil service, right?"

"Yes."

"What kind of work did you do?"

She looked out the front window. "I was a crisis counselor for the National Board of Health and Welfare."

He couldn't help himself. Slaton began to laugh.

Magnussen smiled as well, clearly seeing the humor.

TWENTY-FIVE

The aura of goodwill that had developed in the cockpit was gone as the seaplane made its final approach to landing. Slaton instructed Magnussen to skim the coastline at low altitude, and after ten minutes he saw an acceptable entry point, a remote cove with no apparent civilization for miles in any direction.

She brought the Cessna to another soft landing, and as soon as the craft settled she began steering toward the darkening German shore. Janna Magnussen, crisis counselor and pilot, looked predictably tense as the shoreline came near.

When she killed the engine Slaton reached into a pocket. His hand came out with the remainder of their agreed upon fee.

Once she'd taken it, he said, "Turn away."

"What?"

"Your face—turn away."

Magnussen gave him a cautious look, but complied, turning toward the opposite window.

Slaton pulled the .22 from his pocket, angled it carefully, and fired his last remaining round. The radio panel exploded.

Magnussen jumped involuntarily. She turned back and saw what he'd done.

"You bastard! You shot my airplane!"

"Only the radios—the rest still works. How much does a new communications panel cost?"

Still shaken, she took a moment to answer. "In dollars? Maybe two thousand."

"Okay. I'll add that in. Twenty-two thousand. Give me a few hour's head start, and you'll have the check by the end of next week."

She gave him a sharp stare. "How will you know if I've earned it? If I waited?"

He only smiled, and said, "Thanks for your help." Slaton opened the door and stepped onto the float. After a hesitation, however, he turned back. "Janna— you saw the sailboat, didn't you?"

"Yes."

"And you saw that it was heading north."

No answer.

"There was a woman on that boat. She's being sought by the police. There are other people looking for her as well, people who might do her harm. I can tell you that she's done nothing wrong—other than getting involved with me. But there is one thing I told you that wasn't truthful." Slaton met her blue aviatrix's eyes. "The woman on that boat is not my mistress. She's my wife. And I love her more than you could ever know."

Magnussen stared at him, and then shifted to her shattered instrument panel. A curiously amused expression came to her face. "Where were you when I was twenty?"

Slaton grinned, then eased the door closed.

Five minutes later he was standing on Continental Europe and watching the little seaplane skim into the sky one last time. He did not wait until it disappeared. Slaton placed his backpack on a large rock and took inventory. A GPS navigation device, a .22 Beretta with no rounds remaining, field glasses, and one energy bar—he had insisted Christine take the others. Thirty-nine U.S. dollars remained in his wallet.

He placed the gun in the right-hand pocket of his jacket, tucking the flap inside for better access—even without bullets it was good for intimidation. The GPS device went into the opposing pocket, along with the compact field glasses. He took out his wallet and removed everything except the cash. A Virginia driver's license, voter's registration, and Prince William County library card, all in the name of Edmund Deadmarsh, went into the otherwise empty backpack. An identity that had lasted nearly a year was now at its end.

He suspected Anton Bloch had performed the most difficult part—once Slaton arrived in Sweden, the legend of Edmund Deadmarsh had been scrubbed from cyberspace, probably erased on cue after one last use. The resulting anonymity was help enough, yet he also recognized a signal from his old boss. *Disappear, David. Find another way.* Slaton had never been told, but he suspected the identity originated with the CIA, Bloch calling in an old favor before he retired. Or possibly MI-6. Whatever the case, Bloch had finished what he'd started. The director who'd given the world Edmund Deadmarsh had taken him away, reciprocal keystrokes to remove every trace.

Slaton found a stone the size of a softball, put it in the backpack, and zipped everything shut. Taking the straps in hand, he gave a half spin like a hammer thrower and heaved the backpack fifty feet out to sea. With one thumping splash it was done. The man born as David Slaton was again a ghost. He had killed many a legend in his time, but never before had it been such a bittersweet parting. If the name Edmund

Deadmarsh had been no more than fiction, for Slaton it represented a very tangible life. Grilled burgers on the deck in Virginia, a week on the beach in Curaçao. The closest thing to normalcy he'd experienced in a very long time.

Now the vestiges of that life were sinking to a deep and dark place. The vestiges of his earlier life had long ago been eliminated. Police and intelligence organizations, for all their efficiencies, were modeled on the idea of matching a known to a known. In Slaton's case it would become no more than an exercise in frustration. Aside from the hazy recollections of a few policemen and acquaintances, perhaps a few distant captured images, there was nothing to compare. There were no pension accounts to watch. No driver's license on which to put a bulletin. No family mobile signals to monitor. The man standing on a German beach this early fall evening, alone and unshaven and empty-handed, was as pure an apparition as could be.

With dark clouds eclipsing everything to the north, the remains of the day were no more than a spray of purple on the western horizon. In the waning light Slaton looked left and right along the coast. Seeing nothing but rugged shoreline in either direction, he turned south and picked up a brisk pace. The *kidon* hit the tree line and was soon lost to sight.

When Evita Levine stepped through the portico of the Isrotel Tower Hotel in Tel Aviv she immediately got the looks she was accustomed to. She pretended not to notice the bellman's stare, and quietly appreciated but did not return an obvious glance from a businessman in an expensive suit. She too was well dressed, reflecting her recently established Ronen Chen expense account, and prominent on her wrist was the newest bauble, a bracelet of white gold and diamonds. She did not bother stopping at the front desk, instead going straight to the elevator and rising to the tenth floor. There she knocked on the usual door.

It opened almost immediately.

He stood there unsteadily, a half-spent bottle of red wine in his hand and a loosened tie round his neck. He looked at his watch, the motion nearly tipping the contents of the uncorked bottle onto his stiffly pressed white shirt, and causing Evita to wonder if perhaps she should have come earlier after all.

He said, "There you are, darling, I was beginning to wonder."

"I'm sorry," she replied. "I couldn't get my husband out of the house."

She stepped inside, kicking the door shut with the heel of her spiked Manolo. Both waited for the lock to catch before embracing. He was a small man, and in her five-inch heels—the ones he so liked—Evita was forced to bend down to meet his lips.

With his hand clutching her bottom, she nipped once at his ear and whispered, "I'm still not used to these little deceptions. I am not a professional like you."

He backed away. "Not to worry, my angel. As always, I have taken every precaution. If it puts you at ease I can call and find out where he is right now."

This gave Evita a fleeting chill. He was only trying to impress her, of course, yet she could never forget that he was a powerful man.

"No, that's not necessary."

He sauntered to the bar, brimming with confidence. "So—tell me about your week."

Evita did, as always keeping to the most insipid truths. She talked about her job at the nail salon, a miserable dinner at her in-laws, and the university rejection letter her best friend's brilliant son had just received. He listened at first, but the longer she talked the more he drank, and his interest inevitably faded. The first bottle of wine went quickly, and by the time the second clanked to the floor they were both on the bed, his shirt gone and she down to her new and very expensive undergarments.

Evita rubbed his hairy chest, slow circles that had the desired effect.

"Enough about me," she said. "Have you had a busy week?"

"Oh, you can't imagine." He let loose a long breath. "There have been meetings every night. The director is a driven man, and he expects no less from those around him."

"It sounds awful. So much pressure. I wish I could ease your load."

He chuckled lecherously.

"No, I mean it. I wish I could put all of Hamas on a leaky boat and send them to sea."

He looked at her drunkenly, a hazy leer that seemed not so different from old Yehud at the bar. "Yes, I believe you would. If I only had more warriors like you."

Her hand went lower, onto his round, furry belly. "And Iran's mad scientist—I would put a bullet in his head myself if the chance came."

"I told you," he said, "we're trying. That cockup in the desert—it never had a chance of succeeding. And the motorcycle fiasco? Lunacy, I tell you." His speech had acquired a familiar viscosity. "But we have one more chance. Hamedi is going abroad, and the director thinks he has found a way. He's brought in a new man to do it, one who will not fail."

"One man?"

"Yes."

"An assassin? How frightful, the people you deal with. How will it be done?"

"I shouldn't say anything, darling. Not this time."

"Of course, I understand." She nuzzled to his ear. "You lead such an exciting life, mon ami. So exciting . . ." Her hand found his mark. "Let's talk about it later."

Ezra Zacharias, director of operations for Mossad, inhaled sharply. "Oh . . . yes . . . much later."

Blix escorted Sanderson into his house.

"I'm fine, Gunnar, really."

"I still think you should have someone with you tonight. What about your sister?"

"She's away on holiday."

"Annika?" Blix said, referring to his daughter.

"I'm not an invalid, dammit! Not yet anyway. Annika is busy enough. And so should you be. Now get out of my house and find this bastard who's making all of us look like fools."

Blix grinned. "Yeah, you seem your old self."

He turned to go, and Sanderson said, "Thank you, Gunnar."

"No problem. Oh, I almost forgot." Blix reached into his pocket and pulled out Sanderson's phone. "Here."

Sanderson took it. "They're letting me keep it?"

"Not exactly—they've pulled the sim card. You'll need to pick up a new one."

"I'll take care of it right away."

"Call me as soon as you're reconnected."

"Thank you again."

Blix left, closing the door behind.

Sanderson sat down at his dining room table. He pushed aside a bowl of stale potato crisps and set down his disabled phone. The room was still and silent. He closed his eyes and slipped off his shoes, and with cold seeping through his socks from the bare stone floor, Arne Sanderson wondered what on earth was wrong with him.

The Stockholm police were paying a great deal of overtime. Officers who'd spent their afternoons swarming over three triangulated locations looking for an elusive American, only to come up empty, had been kept on duty. By sunset teams were stationed at each of the three sites, walking arm-in-arm with bright flashlights in search of evidence. Others were committed to patrol subway and ferry terminals. A dozen officers spent their Tuesday evening watching travelers at Arlanda Airport, and two men had been posted, rather hopefully, in the lobby of the Strand Hotel. Neighboring counties had been alerted, and immigration counters across Sweden received notice to watch for an American, possibly traveling under the name of Edmund Deadmarsh, who was suspected of shooting a police officer.

Anna Forsten gave two news conferences that evening. The first provided a terse overview of the recent Strandvägen attacks, a dry and procedural account that was trumped on most news stations by sensational eyewitness video, taken with a mobile phone, that had a certain *Blair Witch* production quality. People could be seen running and screaming, and shots were clearly audible as a young man crashed his scooter and went skidding across the pavement in front of the Renaissance Tea Room. The police acquired a copy of the video, but quickly declared it to hold little evidentiary value.

Sensing her grasp on things slipping, Commissioner Forsten held an impromptu second act on the sidewalk outside her office. In a brief but well-articulated statement she emphasized that things were firmly in control, her legions of crack investigators making significant progress toward capturing the fugitive. Dozens of questions were lobbed, like so many verbal grenades, as Forsten backed into the fortress that was National Police Headquarters. She answered not a single one.

TWENTY-SIX

At the very moment Commissioner Forsten was back-pedaling across a Stockholm sidewalk, the man she was looking for was standing on a more quiet slab of concrete some three hundred miles south in the port of Sassnitz, Germany. From his arrival point, Slaton had hiked the width of Jasmund National Park, a four-mile excursion through the brooding heaths and moors of northern Rügen Island. Where the park gave way to a narrow road, Slaton turned left toward a glow of lights in the distance. Twenty minutes later he arrived in Sassnitz.

Now, standing in front of the rail terminal, he looked out and marveled at his good fortune. Slaton could not imagine that a better selection of transportation alternatives existed in any square mile of Europe. He saw a ferry port that dealt the full spectrum—passengers, cars, and long-haul trucks. A rail terminal lay directly behind him, and on the horizon was a shipping yard. In the harbor a small cruise ship had docked next to the fishing fleet, and an assortment of leisure craft lay moored in private slips. There were small bulk carriers and cargo ships, and around these, loading cranes and forklifts sat ready to connect everything to trucks that would spread their payloads across Germany and beyond. Yet if the possibilities seemed overwhelming, they narrowed considerably when he measured his means against his objective. He had thirty-nine U.S. dollars in his pocket. On that he had to reach Switzerland.

Patiently, Slaton reckoned how best to attack the problem. He walked toward the ferry terminal with a cool wind at his back, the air scented with evergreen and the acrid residual of wood-burning fireplaces getting an early-season workout. As the long northern dusk lost its grip, the walkways fell increasingly sectioned, deep shadows broken by shards of electric light. Slaton lingered in the darker recesses to study his options. His attention settled on a large ferry where vehicles were unloading, and after twenty minutes the answer to his problem lumbered down the big metal off-ramp.

He kept to the shadows and watched, and soon two more vehicles of the same type rolled off in direct succession. He followed the little convoy's progress and saw them park, one by one, in a well-lit holding yard. He watched the drivers dismount and deliver the keys to a kind of dispatch shack. Slaton could not see inside the shack, but he imagined rows of keys hanging on hooks, or perhaps tagged and put in drawers. Either would serve the German penchant for organization. He kept watching, and in thirty minutes saw nine more of the type, nearly identical to the first, driven off the ferry, parked, and the keys delivered to the shack.

Satisfied he understood the process before him, Slaton began a well-practiced reverse flow. He searched for faults in the system, and saw a number of possibilities. He then studied the parking lot itself. The apron was massive, nearly a half mile in both length and width, and surrounded by a wire fence. The lot was roughly half full, a hodgepodge of trucks and cars and trailers and containers. Some would be gone in minutes, while others might expect spring flowers to blossom beneath their undercarriages. Of particular interest, Slaton noted that there was only one entrance, governed by the shack, where a heavy-set woman gave cursory inspections to everything that came and went.

He looked once more at his targeted vehicles and knew it had to be. It was a perfect match for his needs, albeit the sort of theft that would require patience and planning, even creativity. His decision made, Slaton stepped out of the shadows and set to work.

The knock on Sanderson's door came at half past eight that evening. He opened it to find his ex-wife.

"Ingrid . . . what on earth?" Seeing the concern on her face, he quickly surmised, "Blix called you, didn't he?"

"How are you, Arne?"

"I wish everyone would stop asking me that."

A gust of wind swept across the threshold. "Are you going to ask me in?"

"Yes, sorry."

Sanderson turned and swept his eyes over the room. As best he could remember, Ingrid had not been here since moving out five years earlier, and he wondered how the place had changed in that time. He saw unkempt furnishings, a carpet that needed cleaning, an embarrassing stack of dirty dishes by the sink. There was no getting around it. "I've given the maid a year's holiday."

"It's not so bad," she lied.

"Can I offer you some tea?"

"Decaf would be nice."

Sanderson put water on the stove, watching with an odd discomfort as she meandered the place they had shared for so long.

"How is my garden holding up?" she asked, peering into the darkness out the back window.

"Honestly? It looks like the Ardennes after a good German pounding."

She smiled. "It doesn't seem like five years, does it?"

"No," he agreed.

"How is Alfred?" Sanderson asked, happy he hadn't said "the toilet king."

"Not well, actually. It's his heart."

Fishing through a cupboard for clean cups, Sanderson stopped what he was doing. He saw her sadness, and said, "I'm sorry, Ingrid. Really I am."

She came closer and looked at him in the kitchen's strong light. "You don't look well, Arne."

"What did Blix tell you?"

"He said you passed out at headquarters today. And he said you've been forgetful—that it's become an issue at work."

"It won't be an issue any longer." Sanderson turned back to the cupboard. "I quit today. It was a rash decision, I admit, but Sjoberg had just pulled me from a big case for no reason."

"I did hear about that. You were working on these shootings?"

"Yes. He was quite unreasonable about the whole thing. But I suppose it was as good a time as any to pack it in. I've given them thirty-five years."

"That must have been very difficult."

"Not the way I did it. But we all knew it was coming. I only wish I could have finished the investigation I was working on."

The tea brewed and then cooled to the point of being useful. As they talked, he thought Ingrid seemed dampened, even spiritless, but given the mood of her visit, not to mention her husband's ill health, he should not have expected more. He did wish it, though. When they moved to better ground—their daughter and her fireman boyfriend, and the attendant speculation about grandchildren—the air seemed to improve. Ingrid even made him laugh once or twice, which was once or twice more than any other night this week. They'd talked for an hour when she finally looked at her watch.

"I should be going. Alfred doesn't always remember his pills before bed."

"Yes, of course."

After an awkward moment, she said, "I promised Blix I'd tell you to see a doctor. If he asks, say I did."

Sanderson smiled. He helped her put on her coat, and she looked at him with something old and familiar.

"This investigation—it's bothering you, isn't it, Arne?"

"They all do."

"No. Not like this."

"Unfortunately, there's nothing more I can do about it."

"Oh, I don't know." She went to the door and took the handle. "You could always get off your ass and finish what you started."

To sink a sailboat was not as easy as Christine imagined. She spent an hour in near darkness hammering and pounding, and in the end used a battery-powered drill to breach what she guessed was an adequate hole below the starboard waterline. When seawater finally began flowing, she disabled the automatic bilge pump and cranked the motor.

She had argued at length with David over the need for sinking the boat, he being of the school that no evidence should ever be left behind, and she assuming a more practical sailor's point of view. A compromise was reached when he agreed that once their situation normalized they would search out *Bricklayer*'s owner and make things right.

With the boat hove close to shore in a cove off Runmarö Island, Christine maneuvered to point the bow toward open water. She shone a flashlight into the cabin and watched the water level, trying to estimate the rate of rise in relation to the engine compartment. When she gauged submersion to be minutes away, she lashed a line beam-to-beam to hold the tiller steady and levered the motor into gear. For the third time in as many days, Christine slipped down the stern ladder in her underwear and eased into the Baltic. It seemed colder than ever.

Clothing under her arm, she waded into ankle-deep water before turning to watch. The boat ran seaward, and veered slightly to starboard as slack settled into the steering arm. She had already used the boat's depth finder to confirm that the water just offshore was deep, even if the very concept seemed ignoble, rather like making a condemned man stand in his grave to verify the correct depth. She heard the rumbling motor sputter, hesitate, and then go silent. So far so good. Already showing a distinct list to starboard, the momentum the boat had gained was absorbed in an awkward pirouette. Fifty yards out, the drunken silhouette of *Bricklayer* fell still on an indifferent sea.

Christine slogged ashore, used the last dry towel, and put on her pants. She wondered how long it would take, knowing that big ships sometimes took hours to go down, even days. There were any number of variables: buoyant compartments, shifting loads, center of gravity. For a long time nothing seemed to happen. The little boat just sat there, its skewed mast clear in the cloud-drawn moonlight. Then it began to founder, moving lower and swaying further to starboard until the gunnel went under. Across the still bay she heard rushing water and spewing air, and minutes later the blue-belted Pearson was flat on her side. As the hull disappeared, she watched the mast go vertical as if grasping for the wind one last time. Then it slipped straight down like Excalibur into the lake.

Christine turned away before it was gone.

Erbek Gurhan handed over his delivery paperwork, and in return was given a set of keys by the frau in the shack outside the Sassnitz transfer lot.

"You are Turkish, no?" she asked.

He nodded. "Where is this one?"

"Spot two hundred and six."

Gurhan grunted.

"My name is Helga."

"Erbek."

"You're getting a late start," she said.

"Tell me something I don't know. I just got the call—the ferry was running late."

"Is it time and a half?"

"You're damned right."

"So then you are rich. Maybe you can buy me a pint tomorrow. My shift ends at twelve every night."

Gurhan stared at her. He had been in Germany for five years, but still was not accustomed to the forwardness of Western women. "I won't be back tomorrow," he said. "This one is going all the way to Munich."

"Then maybe the next day."

Gurhan grunted a second time and turned away. As he padded across the gravel siding, however, he kept thinking about the woman in the gatehouse. She was lively enough and not bad to look at, although too many after-work pints had dulled her shape. And she had to be at least fifteen years older than he was—it would be like going out with his mother. Gurhan sighed. *A spirited woman with a slack body. Why can I never find the inverse?*

He found spot 206 at the back of the lot, and there his night was ruined. A mechanic with a work light was beneath the small motor home, his legs jacked out from under the front bumper.

"What is wrong?" Gurhan asked, bending down toward the ground.

The mechanic, dressed in greasy coveralls and with a wrench in his hand, slipped out from under the camper. "The engine starter is bad. I have to replace it."

The man had light hair, but Gurhan thought his accent was not German. Probably a Pole or a Latvian, he supposed, another expatriate brought in to do the dirty work. Not that it mattered to a Turkish delivery driver. "When will it be ready?" he asked.

"I cannot get a new part at this hour. Tomorrow, I think. Probably close to noon."

Gurhan cursed under his breath. "They just sent me here from Stralsund. What will I do until then?"

The mechanic shrugged and pushed back under the bumper.

Gurhan stood straight and looked at his watch: 11:45. He looked at the gatehouse and saw the frau whose shift was nearing an end. From a distance she seemed more attractive, and from any range utterly bored. *What the hell*, he thought. He started walking back to the shack.

"Hey!"

He turned and saw the mechanic's head again.

"I'll need the keys if I am going to make this work."

Gurhan didn't hesitate. He tossed them across the divide, a poor throw actually that was headed for the grill. Then the blond man swept out his hand and snatched them cleanly from the air.

TWENTY-SEVEN

By three a.m. Slaton had skirted Berlin and was sweeping through the heart of Germany, nearing Magdeburg, a modern and vibrant industrial city that seemed to have no recollection of being plundered by the Holy Roman Empire, or later bombed into oblivion by Allied air forces.

Sassnitz was a hundred and fifty miles behind, and by daybreak Slaton would have two hundred more. Rain had begun to fall, the kind of dense October drizzle that might not break for days, and the camper's tires hissed over wet asphalt as the headlights skipped their predictable pattern over glistening white lines. Striking a pothole, the vehicle rattled down to its bones, and somewhere behind him Slaton heard a drawer slide open. The RV had seen a lot of use. It smelled of mold and cheap cleanser. Slaton didn't care in the least.

He studied the rearview mirrors, and for the fifth time tonight cataloged the headlights drifting behind him. Vehicle headlights, he knew, produced unique signatures at night, and with some diligence could be logged and tracked. The shape of various lenses, their geometry and spacing, not to mention brightness and color. Taken together, it was all as telling as a written signature, and any vehicle following for a length of time could be readily identified. Slaton saw none behind him now that looked familiar.

He reckoned he would have to stop for fuel once before reaching his destination, and this would likely exhaust his remaining cash. The camper, a three-berth model, had been an ideal choice, and Slaton knew precisely why it had arrived at the docks of Sassnitz in mid-October. It was the sort of rental vehicle that drew a premium price in Scandinavia during the summer months, but with winter fast approaching the fleet was being repositioned south for the offseason. Spain or France. What he'd originally envisioned as a straight-out theft had gone smoothly. He'd watched the intended driver and the gate guard walk away together at midnight, and from there it was simple enough. Slaton had driven through the gate and waved to the new shift, a slim dark-skinned man. If challenged, he would have reverted to his role of mechanic, claiming the need for a test drive to certify his repair. That would have gotten him out the gate, but also resulted in a considerably shortened window of use. As it turned out, the watchman had only returned his wave, and Slaton drove away reckoning that his theft would not be noticed until midday tomorrow.

Just like riding a bike, he thought. *Or stealing one.*

His plan evolved further ten miles outside Sassnitz when he discovered the routing slip hanging from the camper's rearview mirror. Destination: Munich. Not a perfect fit, but too good to pass up. Slaton would simply deliver the RV himself. When the unit showed up in the right place at the right time, there would be little alarm over what was clearly a scheduling foul-up in which two drivers had been booked for the same delivery.

Traveling west on the E30, he came to the junction that would take him south toward Leipzig and Nuremberg, and the low emerald mountains of Bavaria. Slaton veered right, toward the exit, and slowed considerably—the steering was sloppy on the slick road, and he wanted no chance of sliding into a guardrail. His journey was taking shape in the best way possible, an oblique path that molded to the contours of what was available. It was an awkward way to travel, to be sure, but had one irresistible advantage—it was even harder to follow.

The man named Rafi arrived at Tehran's Imam Khomeini Airport at 9:50 that Wednesday morning, Iran Air Flight 528 from Amman running its customary one-hour late. When he reached the curb he saw the usual car waiting, a black Mercedes limo. It was the eighth time he had run this gauntlet, a nuisance he blamed—as with Damascus's faulty sewers, Gaza's dust-laden air, and the price of vegetables in Beirut—on the meddlesome State of Israel. The Jews, he'd been told, were getting better at monitoring the Internet, and because of it Rafi had not been able to use his mobile phone for anything of importance in a year. In effect, he had been relegated to the role of foot messenger. Indeed, as a man who knew his history, Rafi equated himself to those brave Persian runners who'd been tasked to skirt the grip of Genghis Khan and his crew some eight hundred years ago, a noble and fearless lot who risked life and limb to deliver vital communiqués.

Yes, he thought, *we have a great deal in common. Only I have enemies on both sides.*

Once inside the Mercedes, he shifted across the

plush leather to get a better flow from the air-conditioning vent. Neither the limo's driver nor the thick man beside him said a word as the big car bolted through intersections heading for MISIRI, Iran's Ministry of Intelligence and National Security.

Rafi looked out the window and took in the blur that was Tehran. He had never actually set foot in the city, yet it somehow seemed familiar. He saw old women selling vegetables from carts, and suicidal young men doubled up on scooters as they weaved through lawless traffic. It could have been Amman or Cairo, any number of capitals across the region. This familiarity ended abruptly, however, when the big Mercedes swerved through a set of brooding iron gates to be swallowed by the headquarters complex of MISIRI.

Rafi straightened in his seat, and soon the big car skidded to the curb and the door popped open. He was hustled through a maze of hallways, and twenty-two minutes after landing in Iran, Rafi entered the utilitarian office of Farzad Behrouz.

The little man remained seated, his fingers squaring a thick envelope on the desk in front of him. "Well?" he prompted, no hint of cordiality.

"It is as you suspected," Rafi said. "There will be another attempt on Hamedi."

"Where and when?"

"I don't know."

Almost imperceptibly, Behrouz cocked his head. "What do you mean? Our source has always been quite . . . forthcoming in the past."

"Our agent explained her situation to me. It is a delicate thing we ask, and I think she was correct to not press harder than she did. Zacharias is not a fool. But there was something. She said the Jews expect

Hamedi to go abroad soon. They see this as an opportunity. If it is true, then you have your answer."

"No," Behrouz argued, "I must have specifics."

"I've told her to keep trying, to schedule another rendezvous."

"She understands that time is running short?"

"Yes, of course. And there is one more thing. Mossad thinks they've found a man who will have more success than the others. A lone assassin."

Behrouz went quiet and leveled a discomforting gaze. It was a look Rafi had not seen before. "Who is this man?" he finally asked.

"I know nothing more."

"Well go back then! Take command of your Jew whore! Give her money, threaten her with exposure, do whatever it takes. Find out who this man is. And I must have the precise time and place of any attack!"

"I will do what I can," Rafi said.

"No," Behrouz replied, "you will do what I instruct. You have two days." From his desk he produced a mobile phone and slid it across the desk. "This is secure. Use it when you have my answer."

He then pushed the envelope across and Rafi took it.

Though he had originally contacted Iran though Hezbollah channels, Rafi himself took credit for the discovery and recruitment of the disconsolate Evita Levine. And as was often the case in this part of the world, aside from being a patriot, he was not above taking a reasonable commission for his work. He knew well the value of information.

Behrouz issued further, very specific instructions, and the next meeting was arranged. When Rafi left the office minutes later, he hoped his next trip here would be his last. There was something about the place that made his stomach turn, a discomfort not worth even the thick envelope of cash in his pocket. It was in the air, he decided, a stagnant and foul odor. The sort of embedded stench that might be imagined to rise from the bowels of a medieval castle. Whatever the source, he didn't want to know.

As he was escorted down the long hallway back to the limo, turning left and right through confusing corridors and drawing the dead air into his lungs, Rafi suspected he knew exactly how those messengers had felt some eight hundred years ago.

Sanderson was awakened by an unfamiliar ringing noise. It took a few groggy seconds to realize that the bells were coming not from his head, but from his phone. He'd purchased and installed a new sim card last night, but had gone to bed before dealing with the settings. His phone had defaulted to its factory ringtone, not to mention its factory volume. It sounded like a fire alarm.

"Sanderson."

Blix said, "Morning, Inspector. I got your message last night, but it was late and there was nothing new to report."

"That's fine. And this morning?"

"One thing. We've found one of the phones Deadmarsh used to call you."

"Where?"

Blix told him.

"You're kidding."

"I thought it was a little theatrical too. I'm on my way there now. If you want to meet me . . . well, I could be your escort."

"I'll be there in twenty minutes."

TWENTY-EIGHT

In 1626 Sweden was at the height of the Stormakts-tiden, or more commonly, "The Great Power Period," and it was the year in which King Gustavus Adolphus, engaged in a fourth consecutive war with the tireless Poles, commissioned his navy to construct the most fearsome and heavily armed warship the world had ever seen. A thousand oak trees were cut to provide timber for her hull, and fifty twenty-four-pound guns were ordered cast to be incorporated onto the mighty ship's high deck. Every quarter of the vessel was to be sculpted with ornamentation, striking designs to intimidate enemies and glorify the prowess of the king. The result, two years later, was the *Vasa*.

On August 10, 1628, Sweden's symbol of strength set sail on her maiden voyage. Her reign of terror, meant to last decades, was in fact measured in minutes. Under the first puff of wind ever to strike her sails, the top-heavy ship capsized and sank less than a mile from port. It was a trauma felt not only by the Swedish navy, but in the collective psyche of a nation. *Vasa*, for all her might and potential, was indelibly registered as a symbol of what might have been.

Nearly four hundred years later, on a crisp October morning, Arne Sanderson stood outside the Vasa Museum with his hands plunged deep into the pockets of his worn overcoat. He eyed the parking lot stretched out before him, much as Gustavus Adolphus had likely once regarded the harbor, and thought, *I do believe we've got this all wrong.*

The cavernous building behind him held the salvaged remains of the great ship, and the morning shift of visitors was already queuing up for guided tours. In front of Sanderson, framed by a slate gray autumn sky, was a nearly empty parking lot, and at the far end he saw a police evidence van and two squad cars. A half dozen officers in sterile gear were busy combing the tarmac. In a burst of enthusiasm someone had cordoned off the entire parking lot as a crime scene, causing Sanderson to wonder—given recent events—how much yellow tape the department kept in stock.

"Morning, Inspector."

Sanderson turned and saw Blix. "Good morning, Gunnar."

"Glad you could make it."

"So am I. And please don't ask me how I'm feeling—I'm getting tired of that question."

"Done."

Blix began walking toward the police contingent and Sanderson fell in beside him.

"Anything new on the investigation?" Sanderson asked.

"Our finest minds are working on it."

Sanderson looked up and saw the wry smile.

"Actually, I just came from the morning meeting," said Blix. "The best news is Sergeant Elmander's positive outlook. He'll be walking with a limp for a few weeks, but should be back on desk duty soon."

"Yes, that's very good news."

"We're still trying to verify that the comatose man

in Saint Göran is a former Mossad director, but the Ministry of Foreign Affairs has the taken lead on that. All we can do is wait. As for the rest—not much, honestly. Some more grainy surveillance footage, but nothing that will do us any good. The usual lot of dubious eyewitnesses. Forsten is operating on the principle that our man is still in Sweden, Stockholm if you ask her. At least a hundred officers are busy watching trains and bus stations and airports. You know the bit— look for a tall light-haired man who's sweating and fidgeting."

"All that behavioral analysis rubbish they've been drilling into us?"

"I suppose it has its uses," Blix said. "But the bottom line hasn't changed—we have a killer at large, and Dr. Palmer still hasn't been found. Oh, and headquarters is ready if Deadmarsh calls your old number again. They've got a new software package that supposedly will give them a near real-time fix on his position."

Sanderson thought Anna Forsten was throwing her investigative spears into a very dark jungle. "We rely too much on technology these days," he said. "There's a place for it, mind you, but it's no substitute for thoughtful detective work."

A constable was manning the entry point, a young lad who looked familiar, although Sanderson couldn't recall his name.

Blix said, "Good morning, Karl," as they both walked past.

Yes, Karl, Sanderson thought.

They exchanged pleasantries with a technician who was picking up shards of plastic with tweezers and slipping them into evidence bags. A woman nearby was taking photographs of bits and pieces that were scattered over a ten-meter circle.

"We were able to track down the three phones he was using," Blix said. "All disposables, purchased Sunday at a little shop in Jakobsberg. We're pretty sure this is the remnants of one of them. Nothing yet at the other two locations, but we're looking."

"It looks as if the damned thing exploded," Sanderson remarked.

"Run over by a car is my guess," Blix suggested.

"I can't say what caused the damage," the tech replied. "But once we get it under a scope we'll be able tell you."

"What about information from the memory?" Blix asked. "Any chance it's usable?"

"Possible, but that will take some time."

"And you haven't found anything other than the phone?" Sanderson asked.

The technician looked up, and for the first time seemed to recognize Sanderson. "Nothing obvious, Inspector. Of course, a parking lot like this—you've always got trash to deal with as well. There was a crushed compact disc just behind me. It's going to take a while to sort through. I think we have enough from the outer case and buttons that we might be able to lift a fingerprint or two. At least a partial."

Blix said, "That is, if he didn't wipe it down."

Sanderson frowned. "If this Deadmarsh fellow can make his passport evaporate, I doubt we're going to find a record of his fingerprints languishing in our files."

Blix said, "He was using three phones within a matter of minutes. Locations all around town. Is there some way to do that remotely? Relay a telephone call?"

The forensic man said, "Never heard of such a thing, but it wouldn't seem difficult. Voice over

Internet—that's readily available. A sharp programmer could come up with something."

"There might be an application already out there," Blix suggested weakly.

"No," Sanderson said. "We're slipping the more basic question. Deadmarsh has gone to a considerable amount of trouble here. Why? What has he gained from all this?"

The forensic man stopped his tweezing. Both he and Blix looked at Sanderson.

"Don't you see? He's got us chasing our asses. The question is, why?"

Ten minutes later a frustrated Sanderson was back in his car. He decided he wasn't going to find anything useful here, or for that matter, at either of the other two sites. His own words kept beating in his head: *He's got us chasing our asses.*

That was his overriding thought as he turned toward headquarters, bound for what was certain to be another wretched encounter in Sjoberg's office. Try as he might, he could think of no better option than to make a last stab at groveling his way back onto the investigation. Even if Sjoberg turned him down, as he probably would, Sanderson might glean something useful from beating around headquarters. Yet as he made his way into town, his foot was uncharacteristically light on the accelerator. Sanderson had spent most of his career dealing with petty criminals, dullards whose methods were as hopeless as their prospects. Deadmarsh was clearly something else. Sanderson racked his brain, sure he was missing something.

How? How did you do it?

He recalled the engine noise he'd heard over the phone. Then he considered the distances involved, along with his first impression this morning. *It looks as if the damned thing exploded.* That was when it struck him. Sanderson braked to a hard stop, swerving to the side of the road, and craned his neck skyward. Just as had been the case yesterday, he saw nothing but a solid layer of cloudcover above, gray and ominous.

Even so—

Sanderson wheeled his car through a quick three-point turn, and his foot went down hard as he accelerated in a completely different direction.

In the predawn hours that Wednesday, Slaton swept through Bayreuth, Wagner's final resting place, and farther on skirted Nuremburg, witness to both the swaggering beginnings and ignominious end of Hitler's depraved Nazi Party. He arrived at the Munich outpost of EuroCamper Rentals at 8:21 in the morning.

Slaton steered through a double-sided gate that no one bothered to guard, and saw a parking lot with perhaps twenty recreational vehicles similar to the one he was driving. Finding an empty slot at the front, near what looked like a small office, Slaton backed the camper in deftly—as any professional driver would.

He took the keys in hand, pulled the routing card from the rearview mirror, and walked toward the office with a weary stride that was not contrived. He pushed through a squeaking metal door into a paintless and beaten room. One wall displayed a poster of a camper like the one he'd just parked, the unit in the picture considerably cleaner, and presented with a smiling family in an otherwise vacant Alpine meadow. The only other thing here that could be called a decoration was a monthly calendar, the October offering a voluptuous woman whose naked body was covered strategically by red and brown leaves, her tanned haunch nestled against the logo of a brake rotor manufacturer. A space heater in one corner was working hard but losing the battle, an ominous sign in early October, and behind a counter Slaton saw a big man sitting on a high stool. His hair was wild and his face grooved, the sort of deep wrinkles that implied not only cigarettes and alcohol, but every vice known to God and earth. The proprietor was leaning on the rough countertop and watching something on a tiny TV.

The man looked up, said nothing, and held out his hand. Slaton gave him the key and the delivery routing card.

"Where is the rest of the paperwork?" the man demanded in German.

German was a language Slaton struggled with, especially after years of neglect, but it hardly mattered. He could decipher the puzzle-like compounds well enough to understand commands, and he could respond with ill-phrased answers as well as any recent immigrant. In his current guise—delivery driver for a rental company—he reckoned that a formal command of the language would only inspire unwanted attention.

Slaton shrugged helplessly. "They give me nothing else."

The man snorted, and asked, "Did you hit anything?"

"No."

"Did you put gas in it?"

"Yes, sure."

"You have the receipt?"

Slaton did. He handed it over and the man took a cursory glance. The German opened a locked drawer using a key from a ring on his belt, and pulled out twenty-four euros, counting twice. When his hand went back into the drawer, deeper this time, Slaton tensed and watched closely—he knew what else was often kept in locked cash drawers.

What came out was a piece of hard stock paper. The man handed it all over in one stack. "Here's your voucher for the train back to Sassnitz."

Slaton relaxed. He was tired, the kind of fatigue that could bring mistakes. He took the money and the voucher, and asked, "Where is train station?"

The man pointed down the street.

"How do I get there?"

"You walk."

"It is far?"

The weathered German smiled. "Yes."

Slaton arrived at Munich Central Station at 8:58. The walk had in fact been two miles, easily manageable by the recent standards he'd been setting. Along the way he discreetly dropped the Beretta into a storm drain, seeing few positives in traveling with a concealed weapon that was empty.

At the station he presented the voucher at a ticket window, explaining that he wished to amend his destination. The agent told him that yes, he could change the ticket, but a fee would apply. Fortunately, the original value of the voucher was far in excess of the new fare, and even with the change fee subtracted Slaton was due a refund of nineteen euros.

He spent six on breakfast, a sweet pastry and dark coffee, and as he waited for his train to Switzerland he found two discarded newspapers, *Bild* and *Die Welt*. World leaders were addressing climate change, the Deutschmark had fallen, and another screen starlet had died in a hotel bathtub. He found only one small paragraph referencing a fading manhunt in Stockholm, the most interesting revelation being that there was a new detective in charge, Inspector Sanderson having been taken off the case for unspecified medical issues. Slaton was glad, because Sanderson had seemed competent, and doubly so because the ensuing handover would lend itself to confusion and lost leads.

At 9:52 Slaton boarded a crowded second-class car. It was a commuter special with few empty seats, and he shouldered to a window beside a young girl, nineteen or perhaps twenty years of age. She had the look of a schoolgirl, long hair and pretty, and sat straight-backed with her knees together and hands in her lap. Slaton could not imagine a more ideal seatmate. Attractive young girls traveling alone knew better than to strike up conversations with strange older men. His seat selection was further validated when a well-dressed businessman sat in the opposing row and was immediately accosted by the man to his left, a middle-aged fellow in a creased coat and crooked tie who was trying to sell investments. Those were eyes Slaton would avoid, as he had no desire to listen to a sales pitch all the way to the Swiss border. And anyway, from a strictly actuarial standpoint, fixed annuities were not a practical investment vehicle for assassins.

At 09:59 the train pulled away.

When he drifted to sleep minutes later, the *kidon* was four hundred miles removed from his entry point in Germany. He had virtually no chance of being traced. His belly was full. And he had thirteen more euros in his pocket than when he'd started.

TWENTY-NINE

The boarding of the 10:15 ferry was nearly complete. Standing in an alcove at the back of the terminal, Christine Palmer—doctor of internal medicine, mother-to-be, and fugitive pirate—stood wondering if the gangway would be pulled punctually.

The clock near the ticket booth read 10:07. The crowd of passengers was larger than she'd expected, and on a Wednesday morning she guessed most were commuting to work, a few perhaps heading into town to shop or meet dental appointments. The voyage from Styrsvik, Runmarö Island, to Stavsnäs would last no more than ten minutes. Indeed, Christine could see the receiving dock barely a mile away, a dark shadow floating on the mist-shrouded bay.

10:08.

Not wanting to cut it too close, Christine decided to make her move. She went to the automated ticketing kiosk and pulled out a credit card imprinted with the name Edmund Deadmarsh. She purchased a one-way ticket, and as soon as it spit from the machine Christine hurried to the boat. An attendant took her ticket with barely a glance, and she scampered across the metal boarding steps as the last passenger. She veered into the covered lower deck, where virtually everyone had sought relief from the cool marine air, and took a seat in the middle of the largest group—three women her own age amid ten preschool children. A playgroup headed to the mainland, she supposed, likely for an outing to a museum or an amusement park. She smiled at the children and nodded to the mothers.

Three minutes later, right on schedule, the Waxholmsbolaget ferry pushed back from the pier and began churning across the bay for the short passage to greater civilization. Christine watched Runmarö slip behind, descending into the mist much as *Bricklayer* had disappeared into the sea last night along the island's deserted southern shore.

The children were being children, running through the cabin and squealing happy sounds, while their mothers chatted amiably and looked equally content. Christine leaned back and put a hand to her belly— her ribs were still tender from her flyer onto the boat in Stockholm. She tried to imagine what challenges these women might face today. Finding nutrition in fast-food lunch menus? A knot on a tiny forehead from a wayward playground swing? It caused her to wonder.

Will David and I ever find such a carefree day in our lives?

Christine looked out over the water. She'd spent one day with David on a stolen sailboat, and hour by hour she had watched him change, a year's worth of transformation lapsing before her eyes. He'd become increasingly alert, listening and watching, expecting threats from every distant vessel and passing aircraft. She recalled the old gun, worthless as it was. David had found it, searched it out. Within an hour of arriving he had probably located every knife and flare gun and blunt instrument on the boat, and had each item stowed in a tactically advantageous position.

Have I lost him so quickly? she wondered. *Or did I never really have him to begin with?*

The ferry began to maneuver, arrival on the mainland imminent. Christine moved quickly toward the boarding ramp, and was the first passenger to step ashore.

The Stockholm Police nearly succeeded.

The transaction on the flagged credit card was immediately highlighted by the Swedish Security Service. SÄPO forwarded the information to National Criminal Investigations, who in turn sent an advisory alert to the Stockholm police—Edmund Deadmarsh had just purchased a ferry ticket on Runmarö Island, and his arrival at Stavsnäs was imminent.

Within minutes, four units of the local constabulary were making best speed to the ferry terminal at Stavsnäs. The first unit to arrive bounded onto the curb at 10:29, and two officers rushed out and began searching for their suspect: a light-haired American man who was likely armed and certainly dangerous. Hands on their holstered weapons, neither the driver nor his partner took notice of a departing cab in which an attractive, and very alert, auburn-haired woman was staring out the back window.

Sanderson arrived at the bunker-like building of Air Navigation Services of Sweden, run by the government-held LFV Corporation, and at the main entrance found himself staring at an imposing security keypad. There was a call button, and Sanderson pushed it and stared squarely into the camera lens over the door. He got an immediate answer.

"Can I help you?" a disembodied voice rang through the speaker.

"Detective Inspector Sanderson, Stockholm police. I'm here on urgent business."

"One minute."

Expecting the door to open any second, Sanderson reached into his overcoat for what he'd snatched out of his desk yesterday. Years earlier he'd taken a summer posting as a liaison officer to Interpol, a relatively pleasant three months in Lyon, France, in which he sorted through the felons of greater Europe. On returning to Stockholm, Sanderson realized that he'd not surrendered his Interpol credentials before leaving, and with little thought had simply shoved them into a desk drawer. The document, of course, had long ago lapsed, but the small print of the expiration date left virtually no chance of this being noticed. And like all policemen, Sanderson knew that when it came to establishing authority, attitude and volume were far more persuasive than paper and ink.

So it was, when the door opened moments later he flashed his old ID at the security guard and barged ahead, barking, "I have to identify all aircraft that were over the city yesterday at midday. Who must I talk to?"

A clearly flummoxed guard said, "That would be the air traffic manager, sir."

"Well don't just stand there with your mouth hanging open, get him!"

Minutes later Sanderson was talking to a very capable woman named Rolf.

"We keep records for a running sixty-day period," she explained. "After that everything rolls into a long-term storage database."

Rolf led him to a dark room where air traffic controllers were busy behind workstations. All wore headsets, and their faces were illuminated by multicolored displays as they guided aircraft with chattering instructions.

"What time yesterday are you concerned with?" she asked.

"Eleven thirty-two in the morning."

She looked at him questioningly, then began typing at a vacant console. "And you're looking for an aircraft that was over the city?"

"That's right."

The screen in front of them blinked to life, and then settled to a black map display that was highlighted with concentric arcs and lines. Seconds later, this background was overlaid with scattered alphanumeric symbols.

"I see six aircraft over the city." She pointed to a pair of white squares that were tagged with data blocks. "These two are airliners. They are at high altitude and moving fast."

"No, I'm looking for something else. An aircraft that stayed over the city for a period of twenty or thirty minutes."

Rolf tinkered with the display, going forward and back in time until her finger settled on one square. "This one. It was circling the downtown area for thirty minutes, very low and slow. I'm not sure why—nobody would have been sightseeing given yesterday's weather."

"No, they wouldn't," Sanderson agreed. "What kind of airplane was it?"

"A Cessna," she replied.

"Where did it go next?"

This took longer, but Rolf did her magic. Elements on the screen began to disappear, and soon all that remained was a line representing the track of their targeted aircraft. It had spun two irregular circles over the city before meandering south.

Rolf said, "It departed on a southwesterly track, roughly a two-hundred-and-ten-degree magnetic heading. Twenty miles south we lose the signal."

"Can you find out where it went after that?"

"With the radar, not likely. This aircraft was flying low and there are hills in that area. But I can tell you who it was." After no more than a few keystrokes, she said, "Sierra Three Two Five Papa. I've seen the call sign before, but not here."

"What do you mean?"

"Smaller aircraft usually navigate around or under our busy airspace." More typing. "It's a Cessna 180 seaplane owned by Magnussen Air Charters. They're based in Oxelösund. I have the address and phone number if you like."

"Yes, very much."

Five minutes later Sanderson was back in his car, and consumed with newfound excitement. He started the engine and was about to engage the gearshift when he paused. As his hands gripped the wheel, the phone in his pocket seemed inordinately heavy. He knew he ought to call in his findings to the command center. But would anyone listen? Would anyone act? Possibly. Yet the information would have to go through channels, bounce across a half dozen desks and email inboxes. By then the lead might go cold. That was what Sanderson told himself, anyway.

He put the car in gear, pressed his foot down hard, and minutes later was accelerating onto the E4 headed south.

THIRTY

The first attempt on Ibrahim Hamedi's life had earned him a lone bodyguard, a man who doubled as his driver. After the second attempt he never left home, or the compound in Qom, without a sizable convoy. The composition of his escort varied based on setting. Military vehicles were preferred for desert travel, but today, snaking through the baffling maze that was south Tehran, he made due with three armored limousines. Hamedi was in the lead car, which seemed to him counterintuitive from a security standpoint. But then, he was no expert. With awkwardly reassuring logic, he had long ago relented that Farzad Behrouz would take every possible measure to cover both their asses.

A motorcade of armored Mercedes was not an unusual sight in certain quarters of the city. In the working-class neighborhood of Molavi it stood out like a circus train. People stopped on the sidewalks and stared. Hamedi looked back through bulletproof glass and saw a distantly familiar place. The street was little different from a thousand others in south Tehran. In a long-settled victory of pragmatism over style, endless strings of tan tenements were crammed shoulder to shoulder, their earthen walls seeming to lean on one another like rows of dominos whose fall had been interrupted. He saw wires for electrical and phone service strung overhead like so much spaghetti, and from the main lines illegal shunts snaked brazenly through windows up and down the street. The scents were as ever, the urban tang of people and the stench of refuse, all cut by cinnamon and saffron drifting from kitchen windows.

Hamedi studied each face that passed, looking for any that seemed familiar. Mohammed, his best friend from grade school, or Simin Marzieh, the first girl he had ever kissed. He was sure they were here somewhere—assuming they were still alive. Hamedi had escaped these circumstances, but he was a rare exception. He did not delude himself that it was a matter of having worked harder to get ahead. Hamedi was the one *inside* the armored Mercedes because he could multiply six-digit numbers in his head at the age of five, and because he had earned his PhD in particle physics at the age of twenty-two. Hamedi had been given a gift from God, and he had not wasted it.

He craned his neck as they turned onto his old street, and soon he saw the building. It was a five-story affair, a weary testament to the color beige baked hard by fifty summers. Then he saw his mother. She was there at the threshold of her first-floor unit, sweeping the front step as he'd seen her do a thousand times. This was her never-ending crusade against the dust and wind, one that she would never win, and probably didn't care to. "It is the battle that is important," she would say. Even from a distance, Hamedi thought she looked different from when he'd last seen her, the back more bowed and the hair a lighter gray. The sharp olive eyes, however, he knew would be unchanged.

"Park across the street," he ordered.

The driver nodded, and a bulky man in the passenger seat murmured something toward his collar. There were six more men in the other cars. The last time Hamedi had come here, a year ago, he'd been alone. That, he knew with certainty, was something that would never happen again.

The cars eased to a stop across the street from his old home. When Hamedi got out, the two men from his car followed and fell in step. "I don't suppose I could ask you to stay here," he said.

The guard in front, a heavy slab of a man in an ill-measured suit, said, "I am sorry, Dr. Hamedi, but you know our orders."

"Very well," he said. "But give us a little peace."

As they crossed the street his mother kept sweeping. He was sure she'd seen them—nothing happened anywhere on the block without her knowing about it—and so this was her greeting.

Hamedi stopped at the foot of the steps. "Hello, Mother."

She looked up at him with the same severe look he'd seen last November. Had it been there ever since? he wondered.

"I suppose you want tea," she said.

Hamedi looked up and down the block. He saw at least twenty people staring at them, gawking from the street, faces framed in nearby windows. "Yes, that would be nice."

Without another word, she turned into the house.

The two bodyguards followed them inside, but kept their distance. One took up a position at the front door, and the other at the back. His mother said nothing else until she emerged from the kitchen with the familiar tray: one teapot, two chipped china cups, and a bowl of honey.

"And what blesses me with this appearance? Surely you have important work to do."

"How have you been?" he asked.

"I am as always—fit and alone."

"You miss father," he said.

"It's been six years. Time has its way. But it is more difficult when one has no other family."

"You have friends."

"Oh, yes. And I will have more tomorrow when word gets out that my son, a man of such standing, has been here to visit mercy on his old mother."

"If you were not always so miserable I would come more often."

For the first time her eyes engaged him directly. "A letter arrived last week from your mentor in Hamburg."

"Dr. Bohrlund?"

"Yes. He said the man who took that position you turned down at the university—he has not worked out. They are searching for a replacement, and Bohrlund thinks the post could be yours if—"

"Enough! I will not hear this again!"

"And I will not listen to weak excuses of what you now do!" she said defiantly. "You had such promise, Ibrahim! In Europe you could have taught science and done worthy research. You could have made the world something better. Instead you've sold yourself to this madness."

"I have sold nothing. What I do, I do in the name of peace." Hamedi looked across the room and saw the shoulder of one of the guards. The man would have no trouble hearing their raised voices. He said in a quieter tone, "You are my mother, but you are not worldly. I don't expect you to understand my work or what will come from its success. But someday you will accept my decisions."

After a prolonged silence, she said, "So why have you come here then? To torment me?"

Hamedi eased himself into his father's familiar old chair. "I am going to Switzerland soon on business. Is there something you would like? That soap I used to bring or some chocolate?"

She snorted. "Don't bother yourself."

Hamedi heaved a sigh and surveyed the small room. His boyhood was all around him, and he felt a peculiar discomfort in having brought the guards here—it was as if they were violating the one place in Iran where he had ever felt safe. He said, "There is something else I could do for you. I could . . ." Hamedi hesitated mightily, "I could get you a better place to live."

His mother's eyes narrowed severely. "A *better* place to live? You mean a place that is away from my friends? Something new and clean, with no marks on the wall or stains on the curtains? One without memories? Or perhaps you only want your old mother in a safer neighborhood, one without so many undesirables."

"I am not without influence, Mother. I could get you a house with a garden in Hashtgerd. It's a nice place—many of the high-ranking military officers and Majlis live there."

She stared at him incredulously. "The Majlis you say?"

Hamedi paused, waiting for her predicted disgust to pass. The big shoulder was still there. "Or . . . I still have the apartment in Hamburg. Perhaps you could go there, even for a short stay. I could arrange a flight for you to—"

"Enough!" she shouted. "This is where your father died, and this is where I will die, God willing."

Hamedi was suddenly sorry he had come. He should not have expected different, but it was a pain he had not felt in a year. He rose from his father's old chair and raised his voice. "Very well! I came to offer my help, but I will take no more of your misery. I'm sorry you consider me such a disappointment, but I will never regret the course I have chosen. Remember that, old woman!"

He strode to the door.

"Ibrahim—" she called.

Hamedi hesitated, almost turned. But then he strode ahead and his two shadows fell in place behind. Seconds later his convoy was under way, churning down the dust-laden street. He supposed her face was there in the window—as always, the cleanest window on Khorrami Street.

Hamedi did not look back.

The matter of entering Switzerland from Germany was something to think through. Slaton knew that with the adoption of the Schengen Area, Switzerland no longer staffed border control points on roads leading into the country. Equally, rail and bus service were not regularly monitored. But this was not an absolute—customs officers had full authority to stop anyone entering the country, and they randomly patrolled trains to ask for identification and search baggage. Carrying no identity papers whatsoever, Slaton was not keen to travel in a vehicle of any sort. On the other hand, he was facing a firm deadline—an appointment to kill a man in four days' time. The latter forced his hand, and he decided that with the precautions of good tradecraft, it would be best to take the train straight through.

Two and a half hours after leaving Munich, the Intercity Express breached the Swiss border near the town of Bregenz, Austria, and crossed the Rhine to afford a sweeping view of Lake Constance. An announcement was made over the public address system regarding the border crossing, but Slaton saw no customs officers, and neither he nor any of the other passengers bothered to reference the folding cards in the seat pockets that served as official notice, in three languages, of the duties, laws, and responsibilities assumed by those entering Switzerland.

The annuity salesman, still at his opportunistic best, had begun chatting up a thickset man across the aisle. Slaton saw the old peddler pull out his wallet, ostensibly to produce a business card, but also managing to put on display an inset photograph of his lovely wife and two daughters. It occurred to Slaton that he had never in his life kept such a picture in his wallet, even in his recent "domestic period" as Christine called it. Would it ever happen? Would a day come when he could walk through the world without the specter of entangling his wife, and now their child, in his violent past? In the last year he had covered much new ground. He had paid a water bill and opened a credit account, albeit under the alias of Edmund Deadmarsh. For the first time in years he kept a legitimate home address, if one discounted the dusty storage facility in Tel Aviv where a few inherited household items had been moldering for years. Yet now he was slipping back, returning to the abyss.

As the train continued westward, the great slabs that were the Alps dominated the horizon, their crests already aswirl in winter clouds and new snow. Slaton shut his eyes, needing to rest, but also in case any promotion-minded customs officer suddenly appeared in the aisle. Yet if his body was still, his thoughts were less so. He was heading for Geneva and an assassination, searching for a course that would solve all his problems. Yet like any gamble, the coin could equally land against him. If that happened, if he lost control, he might lose Christine forever. At the moment there was only one option—Slaton had to keep moving forward. Keep searching for a way out.

With a change of trains, he could be in Geneva by early afternoon. He would not, however, go that far today. The man he was to kill might soon be in Geneva—but the money was in Zurich.

At 3:15 that same afternoon, as the *kidon* was spanning Switzerland, Arne Sanderson pulled up to the building labeled Magnussen Air Charters in Oxelö-sund. He parked his car, and through a drizzle-obscured windshield saw an airplane at the dock with the registration number Rolf had given him: S325P.

A slightly built woman was tending to something in the cockpit. Sanderson got out of his car, shrugged his collar higher, and walked over to announce himself. "Excuse me—may I have a word?"

The woman, who was standing precariously on one of the floats, leaned outside.

"I'm Detective Inspector Sanderson, Stockholm police." He flashed his old Interpol credentials and she glanced at them.

"It's about damned time!" she said.

"Sorry?"

"I called the local boys this morning. Told them I'd had some trouble."

The woman stepped onto the dock and offered a hand. "Janna Magnussen."

"Yes, good to meet you," Sanderson replied. "What kind of trouble did you report?"

"A hijacking, of course."

Sanderson blinked, caught off-guard. "You mean an air hijacking? As in when someone forcibly takes control of your airplane?"

"Yes."

"Maybe we should start at the beginning."

Janna Magnussen's eyes twinkled. "Yes, that might be for the best." She looked up at the inclement sky, and said, "Why don't you come inside, Inspector."

THIRTY-ONE

In the office they stood split by a navigation table where a map of Sweden was pressed under a scarred sheet of Plexiglas. Sanderson saw that various points around the country, mostly remote lakes and coves, had been circled with markers and then connected by lines to Magnussen Air Charter's Oxelösund hub.

"He hired me out for a charter," she said. "I took him out Monday morning and dropped him on an island. Picked him up at the same place yesterday morning."

"What did he look like?"

Her description left no doubt in Sanderson's mind—they were talking about Deadmarsh.

"Where exactly did you drop him?"

Magnussen referenced the map and pointed to the cove on Bulleron Island. She described her delivery and the next day's pickup, then circling over Stockholm while Deadmarsh threw mobile phones out the window. She told him about the gun and a forced flight to the German coastline. Her story rang true to Sanderson, and at the end he was left with two questions.

"Do you know who he met on that island?"

"He told me it was his wife. She had a sailboat."

Again, this made perfect sense. Sanderson asked, "And where did you drop him off yesterday?"

Magnussen pulled a different chart from a cabinet and unfurled it on the table. Sanderson saw that it covered the Baltic and northern Europe.

She tapped her finger on a spot high on the German coastline. "Right here. It was nearly dusk last night."

"When did you arrive back here?" he asked.

"About ten o'clock last night."

"And you waited until this morning before making a report to the authorities?"

"I was rather shaken last night."

Sanderson said nothing.

"Even when I called this morning I don't think the constable believed what I was telling him. You have to admit, it sounds rather fantastic. He asked if I'd been drinking—which I have been known to do."

"You shouldn't have waited," Sanderson said. "To not immediately report something like this is a crime in itself."

"It's also a crime to impersonate a police officer."

For the second time in a matter of minutes, she had him off-balance.

Magnussen gave a wry smile. "Your credentials expired years ago, Inspector. I have very good eyesight."

"And I have very little patience for games. This man is dangerous. Did he offer you money? Is that why you've given him a head start?"

"Possibly. But I could also say I felt threatened. He shot my airplane—I can show you the damage."

"Anything else?"

She cocked her head to one side. "In all honesty—I rather liked him."

Sanderson leaned forward on the table, feeling suddenly weak.

"Are you all right?" she asked.

"Yes, I . . . I'm fine."

She looked at him doubtfully, then said, "So now you know my story. But what are *you* doing here?"

"I'm a policeman."

"Not according to your paperwork."

"All right, I'll grant you that. I'm here unofficially. Until recently I was heading up the search for this man. I was put off the case for a medical issue, but I don't like leaving things unfinished."

"I know who he is," Magnussen said. "I've been watching the news reports—all that uproar in Stockholm."

Sanderson nodded.

"So where do we go from here?" she asked. "Will you call back to headquarters and tell them everything I've said? Or would that put you in an awkward position?"

He said nothing.

Magnussen took a rag and began erasing a line on her map. "We're both in a fix, aren't we, Inspector?"

"Perhaps we could adopt a broader view," said a circumspect Sanderson. "You were abducted by this man. He threatened you at gunpoint, so you felt intimidated for a time. But eventually you called the police. I don't see that you've done much wrong."

"Even if he were going to send me money? That's what you suggested."

"Did I? I'd already forgotten about that. My memory isn't what it used to be."

"Would you vouch for all this?" she asked.

"I might. Under the right circumstances."

"Which are?"

Sanderson told her.

Janna Magnussen gave him a wide grin "You know, Inspector—I think I'm beginning to like you as well."

For two hundred years Zurich's Bahnhofstrasse has been the recognized financial center of Switzerland. It is where banking icons Credit Suisse and UBS have long made their homes, housed in buildings that are as solid and enduring as the Alps, yet muted with just enough architectural vagueness to give clients—they are never called customers—the impression that while their money is unerringly present, it is not necessarily accounted for. The balance of the street's tenants are a more candid bunch. Gucci, Coach, and Cartier are all here, and their sales staffs clearly well fed. Bahnhofstrasse is clean, safe, and polished. There is not a crack in the sidewalk to catch a Christian Louboutin heel, and the shells dropped by squirrels onto the heads of tolerant passersby are soon swept clear. It is a place with a great many attributes. What it does not have is public phones.

For a two euro tip, Slaton made his call from the bar of a waking basement nightclub. He dialed a number he had memorized years ago, and it was answered efficiently, almost certainly by the same woman he'd spoken with the last time he'd called.

"Krueger Wealth Management."

"Yes," Slaton said, "I'd like to make an appointment with Herr Krueger."

"Are you an existing client, sir?"

"I am. The name is Natan Mendelsohn. Please inform Herr Krueger that I will join him for dinner this evening at Il Dolce. Seven o'clock."

A hesitation. "Sir, Herr Krueger is already committed this evening to meet a long-standing client who—"

"Just give him the name, the time, and the place. He will see me. And tell him to please bring the package he's been holding."

Slaton did not wait for a reply.

Arne Sanderson did not like airplanes. He particularly did not like small airplanes. Small airplanes that took off and landed on the sea, in his mind, were a clear defilement of physical laws.

All the same, here he was.

They had taken off three hours earlier, Sanderson watching the Swedish coastline slip in and out of view amid the clouds until it disappeared completely. Since then Magnussen had been flying on instruments in heavy weather. In a way Sanderson was happy, because the gray shroud around them gave no perception of height or speed or movement—they were simply floating in a bubble of moisture with no sense of up or down.

"How is the weather where we're going?" he asked.

Magnussen pulled her headset away from the nearest ear. "It's still good," she said. "We should have no trouble landing. I'll have you at the seaplane dock at Sassnitz in roughly twenty minutes. Do you have your passport? There are immigration controls."

Sanderson was happy that it had been in his car. "Yes, I've got it. But I have to ask you again—are you sure this man didn't give you any idea where he was heading?"

She shook her head. "Sorry. But from his point of view, why would he?"

Magnussen pushed the plane into a descent and

soon they were skimming under the clouds, the northern coastline of Germany rising in front of them. Sanderson gripped his armrests as the sea came closer, and his eyes were shut tight when the airplane settled to the water with surprising smoothness. Minutes later he was standing on a floating dock, much like the one from which he'd boarded back in Oxelösund. Magnussen had a brief conversation with a man about fuel before walking over and offering her hand.

"Our bargain is complete, is it not?"

Sanderson shook her tiny hand. "Such as it is. Have a safe flight back."

"What will you do from here?" she asked.

Sweeping his eyes across the place, Sanderson said, "I'll be damned if I know."

THIRTY-TWO

It was a mystery to many how Walter Krueger, a man of reputable upbringing and high acquaintances, had gone adrift at the crest of life. He'd been born into a solid Zurich family, and as a young boy attended the most prestigious private academies. On graduating from university he married a woman of impeccable pedigree, not the least of whose attributes involved being the lone daughter of a prominent banker. So it was, when Krueger began his corporate climb it was with a solid midlevel job at one of the largest banks in Switzerland, rapid advancement a given. His home life showed equal promise when it became apparent that his wife's bland figure disguised a thriving fertility. Within eight years of landing at Bank Suisse, Walter Krueger was the assistant director of investor relations, and he had to his credit six children, a ski chalet in Klosters, and a raging peptic ulcer. For a Swiss banker, life was as it should have been.

Then, one early spring day four years ago, Walter Krueger had lost it all. The investigation was born from a trivial act of spite—a low-level clerk, terminated for failing a drug test, had before he was sacked manipulated routing numbers and forged his supervisor's signature, having the effect of diverting the bank's entire quarterly tax disbursement to a vice president's personal brokerage account. The mischief was quickly sorted, but not before the bank examiners had stuck their noses in. During the course of their inquiry Krueger fell under separate scrutiny, in particular his dealings with a wealthy Israeli, rumored to be an arms dealer, who generated great sums of dollars to be legitimized in the form of Swiss government bonds and U.S. Treasury certificates. With the bank regulators circling, Krueger was called to a meeting with the firm's board—his father-in-law centered between four equally unsmiling men. Krueger walked out of that meeting unemployed. He was permitted by the bank to keep the contents of his desk, and by his father-in-law to keep his wife and children. The client in question was quietly asked to do business elsewhere, and the sated bank examiners flapped onward to the next carcass. With Walter Krueger sacrificed, everyone went back to the business at hand.

This was where Krueger had surprised many of those who knew him. At the age of forty-one, and shored comfortably by his wife's fortune, he could well have retired to the chalet with Greta and their six children. He did not. Perhaps harboring an ill vision of some kind of Von Trapp existence in the Tyrolean Alps, Walter Krueger took a different path. If his reputation was ruined, his qualifications remained intact, and he struck out to open his own private bank, leasing a small suite in a bland building in the shadows of the Bahnhofstrasse giants.

His first client, by no coincidence, was a wealthy Israeli looking for less obvious rinse cycles for his soiled assets. His name was Benjamin Grossman, and he was indeed an arms merchant. Krueger set out by retaining a good lawyer, actually an entire firm, and was soon testing the curbs of law and privacy to manage Grossman's money. It was a delicate operation, but the fees and margins Krueger demanded, and that Grossman allowed, were percentages that would have given his father-in-law palpitations.

The workings of Israel's top arms merchant did not escape Mossad. Certain branches of the Israeli government—Shin Bet and Aman among them—had logged substantial files on the opaque dealings of Benjamin Grossman, indeed enough to shut him down had they been of that mind. But Mossad's director at the time, Anton Bloch, was always one to put opportunity above justice. He reasoned that a recognized and well-financed arms dealer, already in cahoots with a dexterous Swiss banker, could prove invaluable for Israel as a *sayan*, a Hebrew word that translated roughly to "helper." Across the world, these were Mossad's enablers, men and women who offered money, influence, and expertise to advance the Israeli cause. In the case of Grossman, all Mossad needed was a trusted agent to make their delicate connection, and they found him—or created him actually—in the persona of Natan Mendelsohn. Krueger Asset Management had found its second client, alias David Slaton.

Il Dolce was as pretentious a restaurant as resided on Bahnhofstrasse, superb food and vintage wine at ruinous prices. More directly, it was a place where business was done. Slaton watched the restaurant from across the street, a bookstore with a good view of the entrance, and saw Krueger arrive, punctually and alone, and disappear inside. He kept watching for five minutes, then walked up the street for a secondary inspection. He saw nothing out of place.

Slaton had scouted the area earlier, and spent ten minutes inside the restaurant, ostensibly to make a reservation. The place was exactly as he remembered. He had met Krueger here on four previous occasions, two of these with the arms dealer Grossman also in attendance. Over Il Dolce's exquisite beef and fowl, the three had coordinated funding and arms shipments for a series of Mossad initiatives, the details always later knotted in the privacy of Krueger's office. In time, the operation with Grossman had gone dormant, Anton Bloch sensing too much risk. It was a loose end Slaton had never had the chance to clean up, and one that he now hoped Mossad had forgotten about.

He found Krueger at the reserved table, a quiet corner near a fire exit. The banker had a menu in hand, but spotted Slaton straightaway.

Krueger rose and extended his hand. "Monsieur Mendelsohn, how good to see you. It has been a long time. You look well." He kept to the English they'd always preferred.

Slaton shook his hand. "It's good to see you, Walter."

They took their respective seats. Krueger was as Slaton remembered: big and plump with a horseshoe of close-cropped hair around his balding crown, a great marshmallow of a man in a thousand-dollar Italian suit. Yet if his exterior was soft, his gaze was as keen as his investment results implied. Slaton's most compelling question was one he could not ask. He wondered if Mossad had come back in his absence to install a surrogate for Natan Mendelsohn. If so, it would be written on Krueger's face right now. It was not. The man looked unbothered, even happy to see him.

"I've been abroad for some time," Slaton said.

"Pleasure or business?" Krueger asked.

"Only business. Men like us have little time for the other, no?"

"*D'accord*. My chalet in the Alps has been gathering dust since last winter."

"Business is good then?"

"Reasonably so," replied Krueger. "The Americans have been pushing our government for more transparency in banking, yet only when it comes to those who owe taxes to their IRS."

The two exchanged a knowing smile and were soon chatting about families, Slaton hoping he remembered correctly the number of children birthed by the fictional Natalya Mendelsohn. The waiter came and took their order, and everyone switched languages. In Zurich business was conducted in English, contracts written in Swiss German, and dinner ordered in French. It all created a degree of confusion, but this was not unintended. If clients did not get what they expected, salesmen, attorneys, and chefs all had a reasonable case for missed communications. Krueger selected duck a l'orange, Slaton grilled trout Ruden. A pair of martinis found their way to the table and, after a toast to nothing in particular, Slaton took the helm.

"Did you bring my package?" he asked.

"Of course." Krueger reached into his jacket and pulled out a sealed envelope, slightly larger than a standard letter. "It has been in my safe for fifteen months now."

Slaton took the envelope, pocketed it, and said, "I haven't seen an account statement in some time—did you bring one?"

Krueger went ashen. "Statement?" A long hesitation, then, "The account you speak of . . . are you not aware that it was brought to zero some months ago?"

"Was it?"

"By your own attorney."

"My attorney."

"The woman who came to see me. The papers were completely in order," Krueger said uneasily, "your limited power of attorney. All perfectly valid and certified. I don't see how—"

Slaton held up a hand to put the Swiss at ease. "Yes, I understand all that. I made the authorization, of course. But nothing at all remains in the account?"

"The account itself is intact, as your attorney directed. Quite clear. But the balance is zero. All funds were transferred to the bank in Tel Aviv."

Slaton considered this. It made a certain sense. There had been perhaps twenty thousand U.S. in the account when he'd last seen it, along with a smaller secondary standing in zero-coupon Swiss bonds. Were Mossad's bean counters only being meticulous? Recovering funds gone astray? Or was there something more? That the account had been left alive struck Slaton as unusual. Procedurally, it would have been more typical for Mossad to close it, effectively cutting all ties to Grossman. But then it occurred to Slaton that leaving the account open was like setting an alarm. If inquiries were made, perhaps by the police or bank examiners, Mossad would be forewarned. Yes, he thought, that made sense. A tripwire—and one that he had just activated. Slaton twirled his martini by the stem of its glass, hoping idly that Krueger would offer to pay for dinner. He needed cash, needed it now, and while there were any number of ways to acquire funds, all entailed a certain amount of time. A certain amount of risk. His entire approach to Geneva would have to be rethought.

"I hope I have acted to your satisfaction," Krueger prattled.

"Yes," Slaton said distractedly, "the timeline of those transactions escaped me for a moment, but it doesn't matter."

Krueger beamed. "*Bon*." The banker then turned tentative, lowering his voice amid the burble of conversation around them—a man about to voice serious concerns. "I am happy to have not disappointed you, monsieur. There is, in fact, a separate matter we should discuss."

"A separate matter?"

"I have been trying unsuccessfully to reach you for many months. The address I have on file, the postal box in Oxford, seems to have reverted. And your previous phone number has been disconnected. I even tried to contact you through your attorney, but she and her staff seem to have taken an extended holiday. They do not return my calls."

Krueger paused, clearly hoping for some explanation. Slaton said nothing.

"I was quite happy to find the message from Astrid today saying that you had returned. Are you aware of our friend Grossman's passing?"

Slaton's head tilted ever so slightly. "No. I'd heard nothing about it."

"It was rather sudden, I'm afraid. Some type of cancer last summer. Such a thing . . ." Krueger turned wistful, creases straining his banker's veneer. "For a man to have so much, only to see life slip away."

"When did he die?"

"August, I think it was, in Basel. He had the best doctors, of course, but there was nothing to be done."

Slaton now understood why Mossad had not installed a surrogate for their dealings with Grossman. With the man terminally ill, and Slaton listed as killed in action, the House of Krueger had to be cleansed—no lingering stray funds, no taxes accruing, no embarrassing contractual obligations. The only loose end was a single open-ended account dangling like a baitless hook.

"I assumed that you knew he was ill," Krueger said, "since the two of you often did business together. In fact, I originally thought this was why you had sent your attorney to conclude our dealings."

"No, that was a separate matter."

"I trust you weren't displeased with my performance."

"No, not at all. But you said you were trying to contact me. Why?"

"Soon after Monsieur Grossman's passing I was contacted by his legal firm." Krueger paused, seemingly puzzled. "Did you know him well—personally, I mean?"

"Not really. Our relationship was strictly business. I know he was Swiss, from Basel as you say, and I remember that he spent a fair amount of time in Central Africa."

"Were you aware that he had no family?"

"No, it never really came up."

"Monsieur Grossman never married." Krueger leaned in conspiratorially. "Between the two of us, I think he may have preferred men." The banker let one hand fall limp at the wrist.

"I wouldn't know anything about that," Slaton lied. In truth, Mossad had solid proof of Grossman's homosexuality, including a number of telling photographs. It was the kind of thing intelligence agencies loved to mine, although in an increasingly tolerant world, garden variety homosexuality was of little use outside politicians and the clergy.

"His parents died years ago," the financier

continued, "and he had no long-term partner, no brothers or sisters. As he neared his end, however, Grossman had the presence of mind to make plans. You impressed him, monsieur. More to the point, he said you were closely tied to a worthy cause, one that he supported wholeheartedly."

The waiter interrupted with two well-presented plates. Krueger wasted no time, ripping into his duck with gusto. Slaton took a more reserved approach, savoring the best meal he'd had in weeks.

Krueger pulled a bone from his mouth with a *plop*, and said, "I should put it to you clearly. In his last days, Grossman met with his attorneys. He made a new will, Mr. Mendelsohn, one that designates you as the receiver of his estate."

Slaton diverted from his own meal. "He left me something to distribute?"

"Practically speaking—he left you everything. In legal terms it is not a personal bequest, but rather a trust, the kind of thing lawyers are paid great sums to create. As a practical matter, however, there are no restrictions regarding the management of the estate. I've already seen to it that all tax matters are satisfied—we Swiss can be very unforgiving about such things. You are the lone trustee, effectively in control of Grossman's legacy. He was convinced that you would find good use for it."

"Yes . . . I'm sure I will," Slaton replied. He was caught off-guard, but in fact had seen such arrangements before. Grossman had no heirs, and the dealings of his dubious life had instilled that most powerful of urges for a man at death's door—a guilty conscience. There was probably more to it. Perhaps grandparents who'd died in a concentration camp, or an old lover who'd been killed by a Hezbollah suicide bomber. If

Slaton were to look closely enough at the colorful life of Benjamin Grossman, it would be there.

"Aren't you going to ask?" Krueger said, giddy with anticipation.

"Ask what?"

"How much."

Slaton did ask.

Krueger told him.

THIRTY-THREE

Farzad Behrouz could see little to distinguish the door he was watching from a hundred others along the dust-caked street in central Molavi. The apartment was situated on the first floor of a five-story affair, a welcome advantage—surprise was far easier to keep without ten sets of boots clambering up switchback staircases. He watched a cat on the front step nose hopefully around an empty saucer. There was one window on the face of the flat, at this hour closed and in south Tehran certainly locked, and behind the glass was a small flowering plant that looked oddly vibrant in the dim light.

The four cars were in position, three on the front street and one in the back alley, the last team not meant to take part, but simply there for containment should any vermin scurry out the back door. Standard procedure. There were no lights on inside the flat, and had not been since nine-thirty—this from the advance surveillance group—which implied that their target had been asleep for roughly an hour. Satisfied, Behrouz chopped a finger from his seat in the lead car to set the assault in motion.

Ten men spilled into the street. It was probably

eight more than they needed, but then shock was always an intended subtheme. The two men in the lead, carrying a hundred-pound battering ram, didn't bother to knock. They hit the door on a dead run and it yielded to a single blow, slamming back hard and then hanging by its hinges in the aftermath at an awkward angle, rather like a drunk clinging to a lamppost.

The cat ran for its life.

Behrouz watched his team disappear with a trace of regret. He'd done his share of late-night door knocking, early in his career, and he remembered the thrill. Tonight, however, unlike the recent synagogue campaign, he could not take part. He wondered what was happening inside, and admonished himself for not having his men wired so he could monitor their chatter. His reasons for not personally taking part were summed up in that American-coined phrase he had grown to relish: plausible deniability. Behrouz was on a limb to even order this raid, and to be seen as actively involved could prove problematic—a definite risk when every urchin on the street had a smartphone with a camera. As the head of state security, there were only a handful of men in Iran who could call Behrouz to account. But no head of state security was without enemies.

Behrouz saw a flashlight beam slash across the window, and then shadows scurried past the open doorway. He heard a crash as something was overturned, and then the woman's voice barked, loud and indignant. He frowned. After twenty minutes, the leader of the search team trotted out. Behrouz rolled his window halfway down.

"Well?" he asked impatiently.

"Nothing."

Behrouz cursed under his breath. To this point the stakes were minimal, but pressing further would raise the risk considerably.

"Do we take her into custody and keep looking?" the man asked.

Behrouz was still for a long moment. They had been watching the old hen for six hours, ever since her son's motorcade had left. And they'd been discreetly asking questions for a week. By all accounts she was a kindly old soul, well-liked by her neighbors. A distributor of cakes to children and supper to the indigent. None of this told Behrouz what he wanted to know.

He finally said, "No. Tell her a mistake was made and apologize. Say the local police reported a drug stash in the building."

The brute looked at him as if he'd just been told to dance the tango. "We're letting her go?"

"Yes, you idiot! Do it!"

The man plodded off toward the house.

The team was clear three minutes later. They tumbled into their cars and the black convoy re-formed, and as Tehran eased toward midnight the team slithered away under a trail of dust. Before turning the corner, Behrouz looked back and saw the old woman appear in her doorway. She paused at the threshold for a moment, hands on her hips in a nightdress and staring indignantly. Then, in a final act of defiance, Ibrahim Hamedi's mother reached out and pulled her shattered door closed.

"You're sure?" Nurin asked.

"Yes," said Ezra Zacharias. "The account was checked on the client's behalf earlier today."

"And why are we monitoring this account?" inquired Veron.

The three men were at the conference table in Nurin's bunker, seated on three opposing corners. The Star of David flag hung limply on a staff behind Veron, as still as the air in their subterranean vault. Daylight had left the city above hours ago, but there were no windows here to prove it. That was what Nurin had never liked about this place—you never had a true sense of what time it was.

"The man who's been giving us trouble in Stockholm," Nurin explained, "he was once involved with this account. After what happened Sunday, I suspected he might attempt to access it. The account has long been inactive, but our man would have no way of knowing this."

"So he's one of us," said Veron.

"*Was*," Nurin corrected. "A long time ago."

"A *kidon*?"

Walking a thin line with his two lieutenants, Nurin decided the best reply was none at all.

Zacharias said, "This attempt to access the account—what does it mean?"

"It means he is in Switzerland. It means he needs money, but hasn't found any."

"Money?" questioned Veron. "For what purpose?"

Nurin chose his words carefully. "He has harmed us once. He may try to do so again."

"But why?" implored Veron. "You still haven't said what the former director was doing in Stockholm. Why did he contact this American woman?"

Nurin sat back in his chair and looked pointedly at the ceiling. Both his subordinates remained silent as he churned to a decision. When the director's eyes came down, they settled on Veron.

"What kind of force can you have in Switzerland in twenty-four hours?"

"Twenty-four hours? We always have one team on alert." Veron spoke with a commander's confidence. "Eight men."

"Do it. I want them standing by in Geneva tomorrow night."

"Geneva?"

"Yes. That's where he's going."

Veron hesitated visibly, everyone knowing his question. *How could you know this?* What he asked was, "And our mission?"

"If I give the word, I want you to find him."

"How? We barely have a description."

Nurin explained in detail where to look, and when, and added at the end, "Look for the man with a rifle."

After another long silence, a clearly frustrated Veron said, "And if we find him as you say?"

"Wait for my instructions. If he is *not* there—I may have another mission for you. Tell your best marksman to be ready."

Four hours after stepping onto German soil, Arne Sanderson was still walking. As night gathered, Sassnitz fell to a film noir landscape. All around him were utilitarian buildings set on industrial grade concrete, the sort of corrugated aluminum boxes no reputable architect would ever admit to creating. Smoke from the exhaust of countless vehicles mixed with chimney risings from pocket neighborhoods, altogether giving the air a rough-hewn edge of diesel and soot.

Sanderson trudged along a gravel railroad siding, head down and collar high, and tried to collate what he knew. Before landing—if that was what you called it in a seaplane—Magnussen had shown him where she'd dropped the American, a small cove a few miles up the coast. From there the shoreline was empty in either direction, and Sassnitz the only civilization nearby. As he sidestepped across the rails, heading for the town's transportation hub, Sanderson was comfortable concluding that this was where Deadmarsh had come.

Unfortunately, it only led to a larger question. Before leaving Sweden, Sanderson had taken the time to reference Janna Magnussen's flight planning table. He'd drawn a line south from Sweden across the Baltic, and in doing so had proved his suspicion that Poland was a more direct escape. There were also any number of other options on the compass. West to Norway, or east to Latvia or Estonia.

Why did you come here? he wondered.

Sanderson crossed the entrance of a holding yard, his feet pressing gravel into wet earth, and he tried to see it all as the assassin would have. A busy transfer point with a constant flow of trucks and boats. A rail yard with scheduled departures to firm destinations. Perhaps there was his answer. Why here? Because from Sassnitz a man could go virtually anywhere in Continental Europe with little chance of being tracked. It was an ideal waypoint. Yet as good as that theory was, it only led to another question. A waypoint to where? Without knowing where Deadmarsh was heading, he was grasping at air.

A gust swept leaves over the ground like so much October confetti, and Sanderson tucked his chin lower. He stopped in the rail terminal and talked to a few of the attendants, language an ongoing obstacle as he mixed halting German with English. *I'm looking for a man who might have passed through yesterday. Six foot one, fair hair, unshaven. Name? I don't know. Where was he going? I'm not sure.* He was persuaded by a night watchman to ask a ticket agent, and the ticket agent told him to try the taxi stand. After ten minutes and six sets of shrugged shoulders, Sanderson gave up on a quest that bordered on the ridiculous.

He went back outside where the night's coolness hit him. He plodded over service roads and circled warehouses, looking for any inspiration. He came upon a large parking apron where trucks and shipping containers were lined in rows. At the back he saw an assortment of parked recreational vehicles. Sanderson walked up to the access point feeling strangely lightheaded. A tiny gatehouse was staffed by a middle-aged woman, and he saw an identification badge hanging round her neck on a lanyard. Her name was Helga. She was engaged in an intense conversation with a swarthy, younger man, but both fell silent when Sanderson came within earshot.

She said something in German that Sanderson didn't understand. He replied with, "Do either of you speak English?"

"Some," said the woman.

"I'm a policeman from Sweden. I'm here looking for . . ." Sanderson drew a blank. His mind seemed to freeze, like a computer in need of a reboot. He looked all around. The lights overhead seemed particularly bright, glowing banks that cast the cargo yard in a watery amber hue. His gaze settled on a light pole that seemed to divide as he looked at it. His head felt like it might split.

"You are all right?" the man asked.

"No, I . . ." Sanderson struggled for words, any words. What came out was, "Could you . . . tell me . . .

tell me if there's a hotel nearby. I'm not feeling at all well."

One point three billion dollars.

The pub was just off Bahnhofstrasse, an English-Irish theme struck in dark hardwood, brass rails, and electric ale signs. Slaton sat alone, parked on a high stool and leaning into a beer the color of Brent Sea crude. It was a necessary prop—without it he'd have been the only person in the place with two free hands.

He sat facing the pub's front window, watching expensive cars stream past in a constant flow, streaks of chrome glinting in the bright streetlights and neon spill. It was eight-thirty on a Wednesday evening, and the pub was stocked with bankers and bookkeepers and civil servants, a general aggregate of upward-aspiring Swiss. They were a well-lubricated bunch, loosened ties over designer shirts, leather-booted legs under tight skirts. Everyone was slapping backs and carrying on in a way that said they had not just arrived. Slaton studied them one by one, perhaps out of habit. He saw nothing to raise a warning flag, yet for some reason kept at it. Watching and listening. He heard conversations that held not a whit of intelligence value. Girlfriends and promotions. Hot investment tips and vacations to Mallorca. He had heard it all before, a hundred different times in a hundred different bars. Yet tonight it sank differently as he filtered the trite and mundane through his newfound prism.

Slaton had worked for Mossad since the day he'd graduated from university. He had never held a proper job, never worried about financial markets or office parties or impressing a boss. The next mission—that had been his creed, his driving principle. An instructor from sniper school had once jested that to be an assassin was akin to being a priest. Morals aside, once you were ordained you could never be anything else. Was it really true?

U.S. dollars. One point three billion.

He'd sat there for a time staring dumbly at Krueger, his fork stuck in a trout. But then, what could one say to such a thing? Benjamin Grossman, heartless merchant of death and closet homosexual, had amassed an absolute fortune. And now he had given it to Slaton, or more succinctly, given it to Slaton to be funneled for the benefit of Israel. In the identity of Natan Mendelsohn, Slaton had never been anything more than an intermediary, his objective to win Grossman's trust and act as his link to the homeland. He remembered discussing Israel and her issues with the man on a number of occasions, because this too was part of his mission—Mossad had to be sure Grossman would make a trustworthy *sayan*. But this?

This Slaton had never expected.

He had faced a great many dilemmas in his years, often matters of life and death. Tonight's revelation was trivial on its face, yet carried an underlying trauma. He would meet with Krueger in his office tomorrow to finalize the trust. Given the size of the bequest, Krueger estimated that full execution would take a matter of weeks as the Swiss authorities stamped documents, verified signatures, and, most importantly, double-checked that all revenue due the canton was collected. The only requirement on Slaton's part was to certify himself to be Natan Mendelsohn, and proof of this was now in his pocket, returned in a sealed envelope after a year in the banker's safe.

At the time it had seemed a good insurance policy,

and now Slaton patted himself on the back for his foresight. He was once again Natan Mendelsohn, and had the Swiss identity card and passport to prove it. Both were Mossad products, although likely noncurrent and erased from official databases. They would be useless for entering another country, and no good to show a policeman. But Slaton didn't need that. Natan Mendelsohn was in Switzerland and would remain there for the rest of his fabricated life. He could use the identity to sign Herr Krueger's papers in front of a lawyer. He could register at respectable Swiss hotels and draw money from respectable cash accounts. On face value the documents were perfect, every stamp and hologram in place, and the photographs of Slaton displaying a textbook fusion of pain and indifference. A man irritated at having to replace expired items. A man who didn't have to be told not to smile. For the immediate future, the identity of Natan Mendelsohn suited him perfectly.

His dinner with Krueger had been a blur after the bombshell, but Slaton had not completely lost his focus. On leaving Il Dolce, in an awkward moment, the newly minted billionaire explained to his banker that he had lost his wallet. Krueger had given him a hundred Swiss francs and arranged for a room at a nearby hotel. Slaton suspected that Krueger would have bought him a hotel if he'd asked—whatever it took to maintain a long-term lock on a ten-digit investment account. At the usurious percentages Krueger charged, he would never need another client.

"Another for you?"

Slaton looked up at a smiling waitress. He snapped back his head, downed the last of his beer, and found himself saying, "Yes, please."

Slaton rarely drank, typically only to remain in

character, but tonight he wanted another. He'd been consumed by a singular thought as he walked here from the restaurant, stumbling through the chilled autumn air without a trace of countersurveillance—he likely wouldn't have noticed if Iran's black-robed clerics themselves had been parading up Bahnhofstrasse. The distraction was still with him as he sat drinking alone, watching the moneyed crowds brush past on newly paved streets and spotless sidewalks.

What if I just kept it? With that kind of money, Christine and I could disappear forever.

The logistics would be simple. Slaton could arrange the details with Krueger tomorrow—have the money distributed to numbered accounts, and then spread far and wide. The Caymans, Aruba, Switzerland. The moral question was even easier. Grossman had been a criminal, but also a Jew, and in the end his conscience had pushed him to leave his wealth to Israel—the country Slaton had nearly died for, but that now betrayed him in the purest sense.

And not for the first time.

Long ago, during his recruitment, Slaton had lost the first woman he'd loved and their child in the most banal of tragedies—killed in a random traffic accident. Yet Mossad had misrepresented that catastrophe, twisting the facts to meet its own ends. They had turned grief into hate, hoping to bias Slaton's psyche in order to channel his physical gifts. In order to create the perfect *kidon*. That had been another regime in Mossad, but the essential manipulation was unchanged. So Slaton would feel no angst in keeping the windfall from Grossman, not today and probably not tomorrow. The only thing left would be to retrieve Christine. Within a month they could be established in a new life in some warm and faraway place. And soon, the three of them, no attachments whatsoever to their old lives. A perpetual deception.

And there, he knew, was the catch. The reason it would never work. It was a lie Christine would never allow. Not for her, and certainly not for their child. Slaton took it no further, feeling like a beggar on a cold street staring at a vacation poster in a travel agent's window—imagining a trip to paradise you would never take. When his beer came he drank it quickly and settled the bill. Ten minutes later he found the hotel where Krueger had booked him a single night's stay. Slaton had never heard of the place, and when he walked inside he realized why. Lustrous marble floors, gilt accents, crystalline chandeliers.

The concierge greeted him and guessed his name. *Bags, Monsieur Mendelsohn? None tonight? Very well . . .* An elegant woman at the desk glanced at his passport and, deferring any bothersome signatures or swiped credit cards, he was soon being escorted to a palatial suite. Once alone, Slaton stood in a room with eighteen-foot ceilings and hand-painted murals. Louis XIV furnishings set delicately on ornate Persian rugs. Now that he was a billionaire, Slaton supposed it was only fitting that he should stay in a five-star hotel.

He could not contain a grin, thinking, *God, Christine, how I wish you were here for one night. In spite of all the rest, this would make you laugh.*

THIRTY-FOUR

Sanderson's eyes cracked open to darkness.

It was not pitch black that he saw but a dim geometry of shadows, black on gray, angled lines overhead. *Where am I?* he wondered. His head hurt and he rose slowly, gradually sitting up in what felt like a soft bed. Yes, he was in a bed. A clock on a nightstand shone bright red numbers: 9:34. Morning or evening?

He had no idea.

His eyes adapted to the gloom and shadows resolved. He saw a bathroom, a closet, and the outline of a small television. He was in a hotel room. With that revelation the dots began to connect. He remembered tracking an Israeli assassin across Sweden to the village of Oxelösund, followed by a harrowing passage in Janna Magnussen's crate of an airplane. Stepping onto the dock in Sassnitz, Germany, and then . . . and then nothing. Sanderson couldn't recall anything more, not even how he'd ended up in this room.

He pushed himself up and trod with sleep-heavy steps to the bathroom. There he was struck by the smell of harsh cleanser and cheap soap. He saw a shower with a rust-stained plug and sagging curtain, gray-plaster walls holding it all in. At the sink he turned on the hot water, got a frigid trickle, but splashed it on his face anyway because he wanted to feel something. His hand cupped his chin to find a coarse stubble, but Sanderson avoided the mirror, not wanting to see what stared back. Thirty-five years of police work took a toll on a man, and whatever ill had found him would do nothing to rejuvenate things.

He walked at a deliberate pace to the front window and fingered back the curtain. A mist-shrouded scene gave him one answer—it was morning. He saw a nearly empty parking lot, and in the distance a busy loading yard full of trucks and trailers. Fog aside, Sanderson thought it all looked vaguely familiar. His more personal haze began to break and he remembered walking—wandering really—in the course of his search for Deadmarsh. Yes, that was it. He'd covered considerable ground and gotten nowhere.

Sanderson glanced up at a flat leaden sky, and asked himself, "What now?"

His detective's brain craved a logical course, but he needed *something* to work with. He had no idea where Deadmarsh was heading, no picture of his suspect to show around. Sanderson had no authority. Not here, not anywhere. He was chasing a man who didn't exist, one whose identity had been obliterated. His suspect knew how to disappear, and had a full day's head start and an entire continent to work with. Against that, Sanderson had no more than his memory of the man's face, a hunch that he was likely Israeli, likely an assassin, and an unverified claim that he was married to a woman who had also disappeared. There, in a sorry nutshell, was the state of his investigation.

He looked around the dank room and saw nothing to indicate how he'd gotten here. *And now I'm forgetting things.* He was fully dressed, his clothes perhaps more rumpled than usual, and his wallet was still in his pocket. The only thing in the room he recognized was his worn jacket hanging over the back of a chair. He knew he hadn't been drinking, yet that was how it felt—like a thick hangover. A night unremembered.

What is wrong with me?

Noticing a room key on the dresser, Sanderson took it in hand, shrugged on his jacket, and ventured outside. The cool morning air clipped his face as he walked to the office. A woman there said he'd already paid for the room, one night charged to his credit card. *Well enough*, he thought. *But why don't I remember?* She had not been on duty last night, and so her only useful addition was that a diner around the corner served strong coffee. Sanderson surrendered his room key and thanked her.

He found the diner, seated himself, and ordered coffee, eggs, and toast from a waitress whose smile seemed permanently embossed—as if tomorrow could only be better. The first overbrewed cup of coffee energized Sanderson, and he began to get his bearings. He pulled out his phone and dialed Sergeant Blix.

"Good morning, Gunnar."

"Morning, Inspector. Where are you? Your daughter called an hour ago and said you weren't at home. She sounded worried."

"I'm fine. It's been a tough week, and I wanted to get away for a few days to convalesce. I'll give Annika a call so she doesn't worry. Is there anything new?"

"On the investigation you mean? That doesn't sound like convalescence."

Sanderson let his silence do the talking.

"The main news is that Deadmarsh used one of his credit cards yesterday."

"Where?"

"He bought a ferry ticket in Styrsvik. Apparently he was heading back to Stockholm from Runmarö Island. We tried to close him down, but there were only a few minutes to reach the docks. We missed him."

You missed him because he wasn't there, Sanderson thought. Based on what he knew, he reckoned that the woman, Dr. Palmer, had ditched her boat and was now aiding and abetting her husband. He considered telling Blix about his own findings—that Magnussen Air Charters had delivered their man to Germany. Sanderson saw two outcomes of this approach. Assistant Commissioner Sjoberg might surmise that his sacked detective was chasing ghosts, in which case Sanderson would be ordered home. And if Sjoberg believed him? Then Sanderson would have to explain why he hadn't called sooner. He felt himself sliding down a slippery slope—and accelerating.

He let Blix talk for five minutes, promised to keep in touch, and then called his daughter and told her not to worry. Sanderson dialed a third number as two eggs were being pushed across the green Formica counter in front of him. Elin Almgren from SÄPO answered.

"Elin, it's Arne."

"Good to hear from you, Arne. How are you feeling?"

"If one more person asks me that I'm going to go on a shooting spree."

She chortled.

"What's happening there?" he asked.

"It's been confirmed—the man in a coma is definitely Anton Bloch, director of Mossad until about a year ago."

"So Deadmarsh was telling the truth."

"He was. The Ministry of Foreign Affairs is paralyzed over how to handle it. SÄPO is operating on the principle that Deadmarsh, his wife, and Bloch are on one side of this fight. Everyone else seems to be against them."

"Including us, bunglers that we are."

Almgren continued without remark, "I can also tell you that one of the men Deadmarsh dispatched at the Tea Room has been positively identified. He was an employee at the Israeli embassy in Stockholm."

"Mossad?"

"Almost certainly."

"Well that's no surprise. So perhaps this is some kind of old guard versus new guard problem? Mossad turning on itself?"

"That's the common wisdom here—although I hate to use that word."

"So what's being done?"

"Everyone is still looking for them, of course. But the head office is quietly backing off, hoping this has run its course."

"And Deadmarsh will just fade away, never to be seen again?"

"Something like that. They're convinced this was an internal Mossad dust-up. Any threat has ended."

"Do you believe it?" he asked.

A pause. "Not really. You?"

"No."

"I can tell you that the National Police are downplaying the investigation. Give this a week, maybe two, and people will forget. Maybe you should do the same, Arne. The man you're after is probably back in Israel right now. Or maybe the United States."

"No, I don't think so."

Almgren waited for his reasoning.

Sanderson only said, "What about his wife?"

"She's the wild card. Caught in the middle of it, I'd

say. Honestly, I wouldn't be surprised if she turned up at the bottom of a very cold body of water. Maybe an old score of some kind has been settled. We've pressed the Israelis for an explanation, but as you'd expect they're keeping a very diplomatic silence."

There was a long pause as she let Sanderson dwell on the information. "Let's assume," he said, "that Deadmarsh actually is an Israeli assassin. Does SÄPO keep files on people like that?"

"An Israeli *kidon*? In our files? No way. Not many countries have people like that on their payrolls, and the ones that do guard identities very closely."

Sanderson sighed. "Yes, I suppose they would, but could you look into it all the same? Anything would help—I'm really up against a wall."

"For you? Not a chance. But you've piqued my interest. Meet me at the Flying Horse in an hour?"

"I can't—I'm not in Stockholm."

Another long silence.

"All right," she said, "I'll call you back."

Sharply at ten that morning Slaton reached Bahnhofstrasse 81 with his customary reconnaissance complete. He was not worried about the police—not yet anyway—but Mossad was a definite concern. He had no idea where he stood with Director Nurin, but having tripped the inactive account there was a chance that Tel Aviv might be watching Herr Krueger. But only if they were very astute—and very quick.

At street level the building was staid and colorless, with a granite foundation that seemed to rise from the bedrock. Yet in the roofline Slaton saw distinct Baroque leanings, theatrical wings and ledges that made him think the place might have once been a church.

Perhaps some long-forgotten denomination that had slipped into holy receivership during one of Europe's Bohemian upswings.

He passed through an imposing set of doors and saw the usual directory of tenants, interchangeable white lettering on black felt. There were five listings—a number that had not changed since Slaton's first visit—and KAM, Krueger Asset Management, still resided in suite 4.

In the office he was greeted by Astrid, the woman he'd spoken with on the phone, and ushered in directly to find a chipper Krueger. Seated across the desk from the banker was a second man Slaton had never met. The stranger's dress, not to mention the briefcase in his lap, suggested he was a lawyer. Slaton, however, was never inclined to simple assumption. He paused at the heavy door, still ajar, which put him one step removed from the thick-walled outer office.

"Good morning, Monsieur Mendelsohn!" said a beaming Krueger. An obligatory hand-pump was followed by, "How did you find your room at Le Chateau?"

"Very nice, thank you. In all honesty, a bit above the standards I'm used to."

"But no more, eh?" Krueger patted him on the shoulder as if he were an old college chum. "Allow me to introduce Herr Holmberg. He is the lead attorney in the matter of this estate."

Slaton shook hands and saw nothing worrisome in Holmberg. The man moved efficiently—not in the way of a killer, but in the way of a bookkeeper, his eyes focused inwardly on documents, his delicate fingers sure and purposeful. His feet were set narrowly, such that he could not rise quickly and keep good balance. His open briefcase was a black leather article with gold-plated locks, and inside Slaton saw a single file that looked unusually thick and heavy. A lawyer, perhaps, who billed by the pound and not the hour. Three pens were holstered in a dividing flap, and next to these three pencils. Slaton could see only the eraser ends of the pencils, but he was sure that each was perfectly sharpened. He stepped away from the door and took a seat.

The model of efficiency known as Astrid produced a silver tray bearing coffee and biscuits, and on this cue the meeting commenced. The lawyer spent a full thirty minutes covering Swiss inheritance law. He explained that bequests to direct heirs were normally compulsory, yet not a concern in this case because Grossman had no family. Holmberg confirmed that the legacy would pass without restriction to Natan Mendelsohn, with the intent of guiding it toward the unnamed charity that he "kept close ties with." Slaton had never before heard the State of Israel referred to as a charity, but he supposed there was no other way for Grossman to have designed things. One cannot name Mossad as beneficiary to an estate.

Ten signatures later, Holmberg was stuffing papers back into his briefcase.

Slaton, having been given a stack of duplicate documents, asked, "Is there a detailed property listing here?"

"Yes, of course," said Holmberg, pointing his gold-tipped pen toward the papers. "Addendum Three contains a precise inventory of all assets, cross-referenced to the valuations in Addendum Six."

What could be more Swiss? Slaton thought, but did not say, as he flipped through and found what he wanted. He nodded approvingly.

With that, the lawyer snapped his briefcase shut

and made a professional exit. When they were alone Krueger began the pitch Slaton knew was coming.

"So, as Holmberg has advised, we can expect no more than a few weeks for probate administration to run its course. Your friend Grossman was right to have put his affairs in order." He sipped from a delicate china cup. "As the sole beneficiary of this estate you are faced with many important decisions. As you know, I have considerable experience in managing private accounts. Monsieur Grossman was, I think, quite happy with my results. I understand that a certain percentage of these funds will go to the foundation you keep ties with. I should advise you, however, that it could be in everyone's best interest to retain a portion of the assets in reserve to . . . shall we say, construct a more permanent endowment. I think you could expect continued healthy returns using a strategy of—"

"Herr Krueger," Slaton interrupted, "please allow me a moment." Slaton pushed his own teacup aside, and his gray eyes leveled on the Swiss. "As you know, our late acquaintance was a man whose business skirted the bounds of . . . shall we say 'propriety.' I should tell you that I too have certain interests I would choose not be open to the light of day. Indeed, that is why we are both here in this quiet little office, is it not?"

Krueger shrugged and turned up his palms on his desk. "*D'accord, monsieur.*"

"Then we should not play games. You have a talent for characterizing money so that it does not draw attention, and subsequently using it to make more. I have a need for that service. The bargain I will give you is this: It is now ten forty-five. By close of business today you will provide me the equivalent of ten thousand U.S. dollars, split evenly between dollars and

Swiss francs. In addition, you will make a reservation in your own name for one week at the Montreux Casino, beginning tomorrow night, and advise the hotel that I am to arrive as your guest. You will then deposit in advance fifty thousand Swiss francs for my use at their tables."

"*Fifty thousand?* Monsieur, this is a good deal of money. There are laws to be considered."

"If I was worried about laws, Herr Krueger, I would not be here but down the street at UBS. I am sure you have cash reserves, other client accounts, money in escrow. You are a private banker and a clever man. You also know that in a matter of weeks the benefits of this legacy will cover everything and more. If you can make these things happen, I will employ you to manage my account on a continuing basis, with a fee structure unchanged from your arrangement with Grossman. Will you agree to these terms?"

Krueger was beginning to glisten, no longer interested in his coffee. Slaton could almost see the commission numbers ringing in his head. "Yes, five o'clock today, ten thousand. And the other. Yes, I can manage."

"Good. But we have more ground to cover."

Krueger actually tugged on the collar of his shirt.

"You will not hear from me for some time, likely many months. When I see you later today, I will execute the papers necessary to allow you to manage this inheritance. My instructions are as follows. When the funds become available, you will split them evenly among ten numbered accounts. From there you will initiate a series of transfers. The Caymans, Bahamas, Aruba—I leave the specifics up to you. In the end, I want nothing—I repeat nothing—to remain in the name of Natan Mendelsohn. Incorporate, set up trusts or foundations if necessary. Once these accounts are established, you may select whatever investments you deem to be in our mutual best interest. Are we clear on everything so far?"

"Yes," Krueger said, "absolutely." He was about to stand when Slaton held out a palm to keep him in his seat.

"There are two last matters. First, the 'charity' referred to in Grossman's legacy. I can tell you that it is not your typical benevolent foundation. In truth, this organization is not a charity at all, and in my opinion not worthy of receiving any of this money under its current governance. As I have been entrusted to steer the inheritance, I will do so in the spirit I believe it was intended. This begins with the instructions you now have."

Slaton paused, and he imagined Krueger mulling the charitable merits of sending fifty thousand Swiss francs to a Montreux casino. To his credit the man remained silent, only nodding like the good banker he was.

"Finally," Slaton continued, his cadence slowing, "you are aware of the late Monsieur Grossman's gray business dealings. I dare say you are not so familiar with mine. To put it simply, those things that Grossman sold, I buy. I operate alone, and in the parlance of our small corner of the world, I am what is known as an 'end user.'"

Slaton let that settle before leaning slightly forward. "I expect you to hold to the most stringent standards of Swiss banking. Our arrangements must be kept absolutely privileged—discuss them with no one. And be very clear on one last point, Herr Krueger. If any, or perhaps all of this money should disappear, you will in fact never see me again. But even if you should find yourself in a very small and very quiet corner of the world, rest assured that I will see you once more. Precisely once."

The banker managed a weak smile. "Sir, I . . . I can assure you that my performance will leave no need for either of us to ever deviate from our arrangement."

The gray eyes smiled back. "Then as you say—we are in accord."

THIRTY-FIVE

Elin Almgren took slightly over an hour to call back. Sanderson, stirring cream into his second cup of coffee from a high stool, picked up immediately.

"Have you found anything?" he asked.

"A new Thai restaurant that makes a wonderful Panang curry."

"Please."

"Sex, Arne. Find some quickly."

Sanderson, patient man that he was, thought, *If she wasn't so damned good . . .*

"Here's what I have," Almgren said. "Our files are thin. Pure intelligence on the sort of man you're after is a nonstarter, at least anything recent. We have volumes on the shooters from Lillehammer and a few less spectacular incidents on European soil. All ancient history. This suspect of yours would have to be in his fifties for any of it to apply."

"No," Sanderson said, "he's nowhere near it. So there's nothing?"

"On the man you're after, no."

"But?" Sanderson prompted.

"It's only a wild idea—one I'm surprised you haven't fumbled upon yourself. Has it not occurred to you that Israeli assassins have been in the news a great deal lately? There were two attempts on the life of Dr. Ibrahim Hamedi this summer. Iran put the blame on Mossad."

"Don't they always?"

"Of course. But we did receive a report from Interpol that identified one of the men in the most recent assault. He was former Israeli Special Forces, almost certainly working for Mossad. Taken together, I'd say that puts him pretty close to your friend. He was a *kidon*."

Sanderson said nothing.

"Well?" Almgren prodded.

"It's not much, but I see what you mean. I suppose it bears looking into."

"Iran's development of nuclear-tipped missiles is Israel's overwhelming concern. So maybe that has something to do with what's been going on in Stockholm."

"Is SÄPO pursuing this angle?" he asked.

"No. But I think somebody should."

"Somebody. Maybe a retiree with nothing better to do?"

"Could be. Just to be a good sport I'll see what I can dig up on Dr. Hamedi."

"Yes, that might help."

"And don't forget, Arne—you owe me another Flying Horse Chipotle Burger."

Iran's Guardian Council was housed, for the day's business, in a nondescript building outside Parliament's contemporary pyramid—an eye-catching and useless place in both form and function.

Behrouz felt strangely alone as he walked up the broad central staircase. He answered this call on a regular basis, and the timing of today's summons was in line with the usual reporting schedule. All the same, a worm of anxiety squirmed in his gut.

The council was already in session when Behrouz arrived, and he was ushered directly in, the members breaking away from less pressing business to give him an immediate audience. Taking the lone seat that faced the long table, he saw he was up against a full contingent of twelve—altogether, a disquieting lineup of dark robes and white turbans.

After cursory words of greeting—along the lines of what one would give a rarely seen neighbor—the chairman said, "Tell us of your preparations for Geneva."

Behrouz was ready. "Our forward team has arrived at the embassy in Bern, and is now finalizing arrangements. They will secure the hotel well in advance of Dr. Hamedi's arrival. We are coordinating with both the local police and Swiss national forces. The United Nations venue is well suited for lockdown during high-profile visits."

"And the other? This 'reception' as they call it?"

"The local authorities are confident they can secure the area. The Swiss have a great deal of experience in hosting diplomatic events. And Dr. Hamedi, for all his importance, is hardly so much a target as the president of the United States or the queen of England."

"That," said another of God's self-appointed emissaries, "is a matter of perspective."

"We should not rely on others," said the chairman. "Do you not have any . . ." he searched for the right word, "suggestion that the Israelis will make another attempt on Hamedi?"

"No, not at this time. But rest assured that I have taken every precaution. On Sunday I will have fifty of my best men on site. No one will get near him."

"That is good," said the robe on the right, a man Behrouz knew to be the leading *faqih*, or Islamic law expert, and consequently the most pious of the lot. "Dr. Hamedi's progress has been nothing short of miraculous. If Allah wills it, he will soon deliver what we have long sought. We all pray for his safety."

Behrouz said, "I think I have proved in recent months that I am capable of ensuring it."

"Your campaign in the synagogues has revealed nothing new?" the chairman asked.

"No, not yet."

A nod from the center. "And have you conducted any other operations as of late?"

"Operations?" Behrouz said, trying to keep a level voice. He watched an exchange of glances along the table, tilted turbans and a flutter of brown cotton sleeves.

The chairman. "We have learned of a disturbance last night in Molavi. Your ministry had no involvement, I'm sure, as your recent efforts have been focused so completely on Geneva."

There was a long and heavy pause. Behrouz knew better than to speak.

"I will leave you with one further thought," the chairman picked up. "As head of our state security apparatus you have performed admirably, and this grants you a certain latitude in running your ministry. But remember one thing, Farzad—you are today not the most critical man in our Islamic Republic. Proceed with care."

"Yes, Chairman, I understand. Thank you for sharing your wisdom."

Minutes later Behrouz was descending the massive staircase, his feet stepping quickly. He checked his phone but saw nothing from Rafi. He was not

surprised that the council had learned of his raid—
the speed of the reprimand, however, spoke volumes.
He had seen it happen to his predecessor, a series of
small missteps that ended badly for the man. Very
badly. He decided it was time to regain the initiative,
lest he face a similar fate. As with most men of his
ilk, Behrouz had spent a lifetime climbing to the top
without consideration for what came afterward.
Today, as he hit the bottom of the staircase, his feet
skidding momentarily on the polished marble floor,
he was beset by a new and disturbing perspective.

On reaching the top, Behrouz realized, there was
only one place to go.

And it was not up.

Sanderson spent a slow cup considering Almgren's hy-
pothesis. Could the troubles in Stockholm be related
to Israel's pursuit of Iran's chief nuclear scientist? It
was a long shot to say the least. If Deadmarsh was
truly a Mossad assassin, the chances were better that
he was hunting down some deserving Hezbollah terrorist. More likely yet was that the erstwhile stonemason had not been tasked to kill anyone. Sanderson
would lay odds that there was no cataclysmic plot at
any level, but rather an alcoholic agent who'd gone
rogue, or perhaps a man chasing his wife because
she'd had an affair with her dermatologist. As any policeman could tell you, the real world was far less a
manifestation of James Bond than Jerry Springer. All
the same, Sanderson had to be sure, which meant dis-
proving Almgren's theory.

Only days ago he'd had Sweden's largest police
force at his disposal. Now, aside from the spare time
of two distant friends, he was operating alone from a

tiny German village. He left a nice tip for the waitress, and asked her if a computer was available for general use. She was happy to point him to a small side room where, for a fee, computer stations with Internet access were available.

The room was a disaster with dirty floors and overflowing wastebaskets, and from the sales flyers on the wall—instant energy shots and roadside assistance insurance—one didn't have to be a detective to realize that the place was here for transiting truck drivers. Sanderson sat on a chair with ripped fabric and foam oozing out the seams, and addressed a brown-stained keyboard on which the lettering of the more frequently used characters had been worn clear. But the machine worked, and he was soon online. Sanderson began by researching articles relating to the assassination attempts on Hamedi. He noted the dates and locations of the botched missions—both occurring inside Iran—and he read the official releases from IRNA, the Islamic Republic News Agency. Not surprisingly, these pieces were scarce on detail and high on rhetoric, taking particular relish in pointing an accusatory finger at Israel.

He moved on to Israeli and neutral news outlets, and then a few blogs where conspiracy theorists congregated. Nothing inspired him. He entered Anton Bloch's name and got hits relating to his retirement, along with a few critiques on the effectiveness of his administration—Mossad chiefs were meant to be anonymous during their active tenure, but apparently fair game once they reverted to the lowly status of private citizen. After an hour the waitress stepped in and brought him another cup of coffee. Sanderson could have kissed her.

He typed the name Edmund Deadmarsh into a search engine and drew blanks. Next he tried

Dr. Christine Palmer—there were apparently four in the world—which produced nothing more enlightening than her physician's website. He backtracked and typed in: Iran, nuclear program, Dr. Ibrahim Hamedi. A number of articles relating to the assassination attempts appeared, along with others of a more critical voice that vilified the mad genius and the weapons project he oversaw. None gave any insight to steer Sanderson in his search.

He closed his eyes tightly and pinched the bridge of his nose. *What? What would prove or disprove?* He opened his eyes and typed: Dr. Ibrahim Hamedi, travel. He opened the first result:

IAEA Requests Emergency Meeting in Geneva
www.reuters.com/IAEAemergencymeeting
October 9—Iran has agreed to an emergency request from the International Atomic Energy Agency for information pertaining to its nuclear program. Recent inspections have been denied by Iran, the Tehran government claiming that certain inspectors are unacceptable. Visa problems have also arisen, although IAEA spokespersons insist that these difficulties are a result of intentional delays by Iran. Independent observers estimate Iran to be only months away from a successful transition of its peaceful nuclear program to weaponization, in particular the mating of a nuclear warhead to its Shahab-4 ballistic missile. Dr. Ibrahim Hamedi, head of the Atomic Energy Organization of Iran, will travel to Geneva and present Iran's case to a group of inspectors and diplomats on October 20.

Sanderson read it again. Could this be why Deadmarsh had run south? The odds were long—but perhaps a ray of hope. An Israeli assassin heading in the general direction of Israel's clearest target? The coincidence could not be more slim. Yet it *was* a coincidence, and if the last thirty-five years had taught Sanderson anything, it was to seek just such connections.

But how to continue? Sanderson had already hidden from Sjoberg a pursuit that had taken him across the Baltic and into Germany. To forward this new theory would get him no more than a one-way ticket home and a follow-up session with Dr. Samuels. He could mention his suspicions to Blix or Almgren, but he doubted they would have any more luck in convincing their superiors—it was simply too thin a link for anyone to chase. At least anyone in their right mind.

Sanderson's time on the computer came to an end. He did not purchase more. He left the restaurant, thanking the young waitress as he passed the main counter, and after a cool five-minute walk found himself in the main Sassnitz transfer terminal. He stopped in front of a machine that sold tickets for the ferry north to Malmö. From there, he could reach Stockholm easily by train, and be home late tonight. An adjacent machine sold tickets for German rail. With a connection, perhaps two, he could be in Geneva by early evening. Sanderson stood still for a very long time with his hand poised over his pocket. North or south? Either was an improvement, he reasoned. *At least I don't have to get on another godforsaken seaplane.*

Comforted by this thought, he made his selection, and ten minutes later was waiting patiently in the busy boarding area.

———

Slaton settled his business with Krueger that evening. He signed the name Natan Mendelsohn to documents authorizing his banker to manage a series of accounts. After this, Krueger handed over the agreed upon funds.

A visibly nervous Krueger asked, "When will I hear from you again?"

"More likely later than sooner. I'll be leaving Zurich tonight."

"Then I wish you happy travels, my friend. Is there anything else I can do before you leave?"

"Two things. First, I owe a debt to a charter pilot in Sweden. I'd like you to send her a check in the amount of twenty-two thousand U.S. dollars. Here is the name and address." Slaton handed over a folded slip of hotel stationery.

Krueger took it without looking. "And the other?" he asked tentatively.

"How many cars do you have?"

"Cars?" the banker stuttered. Slaton had once again made a diagonal move in Krueger's parallel world. "Well . . . two. A Range Rover and an Audi."

"Which did you bring here tonight?"

"The Rover."

Slaton smiled thinly.

Without even being asked, the banker handed over a key.

THIRTY-SIX

Christine stood in front of a bank on Kungsgatan Street trying to avoid the gaze of passersby, and hoping that no one would pay attention to a distracted American woman loitering near an ATM. It was shortly after closing time, and for the last thirty minutes she had watched tellers and mortgage officers vacate the branch office, one by one, until a security guard locked the door behind them. She'd studied each bank employee, but none fit the profile she was looking for. David, of course, had anticipated this and briefed her on a contingency plan. Given the time of day—the Thursday evening rush to get home—Christine was sure she would find her man soon enough.

As planned, she'd spent the previous night with her friend Dr. Ulrika Torsten. Christine had lied convincingly, a breathless account of her escape from the Strandvägen shootings, and ending with an offhand mention that the police had sought her out for an official statement. All variations of the truth. She'd built on this by telling Ulrika that the whole affair had left her shaken and in need of a quiet place in Stockholm to relax for a few days. When she added that her husband would arrive in a few days to escort her back to the States, Ulrika had insisted that Christine stay at her home.

So it was, for one night she had imposed on a friend's gracious hospitality. But late this afternoon Christine gave her regrets for dinner, missing out on a home-cooked meal, and claimed the need for fresh air and an invigorating walk. She was now back at work. David's work.

It took fifteen minutes, but the candidate she saw was perfect. Slightly on the tall side, perhaps a bit blonder. Otherwise, a perfect match. He was moving fast with a briefcase in one hand and an umbrella in the other.

She hurried away from the wall near the ATM.

"Excuse me!"

The man stopped.

"Do you speak English?" she asked.

"A little, yes."

"Could you please help me? I'm trying to get money from this machine, but the instructions are in Swedish." She gave him her most engaging smile and made sure her wedding band was behind her hip.

The man smiled back. Just as David had said he would.

The use of Deadmarsh's credit card at a midtown ATM machine registered almost instantly with the Stockholm police. The nearest officers were dispatched, and reached the bank in five minutes. They were three minutes too late.

Headquarters built a head of steam, and Commissioner Forsten and Assistant Commissioner Sjoberg were soon meeting in a side room with technicians. They poured over video that had been fed directly from the bank's security office, and everyone saw a tall blond man in an overcoat withdrawing money from the machine.

"He withdrew a thousand kronor," Sjoberg said. "He's running low on cash. Maybe he's trying to get out of the country."

"Are we sure it's him?" Forsten asked.

Sjoberg looked at the screen uncertainly. "It's not the clearest image . . . the lighting is poor. Let's ask someone who's seen him."

Sergeant Blix was summoned to join them. When he arrived Forsten explained, "An hour ago there was a cash withdrawal on Deadmarsh's credit card. We have video from the bank surveillance camera. Unfortunately, since his passport dumped we don't have a decent photo to compare. Of all the people in the building, Blix, you had the best look at him."

The video footage looped and Forsten froze it on the clearest image. "Well?" she asked. "Is that him?"

Blix stared at the grainy black-and-white image, but didn't answer immediately. He finally said, "It does looks like him, but it's hard to say. I can't be certain." Under two disbelieving looks, he tried again.

"It's a good likeness," he said, "but something about it . . ." Blix's face contorted as he racked his brain. "He's keying the numbers with his left hand."

"Was Deadmarsh left-handed?" Forsten asked.

Blix shook his head. "I'm sorry, but I can't remember."

"I know who could give us a definite answer," Sjoberg said.

They all stared at one another in turn.

"All right," Forsten ordered, "call him in."

"Ah . . ." Blix hesitated, "I'm not sure Inspector Sanderson is available right now."

"What do you mean?"

"I believe he's taken a holiday," Blix replied.

"Holiday?" Sjoberg burst.

"Well, sir—you did just let him go."

Slaton exercised his newfound wealth in customary Zurich fashion—with a shopping spree on Bahnhof-strasse.

In perhaps the world's epicenter of casual self-indulgence, he caused barely a ripple with his shotgun approach: a pair of Peter Millar twill trousers were partnered with a button-down cotton shirt and Chanel tie, followed by a charcoal Armani sportcoat, and finally a set of black Nike warm-ups with trail shoes. Just off Bahnhofstrasse, he paid a reasonable price for a down sleeping bag and a Prada travel case—somehow relegated to the clearance rack—and an unreasonable one for a Movado wristwatch, a high-end sport version with luminescent dials. With full arms and half-empty pockets, Slaton decided he'd done enough damage for one evening.

He found the Rover in Krueger's reserved parking spot, an upgraded model with four-wheel drive and a massive engine. Before leaving the garage he circled the Rover's exterior once, checking that all the exterior lights were operational, and that the license plate and vignette, or autobahn sticker, were current and not obscured. He would be driving a perfectly valid vehicle, and wanted no excuse for a random traffic stop. Slaton brought the machine to life and was rewarded with a heavy purr under the thick leather and walnut trim. He wheeled out of the parking garage into a thin mist, turned north and gathered speed.

He swept past the up-lit spire of St. Peter's Church,

rounded the Swiss National Museum, and ten minutes later was merging comfortably onto the N1. The lights of Zurich began to fade, and using the cruise control to govern his speed, Slaton struck westward into darkened countryside toward the Limmat Valley. Estimating a three-hour drive ahead, he should have used the time to refine his next steps, or at the very least reflect on a long and productive day. Slaton was making progress, nearing his target, and he now had unlimited funds at his disposal. Yet try as he might, he couldn't concentrate on the mission.

The reason was clear enough.

The simple life he and Christine had built in Virginia was gone, and certainly unrecoverable. Now he was racing across Switzerland, his vehicle acquired by way of coercion, and once again being hunted by the authorities. With terrible suddenness, the past year had fallen to little more than another assignment, a temporary operation, pleasant as it was, that had come to its natural conclusion.

Had life in America really been any different? he wondered.

Not a day had gone by when he hadn't lied to keep up the legend of Edmund Deadmarsh. The sounds of fireworks and cars backfiring still stiffened his spine. He invariably kept a ready supply of cash in their home, and without fail filled the tank on the Ford when it was half full—the Ford because it had twice the horsepower of the Honda. In Virginia he'd taken the same precautions he always had, the lone difference being that he cared about his partner in a very different way.

Her parting words drummed in his head.

If you kill this man in Geneva . . . don't ever come back to me.

Against this was Nurin's countering promise—the assassination of Hamedi was his only chance to return to a normal life. Catch-22. If he killed the man, Christine would leave him. If he didn't, Slaton would have no life to go back to. It was a collision of ultimatums, a mathematical equation that seemed unsolvable. All he could do was keep looking, keep moving to find a better angle. Like the sniper he was.

Find the perfect shot.

And so Slaton drove onward, the Rover pointed west at a measured pace as he traversed the left half of Switzerland.

THIRTY-SEVEN

His eyes opened instantly to a sharp noise.

Slaton immediately tensed, but didn't move other than to shift his gaze toward the uncorrelated motion, a dark silhouette behind the Rover's frosted side window. Someone was outside, very close, their hands low and out of sight. That was always the most important thing—the hands. Slaton kept still, and soon the shape sank lower and disappeared. He heard a car door close, a cold engine labor to life.

The car parked in the adjacent spot began to back out.

He rose to an elbow, his breath going to vapor. He was laying in the Rover's cargo area, wrapped in the heavy sleeping bag and with the rear seats folded down. Slaton had arrived in the waning minutes of Thursday, exiting the A1 at Mont-sur-Rolle, and from there traveled no more than three hundred yards south. He'd parked in a small lot outside the Rolle train station, choosing a tight spot between a panel van and the big Mercedes sedan that had just pulled away. Rolle was centered midpoint along the curved northern shore of Lake Geneva, roughly twenty-five miles from the city of Geneva. Today Slaton would close that gap.

He climbed in front, started the engine and spun the heater knob to full. Rubbing circles in the fogged left and right windows, he surveyed the area around him. He saw an empty parking spot immediately to the right. In the distance, others that had been vacant were now filled by morning commuters. Otherwise, everything looked as it had when he'd arrived six hours ago. The heater blew for five minutes before starting to make a difference. In the backseat he changed clothes, trading the rumpled attire in which he'd slept for the khaki trousers, button-down shirt, and designer tie. He stopped at the train station restroom, and at a washbasin Slaton did his best to revive his coarse appearance. By six-thirty he was waiting on the platform, a ticket in one hand and a newspaper in the other. He stood with ten other commuters who in aggregate could not have matched him more perfectly. A train slid to a stop right on schedule—the Swiss being timekeepers of the world—and the crowd shuffled aboard in an orderly fashion.

Slaton was increasingly alert. His eyes flicked across every person, and in the tight confines of the car he backed against a bulkhead and shifted his stance regularly to alter his vantage point. He was sure he had separated cleanly from Stockholm, and then Zurich. But Geneva was something else. In Geneva he might well be expected.

The run to the city took twenty-seven minutes, the train shouldering to the shore of the serene lake while the massive form of Mont Blanc roused in the distance, its snowcapped peak struck brilliant in the new morning light. No one around him seemed to notice the spectacle. He watched young professionals tap their phones in the name of urgent business affairs, while their older counterparts probed newspaper financials, presumably to calculate how much more or less they were worth on this glorious morning.

Slaton scanned *Le Courrier*, a French-language local paper. French was one of his better languages, and used widely in Geneva—no surprise as Switzerland's westernmost city was virtually enveloped by her sister state. On the front page he saw an article regarding a speech in which the Israeli prime minister had strongly urged the United Nations to take a harder line on the "pariah state" of Iran. Slaton saw nothing in *Le Courrier* about the recent shootings in Stockholm, nor anything about Anton Bloch's identity, which had certainly been verified by now. That the police were holding this out of the headlines did not surprise Slaton, yet he knew it was a risk for whoever had taken over for poor Inspector Sanderson. He wondered briefly what the little detective was doing right now. Was he still involved in the case on some level? If so, Slaton hoped the ice blue eyes were not boring into Christine, but rather darting over old files and endless camera footage, losing focus as they tried to match unmatchable fingerprints.

Searching for a man who didn't exist.

Slaton had a fleeting urge to contact Christine. He imagined how it would feel to hear her voice, to know that everything was all right. It was, of course, no more than a teasing thought. He had not briefed her on any method of making contact, and with good reason. Slaton had seen more than one mission blown in the name of comfort. He had seen men tracked down and shot because they'd exposed themselves in order to say good night to their child. He'd seen a wedding party bombed because one guest had allowed sentiment to override reason. Slaton knew exactly what came of such breaches, and he would not allow it. He could only trust that Christine was safe. Trust that he had done enough, and that she was making good decisions. Because right now, his concealment was the best weapon either of them had.

Slaton disembarked at Geneva's Sécheron Station under a splendid sky, and he dispersed with the other commuters into the heart of the city. Geneva was a place Slaton knew well. He had come here twice before, once as a teenager to attend the nearby Montreux Jazz Festival, and again years later to kill a man. Both aims had been achieved and, for reasons that escaped him, seemed fixed in his mind with equivalent weight. On one shore of Lac Léman he had spread himself on green grass and listened to Ray Charles play his glorious standards, and on the other he had spread himself on a rooftop ventilator to put under his reticle a Yemeni bomb-maker, a proven and indiscriminant killer of women and children. Two fulfillments that could not have been more divergent, yet both set here, on a pristine lake charged by Alpine water, crisp air flowing under a faultless blue sky.

He walked west along Avenue de la Paix, and in a matter of minutes arrived at Geneva's United Nations Office. The main building, originally built to house the League of Nations, was as grandiose as the ideals it represented, a blunt ivory tower of stone and columns and square edges. All around were offshoot wings fronted by broad lawns and reflecting pools, and on a central pathway the flags of the world were aligned in perfect harmony. It was a splendid and pompous place that Slaton might have ignored but for one reason. This was his starting point.

According to Nurin's file, Ibrahim Hamedi would

present Iran's case to the world from this stage. At seven in the evening, two days from now, he would stand at a podium in the grand hall and, in all probability, lie about Iran's program of nuclear weaponization. He would then mingle with the invitees for precisely twenty-three minutes—this also from the file—before being hustled to a side entrance and a waiting motorcade. Three cars, or possibly four, would turn up Avenue de France and make two miles at speed before merging onto Quai du Mont Blanc. There, minutes removed from his diplomatic duty, Iran's chief nuclear designer would be deposited at Lake Geneva's northern shore and walk, amid a thick and watchful security contingent, to his next appearance.

And there the *kidon* would be waiting.

THIRTY-EIGHT

The A-320 airliner slid smooth and true through the thin air at 35,000 feet. A distracted Ibrahim Hamedi looked through the oval window and saw the Black Sea to his left. On the right he could just discern the distant Caspian Sea, and so the thin mountain range before him, capped by Mount Elbrus, had to be the Caucuses.

Hamedi had always been good with geography, and on long flights he found it a useful diversion to reckon his position. A pilot had once taught him the trick. You started with the most prominent features—mountain ranges, oceans, and lakes—and then applied an approximate compass orientation. With a basic knowledge of natural features, the rest quickly fell into place. It worked well enough, he supposed, but over the years had become a less pleasurable exercise. For Hamedi it only emphasized the world's overriding problem—if topography was unwavering, the underlying political and cultural lines were far more unsettled. The Caucuses were a case in point, once claimed by Iran and later dominated by Russia, it was one of the most ethnically and linguistically divided regions on earth. Yet from where Hamedi sat, with his God's-eye view, things looked peaceful, even bucolic.

He supposed it was something of a metaphor for the human condition. Appearances can be illusory.

The flight was a chartered affair, the crew and aircraft having been rented from an Emirates-based leasing company. As such, the six flight attendants were all attractive young females who scurried about the cabin and did their best to make everyone comfortable, serving meals and drinks, fluffing pillows and tucking blankets, their boundless smiles never wavering. It was the sort of pampering that would not exist on an Iranian state-owned aircraft. Hamedi was seated in the first-class section, and behind him in coach was a security detail and support delegation of nearly sixty. He closed the window shade and forced himself back to the cheerless reality of the figures in front of him, an inventory of critical machine tool parts. His index finger was halfway down the page when the only other person authorized the comforts of the first eight rows came up the aisle and took a seat across from him. Behrouz had earlier looked tired and drawn, but he now seemed revitalized as he pecked on a laptop computer.

"This Wi-Fi device is impressive, is it not?" Behrouz said. "I have just received a message from our advance team. The preparations are running on schedule, both at the hotel and the United Nations building. I even have a picture of your cruise ship." Behrouz turned the computer around and Hamedi saw a gleaming white yacht.

"I'm glad you are satisfied," he replied dryly.

"Aren't you looking forward to it?"

"What I am looking forward to is confirmation that the last tranche of fissile material has arrived at Qom from the Natanz complex. These final two shipments have taken weeks."

"Such logistics are not always easy. Much of the delay was due to your own restrictions, Doctor—you insisted on multiple deliveries."

"Highly enriched uranium is our most valuable commodity—and you know how rabid the Israelis are about this. If we coordinated a single transfer and their spies caught wind of it? Can you imagine? They would commit every agent on their books to attacking or even stealing our hard-won prize."

"Now there is a terrible thought," Behrouz lamented. "But I will let you in on a little secret to put you at ease. By the time we land in Geneva, the last shipment will be in place."

Hamedi looked at Behrouz and saw he was serious. In what would have been a first, he nearly smiled at the little cretin. "It's about time."

Behrouz went back to his laptop. He seemed enthralled, and Hamedi supposed he should not be surprised. The security man had climbed through the ranks before the age of technology had arrived in Iran. Behrouz had risen on broken legs and execution killings, the kinds of things that were not furthered by an understanding of bytes or pixels. He considered briefing the man on the vulnerabilities of unsecure signal networks, but decided not to waste his breath.

Behrouz tapped his screen, "I have taken to tracing my ancestry. It's fascinating what one can learn these days. Have you ever tried?"

Hamedi flipped distractedly through his papers. "My family has been in Persia for a thousand years, or so my mother tells me. As a busy man, that is all the genealogy I need."

"How is she, by the way? I understand you visited her recently."

With that, any truce that had developed between

them dissipated. "Must you track everything I do?" Hamedi snapped.

"Yes. That is my job."

"And it is my job to engineer the ultimate weapon for our nation. My mother is the same as ever. A sharp tongue and no love for her failed son—but then, I'm sure my escorts gave you a full report. Now be quiet and let me work in peace."

Behrouz stared, waiting until Hamedi met his gaze. "Use caution, Doctor. Someday you may need a man in my position."

"No," Hamedi countered, "*you* use caution, or I will see to it that someone more to my liking is put in your position."

The two locked a hard gaze, until Behrouz rose from his chair and disappeared down the aisle. Hamedi tried to refocus on his work, but it was hopeless. He opened the combination locks on his secure portfolio and stuffed the papers inside. He slid the window cover back up, hoping to find a prominent feature below. He saw nothing but thick gray clouds and a frost of ice on the window.

Without warning, the troubled, intricate world beneath him had disappeared.

From the United Nations complex, Slaton walked the projected motorcade route—projected because a thing like that was always subject to change, at least if the police knew what they were doing. Arriving at the docks he got his first look at the target area. He bought a sausage and a strong cup of tea from a street vendor, and took a seat on one of the countless benches along the waterfront.

Situated behind him was a modest peninsula that

jutted into the lake like a distended belly, and there kiosk owners were raising their covers for the day, balloons and T-shirts going up for sale. Farther on he saw an old-fashioned carousel spinning its first turn of the day, a handful of mothers and children rising and falling on roundabout animals. The lake hummed with activity, dozens of watercraft running in different directions, each at their own speed, and on the far side of the lake was Geneva's signature landmark—the world's largest fountain, the Jet d'eau, spewed a frothing stream of white four hundred feet into the sky.

Slaton tuned out all this activity to concentrate on what lay immediately before him—two finger docks that stretched into the lake from Quai du Mont Blanc. There were other, less substantial berths along the shore in either direction, but these were meant for small craft. The two main piers led to deep water, and each was apparently designed to sustain one large yacht at its T-shaped ending. The more distant pier was already occupied by an old paddle steamer, one of a quaint fleet that still plied the lake, a top-heavy-looking beast that rested low on the water, and whose broad white awnings would keep dry a profitable contingent of tourists. Other than its geometric positioning, however, the picturesque paddle steamer was of no interest to Slaton.

It was another ship he had in mind.

He already knew her name: *Entrepreneur*. According to Nurin's file she was owned by a Frenchman, an octogenarian pharmaceutical magnate, and at one hundred and thirty feet along the waterline was nominally larger than the old relic moored in front of him. So it was the vacant dock, reaching into the lake with an empty grasp, that became Slaton's primary focus.

Come Sunday evening, this was where *Entrepreneur* would be berthed.

Her absence today was relevant in a number ways. It meant the yacht was not a permanent fixture here, not anchored to a wharf, as was sometimes the case, to serve as a billionaire's overpriced barroom. It also meant that *Entrepreneur* was seaworthy, perhaps sailing at this very moment across fifty miles of blue lake, or possibly moored at a similar berth in Montreux or Lausanne. More likely still, she was in a shipyard with her crew swabbing decks and polishing fittings for the upcoming diplomatic mission, much as the staff of a mansion would prepare for a grand ball. Whatever the case, she was a vessel with captain and crew, and thus quite capable of a starlight cruise to view Switzerland's gleaming showplace city. This point—that a voyage was planned Sunday evening—had been alluded to in Nurin's information, but not confirmed. Of course, from the director's viewpoint any cruise would be moot. If all went by his plan, Hamedi would never reach the ship.

Slaton examined carefully the sphere of possibilities around him, and he began to calculate. He estimated the dock to be two hundred feet in length. At a normal pace, a man might cover such a distance in twenty-five seconds. And there, in essence, was the challenge put to him by Director Nurin. In that interval, somewhere between Quai du Mont Blanc and *Entrepreneur*'s angled-steel gangway, Slaton was to put one well-placed, high-velocity projectile into the head of Dr. Ibrahim Hamedi.

The chief surgeon at Stockholm's Saint Göran Hospital, Dr. August Brune, needed to make a decision.

He was increasingly confident that their mystery patient, who had been in an induced coma for nearly a week, was ready to have the final bullet removed. The problem was authorization. The man had no family, and in fact had not even been identified. The hospital's Ethics Board had advised him that a court-appointed advocate was the preferred course, but this took time, and the impending weekend did nothing to raise the chances of finding a magistrate. An impatient Dr. Brune decided to voice his concerns to the police, who'd been keeping a curiously constant presence around the patient's room. In less than an hour, two men appeared at his office door.

"Can I help you?" said Dr. Brune.

The men introduced themselves. One was from the Swedish Ministry of Foreign Affairs, and the other a representative of the Israeli embassy.

The Israeli said, "We've come to discuss the patient in room 605. We know who he is, and I have papers signed by the family that grant us authority to make decisions regarding his treatment."

The Swede concurred. "The Ministry of Foreign Affairs has made extensive verifications—everything is in order."

Dr. Brune looked at the documents. He had never seen anything like it, but the sheer weight of the paper seemed convincing enough.

The Israeli said, "What do you advise as the best course for the patient?"

"He is stable. I would recommend surgery to re-move the final bullet lodged in the upper lumbar region."

The Israeli nodded. "Agreed."

Brune looked at the two men. He could request to speak directly with a family member, but the set in these men's jaws told him that wasn't going to happen. An unusual situation, but a license to proceed, in his opinion, in the best interest of his patient.

"Very well, then. I'll schedule the operating theater for tomorrow morning. But there is one thing I'd very much like to know—does this man have a name?"

The Swede nearly answered.

The Israeli cut him off.

"No."

Had it happened a half second later, when his gaze was more fully averted, Slaton might have crushed the kid's larynx.

The flash of motion came out of nowhere, close and quick to the left of his bench. With only an instant to evaluate and react, Slaton set his base, raised a blocking forearm, and cocked his right arm back for a counterstrike against the scrawny attacker lunging in from the periphery.

The Frisbee hit him in the lower lip.

The teenager altered his trajectory at the last second and tripped over Slaton's squared leg, tumbling onto the worn grass in front of the bench.

Slaton eased.

"Pardon," the kid said as he stood, dusting himself off. His wide smile was a further apology—and proof that he had no idea how close he'd just come to dying.

Slaton licked his lower lip and tasted the coppery tang of blood. He grabbed the Frisbee, which had landed on the bench next to him, and handed it over.

"Merci," said the kid before winding up and backhanding the disc to his partner in the distance.

Slaton tracked its flight across the lawn and wondered, in what was becoming a recurring theme, if he would ever be as competent at life as he was at death. For today, he reckoned, it was best left an idle thought.

He got up and began walking, and from the docks roamed west along the lake's curved edge. He passed vendors selling food and soft drinks from carts, and regarded a field of small daysailers moored along the breakwater. After a hundred yards Slaton paused, as tourists did, and pondered the scene before him with his hands clasped behind his back. He was looking at the second point of Nurin's plot, the Pont du Mont Blanc. It was a modest item, as bridges went, a three-hundred-yard span to connect the left and right banks of Geneva where the lake funneled to become the throat of the Rhone River. The design was simplistic, neither high nor arching, but six flat lanes of asphalt intended for cars to pass over, not ships to pass under.

When Slaton had originally drawn Nurin's scheme in his mind, he'd thought it amateurish. Now, with the physical geometry presented, he reconsidered. The bridge was set low, crouched on ten concrete and steel buttresses. From where Slaton stood he saw countless gaps in the understructure, a repeating warren of shelters and shadows where a patient man could easily conceal himself on a black evening. He imagined a prone shot, laying across a beam, or even splayed directly on one of the concrete buttresses. Distance was not an issue—from the bridge to the target area he estimated no more than two hundred yards. A simple shot.

He also granted that escape was realistic. The bridge was teeming with traffic—vehicles, bicycles, people on foot. This would change come Sunday night, still a busy thoroughfare but with a different character, more private vehicles and everyone moving casually on the leeside of the weekend. There would certainly be defenses, the Iranians undoubtedly and a modest contingent of the canton's finest. But there would be no all-out lockdown. If Slaton saw that, a swarming defensive perimeter, it meant that the director had failed to contain his leak. Altogether, he decided Nurin's plan was not a great one. But it *was* viable, and this made Slaton suspect that Nurin had already lied to him. He'd claimed that no one else in Mossad had knowledge of the plot, yet there was enough tactical awareness here to suggest otherwise. Had the director called in help? Had he taken advice from someone versed in such mechanics?

Someone like me?

Slaton spent another hour roaming the area. He circled the Brunswick Monument, pretending to study the carved stone lions that stood noble sentry, notwithstanding the humiliation of pigeons perched on their noses and loins darkened by summer mildew. With a walking guide in hand he crossed the bridge to the left bank and stopped at prominent buildings, marveling at high facades and rooftop spires, and viewing his kill box from every conceivable angle. He took a tour of the harbor, riding in a small boat with open seats that circled the Jet d'eau and wetted everyone with mist, and puttered past the tiny lighthouse at the end of the jetty, and whose guide rambled historical snippets and converted jokes into three languages, the punch lines invariably dimmed by translation. By noon Slaton was back ashore, his head full of geometry and his stomach empty, and he decided to cross the busy Quai du Mont Blanc in search of a café.

He was standing on a corner, waiting to cross and still reckoning vantage points, when his well-ordered thoughts swerved into a ditch. The trigger was a scent.

Three women stood beside him, and somewhere sprayed to the nape of a neck was a tester of Christine's favorite perfume. Slaton's mind lurched through a series of disjointed images, and in the end one jagged question drilled into his mind.

When would their child be born? Slaton realized that he didn't know the due date. Realized that he hadn't even asked.

How could I not have asked?

He stood stunned for a moment, dazed and bewildered as traffic thundered past, and as the three women giggled and carried on a chattering exchange. He was saved when the streetlight changed. The prattling threesome set off at a brisk pace, taking the familiar scent with them. Slaton followed after allowing a gap, and by the time he stepped onto the far side of the street he had righted his mental ship.

He turned down the sidewalk and picked up his pace, the day pleasant and the sun bright. As he'd done all morning, the *kidon* appraised the setting before him. Faces and bodies and traffic all went under his capable eye. Unlike the rest of the morning, what he saw set off an alarm, and his easy stride froze to a stop on the sun-drenched sidewalk.

THIRTY-NINE

Slaton watched two black Mercedes limousines glide to a stop at the reception awning of the Hotel Beau Rivage. The first car had metal brackets bolted to the leading edges of the front fenders, a dead giveaway that was reinforced by a set of diplomatic license tags. Four swarthy men emerged from the two cars, and after a brief discussion disappeared into the hotel.

Not yet convinced of his good fortune, Slaton waited and watched. He saw a fifth man pry himself from the driver's seat of the lead car. He stepped to the curb, leaned on the driver's door, and lit a cigarette—a man settling in to wait. Slaton had no doubt that these were embassy cars, but which embassy? After a brief internal debate, he opted for the direct approach.

He walked straight up to the driver, and said in English, "Excuse me, do you know where the bus to Valais stops?"

The man looked at him and shrugged.

"*Où le bus est au Valais?*" Slaton prodded in French.

"No, no. I do not know," the man replied in brusque English.

"Okay."

"Ask bellman," the driver suggested, more to get rid of Slaton than to help him.

"Yes, a good idea." Slaton turned toward the hotel entrance.

The man had not said enough for Slaton to place the accent. It *could* have been Iranian, he thought, but possibly something else. Less equivocal was what he'd seen on the car's front seat, yesterday's edition of *Abrar*, the Farsi-language daily.

At the hotel's entrance Slaton passed between twin stone flowerpots that welcomed guests with bursting waves of yellow and violet, not to mention the most pleasant of fragrances. Inside he found a gilded and ostentatious place, a property that was certainly, as was common along Quai du Mont Blanc, steeped in historical significance. Here, Slaton supposed, the leaders of past ages had dined well over petty arguments, and signed evening treaties in advance of midnight trysts. As such, it was the kind of place that would appeal to their contemporary counterparts who, in spite of the intervening centuries, would pursue their diplomacy in the same enduring manner.

For Slaton it all made perfect sense, and he smiled inwardly at his turn of good luck.

He had just stumbled onto Ibrahim Hamedi's advance security party.

The Hawker 800 touched down smoothly on runway 23 at Geneva International Airport. It was, as business jets went, a generic item. There were no corporate fin flashes or flags of state emblazoned on the tail, no billionaire's initials cleverly incorporated into the aircraft's registration number. It was simple, white, and anonymous. The craft shunned the left high-speed turnoff that led to the passenger terminal, instead slowing for a hard right turn toward the corporate ramp on the airfield's less traveled northern side. The sleek jet was guided to a stop by a waiting ground crewman, and chocks were put in place as soon as the parking brake was set. At the end of its two-thousand-mile journey the plane came to rest, as a curiosity, no more than a hundred yards short of the French border.

The boarding door was flung down and, before the engines had even stopped spinning, a car bearing the emblem of the Swiss Customs Administration pulled up. The Hawker's captain had made advance arrangements. Two inspectors, a man and a woman, got out of the car. The man went straight up the boarding stairs and disappeared. Moments later, the copilot stepped down to the ramp and opened the cargo bay door, cuing the female inspector to lean inside and nudge a few bags. Altogether it was the sort of gentle reception reserved for those men and women who came to Switzerland with important business in mind. The dance went on for no more than five minutes, after which the customs officers walked back to their car, and—in a closed circuit image that would be reviewed most unfavorably in three days' time—the lead officer waved good-bye and gave his best wishes to the flight crew for a pleasant weekend's stay.

As soon as the car was out of sight, eight men disembarked from the Hawker. Each was dressed in a sober suit and tie, and each carried either a briefcase or a leather satchel. Behind dark sunglasses their faces were uniformly blank—eight ordinary men preparing to undertake correspondingly ordinary business. Anyone observing from a distance might have noticed that a few of the men seemed uncomfortable, tugging at their shirt collars and looking stiff in suits that were cut too tight at the shoulder. All were between the age of twenty-five and thirty-five, and all—noticeable even beneath their ill-fitting business attire—were in prime physical condition. There was little interaction among the eight as they walked to the tiny corporate arrivals terminal in what almost appeared a loose marching formation.

Nineteen minutes after landing—two ahead of schedule—Switzerland's newest visitors were concealed in a pair of waiting SUVs and accelerating out of the parking lot to the squeal of rubber over asphalt. The Hawker and its crew did not, in fact, stay the weekend. Without so much as taking on fuel, the jet was back at the runway minutes later, with its flight plan filed and engines spooled, awaiting clearance for takeoff.

Sanderson was awakened by the sound of a jet flying overhead. His eyes cracked open and he saw a scene very much like yesterday's—a strange and chilly hotel room, and an alarm clock that suggested he'd slept through the greater part of the morning. He had arrived in Geneva late last night after an exhausting day of travel, his misery compounded by a late train and a missed connection. But arrive he had.

Sanderson rose and went to the bathroom, and for the first time in weeks his head didn't hurt. He did, however, have an unusually stiff neck, likely from having slept in an awkward position. He was happy to find a clean towel and a bar of soap. The room had been reasonably priced by Geneva's standards, which was to say a rate that stretched his policeman's salary to the breaking point. Or was it his policeman's pension? He showered and dressed before checking his phone for messages. There was nothing from either Almgren or Blix, and this struck him as a disappointment. Sanderson was a patently methodical man, but one could not be methodical without facts to sift through. At the moment he had no more to work with than a single far-fetched idea—that the American he was chasing had come here to gun down a visiting Iranian scientist.

Where to start? he wondered.

He racked his brain, and the only thread of hope that came to mind was a tenuous one. His research had told him that Dr. Hamedi would present Iran's case in a speech at the United Nations Office at Geneva. It seemed as good a place as any to start. Sanderson went to the front desk.

"Can I help you?" the clerk asked in English.

"Yes, the United Nations Office. Is it far from here?"

"Not at all, monsieur. Only ten minutes on the number six bus—you can catch it right outside."

Sanderson thanked the man, pulled up his collar, and went outside to wait on the curb.

Slaton decided he should not be surprised that the Iranians were here. In truth, he should have anticipated it. He entered the lobby and saw them at the front desk: four dark-skinned men, one with gold-rimmed glasses doing the talking, and the other three studying the room with sharp eyes. Soon they were all walking toward the elevator, escorted by a tight-lipped man in a fine suit and a uniformed security guard. Presumably the hotel manager, who gestured airily to emphasize the property's finer points, flanked by his head of security.

Slaton made a quick study of the lobby. A central fountain was surrounded by tall columns and a polished marble floor, and rising from this were five floors of gilt railing, interleaved with hand-carved angels and cherubs that made certain heavenly promises about what lay above. It was a resolutely stylish place, the sort of hotel that would advertise Old World charm or *savior vivre*. The kind of place where each guest room would hold unique furnishings, and where the more exclusive suites kept names in lieu of numbers.

As soon as the Iranians and their escorts disappeared into the elevator, Slaton walked briskly to the stairwell. He pushed through a heavy fire door and climbed the steps three at a time. The Beau Rivage was a five-story concern, and with the ground level obviously committed to common areas, Slaton took a chance and skipped the second-floor landing. He paused on reaching the third. Standing still against the hallway door, he listened but heard nothing. He cracked the door open slightly and saw the elevator door twenty paces up the hall, an elderly woman waiting with the Down button illuminated. Slaton turned and headed up, pausing again at the fourth floor. This time he heard them.

The manager's voice prevailed in lilting French, yet Slaton also registered a barely audible background chatter in Farsi. He didn't speak the language, but he knew enough to recognize it. Sensing that the voices were receding, Slaton edged the door open to see the group bunched in the hallway. He planted his foot to hold a sliver of light at the door, but kept to the stairwell's darkness as he listened to the manager's well-practiced pitch.

"*Your primary rooms are adjacent to one another.*

A beautiful view of the lake from the main suite, and from the other you can see Mont Blanc. Security? Of course. Marcel here will be at your disposal tomorrow from the moment your delegation arrives. We at Beau Rivage keep a long and proud history of hosting dignitaries for important events. A common door between the rooms? Yes, of course, monsieur."

He chanced a look and saw an open door midway down the corridor. When they all disappeared into the room, Slaton let the door slip shut. He went back to the stairs, but instead of descending he climbed up to the last landing. There he noted that the roof access above the fifth floor was barred and secured with a rusted padlock, a modification that would likely not be appreciated by the canton fire marshal. He turned into the vacant fifth-floor hallway, strode halfway down and stomped his foot hard on the carpet. Slaton was rewarded with a hollow thump that told him what he needed to know—under the gold and blue runner, with prints of rose petals and fleurs-de-lis, was a plywood understructure. Two minutes later he was back outside and negotiating his way across the busy street.

The Iranians spent another twenty minutes inside, probably getting a tour of the hotel's security center, which Slaton imagined to be no more than a few closed-circuit video monitors and a bank of phones. When they all came outside and bundled back into the cars, Slaton counted from a bench near the distant carousel and got the number he wanted—five Iranians. This meant no one had been left behind to sanitize the room for listening devices or cordon the area against further incursions. The cars pulled away, and Slaton again noted the diplomatic tags. The vehicles had been drawn, he was sure, from the motor pool of the Iranian embassy in Bern, this a two-hour drive up the A1, the busiest highway in Switzerland.

Things were falling into place quickly. With the cars out of sight, Slaton stood and looked at the dock and the surrounding lake, working everything through a careful sequence. He challenged his blueprint, trying to identify fatal flaws and insert unexpected complications. All plans had them, no matter how well drawn, and in the end it always came down to a matter of probabilities. So he did the math, and was satisfied with the results.

He struck out at a brisk walk back to Sécheron Station, regulating his pace in order to meet the scheduled one-fifteen departure back to Rolle. Slaton's planning was done. He knew what he was going to do.

Even better, he had an audacious idea of how to do it.

Sanderson was riding the number 6 bus, skirting the verdant edges of Geneva's Botanical Gardens, when he saw Edmund Deadmarsh striding past on the sidewalk. His blue eyes went wide. He bolted up from his seat and watched Deadmarsh slip past the windows frame by frame, like a film clip in slow motion. The bus was maneuvering, weaving through a lane change, and Sanderson's hips rattled against seat backs and shoulders as he scrambled up the aisle toward the front. He was halfway there when the driver veered into a right-hand turn.

"Stop!" Sanderson shouted. *"Vous Arret! Polizei!"*

Three languages. None worked. The bus continued onto the side street.

Sanderson looked back over his shoulder, but the

angles had changed and he no longer saw Deadmarsh. The bus straightened out just as Sanderson reached the front.

"Stop!" he screamed.

Sanderson now had the driver's full attention—a set of wary eyes looked back at him in the big central mirror.

"*Polizei!* Let me off here!"

He slapped the big silver arm that controlled the door, and as soon as the bus shuddered to a stop the driver was happy to comply. Sanderson half jumped, half fell to the pavement, and began running back to the corner. He made the turn without stopping, his eyes raking the sidewalks for a man in khaki trousers and a dark shirt. He was nowhere to be seen. Halfway up the street he stopped and spun a wobbling circle.

With his lungs heaving, Sanderson's attention went to the walking paths that led into the Botanical Gardens. He sprinted to the nearest and soon found himself winding through an emerald garden of sculpted topiary and trimmed lawns, moving as fast as his old legs would carry him. He reached an intersection where one path split into three, and there Sanderson stopped. He spun another hopeless circle looking in every direction, but saw only miles of blacktop possibility. The three paths each branched to others, all curving behind hedges and looping around trees. Back across the street he saw other sidewalks, some leading to the lakefront, others encircling the massive World Trade Organization building. People were milling in every direction, shunting between workplaces, running errands, and strolling the gardens.

Edmund Deadmarsh was nowhere to be seen.

Sanderson bent down and put his hands on his

knees, completely out of breath after his furious burst of effort. "Dammit!"

Paul Sjoberg was nearly frantic, but he'd done all he could. When the unexpected message had come this morning he'd tried to get through to Sanderson, but had no luck. He next summoned Gunnar Blix to his office—as far as he knew, Sanderson's closest friend on the force—and explained the situation.

A stunned Blix tried to help but said he didn't know where Sanderson had gone, leaving an exasperated Sjoberg to claim, "It's bad enough I can't find a killer, but now I can't even find my own damned detectives!"

His last idea was to call Sanderson's ex-wife, Ingrid. She didn't pick up, so Sjoberg left an urgent message to return his call without going into details.

Out of ideas, he sat at his desk and stared at the email:

A/C Sjoberg,
While patient confidentiality is normally paramount, I have no choice but to breach it in this instance for the well-being of the patient in concern. By his recent MRI, Inspector Arne Sanderson has been diagnosed with a low-grade brain stem glioma. While there is a favorable chance that this tumor is benign, without prompt treatment other life-threatening complications are imminent. It is imperative that we find Inspector Sanderson and present him for an immediate consultation with an oncologist.
E. Samuels, M.D.
NPB Health Services

FORTY

The waitress slid a beer in front of him, and Sanderson took his first sip flummoxed that he wasn't able to convert the prices on the menu from Swiss francs to kronor. He knew the rough conversion rate, but the math simply escaped him. He pushed the menu aside and wrote it off to fatigue.

The pub was on Avenue de France, across the street from the Sécheron rail station. He'd canvassed the area for three solid hours searching for Deadmarsh but had not seen him again. Given the direction his suspect had been walking, Sanderson's best guess was that he'd been heading for the train station. If so, the American—or Israeli or whatever the hell he was— would be miles away by now. Nevertheless, Sanderson had opted for a stool at the front of the pub in order to watch passersby through the big bay window. It had been the briefest of encounters, but there was no doubt in his mind—it *had* been Deadmarsh. And even if he'd gotten away, Sanderson recognized the larger positive that overrode this setback—his narrow assumption had been dead on target. The man was a killer, and he had come here to undertake a political assassination. Which meant he'd be back.

But what to do about it? he mused.

Sanderson saw three options. He could call Sjoberg and explain that he'd tracked Deadmarsh to Geneva. The AC might give his sighting the credence it deserved, but the more likely outcome was that Sjoberg would reject the political assassination scheme, deem Sanderson deranged, and order him home. Alternatively, he could slip the news to Elin Almgren and let her run things up the chain of command at SÄPO. This, however, was equally problematic. Almgren was already assisting him outside formal channels, and the first thing her superiors would do would be to verify things with Sjoberg, or perhaps Anna Forsten, either of whom would certify Sanderson to be an unhinged cannon. In both cases there was some chance of getting proper surveillance in Geneva, but more likely a pair of men with a soft-sided wagon to retrieve Sanderson himself.

The third option, of course, was to hunt down Edmund Deadmarsh himself. The drawback of this was obvious enough. What if he succeeded? The man was a highly trained killer and presumably armed. And while Sanderson had spent his early years on the force in some of Stockholm's toughest quarters, the man he was hunting was easily half his age, and—something that had not escaped his eye—in superb physical condition. He remembered the gray eyes that kept moving, the way he'd positioned himself in the car to see yet not be seen. Today Sanderson had spotted Deadmarsh from behind the darkened windows of a bus. Tomorrow such an encounter might easily be reversed, and given his present circumstances—unarmed and without backup—Sanderson would not be an odds-on favorite in any confrontation. If he somehow cornered Slaton his only option would be to call the police and plead, in the most rational terms he could muster, for them to arrest a man for an assassination that had not yet occurred.

The waitress, a thin woman with overmanaged blond hair, slid a plate of fresh bread and cheese in front of him. Sanderson began carving as he sorted through his doubts. Perhaps his colleagues in Stockholm would work things out, make the same connections he had, and issue an alert to the Swiss authorities about a lurking assassin. It was plausible, he supposed, yet Sanderson found himself hoping otherwise. He quickly recognized this for what it was—the self-interest of redemption. Edmund Deadmarsh could be his ticket back in. If Sanderson stopped the assassin single-handed, he would become an instant legend. If he blew it, of course, he'd be facing retirement. But then, that was where he already was.

Sanderson looked at his watch, then pulled out his phone and placed a call.

His ex-wife answered.

"Hello, Ingrid."

"Arne! Where on earth are you? I just got a message from Paul Sjoberg. He says he needs to get in touch with you about something urgent, but that you haven't been picking up and aren't at home."

"Yes, I've been ignoring his calls. And he's right—I'm out of town. I'd appreciate it if you didn't talk to him. He'll only make my job more difficult."

"Your job? What are you doing?"

"Exactly what you told me to do."

After a long silence, she said, "Are you having any luck?"

"Surprisingly, yes."

"I'm not sure I like that answer. Blix told me this man is very dangerous. I think you should get in touch with—"

"Ingrid," he interrupted, "I need you to do something for me right away. And please do it without questioning my motives. You have to trust me."

"I always have, Arne. You know that."

"Good. Do you still have your key to our flat?"

"Yes, I think I might."

"If not there's a spare under the pot by the back door—the one with all the dead tulips. I need you to get something from the house and send it to me express overnight." He told her what he wanted and was met with silence. "Can you do this for me?"

He heard a long intake of breathe, then, "Yes, Arne. I'll do it."

Christine was looking at the picture of domesticity. Her colleague from residency, Ulrika Torsten, had just arrived home from work and was reading a story to her thirteen-month-old son. Her husband was making dinner in the kitchen. Unavoidably, she contrasted this to her own circumstances. In order to aid her fugitive husband, she was hiding out with friends after giving them a far-fetched story—lies given and accepted with equal ease.

She hated every minute of it, and hated that David had put her in this position. Yet there was never a question of following through. By some profound influence, she felt closer to David than ever, and she knew that he despised the lies as much as she did— probably more. She also knew that at this very moment he could be risking everything to protect her and their child. For all the trouble that dogged him, Christine was rock-solid in one belief about her husband. More than anything, he wanted what she was witnessing right now—a quiet Friday night at home with his family.

Goodnight Moon came to its end, the mouse and clock having run their ritual courses, and Ulrika held up a bottle and asked, "Would you like to give Fredrik his supper?"

Christine smiled. "Yes, please."

The babe was handed over with a warm bottle, and she tried to make Fredrik comfortable. The child latched on and relaxed instantly in the crook of her arm. Christine felt a protective instinct that was distinctly maternal, and this caused her to wonder how David would react in the same situation. Would the *kidon* be changed by holding his child in his arms?

"You're a natural," said Ulrika. "He always screams when Anders feeds him."

"Not true," rang a voice from the kitchen. "That is only gas."

Christine smiled, and said, "I'm glad I can do something to help. Dav . . . Edmund said it might be Sunday before he can get a flight."

"It's no problem. You can stay as long as you like, Christine. Edmund is welcome as well."

Ulrika went to the kitchen, and Christine found herself mesmerized by Fredrik. He was a beautiful child—but then, weren't they all? His mouth suckled in a slowing rhythm, and before the end of the bottle he was fast asleep, a white dribble running over his cheek that she wiped away with the ever-present slop cloth.

"I think he's done," she called out softly.

Ulrika reappeared and Christine tried to rise without waking Fredrik. Halfway up she felt an excruciating pain in her midsection. She fell back into the chair.

"What's wrong?" said Ulrika, taking Fredrik.

"I don't know," Christine said, grimacing. "I had a fall the other day, bruised my ribs. They've been sore ever since, but not like this."

"I should have a look. Perhaps we can get an X-ray to see whether—"

"No, no! I can't have an X-ray because I'm—" She stopped there, tearing up as pain seared through her upper body.

Ulrika looked at her with concern. "I'm going to put Fredrik to bed," she said. "Then I'm taking you to the emergency room."

Slaton retrieved the Range Rover in Rolle and headed north on the A1. He estimated a two-and-a-half-hour drive to Basel, the city that divided the Rhine and was forever fixed as the junction of France, Germany, and Switzerland. With the sun falling low, what had been a glorious day looked ready to descend into something else, dark clouds riding the northern horizon. Slaton scanned through radio channels until he found a weather report. It promised a foul early weekend, with improvement late Sunday. For what he had in mind, a useful forecast.

Keeping with the flow of traffic Slaton passed through Bern, home to the Iranian embassy of Switzerland, and on the far side of the city made a series of stops. At a hardware store he purchased a small tarp, two heavy canvas duffel bags, bolt cutters, and a keyed padlock. A retail mega-box store provided three inexpensive suit coats and an assortment of spray-on fabric protectants. He worked quickly, paid cash, and kept minimal contact with the sales associates.

Back in the Rover, Slaton maneuvered to a quiet

corner of the parking lot and spread the three jackets across the backseat. All were dark in color, but each knit using a slightly different blend of fabric, one mostly wool, the others leaning toward synthetics. He took the aerosol fabric protectants and applied a heavy band to the left and right shoulders of each jacket. To get the first coating to dry more quickly, he opened the windows for better ventilation. He then waited, leaning on a fender and sipping water from a plastic bottle as traffic on the autobahn built to its daily crest. After fifteen minutes he applied a second layer, but only to the right shoulder of each jacket. Three jackets, three brands of clear solvent, with a heavier application on the right side. Satisfied, he left the jackets in place to dry.

Slaton's next stop was a travel station where he filled the Rover's gas tank for the last time, and finally a pub where he enjoyed a bowl of thick barley soup and warm bread. He was back on the A1 just in time to blend into the leading edge of Friday's rush-hour traffic, set perfectly to arrive in Basel shortly after nightfall.

FORTY-ONE

Sanderson decided he'd been staring through windows long enough. He asked the waitress if she knew where the nearest canton library was located. She did, offering directions along with a warning that the branch would soon close for the day. He settled his bill and set out on aching feet.

If he was going to have any chance of finding one person in an urban sea of a million he had to narrow his field, yet with no actionable intelligence to work from Sanderson saw only one course—it was time to start thinking like his quarry. If Deadmarsh was indeed here for an assassination, his first job would be to find out everything possible about his target. Sanderson, therefore, would do the same. His began his inquiry as he walked with a call to Elin Almgren.

She picked up immediately. "Good to hear from you, Arne. Any luck?"

"Perhaps."

After an extended pause, she asked, "So how's the weather in Geneva?"

Sanderson didn't remember mentioning where he'd gone. "You can be maddening, you know that."

"You asked for any information I could give you on Dr. Ibrahim Hamedi, and the first thing I saw was that he's going to be in Geneva this weekend. Would you like the rest?"

"I sense I'm running up a catastrophic bar bill."

"That you are. I've found a lot on Hamedi, although not much that's going to help you. He's a top-flight physicist, well respected in academic circles. He was offered a teaching post in Hamburg, and also a research position with CERN on the big particle accelerator project outside Geneva. He rejected it all to go back to Iran and build ballistic missiles with nuclear warheads. Or course, this is all publicly available information."

"Tell me something that isn't."

"All right. Anytime a nuclear scientist is suddenly recalled to a place like Iran, questions get asked. Germany's BND, and their Swiss counterparts, the FIS, both made quiet inquiries after he left. It was the usual raft of questions. What kind of expertise did Hamedi have. Had he shown any unusual political leanings or frequented particular mosques in the Hamburg area. Did he have family members back home who might be at risk. No one who knew Hamedi thought he had any affinity for the Iranian regime, and in the end the investigators drew nothing but blanks. There was not the slightest indication that Hamedi was anything other than what he appeared to be—a brilliant scientist returning home to take part in a government program. Despite the objectionable nature of the work, there was nothing anyone in Europe could do about it."

"Can you tell me where he's staying in Geneva?"

"You want me to ask about the projected movements of a man who's been a serial assassination target? That's one way to get highlighted. If you want me to keep this little inquiry of yours quiet you'll have to come up with something less direct."

"Yes," Sanderson relented, "I suppose you're right."

"I wish I had more for you. I'll keep an eye out all the same."

"Thanks, Elin."

"And Arne . . . please take care of yourself."

Sanderson arrived at the library thirty minutes before closing time. He spent the entire half hour researching archived news articles about the head of Iran's nuclear weapons program, in particular the years Hamedi spent at the University of Hamburg and the names of colleagues he worked with. The most promising findings Sanderson printed for later study, and at 6:02 that Friday evening he was the last patron to leave the building, a stack of papers under his arm and a stern-faced librarian bolting the door behind him.

Slaton arrived at the warehouse outside Basel at eight o'clock that same evening. A city that clawed outward into both Germany and France, Basel had long been an industrial center, with a particularly vibrant presence in the pharmaceutical field. As such, it was a place with no shortage of office parks and warehouses. Of specific interest to Slaton was an address owned by LMN Properties, a shell company whose vague title—the late Benjamin Grossman freely admitted—had been lifted shamelessly from the middle of the Roman alphabet.

Slaton had been to the building twice before in his dealings with the arms merchant, so he was sure he could find it. He was equally sure that the property remained in Grossman's holdings, this confirmed by the detailed inventory records provided by the estate lawyer, Herr Holmberg. The only open question was what remained inside. Slaton knew what the storage facility had once housed, and it was not, as alleged in Holmberg's Addendum Three, a waypoint for pass-thru inventories of "seat cushions, wicker baskets, and scented candles."

Slaton steered the Rover through blocks of low office buildings and disjointed parking aprons. The buildings varied in size from stand-alone corporate headquarters to space-sharing small businesses, all interspersed with the odd vacant property awaiting new tenants. He saw a handful of other cars in the area, and lights blazed brightly in random windows. Building 17G, however, nestled in an inconspicuous and ill-lit corner, rendered no more than four empty parking slots and a pitch-black entrance. Slaton maneuvered into the nearest spot and backed the Rover tight to the front door. He retrieved the bolt cutters, already hidden in one of the canvas rucksacks he'd purchased, and made his way to a threshold that had likely not been crossed in months.

The sign on the front door was stenciled in simple block letters: LMN, followed by GmbH to denote the Swiss equivalent of a limited liability corporation. There was no accompanying corporate logo, nor any artful designs or feathered script. Indeed, he saw only two other bits of information posted at the entrance. A phone number to call should the place catch fire, and beneath this perhaps the most telling detail—notice that this particular LMN facility would be open, *BY PRIOR APPOINTMENT ONLY*.

A security keypad at the door posed the first test, its tiny light shining red—the universal color of denial. Slaton knew what the combination had been a year and a half ago, and he doubted it had changed. Holding his breath, he typed the sequence: 4-7-7-2-3-5.

The keypad translation for "Israel." The red light changed to green, followed by a click, and he was in.

Slaton snapped on the lights and happily they worked, some midlevel cog in Grossman's machine having kept up with the utility bills. The air inside was stale, and he was greeted by a dead mouse at the dusty reception desk. He bypassed it all quickly to reach the final impediment. The bulk of the building's square footage was dedicated to storage, this room behind a secondary door that was secured by a simple padlock—a padlock to which he did not have a key. The capable Herr Holmberg would provide one in due course, but the bolt cutters were far more timely. The lock snapped easily, and Slaton pulled the door open with an audible creak. He heaved a sigh of relief.

His luck was holding.

Everything was still here.

On arriving at his hotel room Sanderson settled onto a bed that squeaked. He began sorting through the articles he'd copied, and one in particular drew his interest, a background piece taken from a conservative Berlin monthly. Two of Hamedi's former colleagues were quoted to express surprise that this rising star in particle physics had turned down a teaching post of considerable prestige at the University of Hamburg. Another close acquaintance swore that at least one private concern, the German conglomerate Siemens AG, had tried to recognize Hamedi's talents with the more tangible persuasions of a six-digit pay package and a German car that would, if one was in the mood, exceed two hundred miles an hour on the autobahn. Hamedi turned down the Porsche as readily as he had the department chair, and when he announced that he'd shunned it all for a job with the Iranian government, more than a few eyebrows were raised.

Sanderson had seen such recalls before, governments calling in financial support and reclaiming doctoral candidates to dark corners of the world. Established scientists like Hamedi were often brought back by way of intimidation, this typically involving threats to family members left behind. Yet according to his peers, Hamedi had seemed willing, even enthusiastic about the position, and as far as anyone knew he had no family in Iran other than his mother, a simple woman in her seventies of whom Hamedi spoke warmly, but rarely saw, and who lived in the same Tehran house where he'd grown up. Sanderson's overriding conclusion: Hamedi was either opaquely patriotic, or more likely stoking his professional ego by assuming control of a vital government project. Either way, his motivation had little apparent bearing on how he would be hunted by Deadmarsh.

Sanderson needed what the assassin needed—information regarding the logistics of Hamedi's upcoming visit. When would he arrive? Where would he stay? Where were the vulnerabilities? The only thing remotely helpful was a much-recycled press release announcing that Hamedi would speak Sunday to a U.N. audience of arms inspectors, government ministers, concerned scientists, and of course, representatives of the media. This pushed Sanderson to his last avenue of inquiry, a cross-check of Hamedi's old colleagues from Hamburg. At least three now worked at CERN, or more formally, the European Organization for Nuclear Research, the mecca of theoretical physics. Sanderson then undertook an inverse search of CERN scientists who'd either taught or performed research at universities where Hamedi had studied and taught. Here he unearthed three more possibilities. Altogether, four men and two women, names he recorded for further pursuit in the morning.

He settled into bed, which did nothing to ease the ache in his neck, and checked his phone one last time. A message from Sjoberg he deleted without a thought. The only other thing was a text message from Ingrid: PACKAGE SENT. WILL ARRIVE TOMORROW. PLEASE BE CAREFUL.

Sanderson briefly considered a reply, but in the end he thought better of it. He turned his phone off and closed his eyes, hoping for a decent night's rest before the trying day ahead.

Slaton was staring at an arsenal. One side of the room was stocked to the ceiling with guns, ammunition, and rocket-propelled grenades. The other was piled high with less spectacular, but equally vital, support gear. Water purifiers, boots, uniforms. An inflatable boat caught his eye, but only for a moment. He saw camouflage fatigues, both the classic green and black jungle design, and a pixelated tan desert motif. He saw the dull gray of projectile casings, the reflective green of optic sensors, and the cold black of weapon stocks. Altogether, the color palette of state-sponsored violence.

On Slaton's first visit here, Grossman explained that he'd purchased the building with a contrarian mind-set, reasoning that there was no better place to hide an arms gallery than in a quiet corporate plantation of fastener wholesalers and snow-shovel distributors. Being near the tri-border area, three miles from France and two from Germany, the location was the essence of convenience. Yet this was not a waypoint for shipments. The European authorities were reasonably competent, and so Grossman maintained his bulk storage facilities in less scrupulous and ever-changing points across the globe. Kinshasa, Cali, Jakarta— warehouses that Slaton had already confirmed were in Holmberg's meticulously prepared inventory. The Basel office of the LMN Corporation functioned, for lack of a better term, as Grossman's wholesale showroom.

Closing the door behind him Slaton went to work, and after five minutes with a crowbar he found most of what he needed. There was a wide selection of gunsights and night vision gear. Some required power, and he inserted batteries into two of the units and connected them to an electrical outlet to charge. His preferred sniper rifle was here, the Barrett 98B, but Slaton was happier to find an MP7A1, Heckler and Koch's capable assault weapon, along with five forty-round magazines, ammunition, and a suppressor. There was also a Glock 9mm, and he checked that it was clear and the action smooth before loading a magazine and slipping the gun into the waistband of his pants. Two extra magazines went into his left pocket, upside down and backward, ready for a quick exchange given his right-handed grip. Slaton then helped himself to ten 2,000-gram bricks of a certain Czech-manufactured product, along with the associated electronics. After a thoughtful pause, he took ten more. Finally, in a dark corner, he found the ensemble of gear that would get him in and out.

Slaton collected his equipment—and on paper it *was* his—and began transferring everything to the Rover, the weapons concealed in canvas as he made the short traverse. Once done loading, he retrieved the three jackets from the backseat along with a half-empty bottle of water. Back in the storage room he spread the jackets over unopened crates at the far end. Slaton took the two sets of night vision goggles, now minimally charged, and killed the room's lights. Alternating between the optics, he carefully inspected the jackets, and after a thoughtful two minutes he declared the German unit superior. He crossed the room with the water bottle in hand, twisted the cap, and shook it over the jackets like a priest sprinkling holy water. He again referenced the German sight, and thirty seconds later had his answer.

Scotchgard.

Slaton used the crowbar to rip a half dozen strips of wood from different crates, doing his best to leave the planks with jagged edges and bent nails. The three jackets and the unwanted brands of stain protectant went into a plastic trash bag. He transferred all of it to the Rover, locked up the storage room with the padlock he'd purchased, then reset the alarm on the outer door. Slaton steered Krueger's luxury SUV back toward the A2 on a secondary road. One mile short of the autobahn, he pulled to the shoulder near a quiet country bridge, waited patiently for two cars to pass, then opened the passenger-side window and sent the trash bag spiraling into a churning tributary of the Rhine River.

FORTY-TWO

Slaton arrived at the Montreux Casino at ten o'clock Friday evening and parked the laden Rover in a quiet corner of the ground-floor parking garage. The broken planks he'd ripped from the crates in Basel went on top in the Rover's cargo area, and he added a few sheets of crumpled newspaper and two spent plastic bottles retrieved from a nearby trash can. After setting the alarm, he circled the vehicle once to make sure the only thing visible inside was a pile of trash.

In the hotel lobby, wearing his new Armani sportcoat and with the Prada travel bag in hand, he went straight to the reception area for preferred customers—a runway of red carpet that was clearly delineated by silver stanchions and thick-braided gold rope.

"Can I help you, monsieur?" queried the man at the desk.

"Yes, the name is Mendelsohn and I'd like to register. I'm here as a guest of Walter Krueger."

"Ah, yes. We've been expecting you. Monsieur Krueger called to make all your arrangements." He went to work on his keyboard, and soon Natan Mendelsohn's identity card was accepted with a careless glance. Two minutes later Slaton had a room key in his pocket, and the desk man was handing over a second plastic card, this one cast with a mirror-like platinum finish.

"This card, Monsieur Mendelsohn, will access your gaming account. *Bon chance!*"

The man raised a finger, and Slaton was escorted to a fifth-floor room by an engaging young woman. After a brief tour of the suite, Slaton declared an urge to hit the tables, a request met enthusiastically by his personal concierge. She led him to the casino floor and introduced him to the cashier, who soon pushed a stack of chips across a well-worn counter that summed twenty thousand Swiss francs.

The gaming floor was like any other. Red, green, and gold were the dominant colors, and waitresses in short skirts and push-up bras did a brisk business serving unlimited alcohol to brooding figures hunched behind felt tables and brass machines. The sounds were equally predictable, the squeals of winners easily overriding the quiet groans of their less fortunate supporters.

Slaton began with blackjack. He played poorly, yet somehow emerged nearly two thousand francs to the good. He switched to roulette, bet heavily to accelerate things, and in twenty minutes had forfeited his gain with another five thousand. Slaton frowned accordingly, and slapped his palm on the green felt each time the maddening little ball went astray. The croupier kept to his task, as did the unsmiling pit boss, and the cameras overhead recorded everything as the casino's new guest from Zurich took a modest pounding on the first night of the seven for which he was booked. After a tedious hour's work, Slaton returned to the cashier's cage, and there exchanged his remaining chips for cash, after losses and tips taking to his room the sum of fourteen and a half thousand Swiss francs.

In his room he showered, shaved for the first time in two weeks, and finally, standing at the bathroom door in fresh clothes, made his last assessment of the day—the layout of his suite. Long convinced that simple precautions were the best, he pushed a Queen Anne bureau across the floor until it was positioned eighteen inches from the door. It was the only way in, other than a flush window with no balcony and a five-story drop. The door might give to a stiff kick, but the dresser would serve as a secondary impediment, perhaps giving a few extra seconds in a worst-case situation. The configuration also lessened the chances that he would shoot any ill-mannered members of the housekeeping staff who forgot to knock. Defensive aspects aside, the gap was also wide enough for him to leave in a hurry should the need arise. Moving to the bathroom, Slaton rotated the door fully open, flush against the interior wall, to create the thickest available cover position. His jacket went on a hook by the door, but otherwise he remained fully clothed, including his shoes. The keys to the Rover, all his cash, identity documents, and two spare 9mm magazines were stowed in the usual pockets.

At the end of a productive day, Slaton drew in a long, soothing breath as he approached the bed. There, and on the adjacent nightstand, he found printed cards advertising Internet service, bedsheets, bottled water, room-service breakfast, and the last suggesting how best to handle his bath towels in an environmentally friendly manner. It occurred to Slaton that there was a person somewhere whose principal duty in life was to compose, print, and distribute such material. He tried to imagine the serenity of leading such a routine and unfaceted existence.

Then again, he thought, *maybe being an assassin isn't so bad.*

Slaton swept the advertisements into a stack on the nightstand before stretching out on one side of the king-sized bed, the Glock near his right hand, safety off. Tomorrow, Saturday, October 19, would be a busy day. He willed his muscles to relax, ignored the thrum of traffic from the street below, and with the casino's spotlights carving through silk window shades, Slaton drifted into what he knew would be a fitful night's sleep.

Sanderson remembered to set the alarm and it went off at seven o'clock sharp. He was happy to wake knowing where he was, but on rising felt dizzy, and the all-too-familiar throb at the base of his skull had returned. Breakfast and a shower did little to help, and he tried to ignore it all as he went to the hotel desk and requested a cab to take him to CERN.

For nearly fifty years the European Organization for Nuclear Research had been centered in Geneva. It was where the most accomplished physicists in the world attempted to deconstruct the universe, an undertaking Sanderson presumed did not recognize weekends or holidays. He directed the cab's driver to take him to the primary complex, a place called Meyrin, and settled in for a long ride, reasoning that anything called "The Large Hadron Collider" had to be situated well clear of population centers. He was wrong. Two minutes after passing the international airport, the driver was holding out his empty hand.

The outer facade had an industrial appearance, and

could easily have been taken for a computer chip or smartphone factory. Sanderson took the direct approach, walking straight to the main entrance through a light drizzle and again portraying himself to be with Interpol. To the guard at the security desk he presented his list of six names, and was informed that yes, one was on site today, a senior researcher by the name of Dr. Ernst Hamel.

Two phone calls and fifteen minutes later, he entered building 40, a structure evidently conceptualized by its architect to represent something in the subatomic regime, although Sanderson could not say what. A large central atrium was ringed by multiple floors of office space, doubtless to suggest a rising column of knowledge. He was guided to a glass-walled conference room where the senior scientist could barely be seen behind a table stacked with lab equipment and books. Hamel strode across to greet Sanderson, clearly having been forewarned, and the two men exchanged pleasantries. He was tall and lean with a well-groomed beard, and there was a directness in his gaze Sanderson instantly liked. His wrinkled lab coat was worn at the sleeves, no doubt from countless hours behind a keyboard, and mounted on the wall behind Hamel was a dry-erase board ten feet long that seemed to be filled with a solitary, never-ending equation, the kind of thing Sanderson would not understand if he spent the balance of his life trying.

"Yes," Hamel said, "I worked with Hamedi for a time in Hamburg. A brilliant man. Is Interpol still worried about him?"

"Still?" Sanderson queried.

"I was interviewed shortly after he left for Iran, the usual nonsense. Did he have any political leanings? Did he frequent particular mosques? I said it then and

I'll say it now—he was a good man, brilliant, and very hardworking. I don't think we ever once discussed politics or religion. He was Muslim, of course, but it wasn't something he pushed on others. Hamedi had an expansive bookshelf in his apartment, one that we combed through together many times—I never saw anything more extremist than a copy of the Koran."

"Actually," Sanderson said, "my reason for being here is more forward-looking. We have reason to believe that an attempt could be made on Dr. Hamedi's life during his visit to Geneva this coming weekend."

"I see. Yes, that is a concern." Hamel clasped his hands tightly behind his back. "I did hear about the attempts in Iran—you know, all that business with the Israelis. It's not the kind of thing my peers and I usually have to deal with. But you think he could be at risk here, in Switzerland?"

"Our information is not exactly concrete, but we must err on the side of caution."

"Of course."

"Tell me," Sanderson said, "will you be attending Hamedi's presentation tomorrow?"

"Yes. Dr. Michel and I worked closely with Hamedi in Hamburg and we were planning to go. But given what you're telling me now—perhaps we should skip the speech and be satisfied with the reception."

"Reception?"

"Surely you know about it—afterward, on the yacht?"

"Of course," Sanderson played. "But I'd like to hear what details have gotten out."

Hamel fished through a pile on his table and came up with an invitation that looked as if it had been printed from an email. He handed it over and Sanderson saw a picture of a yacht named *Entrepreneur*, along with a schedule for a reception involving an evening cruise that would take place immediately following Hamedi's speech. *8 p.m. to 10 p.m. Hors d'oeuvres and wine, live entertainment.*

"Yes, we've had a close eye on this," Sanderson said. "By your understanding, who will attend this event?"

"It looks a big enough boat, but all I can tell you is that ten, perhaps twelve of us from CERN have been invited. Two or three of Hamedi's old colleagues from Hamburg are coming as well, I think. And the U.N. people, of course—the chief weapons inspector and his staff. I'm sure the Iranians will have a delegation."

"Oh yes, you can be sure of that," Sanderson said. For ten more minutes he cast questions at Hamel, but caught nothing more of interest. Sanderson bid the professor a courteous good-bye and rode the elevator down buoyed by his results. His next step was obvious, and at the entrance he called for another cab and was soon on his way to the waterfront.

For the first mile Sanderson found himself scanning the sidewalks for another glimpse of Edmund Deadmarsh. He forced himself to stop. It was like expecting lightning to strike the same spot twice. He settled back into the seat and turned on his phone, hoping for salvation from Elin Almgren. He found six messages, three each from Blix and Sjoberg. "Good Lord!"

With two quick touches Sanderson deleted them all. He turned his phone back off.

Blix knocked on Sjoberg's office door and was waved in.

"Have you been able to contact Sanderson?" Sjoberg asked.

"I'm afraid not, sir. I keep getting his voice mail."

"Yes, I've been getting the same. But let's keep trying. What else?"

"I've had a busy morning. Our technicians were finally able to isolate the engine noise in the background of those mobile calls Deadmarsh made. They've confirmed the acoustic signature as being from a Lycoming."

Sjoberg stared dumbly across his desk. "What the devil is a Lycoming?"

"It's an engine that has only one use—small aircraft."

Sjoberg thought about it. "So he dropped those mobiles from an aircraft?" The assistant commissioner rose from his chair and stood looking out the window. "The ferry ticket in Styrsvik, the ATM here. He's been leading us a merry chase, hasn't he?"

"It would appear so. As soon as I saw this I sent a man out to the air traffic control facility at Arlanda. I thought we should go back and try to identify the airplane."

"Yes, that's good. Any luck?"

"I'm afraid so," replied a hesitant Blix. "The supervisor there knew exactly what we were looking for. She said it was a seaplane, based down in Oxelösund—even had the name of the charter company before our man asked."

"How did—" Sjoberg stopped mid-thought. He slammed an open palm on his desk. "Sanderson, the bastard!"

"I'm afraid so. The woman at Arlanda confirmed it. He's got a three-day head start on us."

Under his breath, Paul Sjoberg cursed like the sailor he'd once been. Seeing a case that was deeply in arrears and falling more so, there was only one option—damage control. He dispatched Blix to Oxelösund to pursue the lead on his wayward detective. The sergeant had just left his office when the phone rang.

"Sjoberg."

"Paul, it's Anna Forsten. Christine Palmer has turned up. Apparently she was admitted to Saint Göran late last night. Get over there as soon as you can."

There was a click before Sjoberg could even reply with his own embarrassing revelations. He rushed to the door and ripped his coat off the hook.

FORTY-THREE

Entrepreneur was a stately presence as she slid to the dock, her sleek white lines a pretty picture on a lake that was made for them. Even darkened skies and steady rain could not dampen her showing, and as her port side nudged the pier along Quai du Mont Blanc, Farzad Behrouz looked on intently while five deckhands in crisp white uniforms secured mooring lines. He already knew a great deal about the ship. He knew that she measured one hundred and thirty feet along the waterline, a custom hull cast by Benetti, the well-known Italian shipbuilder. He knew she'd been carted here, all eight hundred tons, in an undertaking that had involved four trucks, two road closures, and six months' worth of permitting. On an alpine lake in landlocked Switzerland, the vessel was a monument to excess, but then, Behrouz supposed that was the point. To her owner—and he was the only one who mattered—the ship had to be an ideal accouterment for the business of light music and martinis on Lake Geneva.

Standing on the dock under a wide umbrella, Behrouz was surrounded by a contingent of eight men, and as soon as the gangway was lowered they set to their mission. The captain was at the rail to greet them, but the Iranians ignored him as they shoved their way aboard, although one man—Behrouz knew him to be the group's comedian—snapped a ridiculous open-handed salute as he passed the skipper. Behrouz was watching his team begin their inspection when his phone trilled.

He saw who it was and thought, *It's about damned time!*

"You had better have good news," he said.

"I am trying," came the delayed voice of Rafi. "But no, nothing yet."

Behrouz bristled. His body went rigid and his face warped in anger, but he could think of nothing to say. He had already threatened the Lebanese in every conceivable way. He had promised to cut off the man's Hezbollah ties, his money, and finally parts of his intimate anatomy, all without result. So Behrouz said nothing. He simply ended the call and stood fuming, glaring up at a dreary sky as a swirling drizzle spackled his coarse black hair.

So lost in fury was the security chief that he did not notice, a hundred yards behind him, a tall and clean-shaven man who slipped quickly between the stone flowerpots of the Hotel Beau Rivage and disappeared inside.

Dr. Christine Palmer knew hospitals well, and those in Stockholm were like any other. She waited until her nurse had cycled through on her regular rotation, then got out of bed. She'd been admitted overnight for observation, but her diagnosis was a relief for an expectant mother—the pain in her upper abdominal region was no more than an aggravation of the injury she'd sustained from her leap across the harbor a week ago. A broken rib, possibly, but this could not be verified by X-ray since her pregnancy test had come back positive. She was still in pain today, but reckoned that the hospital was done with her. The reason she hadn't been discharged likely had more to do with the police. She had not seen them yet, but since she'd given her true name when she was admitted, Christine knew it was only a matter of time.

She peered into the hallway but didn't see her nurse. Still dressed in a hospital gown, she spotted a wheelchair across the hall, which she thought might draw less attention than simply ambling down the hallway. She was one step out of her room when she heard, "Going somewhere?"

To her left was a fair-skinned man with graying blond hair. He said, "I'm Assistant Commissioner Paul Sjoberg, Criminal Investigation Unit of the Stockholm police."

"It's about time," she said. "Where have you been?"

"I was going to ask you the same thing."

"That's a long story."

"I have all morning," the policeman said.

Christine pointed toward the chair. "I wasn't going to leave, if that's what you're thinking. I believe I have a friend on another floor."

He seemed to consider this. "Perhaps we could go see him soon. But first, I think we should talk."

Sjoberg put her in the wheelchair, and then pushed her back into her room. He took a seat on a yellow visitor's chair so ugly it would have looked at home in any hospital in the world. He said, "I'm not sure where to begin. This interview ought to take place in a proper room at headquarters—you can expect that soon. But right now time is critical. I want to find your husband. He *is* your husband, isn't he?"

She nodded.

"Are you aware that he killed two men here in Stockholm?"

"He told me that was—" Christine hesitated, then, "let me start at the beginning."

And she did, a recap much like the one she'd given David on *Bricklayer*. She followed with a brief account of her exploits since their split at the island of Bulleron. She said as little as possible about David's activities since arriving in Sweden, and nothing at all about his past. After fifteen minutes Sjoberg asked the question she knew was coming.

"Where is he now?"

Christine closed her eyes and took a deep breath to brace herself. This was the question David had predicted. And the one he had asked her not to answer. It wasn't the first time he'd put her in an awkward position. Would it be the last? Would the lies ever end? Once again David's past was drawing her in like the relentless pull from a black hole.

She shook her head.

The policeman's teeth clenched behind tight lips. "But you *do know* where he's gone," Sjoberg said accusingly.

A nod this time.

"You should be aware of your position, Dr. Palmer. You are admitting to me that you know the whereabouts of a suspected killer. To not give this information leaves you subject to prosecution. A woman in you condition, expecting a—"

"Don't you bring our child into this!" Christine snapped with a vitriol that surprised even her. "I may have done wrong, and possibly my husband, but the child I am carrying is no part of this!"

Sjoberg turned and took a few steps away, chin on

his chest, hands clasped behind his back. He finally turned and issued what had to be his most severe gaze. "You are making things worse for everyone, your husband included. I've talked to your doctor and he tells me there's no medical reason for you to remain here at Saint Göran. That being the case, I'll insist you come with me to headquarters for a proper interview." After a long pause, his tone lost some of its authority. "But before we leave, perhaps we should go see your friend—if you still want to."

Christine nodded to say she did.

Sjoberg guided the wheelchair through two halls and an elevator, ending at the window of a critical care room. A uniformed policeman was standing guard at the door, and behind wire-fenced glass Christine saw Anton Bloch. He had a breathing tube and multiple IVs, and his chest rose and fell rhythmically to the post-operative tune she knew all too well. It was a sad sight, but a victory of miracles compared to her last vision of him—bleeding and lifeless on a concrete floor. He also seemed pale and drawn, to the effect that he seemed to have aged years in the last week. In a curious thought, it occurred to Christine that she had met a number of Mossad field operatives, and none were near Bloch's age. Was it because few survived that long? Those left standing, by default, became management? *A good question for David when I see him again,* she thought. *If I see him again.*

Having allowed her a few moments with her thoughts, Sjoberg finally said, "You know who this man is, don't you? Or perhaps I should say, what he once was?"

She nodded, once again preferring motions to words.

The policeman leaned down and put his smooth face in her peripheral view. "Dr. Palmer, I don't know who your husband is. I don't know what he's trying to accomplish. But I fear if it continues, he will end up like the man we're looking at—or worse."

Christine didn't reply right away. As she stared at Bloch she felt her chin quiver, felt her eyes began to water. But then she was revived by something else. Trust. David had never let her down, and she had to trust him now more than ever. Buoyed by that, she looked Sjoberg firmly in the eye.

"No," she said, "I will not tell you where he's gone."

FORTY-FOUR

"I'm going to kill someone, I tell you!"

The Beau Rivage desk manager looked up most uncomfortably. "I beg your pardon, sir?"

Slaton kept to Continental-hued English, an accent that might have sourced him from any of a dozen of the upper countries. "That idiot at L'Ambassadeur. I booked his five best rooms for the second weekend in November, and now he tells me he has plumbing issues that must be addressed. He says he can give me no more than two rooms, and that the bridal suite is unavailable."

"*Quel désastre, monsieur!* How can I be of service?"

The desk manager in front of Slaton was not the man who'd been on duty yesterday, the one he'd seen guiding the Iranians. A nametag presented this man as Henri. He was small and round and impeccably dressed, a confectioner's bonbon suited in dove gray silk and a red tie.

"My sister is marrying the Viscount de Vesci that Sunday. The wedding is booked for the Basilica Notre-Dame, and I have been cursed with the thankless job of finding lodging. I would need your best available suite—you have a balcony on the top floor that overlooks the lake, yes?"

"Our finest."

"And four more rooms for the rest of her party. Can you save me?"

"L'Ambassadeur," the hotelier said, adding a *tsk*-ing noise as if to say, *It is only to be expected.* "Let me see what can be done." He toyed with a computer for a short time before saying, "Yes, yes. The Bertrand Suite is available that weekend. And the other rooms—I can do something."

"You are a miracle worker," Slaton said. "But I must see the room before I can commit."

"Ah—regrettably, monsieur, that room is occupied by a guest this weekend. Perhaps if you came back—"

"No! I have to settle this before I leave for Oslo tomorrow. There is no need to go inside, but I must see the room to be sure." Slaton leaned in conspiratorially. "And ask an exorbitant price. Our father is footing the bill, but he will not even attend—too busy on his yacht in the Caribbean with his third wife. If the bastard won't sit through a full Catholic mass at his eldest daughter's wedding, he is due some kind of pain."

Henri cocked his head deferentially, perhaps a man who knew better than to become involved in family discord. Or perhaps a man who worked on commission. "I think I might have seen Madame Dupre enter the restaurant just a few moments ago."

Slaton grinned approvingly.

They went to the elevator, the manager with a key card in hand. As they waited for a car to arrive, a contingent of three swarthy men stepped into the lobby from the street. Slaton knew immediately that they were Iranians. Indeed, he knew they were part of Ibrahim Hamedi's security detail. He knew because he recognized the smallest of the three—as would anyone employed by Mossad in the last five years. Slaton was looking across the lobby at Farzad Behrouz, minister of intelligence and national security for the Islamic Republic of Iran.

Raymond Nurin stood at a fourth-floor window with his arms crossed, the smoke from his cigarette curling upward unbroken in the room's stagnant air. The office, in a little used corner of the administration wing, had been vacant since Nurin's directive to downsize the department last spring. He'd quietly seen to it that the room was left unused, an order that had generally been adhered to, notwithstanding the leopard-print thong he'd found wadded under a desk last July. There was nothing special about the room itself, a testimonial to particleboard office furniture and dry-erase markers, but the view was first rate. The windows here were the largest in the building, and a welcome relief from the bunker below with its artificial light and charcoal-filtered air. In the distance Nurin could see scalloped beaches, and blue-green waves rolling in from the Mediterranean. The day was unseasonably warm, and the masses of Tel Aviv had descended for a last fling with the sun before winter stole it away. Nurin imagined the carefree throngs. Crawling, splashing, flaunting, ogling—all a matter of where one was in life's sequence.

He turned away.

The events he had set in motion were not progressing as planned. Or if they were, he had no way of knowing it. To be director of Mossad implied a measure of influence, a command of events. As it was, Nurin felt like he was free-falling through a blackened void. He'd heard nothing from Slaton, but that was to be expected. Veron's Direct Action team was established in Geneva, yet until given a mission they were a rudderless bunch. And yesterday Hamedi had arrived in Switzerland with an unusually large security force. Everything was in place, so far as could be planned, yet there was one menacing variable—the thing that had cost him no end of sleep this past week. Would Slaton turn up under the bridge on Lake Geneva? And if so, just how competent *was* this *kidon*?

God I've screwed this one up.

Nurin stabbed out his cigarette in a full ashtray. He decided it was time to play his contingency card. Hamedi would never be this vulnerable again, not until it was too late, and there was no way to predict Slaton's intentions. Knowing he had to do something, Nurin pulled out his phone and arranged a meeting in his office.

Ten minutes later Nurin was back in his bunker. Veron had already arrived, and Zacharias soon joined them. Nurin was about to speak when Zacharias took the initiative.

"The girl, Dr. Palmer, has turned up in Stockholm. She was admitted last night to Saint Göran, the same hospital where Bloch is recuperating from his operation."

"Admitted you say?"

"It's nothing serious. The police have certainly questioned her by now, but I doubt she can tell them much."

Nurin wasn't so sure, but it was another complication he had no time to think about. He addressed Veron, "Is your team in place?"

"Yes, they've established a safe house in Geneva and are standing by for instructions."

"All right then, let's give them some. Here is what they will do . . ."

For Israel's most accomplished assassin to find himself in an elevator with the head of Iranian state security was not without prospects.

Henri was prattling a well-rehearsed monologue about the hotel's superior amenities, in particular the thread-count of its Egyptian cotton sheets. None of the Iranians seemed to regard Slaton critically as they shouldered into the car, the bodyguards perhaps anesthetized by Henri's all-too-predictable pitch, a version of which they had already endured.

Slaton studied Behrouz up close, and saw a small man with narrow-set eyes and a rutted complexion. He was reasonably well dressed in a suit and tie, and his two sidecars were similarly fashioned, although each of them involving twice as much fabric. Possibilities stirred as Slaton weighed the situation. Might he modify his original plan?

He could kill Behrouz in seconds—from where he stood, the neck being the quickest and most efficient method—but the other two would react. The Glock was tucked neatly in his rear waistband, ready for a right-handed draw, but the two guards had spread apart well. If Slaton went that route he would be facing, quite literally, the proverbial gunfight in an elevator. He might survive all that, might even reach the fourth floor with his gun in hand to mount an assault on the room where Ibrahim Hamedi was perhaps vulnerable. Yet there were other outcomes less to Slaton's liking. Improvisation was one thing, ill-considered chaos another. The latter bred outcomes that might endanger Christine, and so he took the idea no further.

Slaton was standing directly next to Behrouz, towering over him, and as the elevator rose he extracted a pack of chewing gum from his pocket, unwrapped two sticks, and popped them into his mouth. He held out the pack of gum as an offering. Behrouz gave a quiet snort, then turned toward one of his men and started chattering in Farsi. On the fourth floor the Iranians exited uneventfully, the two big men hanging with Behrouz like sharks trailing a remora—a peculiar contradiction to the natural order of things.

One minute later Slaton and Henri were on the fifth floor, the little man knocking on the door of a room named Bertrand. When there was no answer, the hotel manager pulled out his passkey and opened the door of the suite. Slaton had carefully positioned himself to be on Henri's right, which put him on the active side of the door, near the lock and handle. With the door ajar, he took one step inside and leaned so as to press the hotelier slightly back into the hallway. As he viewed the room, Slaton reached behind his back and stuck the wad of gum that had been in his mouth onto the key card from his own room at the Montreux Casino, then jammed the whole arrangement into the receiver of the striker plate.

"Yes," he said, "this will be perfect. A wonderful view, I'm sure."

"The best in Geneva," affirmed a beaming Henri.

Slaton too smiled as he reached for the handle and carefully pulled the door shut. The desk manager steered them back to the elevator, and in the lobby minutes later the man who would soon be brother-in-law to the Viscount de Vesci agreed to return the next day to formalize their arrangements. Good wishes were exchanged, and as he backed away, Slaton asked, "Where is the men's room, please?"

Henri pointed toward the stairwell as he began addressing another customer.

Slaton waited until the hotelier was fully engaged before bypassing the restroom, and for the second time in as many days he shot up the stairs taking three at a time.

FORTY-FIVE

Slaton didn't get far. At the third-floor landing he came across a guard, an unsmiling stump of a man who would not allow him to continue upward—at least not without making a comment on his radio. The Iranians weren't the best, but they were capable enough. And while such an alert might not be fatal to Slaton's mission, it would pose unnecessary complications. So he nodded cordially to the man, exited the stairwell into the third-floor hall, and followed it to the end. There he found a service elevator he'd noticed earlier, and an empty car soon arrived. A minute later Slaton was at the fifth-floor Bertrand suite removing his shim from the door.

Once inside, he engaged the chain latch and took a closer look at the room. One main sitting area was joined by a single bedroom, all of it dressed to advance the idea that the place had kept queens and diplomats of past ages. There were fine chairs and delicate lamps, and a tasteful assembly of oil-on-canvas landscapes graced the walls. White floor-length curtains caught the breeze from a partially open window, but otherwise the suite was as still as a photograph. Slaton made a quick tour of the place and found one suitcase, unpacked, and a short line of expensive

clothing hanging in the main closet. Madame Dupre's passport was on the dresser, the picture showing
a woman in her early fifties, but the date of birth ar-
guing otherwise. The bed was unmade and the bathroom floor littered with spent towels. The maid had
not yet arrived today.

Slaton went to the main closet hoping the suite was
an exact mirror of the unit below. Were he dealing
with a security force from a Western government, Slaton knew the opening he was about to exploit would
not exist. Top-tier services blocked out entire floors
above and below a principal's room. The fact that
Iran had not, he granted, wasn't because they lacked
good sense or due diligence. The simple answer was
that the Swiss franc put the Iranian dinar at a massive
disadvantage.

From under the lapel of his jacket he took a heavy
utility knife, a small handsaw, and a flashlight, the
generous pockets of Armani having been ample for
his burglar's ensemble. The sheer length of the closet
posed his first challenge. It was at least twelve feet
long, and not knowing where to aim, Slaton decided
to make his cut in the center. With Madame Dupre's
full-length silver fox hanging over his head, he used
the knife to make three clean slices in the carpet, resulting in a square two-foot-wide opening, three edges
cut and folded back over the fourth. Underneath he
found thick foam padding and gave it the same treatment, which left him facing a section of wooden floorboard. The plywood was not overly thick, and had
certainly softened over the years, but it still presented
a problem.

Slaton studied the ceiling overhead, taking it for a
mirror of what he would find below—a lightweight
lattice of decorative panels mounted on a grid of

metal stringers. It was common construction, simple and cheap. The problem was that the panels did little to attenuate noise. He began with the knife, but made barely an outline before turning to the handsaw. It was slow and tedious work that would have been far easier with an electric saw. Unfortunately, in a complication he'd faced before, the resultant noise would be like setting off an alarm.

The blade bit and chewed through old wood, and his bricklayer's hands went numb from pressuring the handle. When the blade finally breached the cavity between floors Slaton stopped to listen. He heard the faint sound of a vacuum, and somewhere a muted television newscast in German. The groan of plumbing as toilets were flushed and the odd thump of a closing door. For a busy hotel, nothing out of the ordinary.

Slaton took off his jacket and set back to work. His fingers soon ached and blisters began wearing into his already hardened hands. Sweat dripped from his brow, and when he checked his watch he saw that he'd been in the room for twenty minutes. He hoped Madame Dupre had a healthy appetite. In a perfect world he would have rented the room for a night and taken his time. As it was, he had to improvise. The thin blade finally met the fourth corner, and with his cut complete he left the saw blade in place and wedged his fingers into the crease, rocking the panel slowly upward. When it came clear he looked through and saw the top of the ceiling panel in Hamedi's closet.

Again Slaton listened. Still nothing unusual.

The dead space between the floors, no more than four inches, was strewn with dust and dead bugs, and he saw that by sheer luck he'd narrowly missed slicing through an electrical conduit. He reached down, dug his fingernails into one soft corner of the ceiling panel, and lifted ever so slightly. It moved, and he was happy to see no light at the opening. The closet door below was closed. There was enough ambient light, however, to see shadows inside the closet. With an urge to move quickly, Slaton slid forward, pulled the panel completely clear, and dropped his head into the gap. Hanging upside down in the darkened lower closet, he looked left and right at a rack of men's clothing. There was one leather jacket, and two of everything else. Dress shirts and trousers, and three feet to his right what he was after—a pair of suit coats. Here, Slaton knew, was the most dubious part of his plan—there was no way to be sure that Hamedi would wear either of them tomorrow evening. Yet like every mission, there came a time to go with the odds.

He anchored his lower body, wedging a knee against the wall, and lowered himself until one arm and shoulder were through the gap. The room was warm, but the sweat beading on his forehead had more to do with the fact that he was hanging upside down in the closet of a heavily guarded Iranian envoy. Slaton reached along the hangar rail, but the suits were beyond his grasp. He quickly extracted himself and pulled an empty wire hangar from the rack overhead, twisting it straight but leaving the hook on one end. On his second try he managed to snag both of Hamedi's jackets and pull them closer. He took note that one was black and the other dark gray. Slaton was reaching for the Scotchgard, and still hanging inverted in the void, when the closet door below suddenly rattled.

Slaton jerked himself up, but there was no time to replace the ceiling tile, which left a gaping hole. He saw light as the door swung open, and then a pair of shoes thumped against the wall. The door shut again. Slaton closed his eyes and breathed out. He distinctly heard voices from the lower room, a casual discussion in Farsi.

He was reaching for the can of Scotchgard again, ready to finish the job, when the second interruption came. A knock on Madame Dupre's door. He heard the mechanical ratchet as the handle engaged, and then a thump when the door caught on the security chain he'd thankfully set.

Someone was trying to enter the room.

Brigit Fontaine, carrying a load of clean hand towels under her arm, called though the cracked door of the Bertrand Suite. "*Femme de chambre,*" she said in her best singsong maid's voice.

She heard no reply, but her guest was certainly inside because the chain was engaged.

"*Madame? Serviettes d'aujourd'hui? Plus tard, ou—*" Brigit froze.

A man was leaning into the gap, and from the waist up—that was all she could see—he was quite naked. He was also covered in sweat and seemed out of breath. He was a tall fellow and, she did notice, rather attractive and muscular.

He smiled at her brazenly, and said in a husky voice, "*Madame est engagé.*"

"*Oh! Certainement . . . pardon, monsieur.*"

"*Trente minutes de plus,*" he said.

"*Trente minutes?*" Brigit repeated. "*Ah! Oui, monsieur, trente minutes.*" Not knowing what else to say, she took an awkward step back.

The door shut gently.

She looked over her shoulder and saw Nicolette down the hall, standing by her cart at Number 12. Brigit scurried silently in that direction and began calling in a harsh whisper. "Nicolette! Nicolette . . . *quel scandale!*"

FORTY-SIX

In spite of what he'd told the housekeeper, Slaton did not plan on thirty minutes.

With the difficult part done, the breach of the floor, he worked quickly. He took the can of Scotchgard, reached down into Hamedi's closet and sprayed a generous three-inch band over the shoulder of each jacket. From his earlier trials he decided that a second coat wasn't necessary. He pushed the jackets back where they belonged on the rail and set the lower ceiling tile carefully in place, then arranged the cut-out section of wood floor at a forty-five-degree diagonal over the gaping hole. He cut away the pad to fit the raised section of wood, and when he folded the carpet flap back it appeared perfectly flat. He then shifted Madame Dupre's luggage stand so that the two X-shaped legs were straddling the hidden hole. The patch wouldn't go unnoticed forever, but Slaton was quite sure it would buy him the thirty hours he needed.

He did his best to clean up, rubbing a hand over the telltale sawdust until it disappeared into the carpet, and then using one of Madame's hairbrushes to groom the thick-pile weave until his cuts were unnoticeable. Satisfied, Slaton was soon standing motionless against the door, glued to the viewing port and waiting for the silence that would send him on his way. Two minutes later, after a whistling steward passed with a room-service tray, he was at the elevator.

He was waiting for the door to slide open when the maid he'd encountered earlier turned a corner. In an awkward moment they locked eyes only a few steps apart. Slaton smiled to put her at ease, and then blew out a long and heavy breath, adding a mock look of exhaustion.

"Madame Dupre," he said conspiratorially. "*Un formidable appétit.*"

The maid's face broke into a look he couldn't quite place—something, he reckoned, between astonishment and delight. Then the elevator arrived and the *kidon* was gone.

Sanderson arrived back at his hotel wet and exhausted, having spent a wretchedly inclement afternoon scouring the United Nations complex and the shores of Lake Geneva. From a park on the southern bank, his chin tucked against a heavy drizzle, he had watched the yacht *Entrepreneur* arrive in all her glory. From the busy sidewalks and pedestrian bridges beyond, sloshing through puddles and getting splashed by passing cars, he had studied a thousand faces. Not one was Edmund Deadmarsh.

He was passing the hotel's front desk when a clerk called out, "Monsieur Sanderson."

"Yes?"

"We have received a package for you, an overnight delivery."

Sanderson walked over and took a small but solid package. "Thank you."

He went to his room and locked the door before

opening the book-sized parcel. Unzipping a packing strip, he opened the flap and pulled out what he'd been waiting for—his service SIG Sauer 9mm. He hadn't carried it regularly in years, but once each quarter he cleaned and oiled the weapon, and exercised both the action and his marksmanship at the firing range. Sanderson had not taken the time to explore Swiss regulations regarding the importation of weapons, but he was surely violating some kind of law in having it sent here. He was equally confident that the shipment of a single handgun, particularly by overnight express, had a miniscule chance of being detected. Not surprisingly, the SIG had slipped through.

He found the loaded magazine separate, and Sanderson confirmed that the chamber was empty. He seated a magazine with the butt of his palm, racked a round into place, and set the gun on the nightstand feeling much better about things.

Ingrid had done well.

The call came at ten o'clock that night, Evita's mobile rattling loudly as it vibrated on the nightstand. She silenced it quickly and waited, but her husband's snoring didn't even change cadence—he'd passed out nearly an hour ago after what was clearly a hard evening session with "the boys." When she saw who was calling, Evita eased out of bed and took her phone into the kitchen.

"There you are," she said in a hushed voice. "It seems like such a long time. I've missed you."

"I'm sorry," Zacharias said. "I've been busy. Very busy. Things are progressing rapidly at work. But I think I can get away for a time. Are you free tonight?"

"Yes," she said quickly, trying for breathless

anticipation. Then for good measure, "I've been longing for you, darling."

They were together less than an hour later in their usual suite.

Evita let the little man lead, as she always did. Indeed, this was how she'd hooked him that first night at the opera house—knowing he had season tickets, and knowing his wife was out of town caring for her ill mother, and standing coquettishly by the refreshment stand at intermission, doe-eyed and cleavaged and flashing glances until he moved to her. They had skipped Wagner's second act that night to talk in a quiet corner of the mezzanine balcony. Zacharias had taken command of the exchange, dropping occasional hints of his loneliness, but speaking more directly about his high position with Mossad. On that first encounter his oblique stories of intrigue and daring had left Evita's mouth set in a perfect letter *O*, a shape that, during the tedious third act of Verdi's *Rigoletto* three weeks later, she mirrored under the crisp cotton sheets of the Isrotel Tower Hotel with a very different end in mind.

Now, twenty minutes after falling into each other's arms, Zacharias lay spent next to her on the bed, their usual wine-laden courtship having been discarded in a frenzy of ripped buttons and tangled elastic.

Afraid he might drift to sleep—he usually did—Evita said, "You seem stressed tonight, my dear. More than usual."

"Yes, yes," he said with a heavy sigh. "But tomorrow it will all be over."

"The assassin you spoke of? He is going to strike?"

He nodded drowsily.

"How so?" she prompted.

Zacharias told her.

When he was done she massaged his hairy shoulders, soft, gentle circles that kept up until he was fast asleep. Evita dressed quickly, but took the time to leave a salacious note on hotel stationery, ending with her lipstick-pressed signature of a full kiss. She was then quickly out the door.

Shortly after, a phone rang in a decrepit hotel on the south side of Saida, Lebanon. After a brief conversation, a relieved Rafi hung up and immediately dialed a second number.

Just after midnight in Geneva, Farzad Behrouz stood on the balcony of his suite pulling a French cigarette to its bitter end. The view was impressive—best if one stood at the outer left edge—but nothing like that of the connecting suite. The balcony to his left gave a sweeping panorama of the city, a million-dollar vista that on this weekend was going completely to waste. He saw the French doors shut tight, drawn curtains backlit by a bulb burning over the desk. Does the man ever do anything but work? Behrouz wondered. He tried to recall if he had ever seen Hamedi when he wasn't hunched over a computer or shuffling through papers. Behrouz, of course, was often consumed by his own undertakings. Yet Ibrahim Hamedi seemed different. And Behrouz, in a long-honed instinct, did not trust men who were different.

He knew a great deal about the scientist. He knew Hamedi was heterosexual, although he had not dated since returning to Iran. He wore a size ten shoe, spoke fluent German and English, and had a scar on his left hip from a scooter accident when he was a teenager. This was all in the records. Yet there was something else that escaped Behrouz, a hidden force that drove the man. He thought he might know what it was, but had been unable to find proof. Indeed, proof of such a thing might not even exist. How to substantiate the blackness of a man's soul?

Behrouz shifted his gaze toward the city, the ominous shadows that were the Alps looming over pitched rooftops in the moonlight. He stabbed the butt of his cigarette into a tumbler just emptied of a sharp twelve-year-old Scotch, and was skimming his eyes over the lake when his phone vibrated.

"Yes?"

"She has done it!" came the eager voice of Rafi.

"Where will it happen?"

"Please understand, this is valuable information. We have put ourselves in considerable danger to acquire it, and perhaps it is worth more than our agreed upon—"

"Tell me this instant!" Behrouz hissed. "Otherwise it will be worth your life!"

A pause, then, "The Jews will attack tomorrow night. On a dock at the lake, in front of a large boat. A lone assassin will attempt to shoot from underneath a bridge—I don't know the name of the bridge, but it is two hundred meters away."

Behrouz stood stunned for a moment, then spun a half circle and saw it right in front of him—the bridge to his right, the first of the spans that overlaid the mouth of the Rhone. From there to the dock, two hundred meters? *Yes*, he thought, *that must be it*.

"What else?" Behrouz said impatiently. "Did she give a time?"

"No. Only that it will happen tomorrow night. If this is not precise enough I could ask her to make another contact. But that, of course, would involve further risk. I am sure she will demand more money."

"No!" Behrouz insisted. "Your whore will make no further contact. Not unless I direct it. If she seems too eager it will raise suspicion. Her target may be decadent, but he is not a fool."

Rafi began to say something else, again involving money, but Behrouz only ended the call. He suspected that none of the money he'd paid so far had gone to the spy. No woman gave herself as this one had for money. She was acting on passion—love, hate, revenge. He pocketed his phone and studied the dock and nearby bridge. Leaning on the balcony rail with a perfect perspective, Behrouz lit another cigarette, and after a long draw began to design his countermove.

FORTY-SEVEN

Somewhere in the distance, in the rising hills that watched solemnly over Montreux, a church bell rang nine times to bring the third Sunday of October to its tranquil beginning.

Slaton allowed himself a late rise, and though he'd slept eight hours, it was with the deficit of refreshment that came from sleeping inches removed from a loaded gun. He went to the window and was happy to see improving weather—yesterday's rain had cleansed the skies, and a sharp autumn breeze snapped at the twin rows of canton flags beneath his window and put a light chop on the lake's cobalt surface. He ordered breakfast in his room, bid the server a courteous good morning, and assured the young man that there was nothing he could do to enrich monsieur's stay.

In a rare allowance, Slaton pulled back the curtains and sat with a reaching view of the lake, his long legs straight and heels crossed on the tiled windowsill. With level eyes he charted the lake as he dug into the heavy tray, mental sketches and checklists gone over one last time. No attempt was made to savor the meal, the only important thing being to fill the void in his stomach with enough dense protein to carry the day.

When he was done Slaton dressed warmly, and in

the Prada bag he packed one extra set of clothing, the cash remaining after his sorry night at the tables, and the Glock and spare magazines. The Swiss identity card and passport of Natan Mendelsohn he pocketed. Everything else Slaton left where it was—clothes hanging in the closet and toiletries strewn about the sink. In three days' time, when Krueger's reservation ended, it would all be rounded up by the housekeeping staff to languish in the hotel's lost-and-found for a matter of months before eventually being donated to a worthy charity.

At the front desk the luckless Monsieur Mendelsohn made inquiries at the concierge station, where an attractive Italian woman, improbably named Victoria Ferrari, was happy to help. He requested recommendations for a route by which to tour the Savoy wine region of eastern France, and a well-versed Victoria said she would gladly help him set an itinerary. He smiled as she highlighted her favorite vineyard tours, and she blushed when he suggested lightly that she might join him, and soon Monsieur Mendelsohn was turned toward the door with a map in hand, clear directions, and a not disinterested Victoria wishing him a pleasant day's journey.

On clearing the parking garage, Slaton pointed the Rover toward the A9, but there turned away from the French border, instead pressing south toward Lake Geneva's far shore. He kept an eye out as he drove, knowing that one last purchase remained, a chore he had intentionally deferred to this afternoon. It would be his largest expenditure yet, but with over fourteen thousand Swiss francs in hand he expected no difficulty in concluding a sale.

Nearing Valmont, Slaton turned left, away from the lake and into steeply rising terrain. He stopped once at the side of the road to drop the passport and identity card, which bore the only high-resolution pictures of him he knew to exist, down a secluded storm drain. He continued to Les Avants, swept briskly through the village, and on the far side steered the Rover away from the main road to ride a gravel offshoot that roamed into thickening forest. Soon he was navigating switchbacks, curving left and right though rolling hills, the compass on the dashboard spinning wildly but keeping in sum an eastward vector.

The timber seemed to rise taller with every turn, and gravel became dirt, but the Rover showed its heritage and kept a firm footing on the shoulderless and rutted road. He did not see another car for two miles, and after a particularly steep rise Slaton began scouting the sidings for a dry clearing. He made his choice and drove slowly clear of the trail, taking care to not hang the differential over a ditch or bend the chassis on a hidden boulder.

Satisfied the vehicle was well hidden, he put the Rover in park and went to the tailgate. Were he of the mind to appreciate the view he would have seen that the lake was presented differently here, framed by stands of pine and fir, and footed by a valley of grass still clinging to the green of summer. Slaton noticed none of it, nor did he register the altered breeze coming strong off the lake, a northwest flow sweeping in from France and rising on the uneven Alpine upslope. His focus was absolute as he opened the tailgate, locked it in place with a pin, and with the wind lashing his hair began to assemble his assault.

Paul Sjoberg was not typically a man to work on Sunday morning. But this wasn't really work.

Stepping from a cold rain, he shook the water from his umbrella under the portico of a grand home on Skånäsvägen. It reminded him of a house where he had once attended a fund-raiser of some sort, although the details seemed a blur. Then again, he might have thought the same about any of the well-tended mansions along this placid waterfront street. Not seeing a doorbell, he lifted a ridiculous iron ring that was hooped through a lion's nose and knocked it against the striker plate. It made a good racket, and Sjoberg struck three times in quick succession, mist spraying from his cuff with each beat.

Ingrid Sanderson—if that was the name she still used—answered moments later.

"Oh . . ." she stammered, "hello, Paul."

"Hello, Ingrid. It's been a long time."

"Yes, hasn't it?" She suddenly went ashen, the way policemen's wives—even policemen's ex-wives—did when grim-faced supervisors came unexpectedly to their door. "Oh, God! Don't tell me it's Arne."

"No, no," he said quickly. "Or actually, yes, but not like that. Nothing dire."

She looked at him guardedly.

Beyond her Sjoberg saw the innards of an opulent mansion, the kind of place in which policemen—even assistant commissioners—did not find themselves without either an invitation or a search warrant.

"You have a lovely home," he said.

"Oh, how rude of me. Come in if you like. But I have to warn you—I'm not sure if my husband is presentable yet."

"Actually, Ingrid, I just need a minute of your time." Sjoberg retreated a step. "A private word, perhaps?"

Ingrid looked back into the house, then pulled an overcoat from a hook near the door. She wrapped it round her shoulders, stepped outside, and shut the door quietly.

"What's this all about?" she asked.

"You didn't return my call."

Her eyes cast down to the well-polished Italian marble. "No, I didn't."

"Arne isn't returning them either. He's turned off his phone and I can't find him."

"Has he done something wrong?" she asked.

"No. He's on leave—it's a medical issue. Has he told you any of this?"

"Yes, I saw him a few days ago. He said he'd quit, and that you and he had had a row."

"We did. But that's over and done. Arne and I have always had our differences, but I have a great deal of respect for him, both as a policeman and a person. Ingrid . . . I spoke with his doctor yesterday. Arne is ill, very ill. He needs to see a specialist right away."

"What's wrong?"

Sjoberg told her.

"Dear God, no. How bad is it?"

"They won't know until they get in and do a biopsy."

She seemed to stiffen. "Paul, do you think . . . do you think he might know about this?"

"I don't see how. His doctor and I have been trying to reach him for days, but he seems to have taken a run after this killer we've all been hunting—which is another reason I'd like to talk to him."

Sjoberg saw a woman who was visibly shaken. She almost seemed to age right there in front of him, her back more bowed, her face coming drawn.

He said, "Please, Ingrid. If you can reach him in any way, tell him to come home. He needs to see a doctor.

That's the only important thing—the rest we can manage."

He turned to leave.

"Paul—" she said.

He turned.

"Thank you."

Sjoberg nodded, then raised his collar and opened his umbrella, and stepped once again into the wet morning.

Back on the porch Ingrid stood gripping the door handle. She made no effort to turn it—it was more a matter of connecting herself to something steady when she realized what she'd done. Her ex-husband was ill, perhaps terminally. Certainly despondent.

And she had just sent him a gun.

Sanderson began Sunday morning studying the layout of the United Nations Office at Geneva. Unlike yesterday, he saw tight security at every corner of the fortress-like building, and he was sure things were equally tight within. A routinely inviting target, the U.N. building would undoubtedly have fixed screening stations in place to inspect everyone who entered, a well-monitored surveillance system, and a security force that was well versed in the perils of hosting presidents and prime ministers. After an hour, Sanderson reprimanded himself for wasting as much time as he had. For a lone assassin to make an attempt here would be absurd. If Deadmarsh was going to strike, he decided, it would be at the waterfront.

Sanderson contemplated walking but he was feeling awful, and so he hailed a cab and collapsed into the backseat with yet another terrible headache.

Reaching into his pocket he found a bottle of over-the-counter painkillers, but a quick shake told him it was empty. He dropped it onto the seat wondering, *When did I use the last of it?* The driver negotiated light weekend traffic, and Sanderson found himself scanning the sidewalks. He saw no familiar faces. All the same, the heavy SIG was a comfort in his pocket.

He was light-headed when he got out of the cab on Rue de la Cloche, his feet feeling as if they were made of lead, and a short flight of steps nearly got the better of him outside Chapel Eglise Emmanuel. Deciding he ought to eat something, Sanderson bought a pastry and container of juice at a confectionary on the esplanade, and gratefully took a seat on a retaining wall in the shade of a chestnut tree on Quai Wilson.

He turned on his phone and saw that Ingrid had called. His finger hesitated for a moment, but then he tapped to return her call.

She picked up immediately.

"Hello, Ingrid."

"Arne, thank God! Where have you been?"

Sanderson thought she sounded rattled—something he had rarely witnessed in their years together. "What's the matter?" he asked. "Is it Annika?"

"No, no, she's fine. It's you."

"*Me?* What do you mean?"

"Arne . . . Paul Sjoberg came to see me this morning. He was contacted by Dr. Samuels. You're not well."

"Tell me something I don't bloody know. As soon as I'm done with what I'm working on I'll—"

"Arne, you fool, will you just listen for once! You've got a tumor in your brain!"

FORTY-EIGHT

Christine spent the night at police headquarters undergoing a battery of coffee-fueled interrogations that tested her stamina, not to mention her resolve. In the end she gave up nothing about David's whereabouts. At the stroke of six in the morning, on the verge of exhaustion, she told them she was pregnant, a fact that Sjoberg had apparently not forwarded to the interrogators. It was a blatantly self-serving use of her intimate condition, but seemed to do the trick. Two hours later Commissioner Anna Forsten of the Swedish National Police came to see her. She explained that criminal charges would be considered, but were not imminent. Christine was free to go, but asked to remain available for further questioning in the coming days. To emphasize this final point, her passport would be held by the police.

From there Christine went straight to Saint Göran Hospital. After a phone introduction from Dr. Ulrika Torsten, she was taken by the supervising critical care nurse to Anton Bloch's room. There she hit another roadblock in the form of a plainclothes security man who might have been Stockholm police or, more likely, she thought, the Swedish equivalent of the FBI. Two phone calls later, Commissioner Forsten authorized

Christine's admittance, reasoning that she was the patient's only known acquaintance in Stockholm. Christine suspected more self-serving motives, and she noticed the guard at the door watching closely as she took a seat next to Bloch's bed.

He was breathing on his own now and, according to a nurse who came and went, the operation had been a success. The patient, however, had yet to regain consciousness. Even asleep Bloch looked his gruff, serious self, and it seemed comforting in an oblique way. She settled into a bedside chair, ready to keep vigil over the man who had put his life on the line to save hers. She had an urge to take his hand, and when she did Christine sensed a shift in the guard's gaze.

That will be in the report, she thought.

The chair's soft faux leather took its hold and she began to relax. She wondered what David was doing right now. He was in Geneva, of course. Lying, cheating, stealing—all the things he was trained to do. But would he take the last step? Would he kill? He had done so before many times, always in the name of his country. But now?

It struck her then, as she pushed back and molded into the soft cushions, that she had put David in an entirely untenable position. On one hand he'd been threatened, told that his wife and child would never be safe unless he carried out one last assassination. But if he went through with it, she had promised to leave him. For the first time Christine put herself in David's place. She asked herself that same question. Would she kill a man to protect her child? Chillingly—and without hesitation—the answer came.

Oh, David. What have I done to you?

She closed her eyes tightly. The room was cool and

quiet, the only noise being the rhythmic beep of a vital signs monitor. Sleep-deprived and queasy, confused and exhausted, Christine put her free hand to her belly. Soon she was fast asleep.

Sanderson sat under the chestnut tree for a very long time. On the lake sailboats heeled against a stiff breeze as they scythed through sun-flecked water, and Mont Blanc was clear in the distance, two colorful hot-air balloons hovering near its black-granite base. As he watched the crowds stroll the sidewalks, it struck Sanderson that nearly everyone seemed oblivious to the glorious morning around them. A couple arm-in-arm were too distracted by one another. A woman carrying groceries was consumed by her chore. And the elderly man shuffling with his duck-handled cane? *Yes*, Sanderson thought. *He's the one who's seeing it.*

Ingrid had talked for half an hour, telling him what he needed to do and who he needed to see. He was glad about that, not because of what she'd said, but simply to have someone there to say it. He would need her in the days ahead, and not for the first time labeled himself a fool for ever having let her go. He promised her he'd come home right away, knowing he wouldn't. Sanderson did, however, take the time afterward to check tomorrow's flight schedule. This in itself—the consideration of a flight—he saw as a clear admission of the gravity of his situation.

Thirty-five years a policeman, Arne Sanderson had witnessed more than his share of misery, and so he was well versed in the five conceptual stages of grief. He also knew he would not bother with them. Denial of facts was not in his nature, and anger he thought self-defeating. He might eventually bargain with God for salvation, but right now had more pressing matters to deal with. And depression? Sanderson thought.

Please.

So it was, he moved directly to acceptance. Sanderson even imagined, in a triumph of positive thought, that his affliction was an advantage of sorts—would it not be easier to chase a dangerous assassin as a man with nothing to lose? So with the throb at the base of his skull acting as a constant reminder, he forced himself to get on with the business at hand. Just as he'd been doing for thirty-five years.

The pastry had been quite good, and he went back to the confectionary and bought another, along with a large white coffee. Calorie counting, he decided, was going to get a holiday. Sanderson set back out on the sidewalk at a measured pace with his hands full of sugar and a gun in his pocket. He scanned faces in the shadows of trees shedding yellow, noted untended vehicles in windswept alleys, and eyed the cold lake as chestnuts crunched under his feet. It was noon on Sunday.

If his thinking was right, he had eight hours in which to find Edmund Deadmarsh.

Christine sensed movement, and she opened her eyes to find Anton Bloch staring at her. It was a weary, medicated gaze, but his recognition was obvious.

She smiled. "Welcome back."

He blinked, as if a grin was too much effort.

Christine kept to protocol and immediately summoned a nurse, who in turn put through a call to the attending physician.

"The doctor will be here in a few minutes," the

nurse said. In English she asked Bloch how he was feeling, and got a grunt in return. She then began tending his IV.

Bloch kept his gaze locked on Christine.

"I want to say thank you," she said. "I know what you did for me. For David."

"Da . . . David?" he rasped. "Where?"

She cocked her head, then gave him a knowing nod. "You've been out for quite some time. Today is Sunday, October 20."

She watched him think about it, and could almost see the slumbering synapses connect—a calendar date in his head highlighted in red. This time it was Bloch who reached out and took her hand in his. Christine felt him squeeze.

FORTY-NINE

At seven that evening Arne Sanderson was sitting on a large rock—not by choice, but simply because that was where he'd been standing when his legs buckled ten minutes earlier. That his body was failing was not unexpected, but he did rue the timing. Another few hours was all he needed.

He was stranded, rather symbolically, near the Feu des Pâquis, a hundred-year-old lighthouse situated at the tip of a jetty that clawed into the lake just east of the main docks. The lighthouse was fashioned in a quaint octagonal design, and had once been used for commercial shipping, a point Sanderson had gleaned from a discarded tourist brochure. Today, however, in the world of GPS and computer-coupled navigation, the old relic served as little more than a photographer's backdrop, backlit and plastered with enough coats of white paint to make the original structural members redundant. Sanderson, of course, had not gravitated here to take pictures. After some deliberation, he had deemed the jetty the best vantage point available—a place with negligible foot traffic, and a commanding view of the docks and surrounding harbor.

He'd spent the entire afternoon roaming the area,

walking more miles than he had in years. In an age of instant messaging and data sharing, the art of patient observation was a fading discipline, but Sanderson knew it well. Much of what he'd seen so far was predictable. Uniformed Swiss police were making an obvious showing, and pairs of swarthy men, Iranians no doubt, tried unsuccessfully to be discreet. He'd made a good survey of the nearby rooftops and balconies, although he reckoned that if Deadmarsh was truly competent—and Sanderson suspected he was—the man would not make things so simple.

He remained convinced that the U.N. building would be too difficult to breach, and his afternoon-long study of the waterfront only added to this conviction. From a defensive standpoint the lakefront was too busy to manage properly, too open and public. At any given moment there were hundreds of people, hundreds of vehicles, all moving in a flow that would be impossible to monitor, let alone neutralize. A simple drive-by shooting at the foot of the dock was a distinct possibility, he reckoned, but the most intriguing weakness involved the boats in the harbor. As Sanderson looked out now, in the half-light of the calm evening, he saw a dozen craft of varied sizes and utilities, their red and green navigation lights a snarl of unpredictable movement.

Yes, he thought, *that's how I would do it.*

For the sixth time he tried to stand. His legs protested, but began to comply. Then, just as he leaned forward to gain momentum, a bolt of lightning shot through his skull. Arne Sanderson sat back on his rock and cursed.

He would have to wait a little longer.

From behind a grand podium Ibrahim Hamedi raised a blunt finger to make his final point:

"And in conclusion, let us remember this. In the Middle East today only one nation has a nuclear arsenal poised for delivery. Though it has never been admitted, the state of Israel is alone in this destabilizing course. Such recklessness casts a shadow across the region that cannot be ignored. Were it not for this, her peace-loving Arab neighbors would have no need to even consider such a capability.

"I tell you today that the intent of Iran's nuclear ambition is honorable. Yet the same cannot be said of the Zionist state and her Western supporters, all of whom keep massive nuclear stockpiles as they complain that others should never be allowed to follow in their steps. This is the path of folly. As a scientist, I can say with authority that technology knows no geographic or political boundaries, and it moves in only one direction—forward. Knowledge is the great equalizer, and it cannot be governed by political cabals any more than the rising of the sun or the movement of the stars. As I speak to you today, Iran does not possess the capability to undertake a long-range nuclear strike. But should she ever choose to do so, it is a matter that will be determined by science and effort, not the self-serving crusades of others."

Hamedi backed away from the podium and struck a defiant pose that was instantly caught in the flash of expectant strobes. His facial expression, soon to be echoed in all the world's media, was something close to a scowl. The subsequent applause was mixed at best, the Iranian delegation clapping fervently against what otherwise might be characterized as crickets.

Hamedi descended to the floor of the assembly hall, and was immediately flanked by his security detail.

He began shaking hands along a somber receiving line of men in well-fit suits and women in sedate over-the-knee dresses. Names were mechanically pitched and caught, and then forgotten with equal ease. His friends from academia lingered near the end, a group who clearly employed a different couturier, and here Hamedi found his warmest greeting—the simple enthusiasm of old friends. Nevertheless, he was not allowed to linger.

Reporters spouted a few questions, as was expected of reporters, and Hamedi summarily ignored them, as was expected of dignitaries. For twenty-three minutes Iran's chief designer made the rounds before ducking his head into the second of four sturdy cars at the side entrance. With two motorcycle policemen blocking traffic, and a helicopter overhead, the motorcade shot onto Avenue de France, turned right, and accelerated south.

The man clad in black scaled the underside of the bridge slowly, transferring his weight carefully and keeping the rifle high and out of view. He used a simple wooden plank to bridge the girders, clearing one span at a time and then sliding the plank forward to the next gap. The end result was a completely invisible approach, save for anyone who was actually underneath the bridge, and when he reached his desired perch the assassin made sure the board was secure and left it in place.

He looked down and saw his firing position—a flat steel beam three feet wide, with a flange on one end that would perfectly support his forward hand. He supposed there had never been a more stable shooting platform on earth. The assassin checked his gun one last time, ensuring that nothing had been damaged or altered during his traverse. He then glanced at his watch. Six minutes, more or less. He would begin his vigil in three. That was when he started taking chances. Logically, once he lowered himself to put his eyes on the target area, it meant that others could put their eyes on him. But in this he felt secure, confident that the bridge's dark shadows would grant him the few minutes he needed. *The only way they will see me,* he thought, *is if they know exactly where to look.*

He breathed deeply and tried to relax, his muscles tense after the awkward positioning maneuver. As he waited for his target to appear, the man pulled out a stick of chewing gum and popped it into his mouth. By feel, he then reached back with his hand to put the wrapper in a side pocket.

"There!"

Behrouz stiffened when the warning came through his earpiece. He pressed the bud to his ear.

"Under the third span!" the same voice said over the tactical frequency.

Behrouz was standing on *Entrepreneur*'s gangway as guests arrived en masse for the ship's departure. He whipped his head around and looked intently at the bridge.

The irritated voice of the tactician in charge bristled over the frequency, "Who is reporting? Use your call sign!"

"Six! This is position six! I saw something fall from the third span. It was tiny, but there was definitely something. I think I saw movement there too, in a small gap."

Another voice, "Position four—I saw it as well. It could have been a feather."

"Should we intervene?" asked the commander over the radio, his taciturn voice making any use of his own call sign redundant.

He was posing this question to Behrouz, and there was a heavy pause on the frequency as everyone waited for an answer. Behrouz had seen nothing himself. He looked anxiously at his watch—the motorcade bringing Hamedi would arrive in a matter of minutes. Yes, he thought, it was just as Rafi had said: *A lone assassin will shoot from underneath a bridge . . . two hundred meters away.*

"Yes!" Behrouz barked into his lapel-clipped microphone. "Do it!"

The commander gave the order.

Six men materialized in less than a minute. Two came from a car parked at the northern foot of the bridge. Another two had been circling as tourists, disposable cameras now dropped to the street. One was tending a skiff moored to the quai, and the last had been changing a tire on a rented bicycle. In an assault that had been mapped out hours ago, they all reached the support span in the allotted sixty seconds, and soon were dropping over the sides of the bridge from six different angles. Behrouz heard torrid chatter on the radio, and his eyes padlocked on the base of the bridge.

The first shots were muted—the Iranians had committed to sound suppressors in order to keep the Swiss authorities out of things as long as possible. The response was not so quiet. An explosion of rifle shots shattered the night.

"Two is down!" came a call on the radio.

More shots.

"Target moving west!"

Another voice, "Four is hit!"

The next round of unsuppressed fire was answered with a nearly continuous volley of muted shots. Behrouz saw a black shadow fall from the underside of the bridge and land in a heap on the concrete buttress ten feet below. The body began moving, crawling to get away, until a final barrage finished the job. The black-clad figure went still.

"Target is hit! He's down!" came the commander's breathless voice.

Soon Behrouz saw his team—the three that were left—surround their target. The final verdict crackled to his earpiece. "We got him!"

The commander of the tactical team was soon at Behrouz's side. "It is done," he said. "The area is secure and the Swiss police have been notified. Three of our men were hit, but two are still alive. We've called for ambulances."

Behrouz saw a police car on the bridge, and then another. A pair of the local gendarmerie had already made their way to the understructure and were shining flashlights on the dead assassin. Sirens blared in the distance, and Behrouz heard a new voice in his earpiece.

"Two minutes from the curb."

The transport detail. Hamedi's arrival was imminent.

He could divert the motorcade, of course, send the problematic scientist to the safety of the nearby hotel. But that would be like admitting defeat. He watched a pair of men who could only be Hamedi's colleagues— thick glasses and unkempt beards—present their invitations to the armed guards at *Entrepreneur*'s gangway.

They seemed completely oblivious to the carnage at the nearby bridge.

"We have a picture," said the tactical commander.

Behrouz referred to his phone and saw a grim photo of their victim. The eyes stared blankly skyward, and one cheek had been ripped away by a bullet. *A fitting end for a hired gun,* he thought.

"One minute until Dr. Hamedi's arrival," the commander announced. "Are we to continue operations?"

As Behrouz considered it, his phone rang, and he saw it was his liaison officer with the Swiss police. He ignored the call but expected a redial soon. It occurred to him that if they didn't all get on the boat now, they'd spend the rest of the night answering to the Swiss police. This made his decision.

He replied buoyantly, "Yes, I don't see why not. Dr. Hamedi has dodged another bullet. Let's bring him aboard."

The commander stepped away to issue the order.

Behrouz found himself drawn back to the photograph he'd just received. A grisly image, to be sure, but he'd seen worse. At least the man had found a mercifully quick end. The lighting was poor and the resolution wobbly, yet certain details were clear. The killer's fingers were still wrapped around his weapon. There was blood everywhere—pooled on the concrete and blossoming on the killer's shirt, streaked over his dark skin and matted in his curly black hair.

So this, he thought, *is Israel's lone assassin.*

FIFTY

Sanderson had heard the gunfire quite clearly. In the excitement of the moment he'd jumped to his feet, but immediately felt dizzy. He kept standing, though, leaning on a white metal rail to watch the proceedings. He was a quarter mile from the dock where *Entrepreneur* lay, her elegant superstructure bathed in yellow light and framed by the lively city. That was where his eyes had gone first, until it became apparent that the disturbance was farther off at the base of the distant bridge, half a mile from where he now stood. Back in the day, as a young constable with his life ahead of him, Sanderson might have covered such a gap with an easy three-minute run. But now, as a broken-down veteran and soon-to-be pensioner? A man with no more to look forward to than needles and scalpels? It might as well have been the moon.

The rally of lights grew at the Pont du Mont Blanc, alternating pulses in the hues of authority—blue and amber and red. There were soon a dozen cars and two ambulances, and regular vehicle traffic across the bridge was halted in both directions. Then he saw a motorcade rocket up Quai du Mont Blanc and pull to a stop at the foot of the dock. It could only be Hamedi's entourage, and their arrival spoke volumes to Sanderson. If Hamedi had not been diverted, it meant any threat against him had been decisively neutralized.

So there was his answer.

Imagining Deadmarsh bullet-ridden and lying in a heap, Sanderson was struck by a bolt of recrimination. Could he have prevented it? Had any policemen been killed or injured? He realized now that it had been a mistake to not call Sjoberg and tell him what he knew. Sanderson had made a lot of good decisions over the years, but his last one had been wrong. And people were dead because of it.

He watched the man who had to be Hamedi get hustled up the pier by a security detail. They all clambered up the gangway and disappeared into *Entrepreneur*, and minutes later he watched the crew lift mooring lines and heard a low rumble from the engines. The big boat pushed away from the dock with a stately demeanor, and on her aft mast the United Nations flag flew in a bright spotlight, flapping smartly in the evening breeze.

So that's it then, he thought. *It's all over.*

The slight detective fell back to his rock, this time not so much a physical slump as a deflation of spirit. Sanderson was overcome by the idea that he'd screwed up. Desperate to prove his continued relevance, he had let his ego get in the way of the job. His chin wrinkled and tightness racked his chest, and he held his throbbing head in his hands. Sanderson forced his gaze away from the evidence, the grandeur of *Entrepreneur* getting under way and the tragedy being cleaned up under the bridge, and his eyes settled on the tiny lighthouse to his left. It was surrounded by a breakwater, a U-shaped pile of white boulders meant to protect the outer jetty. In the half-mote between the two, bob-bing in the early-evening shadows, Sanderson saw something that seemed curiously out of place.

He saw an untended jet ski.

Oded Veron put down the phone in Mossad's opera-tions center. He was clearly livid, his face red and veins bulging on the sides of his thick neck. Two strides later he was inches from Nurin's face. The director held his ground, knowing that calm was his best defense against an old soldier who made his living by intimidation. All the same, he would not be surprised if a blow came.

"You sacrificed my man!" the Direct Action com-mander screamed. "You sent him in with his hands tied. You told him exactly how to do his job, and when things went to hell you ordered his support team to back away! What the hell is going on?"

Nurin glanced at the room's third party, Ezra Zach-arias, who nodded knowingly.

"Yes, I'll explain everything, Oded. I owe you that much. But right now we have to know exactly what is happening. Please give me a few more minutes."

Veron backed off, still seething, and strode to the far side of the room. He sank heavily into a plush chair, soft leather crinkling under his bulk.

With that storm abated, Nurin turned back to the information flowing in from Veron's team in Geneva. He was relieved that Slaton had aborted the mission. Difficult as the evening was, Nurin realized that he should have done things this way from the beginning. Using Slaton had been a desperate measure.

No, he thought. *It was a sign of weakness.*

Zacharias spoke up. "Sir, I think there is something I should take care of?"

Nurin nodded. "Yes, Ezra. It's time for you to wrap things up on your end."

Without another word, Zacharias left the room.

After stepping aboard *Entrepreneur*, Hamedi endured a succession of handshakes that seemed to have no end. Strangers claimed they were glad to meet him, which he doubted given his present reputation, yet he smiled and said the same in return, thinking, *Soon each of you will have a story to tell.*

On clearing the arrival contingent, a man Hamedi recognized as Behrouz's number two pulled him aside, and after a quiet word ushered him toward a remote corner of the ship's quarterdeck. They passed heavy tables stocked with hors d'oeuvres, crab quiche, and Provençal tarts, and to one side was a well-stocked bar where a pair of young women in black uniforms were busy pulling corks. Hamedi felt a rumble in the deck that told him the boat was maneuvering. Empty teacups began chattering on the tables. He was guided round a makeshift stage where the members of a tuxedoed string quartet were making final delicate adjustments to their instruments. Hamedi's escort came to a stop behind the stage backdrop, a thick velvet curtain that put them completely out of sight.

The guard said, "The minister of security has requested a private word with you, Dr. Hamedi."

"A word about what?"

The man walked to the port rail and pointed across the water.

For the first time Hamedi noticed the sea of lights pulsing around the northern half of the first bridge. He said, "You mean . . . it has happened again? The Israelis?"

"Yes, only minutes before you arrived. But everything is under control. It appears to have been a lone assassin—he did not survive our counterattack. Colonel Behrouz," the man continued, using his boss's old Revolutionary Guards rank, "wishes to give you a full account."

The guard disappeared, but Hamedi had a sense he was waiting just on the other side of the backdrop. He went to the rail and stared at the disquieting scene. On the previous two occasions he had been forewarned by Behrouz. A third attempt, of course, was always a possibility, but the idea had slipped from Hamedi's head amid the blurring course of his work and the preparations for today's speech. Now reality stared back at him, blue and red strobes reflecting from the lake like lasers.

"A third attempt?" he whispered to himself. "Why do they not stop?" The guard had said it was a lone assassin, but this seemed small relief. A shaken Hamedi hoped it was the last.

The boat was moving, and the city seemed to rotate as she slipped further from the dock and began picking up speed. Hamedi closed his eyes tightly. The prayer that came to mind was the first his mother had ever taught him, and he versed the words softly under his breath, mimicking her distinctive musical cadence. Hamedi was not quite finished when he sensed a presence behind him. He abruptly went silent, and turned to see Farzad Behrouz. The look twisted into his pockmarked face was nothing less than exultation.

"Yes," Behrouz said. "Yes, I knew it all along. Only the proof escaped me—and now I have it."

Hamedi opened his mouth but no words came. Thoughts he had not harbored in thirty years surged to the forefront. Dangerous, reckless thoughts. It is a curious paradox that those brilliant men and women who design nuclear weapons are not, on balance, inclined to physical violence. Yet as a boy Ibrahim Hamedi had seen more than his share of scraps, and so he knew where his fists were. He had, of course, never killed a man, but there was a first time for everything. A lifelong disciple of physics, Hamedi resisted the urge to work things through mathematically. Mass and momentum and conservation of energy were all good and fine for a classroom, but right now he thought it better to simply lunge for the little cretin's throat.

Behrouz saw it coming and opened his mouth, presumably to call for help.

Neither man's intent came to pass because in the next moment, under the vigorous opening notes of Brahms's String Quartet Number Three, they were both slammed to the deck by a massive explosion.

FIFTY-ONE

Slaton's head was just out of the water, having risen from the lake mere seconds before the explosion—the only sure way to protect his ears from the concussive effect of the blast. Even fifty yards away and above the surface, the submarine blast was deafening. A wave of energy struck his wetsuit-clad body as it transferred through the frigid water, but Slaton's eyes remained locked on the slow-moving ship. *Entrepreneur* seemed to hesitate for a moment, teetering on a foaming section of lake a hundred yards from the dock, her silhouette framed by the city's shimmering reflections.

Water dripped from Slaton's camouflaged boonie hat, but he remained completely motionless. One eye was fixed to his thermal imaging optic, but at any instant he could shift to the fixed night sight of the MP7. His stillness was a stark contrast to the scene forty yards away. *Entrepreneur* was foundering quickly, her back broken, and the bow and stern had already begun to list in opposite directions. Water frothed from a breach amidships and flames belched from the waterline, the latter a result of compromised fuel lines that would soon carpet the lake in fire. All anticipated. For a brief moment Slaton wondered if he'd overdone the Semtex. But only for a moment.

Smoke on the water . . . The classic Deep Purple song, recounting a fire on the opposite shore of Lake Geneva, was tonight being rewritten.

He kept the MP7's black barrel trained loosely on the stern section—the site of the gala, and where nearly everyone had been at the moment of detonation. Forward of the breach he saw only a handful of crew and hired help. The guests were surging aft, away from the blaze. Again, precisely as anticipated. Slaton began shifting his optic with sharp, mechanical corrections, settling on each flailing body for the necessary two seconds. With roughly forty people to sort through, he concentrated on small groups, knowing Hamedi would be quickly surrounded by security staff wanting to steer their principal to safety. And on this sinking ship, safety meant one thing—at the stern, hanging on a pair of davits, a skiff with an outboard motor. There were other lifeboats, of course, but these were less obvious and not yet deployed, so Slaton reasoned that Hamedi's guardians would move aft and commandeer the seventeen-foot Boston Whaler. Any quaint laws of the sea regarding women and children would be decisively overruled by their submachine guns.

The crewmen were distributing life jackets, but this too Slaton had foreseen. He hoped he had predicted every complication because the next two minutes would be critical, indeed the part of the plan that had concerned him from the beginning. Amid the smoke and chaos of a sinking ship, he had to identify Ibrahim Hamedi. Slaton kept shifting, looking through the sight and studying thermal images as rising flames licked the water. Waves of smoke rolled through his field of view, obscuring the ship for brief intervals, but Slaton held fast, held patient, long enough to eliminate potential targets one by one. On his fifteenth shift the *kidon* caught a glimpse of what he was after.

A group of three, the men on the flanks brandishing weapons and hauling the man in the middle by the elbows. Slaton had to be sure, so he kept watching. When one of the guards stumbled he got a clear look and saw what he wanted—one clear band over the left shoulder. It wasn't a brilliant difference—you would have to know to look for it in the first place—but the variance in thermal signature was conclusive. Two subtly discrete coefficients of heat retention in the cool evening air.

Scotchgard.

Hamedi.

For the first time Slaton's finger engaged his trigger. The *kidon* knew who to kill.

Slaton submerged and began breathing again through the high-pressure regulator, kicking briskly to close the gap. Sight was useless in the pitch-black lake, so he went with dead reckoning, using his initial bearing and knowing precisely how fast he could swim at flank speed in full scuba gear—the kind of thing a *kidon* had to know.

He surfaced, by the luminescent hands of his Movado watch, twenty-eight seconds later, this time rising without any attempt at stealth. He saw a crewman trying to run the davit motors to lower the Whaler, but it was fast becoming an exercise in futility as the lake rose to meet *Entrepreneur*'s sinking stern. So the sailor waited, and when he had enough slack he simply untethered the runabout. The crewman was the first to climb in, and Hamedi went next, half-guided, half thrown into the boat by his minders, one large and one small, who quickly followed. As the crewman went to the helm, four more Iranians—looking ridiculous in dark business suits, orange life jackets, and carrying submachine guns—reached *Entrepreneur*'s disappearing stern. Two made the leap to the drifting Whaler. Two didn't.

With the gap increasing between the boats, Slaton's target was effectively separated and his defenses quantified. Four guards and a crewman had reached Hamedi, two others remained nearby. Slaton shifted from the viewing optic to the MP7's sight. It was time to live by an assassin's rules. Anyone with a weapon died. And those with the biggest weapons died first. From twenty yards his first target's head appeared massive. Slaton widened his legs to stabilize in the water and settled his sight, already planning his next two shots. He gave a quick double tap, and a guard who was trying to step across—one leg on the yacht and another on the Whaler—crumbled into the divide between the boats. The second man on *Entrepreneur*, his semiautomatic still strapped to his chest, had a bullet in his head before his partner hit the water.

Slaton's gun was suppressed for sound, but the guards were trained and so they knew they were under attack. Using his long fins, Slaton spun left and settled his sight on the Whaler. One of the guards was tall and obvious, and Slaton traded shots with the man. A round from his MP7 found home as the water to his right exploded. Uncomfortably close.

Then he heard shouting. *"There! In the water!"*

More shouts from the sinking yacht. The *kidon* submerged.

With strong kicks Slaton swam straight under the Whaler, the boat's dark outline clear in the dancing orange reflections. He popped up this time on the shore side, his MP7 ready and new angles of fire already fixed in his head. But he could not shoot indiscriminately. With the optic he positively identified a guard at the bow, fired and watched him go overboard when hit. Hamedi's protection was now down to two—but they began learning. They fell to the deck and disappeared, leaving Slaton no shot. Rounds suddenly exploded all around him, the water churning like a blender. He snap-sighted on a figure near the stern of the yacht, but before he could fire his MP7 jerked to one side. Slaton felt stinging pain in his scalp and saw that his gun sight was gone, nothing but the jagged metal bracket remaining. He answered with a quick, unsighted double, and his target twisted but stayed on his feet. Slaton fired again from twenty yards and finished the job.

He submerged again knowing time was short. It was time to get close.

It was time to take Hamedi.

Behrouz was scrambling on the deck of the Whaler when a foot caught him in the face. He looked up and saw Hamedi backing away.

"The Israelis!" the scientist screamed. "They are after me again! Don't you see that?"

Behrouz didn't know what to think. The Israelis *were* attacking. But what of the words he'd heard slip from Hamedi's mouth only minutes ago? There was no time to think about it. He screamed at the white-uniformed crewman at the little boat's helm. "Get us out of here!" Behrouz pointed his handgun at the man to leave no room for questions.

The crewman's eyes went wide—wider than they already were with bodies and mayhem all around. He cranked the outboard motor and it came to life, and from a kneeling position the man put the motor into gear and slammed the throttle forward. There was a roar from the back of the boat but nothing happened. They went nowhere.

"What is wrong?" Hamedi shouted.

"I don't know," the helmsman said. "We must be hung up on something. Maybe a line."

Bravely, the man lifted his head above the gunnel and looked over the side. Then he moved aft and looked over the stern.

"The propeller is gone!" he shouted.

The propeller, in fact, had been removed forty minutes earlier and was now resting on the bottom of Lake Geneva. The crewman, befuddled by the missing prop but growing more confident, leaned in for a closer look. He never saw the gloved hand come out of the water.

Slaton got a fistful of uniform collar, braced against the boat's hull, and pulled the sailor over his shoulder and into the lake. Having removed his scuba rig, he vaulted over the stern with the Glock ready. He was breaching the point of least freeboard, the most vulnerable position to defend, so he expected Hamedi's two remaining men to have their weapons already trained in his direction. He only saw one, and much closer than expected. Only an arm's length away.

In an instantaneous decision, Slaton shifted his momentum and threw himself on the man.

He crashed in hard, but his hand struck something and the Glock flew from his grip. The man was big, but he was flat on his back. Slaton lashed an elbow to the head that slowed the Iranian, but he kept fighting—the determination of an old soldier who'd battled for his life before. They grappled and locked arms, heading for a stalemate that was not in Slaton's favor. He sensed something under his free hand, and recognized by feel what it was. Working a hand free, he pulled the anchor line until he had enough slack, then managed to loop it around the man's neck. One handed, he had little leverage, but then he caught a break—his adversary panicked.

The big Iranian put both hands to his throat and tried to pry the rope away. That was all Slaton needed. He didn't pull, but twisted, tightening the noose in a powerful grip. The Iranian struggled fiercely, but that only used more oxygen and made his life that much shorter. In less than a minute it was over.

But a minute was far too long.

Slaton rolled away and saw the boat's last two occupants. Ibrahim Hamedi was backed against the starboard side. Across the beam, down on one knee, was Farzad Behrouz.

Slaton's Glock was in his hand.

FIFTY-TWO

Slaton went still, the only option when looking down the barrel of a 9mm.

Behrouz said, "Almost, Jew. You almost did it."

Slaton said nothing, and the Iranian's eyes seemed to narrow with suspicion. He thought Behrouz might be having a flashback, remembering his face from yesterday's encounter in the elevator. But then Slaton was taken completely by surprise.

Hamedi kicked out a leg, perhaps to get his balance in the rocking boat, and for some unfathomable reason Behrouz took it as a threat. He shifted the gun and pointed it at the scientist. Only a few feet away, Hamedi backed against the fiberglass hull, fear etched into his broad face.

Behrouz appeared baffled, unsure. His bewilderment was compounded when someone shouted his name from the sinking yacht. At that moment an acrid wave of black smoke washed over everything and, as if to make the chaos complete, a muffled explosion shook the night. Slaton guessed the blast was not from a grenade or a gun, but rather a death throe from the ship, probably a pressure door giving way behind tons of water or a keel beam buckling.

He watched the two Iranians intently and saw a

passionate mistrust between them. The implications of this defied logic. Why was the security chief threatening the man he was duty-bound to protect? Slaton wasted no time on analysis. With a hunter's instinct, he saw Behrouz's hesitation as his chance. The man was ten feet away, too far to reach before the gun could swing again. But Krav Maga did not fail. The rope was still looped around the dead man's neck, yet there was more of it, a hundred feet of braided nylon painstakingly coiled by some meticulous crewman. And at the end of that, inches from Slaton's left hand, was what he needed.

"You've made a mistake!" Hamedi pleaded, staring at the gun. "You don't understand!"

Behrouz seemed more confused than ever, and that was Slaton's cue. He reached for the rope.

The Iranian sensed movement and tried to shift his aim. Slaton had five feet of line to work with, plus the length of his arm. At the end of that radius was his weapon. With only one chance, Slaton twisted sideways and whipped a ten-pound galvanized anchor into a sweeping arc that ended perfectly at the side of Behrouz's skull. There was an audible crunch, and the little Iranian crumpled to the deck, dead before he hit.

Slaton never stopped moving. He sprang to his feet as a fearful Hamedi rose and tried to defend himself. Shots rang in from the foundering yacht, and Slaton launched himself shoulder first, flying across the gap toward the panicked scientist.

Both men went headlong into the frigid lake.

Bullets ripped the water, their trails effervescent shards of orange and white light.

Slaton had a handful of Hamedi's collar and was

dragging him lower. The scientist was a large man, but thankfully he didn't resist right away. He was in shock after having endured an armed assault, and then being pitched into an icy lake. Slaton pulled and kicked toward his only chance—the scuba rig hanging beneath the Whaler by a quick-release knot. He was nearly there when Hamedi began to struggle. They'd been under only seconds, but the Iranian was not prepared, not trained, and the lack of air induced panic.

Slaton looked up, but without a mask he could see no more than the shadow of the small craft. It was enough. Aft, starboard side, a ten-foot line hanging straight down from the surface. There was Slaton's salvation. Hamedi began thrashing for all he was worth, fighting the man who he imagined was trying to drown him, fighting the insistence of his lungs to breath. In a matter of seconds, everything would be for naught. Slaton paused just long enough to deliver a short, compact elbow to the side of Hamedi's head. It did the trick, stunning the man, and with one last heave Slaton reached the regulator with his free hand.

He ignored his own mouth, instead feeling blindly for Hamedi's face and stuffing the mouthpiece between his lips. Slaton hit the purge button, forcing air out of the system and into the scientist. Either by basal instinct or good sense, Hamedi began breathing, sucking long draws from the tank. The rig was a standard octopus setup, two regulators, and as his own lungs strained Slaton found the second mouthpiece and took his first breath after a minute of strenuous work. He disconnected the rig, put one strap over a shoulder, and then donned his mask and fins.

The *kidon* began kicking furiously.

Direction was everything.

Slaton referenced the luminous compass on his diving rig and pushed southeast. Overhead he saw all colors of light playing the surface, yet they were patternless and chaotic. Not yet searching. In twenty minutes that would change. By then *Entrepreneur* would be resting on the bottom of the lake, and things would begin to organize.

The lighthouse was less than a mile away, and when he got closer it would act to the inverse of its design—it would guide Slaton straight toward the rocky jetty. His problem was speed—he was dragging a full set of gear and a two-hundred-pound physicist. Hamedi had at least gone still. Slaton knew he hadn't drowned, because the regulator's exhaust port was venting a rhythmic flow. More likely the man was dazed from prolonged immersion in fifty-degree water. Slaton's thick wetsuit gave him protection, but the scientist would soon succumb to hypothermia.

Slaton did everything he could to lighten his load. He ditched all his equipment, including the damaged MP7, until the only thing left was the scuba rig. The next twelve minutes were an underwater sprint that felt like a marathon. It was the most challenging physical test he had ever faced, and there had been many, both in training and in the field. His lungs heaved and his legs burned. He shifted to different strokes as cramps set in, and following a long-honed practice Slaton translated his pain into anger. He cursed Mossad and Director Nurin, cursed Iran and the depraved genius he was dragging behind him.

Finally, he saw the glow of the lighthouse.

Nearing the jetty he popped his head up once to confirm his bearings. Slaton didn't allow Hamedi to surface, knowing a taste of fresh air would only incite further panic when he was pulled down again. With legs that felt like rubber and straining lungs, his pace declined markedly over the last twenty yards. When he broke the surface the second time they were on the calm backside of the jetty.

The sky overhead was clear, populated with stars and planets that were every bit as tranquil as the scene behind him was chaotic. Hamedi sputtered and coughed, and spit the regulator from his mouth. He began gulping air like a just-landed fish on the deck of a boat.

The jet ski was right where Slaton had left it, and he ditched the scuba gear before muscling Hamedi over the slick rocks. The tiny cove created by the breakwater was out of sight from the quai. In the distance he saw what was left of *Entrepreneur*, her white steel stern rising, air venting from portholes and blown-out windows. There were a half dozen smaller boats circling, shining spotlights and plucking survivors from the water, and at the nearby dock a shoreside contingent of police and Iranian security men scoured the water for their lost scientist.

Hamedi tried to say something, but it came out as no more than a croak. Slaton hauled him the last few yards to the waiting watercraft. He had purchased the fastest model he could find this morning, twelve thousand cash for a two-seater that would reach seventy miles an hour on their run across the lake to the quiet overlook where the Rover was waiting. From there, Slaton would call Director Nurin and make his bargain.

He tried to wrestle Hamedi onto the watercraft, but the Iranian began struggling again.

"Get on!" Slaton ordered.

Hamedi said something else unintelligible, still coughing uncontrollably from his underwater ordeal.

Then another voice rang in from behind. "Stop! Don't move!"

Slaton froze. It was a voice he recognized.

He turned his head and saw Detective Inspector Arne Sanderson. One hand held a gun unsteadily while the other gripped the iron railing that encircled the lighthouse. He was in a wide-set stance, but swaying like a sapling in the wind. If Slaton were to guess, he'd say the man had been shot—he looked like he might pitch over at any moment. Slaton checked behind Sanderson, and as far as he could see up and down the jetty there was no one else. Neither did he see a radio bud in the detective's ear, nor a microphone on his lapel. Slaton remembered the news article—Sanderson had been taken off the chase for unspecified medical reasons. *The detective is here alone*, he thought.

"I'm not as good a shot as you," Sanderson said, seeming to read Slaton's thoughts, "but from ten meters I won't miss."

Slaton was about to reply when Hamedi, finding strength from some reserve, stood straight. He pushed Slaton away with a stiff arm, and shouted, "Do you not realize what you've done? You have ruined everything!"

Slaton stood absolutely still. Absolutely stunned. The words themselves were not a revelation. The shove was weak and meaningless. What shocked him to the core was that Hamedi had spoken in perfectly succinct and fluent Hebrew.

FIFTY-THREE

"I am a Jew, you fool!"

Hamedi said it a second time in English, and the words themselves sank.

Slaton's tactical mind-set aborted, tripped by the one thing he could never have imagined. Every problem he'd solved, every motive and strategy was suddenly put in a mirror, refracted by four simple words.

I am a Jew.

Hamedi's hair was matted to his forehead and he was shivering uncontrollably. But there was unshakable conviction in his voice. "I was born in central Iran," he said. "But I was born a Jew. There are over twenty thousand of us across Persia, and we have been there for three thousand years. My parents—"

"Enough!" Sanderson shouted. "Whatever your story is you can tell it to the proper authorities. Keep your hands where I can see them, both of you!"

In dense silence the three men stood still, each wrestling a distinct set of problems. It was Sanderson who made the next move. He said nothing, but lifted his gun toward the sky with an unsteady hand.

Slaton knew immediately what he was going to do. The detective was clearly ill, certainly incapable of an arrest. So Sanderson was going to fire a shot into the air that would bring the police swarming.

"Wait!" Slaton said. He pointed to Hamedi and addressed Sanderson, "You know who this is, don't you?"

Sanderson nodded tentatively. "I'll assume it's Dr. Hamedi, the man you came here to kill."

"Really? Think about that. I sank a ship and shot a half dozen men to get this far. Dr. Hamedi is still standing."

Sanderson's eyes narrowed. "So what the hell is going on then?"

"That's what I'd like to know," Slaton seconded.

They both stared at Hamedi.

Sirens blared in the distance as the three men stood in the lee of the breakwater.

They were less than a mile from the ruin on the lake. *Entrepreneur* had disappeared, her only remnants a field of charred flotsam drifting amid the sheen of unspent fuel oil. Nearby docks and bridges were overrun with first responders, and the traffic on Quai du Mont Blanc had come to a standstill. The jetty had so far been ignored, the distance enough of a buffer. But for how long? Slaton wondered. Soon the search for survivors would spread to their position. Did he have ten minutes? Fifteen? Whatever the interval, he had that long in which to salvage his life. Yet Slaton knew he was helpless until he understood.

Sanderson's gun was at his side as Hamedi told his story.

"I was born in a small village outside Isfahan. My parents brought me up in the faith, but by the time I was three it became apparent that I had certain academic gifts. My mother was disconsolate that my talents would be wasted. Jews in Iran, you see, have little hope of a proper education. So my father moved us to the anonymity of Tehran, and we took a Persian name. My mother kept with my religious education but always behind closed doors. Able to attend good schools, I advanced more quickly than anyone imagined. As you know, I studied in Europe at the best universities. Yet I never forgot my upbringing, my ancestry."

"Did Israel ask for your help?" Sanderson asked.

"No. Israel knew nothing of my background. It was only something in my head, a desire to work for the homeland, perhaps retribution for all those Jewish boys I knew long ago who were beaten and bullied, the ones who never had a chance to succeed. I was given wonderful opportunities in Europe, but one day a woman from the Iranian embassy came to see me in Germany. She was very up front, telling me that Iran needed help with certain aspects of the nuclear program. She didn't come right out and talk about missile advancements and warhead design, but we both knew what was at stake. I spent many sleepless nights afterward, thinking about what she'd said, what they wanted from me."

The siren of a police boat suddenly blared behind the breakwater, and Hamedi went silent. The siren and churning diesel altered pitch as the craft passed, and soon the sounds mixed into the disharmony of the nearby rescue. The white octagon of the tiny lighthouse was bathed in a kaleidoscope of flashing lights and stray search beams.

"I don't understand," said Slaton. "You claim sympathies to Israel. So why go back and help Iran with the program that is her greatest nightmare?"

Sanderson answered that question, his detective's brain less handicapped than his body. "Because you didn't go to help."

Hamedi didn't comment on that, but asked Sanderson, "You are a policeman?"

"Yes," said Sanderson, "at least in Sweden I am."

"And a good one, I think."

Slaton said to Sanderson, "I thought you were taken off the case."

"Officially I was," Sanderson said. "But I don't like unfinished business."

Hamedi then addressed Slaton. "And you? You are Mossad? A *kidon*?"

Slaton nodded.

"So there you are," Hamedi said. "We stand here on three different points of a triangle. But what I will tell you next may change that geometry." He stood next to the jet ski, cold water up to his ankles, dripping hair matted to his head. His voice, however, was steady and brimmed with confidence. "When I went back to Iran I worked very hard. I made several technical and organizational changes to advance the primary goal of the project—the integration of ballistic missiles with nuclear warheads. In time I was given greater authority, and eventually came to oversee the entire undertaking. I suppose I knew all along what I was going to do, in a general way, but the details fell into place quite naturally. In recent months I've issued orders for the most critical components, including all highly enriched uranium, to be consolidated at the Qom facility outside Tehran. Thanks to my efforts, Iran's entry into the nuclear arena is imminent. Five days from today, our first missile-capable warhead is scheduled for an underground test. But it will not happen as planned."

Sanderson and Slaton were completely absorbed, silent as they waited for the rest.

Hamedi's voice edged into triumph. "Four days from now, this coming Thursday, I have planned for an early arrival of that blast. In a few milliseconds I will destroy the entire Qom complex and everything within. By my estimate, enough damage to set back Iran's nuclear plans for seven years, hopefully longer."

Slaton stood stunned for a time, but then arguments came to mind. "But this doesn't make sense—Mossad has been trying desperately to kill you. I was sent here for just that reason. Why didn't you get word to them, explain what you were doing?"

Hamedi looked at Slaton uncomfortably. "I did."

For the second time in a matter of minutes, Slaton's well-defined world overturned. Yet it all made sense in a startling way.

Hamedi went on, "My contact with Israel has been very limited. But I can tell you that the director of Mossad has known of my intentions since early this summer."

"Early summer," Slaton repeated. "So the assassination attempts, including tonight—they were only for show. None were meant to succeed."

Hamedi nodded. "Quite the opposite. All were guaranteed to fail. You see, a serious complication arose. One man in Iran became suspicious of me—a man you conveniently eliminated tonight. Farzad Behrouz has been digging into my past, searching synagogues for records of my upbringing, interrogating my mother and searching her home. He was on the right track, but never found proof. Not until tonight when he heard me recite a small prayer in Hebrew. Then he knew."

Slaton remembered Director Nurin's plan. *It will tell you where and when to strike . . . a tactical*

opening that is ideal for a man with your gift. Use it.
The director had set him up to die, and in doing so
had put Christine at risk. Slaton had to understand
completely. "How did it work? Was Nurin feeding the
Iranians intelligence? Was he actively sabotaging his
own strike teams?"

"Yes," Hamedi said. "Behrouz told me he had an
agent who gave accurate warnings—where and when
the attacks against me would come. This agent was
clearly planted by Nurin."

"So good men were sent to the slaughter, sacrificed."

Hamedi, his face riddled with angst, said, "Yes. This
part filled me with sorrow, but clearly the director
thought it necessary. I tried to consider things from his
point of view. A military attack on Iran's nuclear facilities would put at risk hundreds, even thousands of
Israeli soldiers. Would that not be worse? Israel is desperate to stop Iran, and my importance to the program has been widely accepted. Clearly Nurin felt
that if he did not make attempts against me it would
only fuel Behrouz's suspicions. He *had* to make it look
as if Israel was trying to eliminate me."

Fifty yards away Slaton saw two policemen scouring the base of the jetty, their flashlight beams scanning the water for survivors. In a matter of minutes
they would reach the breakwater.

"But now," said Sanderson, "Behrouz is gone?"

"Yes," Hamedi confirmed. "Our friend here was
quite innovative, but there is no doubt—he is dead."

"And no one else in Iran shares his suspicions about
your background?"

"I don't think so," Hamedi said. "Behrouz always
retained a card-player's mentality—something like
this he would have kept to himself until he was certain. Others helped in his search, of course, but they

were only low-level people with no understanding of his larger suspicions."

"So," Slaton reasoned, "if you were to turn up as a survivor tonight—you could still go back to Iran and carry through your plan?"

Hamedi thought about it. "Yes. With Behrouz eliminated, I'm sure there will be a fight for his position—one that will last weeks, if not months. For the time being all security will be focused on one thing—the imminent test. I am more secure now than I was an hour ago, and all I require is four more days. Allow me that, and I can give Israel her greatest victory since the Six-Day War."

Sanderson drew a heavy sigh. "I'm not a political man by nature, but clearly the world could use a little more time with Iran. I could turn Dr. Hamedi in, say that I found him in the water. He'd be back in Iran tomorrow. And I have to confess this would also get me out of a rather deep professional hole I've dug for myself."

The policeman and the scientist looked at the assassin.

With the gun still in his hand, Sanderson spoke for them both. "That leaves you, sir. Now that we all know the truth of what's going on . . . is there any way this can end well for you?"

Slaton pulled the diving hood back off his head, and the cool night air washed over him. It didn't help—he was drowning under too many variables and intricate angles. He was a Jew as well, and could not deny a desire to help the homeland—in spite of what Israel's guardians had done to him. But more important was Christine and their child. In a crushing moment, Slaton felt his life in Virginia slipping away. Perhaps he'd been a fool to even imagine a normal existence, but if he let go now he was sure it would be lost forever.

Looking grimly at his odd bedfellows, a Persian-Jew scientist and a Swedish policeman, he said, "All right, gentlemen. Here is how we will do it . . ."

FIFTY-FOUR

The sorry state of Nurin's psyche was certified when he looked down and realized that he was holding a lit cigarette in each hand. Hunched at the control desk in Mossad's operations center, he discreetly doused one in an ashtray and took a long pull on the other.

There were three large video screens in front of him—one the direct feed from Veron's Direct Action team, and the other two alternating between commercial news feeds, which had a tendency to loop the most spectacular clips. All showed the Armageddon-like scene that was the western reach of Lake Geneva. There was smoke and fire, and an army of first responders trying to cope with a maritime disaster—not a well-rehearsed scenario, Nurin supposed, for a traditionally neutral Alpine state.

"Still nothing?" Nurin barked.

"No sir," replied the female communications manager seated to his left. "The DA team is searching on foot now, but no sign of Hamedi."

"Dammit! Where the hell is he? Send the directive again—if they find him I want absolutely *no contact*. He is to be turned over to the Swiss authorities."

"Sir, I've already sent that order twice—"

The woman stopped in midsentence, perhaps feeling Nurin's stare. She began typing.

Nurin turned and saw Veron still squeezed into a narrow chair at the back of the room—the wood looked like it might splinter under his bulk. Thirty minutes ago the shooter from his DA team in Geneva had been fighting off an Iranian counterattack. When Veron tried to send in the rest of his team to support their comrade, Nurin immediately countermanded the order. Now the director would have to defend his actions, and it wouldn't be pleasant. They had all been listening to the tactical channel audio. They'd heard the shooter as he engaged the Iranians, his dialogue cool in the chaos of a gunfight. Then he went down, pleading for help. Other voices picked up, the rest of the handpicked DA unit screaming for permission to engage. Nurin had ordered them to stand down.

Now the tactical channel was quiet, and Veron sat sulking at the back of the room. He looked like a human balloon that might burst at any moment. Nurin walked over and sank heavily into the chair next to Veron.

"Tell me, Oded," he began in a quiet voice. "Through all your years of command in the field . . . was there ever a time when you sent a man into a bad situation, one you knew he wouldn't come back from, in order to get a vital mission done?"

Veron didn't answer directly. Instead, he asked, "The others this summer? Tehran and outside Qom? They were sacrificed as well?"

Nurin braced, not sure how a type-A soldier like Veron would handle that answer. But he gave it anyway. "Yes. I sent six men into situations that were guaranteed to fail. Six men, Oded. I know that number exactly, and their names and faces are burned into my mind. You don't know how this has weighed on me." When Veron turned to stare at him, Nurin added, "Or maybe you do."

"But why?"

"Hamedi is one of us, Oded." Nurin finally broke his secrecy, explaining Hamedi's plan to ruin Iran's nuclear program in a single moment.

Veron considered it for some time. "Yes, then I see why Hamedi must survive. But was it necessary to throw away so many lives?"

"In our limited contact, Hamedi told us that Farzad Behrouz had become suspicious of his background. He was raiding synagogues and interrogating old friends to find proof. The entire plan was at risk. To the world's eye, Hamedi had become the driving force behind Iran's nuclear weapons program. If we did not make attempts against him? That would have fed the suspicions Behrouz was harboring."

They both watched the three video screens, the most impressive being a feed from one of the local Geneva television stations. In a segment that had been running repeatedly for twenty minutes, *Entrepreneur* lay broken in the water, the lake boiling around her like a frothing fire. Thick smoke, black in the city's footlights, swirled wildly into the sky.

"But now . . ." Nurin said in a hushed whisper, "Hamedi has disappeared. Slaton has ruined everything."

Veron stiffened—ears that had been assaulted by the thunder of a hundred battles were still sharp enough. "Slaton? *David* Slaton?"

"You know him?"

"I know of him—the *kidon*. He was a legend. But he was rumored to have been killed in England."

Nurin shook his head. "No, Oded. He lives."

Veron looked up at the monitor and stared at the incredible scene of destruction. "Then God help us."

"No," Nurin countered. "God help Ibrahim Hamedi."

As Gardien de la Paix, intern level, Daniel Kammerer had been with the Geneva gendarmerie for a mere eight months. As a consequence of his junior status on the force, he was without fail given the most tedious and uninteresting assignments. At soccer matches he was relegated to standing at turnstiles to usher away the most blatant hooligans. At the recent wine festival he'd been assigned latrine duty, making sure the tipsy crowds relieved themselves in an orderly Swiss manner—lines respected, and no men allowed to appropriate the women's portable toilets. And tonight, with a calamity of unprecedented drama playing out less than a mile away, Kammerer was stuck playing traffic cop, or more succinctly, shunting traffic away from the cordoned Quai du General Guisan toward Rue du Rhone and the safety of central Geneva.

He was diverting a delivery truck toward a side street, and enduring no small amount of honking and fist-shaking, when the event that would keep him writing reports until early the next morning began. The first thing that drew his attention was a shout. The words made no sense to young Kammerer because they came in a language he did not understand. The strident tone and volume, however, were enough to warrant a look. He right away saw three men standing midway along the Pont des Bergues footbridge, the second of the numerous spans connecting the left and right banks of the Rhone, and just west of the troubled Pont du Mont Blanc crossing where, according to the captain on the radio, more senior officers were searching for a missing Iranian diplomat in the aftermath of the spectacular attack.

Kammerer watched for a moment and heard more shouting. Two of the men, one dressed in black, were standing close to the bridge's eastern side, backed against the hip-high metal railing. The third was ten steps away, centered on the bridge's width and pointing an accusing hand at the others. In his short tenure on the force Kammerer had already witnessed his share of altercations, most involving alcohol. Yet there was something about this scene that seemed very different. Something that troubled him.

He abandoned his intersection, leaving the delivery truck at odds with a stalled motor scooter, and began closing the gap. He was twenty yards from the foot of the bridge, fifty from the rising dispute, when he realized that the man in the center of the bridge was not pointing his hand, but rather a gun. He also saw that one of the men backed to the rail was restraining the other with an arm wrapped around his throat.

Kammerer went for his radio, but the frequency was momentarily blocked by someone's long-winded traffic narrative. He broke into a run, and shouted, "Police! *Arrêtez-vous!*"

The three men ignored him.

Kammerer finally heard a break on the frequency, but in the heat of the moment, with his heart thumping in his chest, the proper radio conventions and protocols escaped him—just as his instructor in training had said it would. But he remembered what she'd said next: *If you forget the correct way, just screw the procedures and say something.*

He did exactly that.

"Pont des Bergues, the footbridge!" Kammerer

shouted into his microphone. "Officer needs help! I see a man with a gun, possible hostage situation!"

Thirty yards from the trouble, Kammerer slowed his pace and drew his service weapon. Before he had a chance to shout anything more, things began to happen in what seemed like slow motion. The man holding the hostage, the one clad in some kind of black suit, pushed his captive away and produced what appeared to be a gun of his own. Before he could raise it, the man in the middle of the bridge fired once, and then kept firing, a hail of shots that Kammerer would report as ten, but later be proven by ballistics evidence to be six. The man clad in black rocked once, twice, and then twisted back and flipped over the metal rail, disappearing into the river.

Kammerer pointed his weapon at the shooter, and screamed, "Drop the weapon!" He said it three times in all, once in each of the languages he spoke—French, English, and Swiss-German. One of them, he wasn't sure which, seemed to work. Or perhaps it had more to do with the volume and situation. Whatever the impulse, the shooter set his weapon on the asphalt, backed away three steps, and very slowly dropped to his stomach and went spread-eagle.

"I'm a policeman!" the man shouted in English.

This Kammerer knew better than to take for granted. He kept his gun trained on the shooter as he closed in, kicked the gun a bit farther away, and cuffed the man, all while keeping an eye on the third man who was standing by the guardrail and looking very relieved. Help soon arrived in the form of three other officers, and things began to organize. Kammerer told the senior man, a captain, what had happened.

"Where is the other?" the captain asked. "The one who was hit?"

Kammerer led him to the rail and they both looked down. Fifteen feet below they saw nothing but the black Rhone rolling slowly westward, her rippled surface cold and empty.

FIFTY-FIVE

For the second night in a row Evita Levine rose in the elevator of the Isrotel Tower Hotel in Tel Aviv. Tonight the call from Zacharias had come late, and indeed caught her by surprise.

She had talked in a hushed voice from the kitchen and made the usual arrangements, yet on hanging up Evita thought she sensed something new in his voice. Or perhaps something that wasn't there. His panting enthusiasm? In any event, she dressed quickly and told her husband, who was nodding off in his decrepit chair behind a television that was running, of all things, an ad for an aerobic exercise video, that her mother was ill and she was going across town to tend to her. Evita had always tried to avoid outright lies, but seeing her liaisons with Zacharias clearly drawing to an end, she tonight allowed herself the expediency of deceit.

The elevator opened, and she walked down the hallway wondering if it was time to break things off. This was a speech Evita had long rehearsed, and one that varied, based on her degree of disgust at the given moment, from a curt letdown to screamed accusations of sexual inadequacy. As she reached the familiar door, however, it all went out of her head. As good as that might feel, there was still reason to be cautious.

He answered her knock immediately, and the first thing she noticed was that he did not have a drink in his hand. The second thing was the way he backed away from her. His usual leer was replaced by a decidedly grim expression that seemed completely out of character. Evita felt the first pang of fear.

"What is it, darling?" She stepped into the room, closing the door behind her. She moved closer and put a soft hand around the nape of his skinny neck. "It's not your wife, I hope. Has she found out?"

"Evita Levine," he said, "you are under arrest for treason against the State of Israel."

She stepped back with wide eyes and a slack jaw. Before she could respond two men appeared from nowhere and pulled her hands roughly behind her back. Evita had no doubt that life as she knew it had just ended, but as was often the case with those in the process of being handcuffed, the question that came to her lips was, "How did you find out?"

Mossad's director of operations gave her a subdued smile. "Don't you see, my dear? I've known all along."

Evita stared at him dumbly. She thought of the nights they'd been together, the things she had done. How she had controlled him. She closed her eyes tightly until a vision of Saud came to mind, her forever-young sculptor with his strong hands and liquid gaze. Evita kept her eyes shut as if to hold that picture, and soon cold tears were streaming down her cheeks.

Six minutes later, and one hundred miles north of Tel Aviv, a second group of Mossad agents, these more tactically oriented, burst into a hotel room where the Hezbollah agent known as Rafi was sleeping off a daylong and well documented bender. The man stirred and, it would be later claimed in the after-action report, made a threatening move toward the nightstand drawer. Perhaps because of this, or more likely since the Mossad team was operating on Lebanese soil, no handcuffs were produced.

Forty nine-millimeter rounds later, the bloody body of Rafi looked as though it had been stapled to the splintered headboard.

Christine had spent the evening at Anton Bloch's bedside in Saint Göran Hospital. She told the police it was because he was an old friend. Bloch, whose rapidly improving condition the doctors found encouraging, knew otherwise.

"It's getting late," he said. "Are you sure you don't want me to turn on the television? There might be something new."

She shook her head.

He had prevailed an hour earlier, and for ten minutes they witnessed the bloodshed in Geneva. The police gave few details, and the speculation by reporters was rampant, neither of which calmed Christine's restless imagination. The few facts were damning enough: an attempt had been made on the life of Dr. Ibrahim Hamedi, leaving one assailant and a significant number of bodyguards dead. The scientist was missing. At that point, Christine had turned the television off.

Now she was pacing back and forth at the foot of Bloch's bed, head low and arms crossed over her chest, and trying her level best to find hope.

"Sit down," he said. "Can I order you some food?"

"I thought I was here for your sake."

"I'm worried too, Christine. But I've had many nights like this. You simply can't dwell on the worst-case scenario. Even if they've identified the shooter, they won't release the name any time soon. Tomorrow is probably the earliest we can expect any good news."

She stopped circling and went to his side. "Good news? From this?"

"It might not have been David," he said. "Nurin could have sent another *kidon* to do the job."

She probed his eyes. "Do you really believe that?"

His pause was too long for a lie. "No. But until we know something more accurate there's no sense in—"

Assistant Commissioner Sjoberg walked through the doorway. He met Christine with a somber gaze that froze her in place.

"Have you seen what's happening in Geneva?" Sjoberg asked, not bothering with any preliminaries.

"We saw something on television earlier," Bloch replied. "A private yacht was attacked, and there was a shootout between an assassin and Hamedi's security people."

Sjoberg's eyes remained fixed, and for a moment Christine thought he was going to chastise her, say something along the lines of, *You knew this was going to happen all along, didn't you?* What he said was, "There was a second confrontation soon afterward on a nearby bridge. The Iranian scientist, Hamedi, turned up. He was being held hostage by a second assailant, a man dressed in black. One of my men, Detective Sanderson, shot and killed the suspect. It was your husband, miss."

Christine's knees buckled and she collapsed onto the side of Bloch's bed.

"Are you certain?" Bloch asked.

"The body went into the river. Until they've recovered it we can't confirm his death. But as for the identity—yes, I'm sure. Sanderson interviewed

Mr. Deadmarsh at length when he was here in Stockholm. He was positive. I can also tell you that Sanderson is an expert marksman. He was very close and wouldn't have missed."

The pain was unlike anything Christine had ever experienced. "No!" she whispered hoarsely. "Please, no!" Then, as Bloch put an arm around her, the torment arrived in full.

Oh, David, she thought, *I did this to you!* Christine doubled over, folded her arms across her stomach, and began to sob uncontrollably.

Dr. Ibrahim Hamedi was quickly identified by the surviving members of his security contingent, which was now under emergency leadership after Farzad Behrouz had been confirmed as a fatality of the attacks, and soon all were being whisked to Geneva International Airport under a heavy police escort. There were tepid protests from quarters of the canton gendarmerie, the detectives there wanting to interview Hamedi as a witness, but a beleaguered Swiss foreign minister intervened, and when Hamedi's chartered jet departed at half past eleven that evening there were substantial sighs of relief both in the air and on the ground.

The second man recovered from the bridge that night was taken briefly into custody, but soon confirmed to be a detective on the Stockholm police force. His gun was taken into evidence, and Detective Inspector Arne Sanderson, who seemed quite ill, did his best to answer questions from a hospital bed at Universitaires de Genève. He gave a precise, if broken, account of his engagement with the assassin, a story that the local detectives decided fit well with the evidence given by young Kammerer.

Rescue operations on Lake Geneva continued into the early-morning hours, and by sunrise every soul on *Entrepreneur*'s passenger manifest—crew, guests, and the gendarme detail—had been accounted for. The casualty count reported in the morning papers was nine dead—eight from Hamedi's security force and the assassin under the Pont du Mont Blanc. Ten passengers and crew members were reported injured, a number that insiders knew was optimistic, and forever left in question, due to the rapid departure of the Iranians. The flotilla of rescue vessels began to dissipate late that morning, and the investigative emphasis shifted to the only remaining loose end—a missing person, the man Officer Kammerer and two civilian witnesses had seen tumble fifteen feet down into the frigid Rhone River.

Under a menacing gray sky, boats with grappling hooks began dragging the tireless Rhone downstream, and pairs of policemen walked both shores, parting stands of tall aquatic weeds and poking in eddies as they searched for the body of an unidentified terrorist who had, by all accounts, taken at least three nine-millimeter rounds from Inspector Sanderson's SIG Sauer. In the opinion of one interviewed police captain, "a not unfitting end for a man who has terrorized Europe from Stockholm to the shores of Lac Léman."

In spite of everyone's best efforts, nothing was found.

After a sleepless night, Raymond Nurin was ruminating in Mossad's bunker when two very unexpected phone calls came. The first, from the operations center three floors above, sent him running to the elevator. He hit the call button, and when the silver door didn't open immediately he bolted to the stairs.

One minute later he was listening to a message that had been taken from a satellite download. "This has got to be a hoax!" Nurin insisted. "The Iranians are trying to spoof us, bring us in."

"No, sir," the tech replied. "The authentication code is valid. He's out there."

"But it's been—what? Three weeks?"

The man shrugged.

"I want Veron in here."

"He's already on the way, sir."

Nurin went to the large map on the wall and looked at Iran. "Where exactly?" he demanded.

Another technician, this a woman holding a printout of the lat-long coordinate set, plotted things on the map and made an X with a Sharpie. "Right here. Seven kilometers east of Cheshmehshour."

In what seemed a disturbing new habit, Nurin realized that he had not considered every contingency. He was still staring at the map in the operations room, still reeling, when the second call came.

"Sir! It's the priority number you flagged!" Nurin tripped over a cable as he dashed to the console and picked up the correct handset.

"Where are you?"

Those three words were the end of his input. He listened for exactly ten and three one hundredths seconds before the line went dead. Nurin put down the handset, and said, "Have the Hawker ready in twenty minutes, fueled for Central Europe. I want a car now—and tell Veron to meet me at the airport!"

As he hurried toward the exit Nurin considered the two calls. They were completely unrelated, but like the good spymaster he was, he immediately began incubating ways to join them in his favor. As Nurin trod down the central hallway, however, his clever schemes went adrift. The map of Iran fixed in his mind, and his calculating nature succumbed to a rare turn of reflection as he wondered, *Where do we find such men?*

FIFTY-SIX

Yaniv Stein sat against his rock—after twenty days anyway, he thought of it as his—contemplating whether crushing the scorpion near his sock-clad left foot was worth the effort. The creature wasn't a threat. Not on the big scale of things. There was perhaps some food value, but food was not his problem. He was out of water. A man could survive for a long time in the desert without food. Water, on the other hand, was nonnegotiable.

In the harsh morning light Stein looked down at his shattered leg. In a way the injury had saved him three weeks ago. The grenade he'd thrown into the truck that night had set off a large secondary explosion—how was he to know that was where they stowed their munitions? Shrapnel from the blast had ruined his leg, but the explosion also proved his salvation—it created smoke, fire, confusion, and most fortuitously, an Iranian corpse that was burned beyond recognition. Nearly delirious from the pain, Stein had removed his outer uniform and done his best to dress the victim as an Israeli commando. He'd then shoveled flaming embers onto what was left of the body until the poor grunt was smoldering again. Finally, in the most painful two hours of his life and under cover of a frenetic night, Stein had crawled eighty yards to this spot, a tiny cavern in the side of a low ridge.

The next two days he spent bettering his camouflage and watching from his hole. Bands of Iranian soldiers came and went. They carted out bodies—first his three comrades and later their own—and then began kicking boot toes through the gory aftermath. The final groups looked more like tourists, senior officers mostly, one of whom nearly made it to his position. Stein was prepared to take the man with his only remaining weapon, his trusted Glock, knowing it would start an exchange that he would not survive. Then the colonel with the big gut had stopped ten paces short and taken a whiskey flask from his pocket, emptying it before heading back to his jeep.

On the third day the visits stopped, the charred equipment left to rot. Since then Stein had been alone. He supposed it was better than capture, yet the subsequent fight for survival had stretched his training and tenacity to their limits. Hydration quickly proved the most serious problem, but after four parched days a desperate Stein had crawled to the donkey's carcass and found two untouched water bladders beneath. A full ten liters that had lasted until this morning.

So today Stein had gone on another search, dragging himself over the sand like a bent snake, turning over burned canvas packs and looking under charred cloth. There had been no water, but he found something even more precious. At the bottom of a crater and half buried in sand—where Dani had been perhaps?—a personal locator beacon. A locator beacon with *one bar remaining on the battery*.

His spirits soared on the discovery, and Stein crawled back to his lair where he dusted off the device under the makeshift shade tarp. They had each been issued one of the units, an ERB-6, the latest in personal satellite technology. Stein spent ten minutes composing his text message, knowing he would likely only have one shot. He included his emergency code word, and a brief mention of his injury. His position on the roof of the Kavir Desert would be accurate to within a few yards, and automatically enciphered before transmission. Stein hit the Send button holding his breath, and watched as the screen churned and finally announced: MESSAGE SENT.

Now he could only wait.

The sun was rising high, cooking night into day, and in the distance Stein saw a dust cyclone swirling. Farther yet, in a teasing image at the base of the northern mountains, he saw the lifting billow of a rain shower. He had turned the beacon off after his one transmission—it wasn't designed as a two-way device—but now he wondered whether there might be one more burst in the battery. Probably not, he decided. With that depressing thought, Stein pulled out his last energy bar. He almost broke it in half, but then shifted his dirt-encrusted fingers to make two breaks. Three pieces. One for each day.

If help didn't come by then, it would almost certainly be too late.

Just after ten o'clock that morning, a bleary-eyed Raymond Nurin found himself walking lengthwise along the southern side of a steep hill outside Montvendre, France. To his left and right he saw long trellises anchored into the rich brown earth, and climbing these, matted in morning dew, were the priceless canopies of Roussette. The grapes had already been harvested and the vines pruned for the season, but that was the limit of his untrained assessment.

Nurin's nondescript aircraft had landed in Grenoble some two hours earlier. There he was told to rent a car, and subsequently guided by a series of texted directions and misdirections. Now, certainly nearing the end of his odyssey, he found himself wandering a family-owned Savoy vineyard with a ticket for the ten-thirty tour in his coat pocket.

This too had been in the instructions.

Nurin had never visited this part of France, and he knew little about wine. He liked red with beef, and knew that some seemed better than others, maddeningly subtle distinctions he could register but never quite quantify. He also knew that the prices listed on restaurant menus varied wildly, a detail that regularly escaped his wife's grasp. Walking over the steep, terraced terrain, he wondered if there was some logic to growing grapes on a south-facing hillside. Better drainage? More sun? Or perhaps cheaper land. If he made it to the ten-thirty tour, he would likely find an answer.

Nurin never got the chance.

"I wasn't sure if you would come."

The level voice came out of nowhere and Nurin froze.

He had never met the man behind him, and wasn't sure why he'd been lured to this meeting. The secure Mossad building from which he normally orchestrated things seemed suddenly very distant. Nurin had spent time in the field early in his career, but he did not delude himself—his mind-set had long ago shifted from tactician to strategist. So he was standing on foreign soil, completely unarmed, and quite alone. And behind him? Behind him was the most lethal assassin Israel had ever built, and by all accounts a man who would like nothing better than to kill him on the spot. Indeed, the fact that he did not already have a bullet in his brain was the greatest positive Nurin could summon from his situation.

And with that lovely thought, he took a shallow breath and turned.

Slaton was there, no more than two steps away, and the director made a quick study. Tall and athletic, fair hair and opaque gray eyes that seemed to look right through him. Or perhaps into him?

The *kidon* said nothing, only responding with his own appraising stare.

"I am alone," Nurin said, trying to keep an even tone, "just as you instructed."

"I know."

"I wasn't surprised to hear from you. When they couldn't find your body I assumed you had egressed Geneva successfully. The Swede, the detective, I saw his statement. It was very convincing. Six rounds fired, three hits at point-blank range. His colorful narrative of how you vaulted end-over-end into the river. Quite compelling. I can only assume that you somehow conspired with this man?"

"No comment."

Nurin nodded. "Very well. And regarding the rest—you are aware of the greater plan?"

"I had a long talk with Dr. Hamedi. He explained everything."

"You did well to find a way to return him to Iran. Even better that you were able to eliminate Behrouz in the course of . . . in the course of events. Hamedi's plan can go forward now."

Nurin saw Slaton's attention dart to a pair of workers walking on a nearby path. They wore work pants and brown T-shirts, and had long shovels slung over their shoulders. Slaton waited for them to pass, then reestablished eye contact.

Nurin asked, "So your plan was to abduct Hamedi? And what would you have done then?"

"I was going to demand your public resignation, along with an admission that you had committed unspecified crimes, the details of which could not be revealed for reasons of national security. You would have gotten prison time. I was going to demand ten years—but I'd have settled for five. One always has to leave room for negotiation."

"Negotiation? With whom?"

"I was going to bring the prime minister here, to the very spot where you're standing. I wanted his personal assurance—in writing—that Christine and I would be left alone forever. Then I was going to hand him Hamedi to do with as he pleased."

Nurin felt more at ease, finding himself on increasingly familiar terrain. "Yes," he said appreciatively, "that was probably the best you could have done."

For the first time Slaton's eyes stopped scanning. Standing on wet earth between wire frames of hundred-year-old vines, the unsettling gaze drilled Nurin directly. "It wouldn't have worked, would it? Not even if Hamedi was the fanatical anti-Semite everyone thought him to be."

"No," Nurin conjectured, "probably not. You might have gotten a degree of retribution—but only against those of us in Israel who were forced to make the difficult choices. A few moments of gratification perhaps, but the outcome wouldn't have changed."

"So for Christine and I there's never going to be a way out, is there?"

"Over the years you have done great things for Israel, David. But in your line of work success comes with a price. Tell me—would you consider coming back? Mossad can always use a man of your talents."

In the ensuing silence Nurin recognized a mistake. He quickly added, "You were very resourceful last night. When you learned the truth about Hamedi, how he was planning to neutralize the biggest threat we Jews have faced in decades, you immediately found a way forward."

"I'm not done yet," Slaton said.

"What do you mean?"

Slaton explained what was yet to come.

Nurin gave the assassin his most circumspect look. "I always suspected you were a good Jew. In the end, you are doing the right thing for Israel, David."

"And you?" Slaton asked. "Do you feel in your heart that you've done the right things?"

"Certainly not. It is the curse of my position. But I can say in good conscience that I have always tried."

The gray eyes turned ominous. "You've sacrificed a lot of good men for this cause, Director."

"No one understands that better than I. Yet in light of what you've just told me—there is one more important matter. In your early days with Mossad, did you ever work with a man named Yaniv Stein?"

The *kidon*'s eyes narrowed. "Many times. Yaniv was a competent operator—a solid soldier who followed orders."

"*Was?*" Nurin repeated cagily. "A curious use of the past tense."

"It's my understanding that he was one of the victims of your disaster in Iran a few weeks ago. Yaniv Stein died outside Qom."

For the first time since arriving in France, the spymaster smiled. "And this, I think, is something we should talk about . . ."

FIFTY-SEVEN

 Three days later
East of Qom, Iran

The little car fishtailed and nearly slid from the road as Ibrahim Hamedi rounded a corner at a patently unsafe speed. He eased off the accelerator, but only slightly, his eyes squinting to see through a dust-encrusted windshield that was further obscured by the low sun. He checked the rearview mirror again, but saw nothing more than a swirling cloud of dust that could have masked a convoy.

The car was owned by his best friend, a brilliant young technician named Hassan. When Hamedi first returned to Iran from Europe, he'd made a private rule to never become attached to his coworkers. This served a dual purpose: it promoted his image as a distant authoritarian, but also allowed for fewer reservations when the end came. And that end was today. Hassan, however, had been the exception. A young man as likable as he was hardworking, he was fresh out of university and an expert in computer modeling. The two had endured countless late-night sessions, hunched over bitter coffee and whirring laptops, in which they formulated implosion simulations and yield efficiency estimates. Yet even against such a sobering backdrop, the kid had made Hamedi smile. Hassan had been his one allowance. Early this morning Hamedi had sent him to Natanz on short notice, hustling him out on a fool's errand and insisting he take the bus that shuttled twice daily between the two facilities. Once he was gone, Hamedi had rummaged through Hassan's desk and found the keys to his rattletrap car right where he knew they would be.

Hamedi's next hour was spent initiating the sequence that had been branded into his mind by a hundred sleepless nights. Warnings overridden. Security codes activated. And the crowning touch, a malware he'd personally written to create a diversion—spurious air-raid warnings to indicate an imminent Israeli airstrike. From his desk on the fourth level, Hamedi had initiated all of it, and then a final keystroke to set the backward-running clock on its silent countdown.

With the unstoppable sequence activated, Hamedi had easily slipped his personal security detail and headed for the elevator. On reaching ground level he saw that his air-raid scheme had been a stroke of genius—every guard and soldier above the subterranean complex was looking nervously skyward from their guard shacks and gun emplacements. No one gave a second glance to the beaten old Fiat that puttered out the gate.

Hamedi was ten miles east now. He referenced the GPS receiver in his hand, and turned off the gravel road onto what he hoped was the correct dirt path. Five miles up the rutted track he saw what he was looking for—a dust-clad Toyota Land Cruiser nestled amid an outcropping of eroded boulders. The truck blended well, tan-colored and eroded in its own way with bent fenders and a baked-on casing of dust and grime. Twin petrol cans were lashed to the rear, and strapped on the roof rack was a sturdy spare tire. Hamedi hit the brakes hard, and the Fiat skidded and disappeared in a light brown cloud. He threw open the door and began to run, but then slid to a stop in the loose dirt. He had almost forgotten his jacket, which held the critical flash drives—Iran's entire nuclear program condensed to fit in the breast pocket of a tweed blazer.

Returning for his coat, Hamedi heard a honk and looked over his shoulder at the Toyota's driver. The man was pointing to a place in the field of stone, and Hamedi looked closer and saw a beige camouflage tarp strung between two large boulders. It blended in so well he'd not even seen it on his approach. Underneath the tarp was a space. *A space big enough for . . .*

Hamedi waved, and soon had the Fiat maneuvered into the camouflaged cavern. He bustled out, this time with his jacket in hand, and for the second time paused. Unsure what to do with the Fiat's keys, he began to put them in his pocket, but then reconsidered and tossed them into the dirt next to the Fiat with the loose idea that Hassan might somehow be able to reclaim his car. Busy as he was, Hamedi did not notice the Toyota's driver shaking his head.

Seconds later he was at the truck's passenger door, and for the first time he saw who was inside. His heart leapt. On one side in the back was his mother, silent but with tears of happiness welling in her eyes. Next to her, on the reclined second seat, was a man—at least Hamedi thought it was a man, so dirt-encrusted and emaciated was the figure. The poor soul was nearly lying flat, and connected to an IV bag that was hanging from the upper riding handle. His face was craggy and withered, but he seemed extremely alert. Hamedi had not expected a third person in the truck, but given the man's condition he easily arrived at a solution—this was one of the men who had trekked through the desert three weeks earlier to kill him. By some amazing turn, he'd escaped the forewarned platoons Behrouz had put in position. Hamedi was pleased, although on seeing the handgun in his lap he hoped the man had been given an updated mission briefing.

"Let's go!" snapped the driver.

Hamedi stared at the Toyota's last occupant. He hadn't been sure at first—clean-cut with fair hair, a lean body he'd last seen covered in neoprene, the face no longer masked in camouflage shading. But the direct gaze and commanding voice left no doubt. It was the *kidon* from Geneva.

"Now!" he insisted.

Hamedi reached for the door handle, but paused. He checked his watch.

"Wait," he said. "Only twenty more seconds."

At first the driver didn't seem to understand his meaning, but then Hamedi turned toward the west. No one said a word as they all looked across the desert. Heat was already rising in the early morning, a wavering mirage that deconstructed the horizon. The facility was just visible ten miles off, a handful of large white buildings surrounded by squat storage hangars, a few antennas and utilities sprinkled in for good measure. These structures, Hamedi knew, were no more than a place marker for what lay below—a massive complex that had been decades in the making. The Toyota's engine had not yet been turned, and so the only thing Hamedi heard was the quick rhythm of his breathing. With five seconds to go even this took pause.

And then it happened.

The speed of light having its advantage, the first sensation was that the complex visibly shuddered, as if a full square mile of earth had bounced on a trampoline. Then a billowing wall of dust skirted the perimeter. There would be no classic mushroom cloud, Hamedi knew, the mechanics being all wrong for that. No spherical fireball, no rising column of heat to generate a Rayleigh–Taylor instability. Underground blasts dissipated energy in an entirely different manner.

The ground wave was next to arrive, the earth rattling under Hamedi's feet in a seismic event that would travel across continents in the next minutes. The audible blast was nearly simultaneous, a low-frequency, muffled thump that echoed off the rock outcroppings. The vibrations dissipated quickly, and in the ensuing calm Hamedi imagined what was happening underground. After extensive calculations, he had positioned the weapon at the principal point of vulnerability in the underground support structure. Thousands of tons of dirt and concrete, originally intended to protect the facility, would now entomb it. Ceilings would collapse, voids would fill, and when the dust cleared— something that would take hours—the world would find a crater half a mile wide and nearly forty yards deep.

This was Hamedi's moment of truth, and his well-considered plan had worked flawlessly. Yet there *was* one thing that surprised him. Something that had not been in his calculations. Hamedi did not feel the predicted elation.

"Get in!" the *kidon* barked, snapping Hamedi out of his trance. The Toyota's engine rumbled to life.

"Yes," Hamedi said, dropping into the passenger seat. "Yes . . . it is time."

Moments later gravel was rattling in the wheel wells as the truck sped northward. Hamedi took an embrace from his mother, and was then introduced to the soldier, a man named Stein. After the greetings ran their course, he found himself again staring over his shoulder, mesmerized by the rising cloud of dust. When he turned away, Hamedi felt strangely nauseous. Were he not a physicist, he might have wondered if it was the radiation whirling in his stomach. After a thoughtful silence he looked directly at the *kidon*.

The blond man seemed to read his thoughts, and asked, "How many?"

"Ninety," Hamedi answered, knowing exactly what he meant. "Possibly a hundred."

The blond man nodded noncommittally.

"Does it . . ." Hamedi searched for the words, "does it ever get better? Any easier to accept?"

This time the *kidon* seemed to think about it. "No, not really. But always remember one thing—you did what had to be done."

FIFTY-EIGHT

Arne Sanderson sat in the passenger seat of his ex-wife's new Volvo, tinkering with the seat controls to find a more comfortable position.

"Can I help?" Ingrid asked from the driver's seat.

"No, I'm fine. Just a bit of soreness from the surgery."

"It's only been two days. Have you taken your pain pills?"

He gave her a severe look. "I won't let you be my nursemaid as well. By the way, I haven't asked lately—how is Alfred?"

"The same," she said.

Sanderson stared out at Stockholm in the late-morning gloom, a steady rain peppering the windshield. "Sjoberg came to see me yesterday."

"Did he?"

"I'm being put up as a hero, you know. Relentless detective, fighting illness and the odds. All that rubbish. Of course there's no mention of the fact that I had been taken off the case, let alone that the assistant commissioner thought I'd slipped my gimbals."

She asked, "Did you really throw your credentials at him?"

"I suppose that was a bit juvenile of me."

Ingrid giggled.

"It felt good at the time." Sanderson allowed a smile, and the ensuing silence was broken by no more than the thrum of passing cars and the hiss of wet asphalt under the Volvo's wide tires.

He said, "They want me to come back."

"Arne, that's wonderful!"

"Is it?"

"Please—don't tell me you've turned them down." Her tone was that of a mother chiding a recalcitrant child. "Arne?"

"I told Sjoberg I'd think about it. But I just don't know."

"The department has been your life."

"Yes, I know. But in those days—when I thought my career had ended—it wasn't so bad. Sooner or later I'll be gone, and the department will get along fine without Arne Sanderson. My thirty-five years won't even be stuffed into a file cabinet—just compressed onto a hard drive somewhere that won't have the decency to gather dust. An electronic urn for the remains of my career."

"And what did you expect? A statue in Stortorget Square? I won't tolerate self-pity, Arne. No one will make a record of my life, but that doesn't mean I haven't been useful. I've made a difference in people's lives, and put a few smiles on faces along the way."

He looked at her and met her eyes for a moment. "Yes. Yes, you have."

Her attention went back to the road as she added, "I see no reason for either of us to go idle—not while we can still contribute something."

She turned onto Sanderson's street, and soon the Volvo was splashing into his rutted driveway. She kept the car going, the wipers flapping rhythmically.

"Can I help you inside?" she asked.

"No, I'll manage."

"I'll check on you tomorrow, maybe bring a batch of my potato soup."

"That would be nice, thank you."

"Did you remember your key?"

He gave her a suffering look, but after a long moment turned serious.

"What is it?" she asked.

"Can you keep a secret?"

"Well, I—"

"No, of course you can't, you're a policeman's wife . . . or were. But I want you to promise me this once."

Ingrid nodded.

"All this business in the papers about me getting the better of the assassin, shooting him on that bridge in Geneva. It's all a lie. My official report, the details of how I came across the two of them—it's fabricated, nearly every word."

"But Arne—why?"

"The whole thing was staged."

"Staged?"

Sanderson confessed, telling her about the three-way encounter on the jetty, Hamedi's confession and the assassin's plan.

"You can't be serious," she said when he was done.

"All I had to do was pretend to shoot the man."

"So this Israeli killer—he's still alive?"

Sanderson looked away, clearly perplexed. He mused aloud, "When I was standing on that bridge, facing the two of them—I wasn't well. I had a terrible pain in my head, fine motor issues. I wasn't thinking clearly. It couldn't have been a more simple task. All I had to do was point the gun at the man and miss, then he was to go over the rail. But my vision—"

"Your vision?"

"At the last moment I remember seeing double. There were two of him, and I was terribly confused and dizzy. You see, I'm not sure, but . . . I fear I may have shot him after all."

She held his hand for a long moment, then reached over and kissed his cheek. "Is there anything I can do?"

"No, you've been wonderful as always. Thank you."

"Take care of yourself, Arne."

"I will. And you take care of Alfred."

Minutes later Sanderson was inside and had the teakettle on the stove. He turned on the furnace, then went around the house and cracked windows open to clear the stagnant air that had built in his absence. On the kitchen counter he lined up enough pill bottles to start his own pharmacy, and finally settled into his best chair. He turned on the television and quickly found a news broadcast. The banner at the bottom told him all he needed to know. BREAKING NEWS: NUCLEAR BLAST DETECTED IN CENTRAL IRAN. GOVERNMENT SILENT AS TO CAUSE. The commentator speculated, because that was all he could do. Sanderson registered none of it. Instead, he weighed the evidence himself, having a good bit more to work with. He sat very still, sifting and making deductions, applying the events of today to what he remembered from Geneva.

The teakettle began whistling three minutes later, and by that time, as he stood gingerly and went into the warming kitchen, Arne Sanderson had a broad smile on his face.

FIFTY-NINE

 Ten months later
Dingli, Malta

Anton Bloch walked gingerly across a wide cobbled street, the uneven brickwork a test to his faltering gait. His long rehabilitation had gone well enough, but he still lacked the strength he'd once had, and the half-mile walk up a steep hill, in the heat of a Mediterranean August, was more than he'd bargained for.

The stone under his feet was an intricate mosaic, clearly a matter of some honor to a craftsman centuries ago. According to the driver who'd brought him here from Luqa, a chatty amateur historian, the Roman legions had arrived two thousand years ago, and in their wake the island was subsequently pillaged by Arab hordes, sacked by the Aragonese, and occupied violently by Byzantines. *So perhaps I shouldn't be surprised he has ended up here*, Bloch mused.

Though his body was travel-weary, Bloch's mind was sharp, and he followed the directions he'd so meticulously memorized. He passed lines of white-stone villas rife with dull corners, and pairs of querulous old women rife with sharp opinions. There were shops and grocers, and the occasional municipal building, the latter distinguished by that universal air of managed demise. Bloch was completely out of breath when he reached the end of the winding lane, where the path funneled open into a broad piazza.

He decided the address he'd been given was most likely allotted to a restaurant on one corner of the square, although the place lacked any numbers to prove the point. The building had yard-thick walls, pockmarked from one invasion or another, and the tables were no more than slabs of bleached stone. Bloch kept to the sidewalk as instructed, and where it ended he paused at a scenic overlook to take in the glistening Mediterranean, a view that had certainly not changed since the day the Romans had arrived. Rolling cobalt swells met the bases of cliffs, having built and traveled for days to reach their churning end. He turned the other way and saw a lazy Monday on the square. Waiters on patios moved languidly in the rising heat to arrange place settings for lunch. Under an olive tree a workcrew was taking a break from plastering the walls of an old church.

Bloch was watching a priest cross the road, black robe flowing and a gold cross dangling from his neck, when David Slaton appeared out of nowhere. He was standing on the sidewalk a few steps away, relaxed but observant. He said, "Thanks for coming." There was nothing more, no offer of a handshake or pat on the shoulder. For a man like Slaton, social graces were no more than tradecraft—exhibited when necessary for appearances, but otherwise superfluous.

"It's been a long time, David."

"Over a year. How is retirement treating you?"

"It was good until you came along. Then somebody shot me in the spine."

"And your recovery?"

"A little stiffness. But maybe I'm only confusing it with old age."

Slaton began moving, and Bloch remembered—the *kidon* was never at ease when still. He strolled the sidewalk and Bloch kept up, wondering if the easy pace was for his benefit. They paralleled an ancient stone wall as light traffic skittered past, and while they walked Bloch studied Slaton. He looked more physically robust than ever. Deep tan and sun-lightened hair, lean muscle straining the shoulders of a loose, untucked shirt. On outward appearances, a man in vibrant health.

"You look fit," Bloch offered.

"I've been working."

"I'm told there are quarries outside town. Men here, it seems, still pull blocks of granite and marble from the earth by hand."

"Do they?"

Bloch looked pointedly at Slaton's roughhewn hands, but said nothing.

"So?" Slaton asked. "Did you do as I asked?"

"I have to say, your method of contact took me by surprise. A check in my name for five million dollars and a plane ticket to America? You never were one for subtlety."

An unsmiling Slaton asked, "Were you tempted to take it and run?"

"No. But be thankful my wife didn't open it first. I'd have a villa in the south of France and two new cars by now."

This time Bloch saw perhaps a crease of humor at the corner of Slaton's mouth. It disappeared as soon as he asked his next question. "Did she take it?"

"I think you know the answer."

"How did you put it to her?"

Bloch sighed. "Not as you suggested. Your idea about a widow and orphan's fund for Mossad operatives lost in the line of duty? Please, David. Do you not know your own wife?"

Slaton didn't respond.

"I told her it was a personal life insurance policy. I said your premiums were dutifully paid, and that she was the legal beneficiary. It didn't matter, of course. Maybe it had something to do with the messenger. You should have hired an actor to pose as an insurance adjuster, a stranger who could arrive at her door with papers to sign and a settlement statement. Or perhaps you might have set up a company with a bland name and simply mailed her a check. But no—one look at me and she wanted nothing to do with the money. By the way, where did you get it?"

"It's not Mossad money, if that's what you mean. Not exactly."

Bloch eyed the *kidon*, but didn't pursue the point.

"Does she have any doubts?" Slaton asked.

"About your death?" Bloch paused, choosing his words carefully. "I'm not sure. Edmund Deadmarsh was declared legally dead in the Commonwealth of Virginia last month. And of course she hasn't heard from you. As you know, I went to see her a few weeks after Geneva, when you first insisted on this madness. She had trouble with it then, but now she seems more . . . accepting. I think she believes that if you'd survived you would have found your way to her by now."

They meandered the promenade in silence, and at the crest of the cliff reached a white stone wall beyond which was a thousand-foot plunge to the deep blue Mediterranean. Bloch knew they were less than three hundred miles north of Tripoli, the roof of the Sahara, yet the arid onshore breeze born of the sirocco seemed at odds with the azure seascape before them.

He said, "Christine permitted me to see your son. He is only two months old but already has your—"

"*Son?*" Slaton stopped abruptly. He turned away, the dry breeze whipping his hair.

"My God!" Bloch stammered. He watched the *kidon* closely, saw his hands thrust deep into his pockets, the thick muscles tensing under his shirt. "You didn't even know that much?"

"The less I know the better."

Bloch pulled out his phone, called up the photograph he'd taken, and said, "Here, David. I took a picture of him with—"

In a flash Slaton whipped around and snatched Bloch's phone. Without even looking at the screen, he smashed it against the stone wall and heaved the plastic and silicon remains spinning toward the sea below.

Bloch said nothing, and for a very long time they stood side by side at the stone precipice. "David—" he finally picked up, "you don't have to do this. I can go back to Tel Aviv. I could tell them that—"

"No!" Slaton cut in. His voice fell to a quiet, hushed tone. "You will go back to Tel Aviv and tell this director and any other that if Christine and my son are ever . . . I repeat, *ever* put at risk, I will start with the prime minister of Israel and work my way down." He met Bloch's eyes. "Are we perfectly clear on this?"

"And your wife and child? You truly intend to never see them again?"

Slaton shifted his stare out to sea.

Bloch shook his head and looked up at the flawless blue sky. He tried to put himself in the *kidon*'s untenable position. He tried to understand. "Tell me, David. Is it possible to care for someone that much?"

Without answering, Slaton turned and walked away. Bloch watched as he moved diagonally across the square, expecting Slaton to vaporize into his surroundings. Instead, he veered to one side of the piazza. The priest was at the church now, overseeing the work crew who'd gone back to plastering what was clearly a Roman Catholic house, the Vatican having long ago wrapped things up here. Slaton steered toward the man and struck up a conversation, a curious back-and-forth that caused the priest to cock his head and put a thoughtful finger to his lips. It was as if Slaton had asked an unanswerable question. Finally, that default solution so often relied upon by men of God was given. The priest shook his head, raised his palms upward, and looked to the sky.

Slaton nodded appreciatively, as if to thank the father for his opinion, and then turned away toward the far side of the square. He picked up his pace over the cobblestone street, shouldered into a crowd at the central market, and in a flurry of white-shirted bronze men and barefoot children playing soccer, the *kidon* was quickly lost to sight.